D1336640

as

ROTHERHAM LIBRARY & INFORMATION SERVICE

11|12 .

CENTRAL

THE WITCHER KEYS

THE WITCHER KEYS

I. R. Johnson

Book Guild Publishing
Sussex, England

First published in Great Britain in 2012 by
The Book Guild Ltd
Pavilion View
19 New Road
Brighton, BN1 1UF

Typesetting in Meridien by
Nat-Type, Cheshire

Printed in Great Britain by
CPI Group (UK) Ltd, Croydon, CR0 4YY

A catalogue record for this book is available from
The British Library.

ISBN 978 1 84624 768 2

Contents

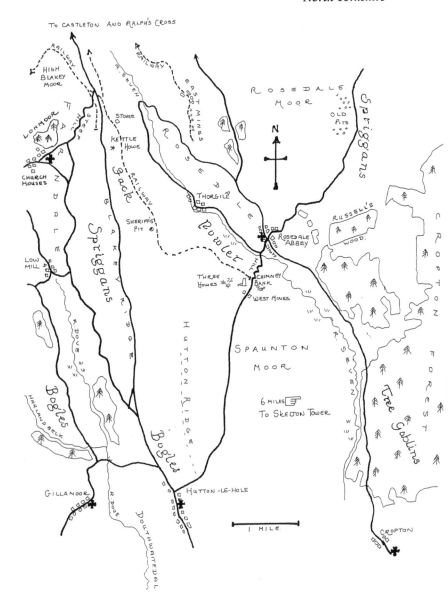

Part of
Farndale and Rosedale
In the county of
North Yorkshire

TO CASTLETON AND RALPH'S CROSS

RAILWAY

HIGH BLAKEY MOOR

LONMOOR

R. SEVEN

RAILWAY

EAST MINES

ROSEDALE MOOR

OLD PITS

Spriggans

STORE

STEEP HILL

KETTLE HOWE

N

CHURCH HOUSES

Jack

RAILWAY

ROSEDALE

THORGILL

Lowler

RUSSELL'S WOOD

SHERIFFS PIT

ROSEDALE ABBEY

CROPTON FOREST

Spriggans

BLAKEY RIDGE

LOW MILL

R. DOVE

THREE HOWES

CHIMNEY BANK TOP

WEST MINES

HUTTON RIDGE

SPAUNTON MOOR

R. SEVEN

Tree Goblins

Bogles

HARLAND BECK

6 MILES
TO SKELTON TOWER

Bogles

GILLAMOOR

R. DOVE

Bogles

HUTTON-LE-HOLE

DOUTHWAITEDAL

1 MILE

CROPTON

Facts and Warnings

A fact ...

During a recent summer, on the edge of a North York Moors village which sprawls untidily across the bottom of a wide and beautiful valley, a bustling and happy home became gradually uninhabitable. The people who tried to sleep there suffered from restless nights and terrible headaches, as a cold, menacing feeling seeped into every part of the house. The entire roof was electrically charged, and every imaginable test was made, but there was not a single wire out of place, and there were no strange fumes or dangerous microbes, either. Nothing.

Out of desperation, two men were asked to come and visit it, extraordinary men called geomancers, and they soon knew exactly what was wrong with the house. There were three ley lines below it, they explained: strange, invisible lines of energy that stretch underground for mile after mile in unwavering, straight lines, and these three crossed at a single point right under that house, just as they had done for countless centuries. This alone was a rare and worrying thing, but there was an even worse problem around the edge of the garden; in fact, a whole army of problems. The geomancers could see them clearly. They could even hear their shouts and jeers, although no one else there could.

This particular army was from a strange and perilous

1

world separated from our own by only the most fragile of threads, an army of little creatures so frightening that they could freeze your blood in a second, an army whose anger was now exceeded only by their loathing of the humans who had unwittingly ruined their meeting place in the trees nearby. The life-giving waters which usually trickled into their roughly hewn stone drinking trough had been thoughtlessly diverted, and so it had been decided that those guilty would be made to pay dearly. They were elementals, no taller than three-year-old children, but troublesome if annoyed, and potentially deadly if enraged.

Needless to say, the water supply was quickly restored and soon afterwards the roof no longer shocked anyone brave enough to touch it. The headaches were gradually replaced by deep, peaceful sleep, too. The elementals were content again ... for now.

... and so, a note of warning:

If you have ever been unfortunate enough to lie wide awake in the middle of the night, convinced that a terrifying, gobliny kind of creature was lurking somewhere under your bed, waiting to sink his teeth into your foot the moment it touched the floor, then this little warning will probably alarm you. I am truly sorry if it does, but it would simply be unfair for you to read even one page further without knowing that the extraordinary beings in this tale (including goblins, sadly) could quite easily be just as real as you and I.

Thankfully, a few of them are even more frightened of us than we are of them, and will do their best to keep out of our way, but never forget that there are countless others, with cold, empty hearts and twisted minds, who fear nothing in this world or theirs. To mock them or their evil ways in anything louder than a whisper would be extremely unwise, for one way or another they would eventually hear of it, and then ... well, you will see.

As for their favourite haunts, it seems that most quiet, shadowy places are perfectly suitable, and I suspect that the countryside close to me now, in an otherwise peaceful corner of the North York Moors, would be one of them. With a good map and some sturdy boots, you could even search there for them yourself – if you're brave enough, that is.

Oh, and by the way, if you do go, be sure to take a good, stout stick with you. It could be far more useful than you think ...

The author

Please see the appendix for further information

The Bronze Key

There was nothing particularly remarkable about the bare garden hedge at Willow Garth Farm, or at least not to begin with. Large orange and yellow horse chestnut leaves had gathered underneath it in deep piles, swept from the lawn by November gales, and a few shrivelled hawthorn berries seemed determined not to drop, but that was all.

Then, strangely, one of those piles appeared to move all by itself, as if a restless hedgehog was trying to make himself more comfortable for the winter, and a few seconds later there was a distinct but faint 'sniff' from the very same place. But this was no sleepy hedgehog. Something far more dangerous and cunning was hiding down there, waiting for darkness to come.

Almost undetectable in their hooded cloaks of woven moss and leaves, two ugly spriggans had been squatting in amongst the lowest branches since long before dusk, patiently watching the old farmhouse on the far side of the lawn, and more importantly, the family who lived there. They were hungry by now, and getting steadily colder, but their spirits sank even lower when a few spots of rain decided to become a heavy shower, which poured down through the hedge above them.

'There's nuffin' goin' on over there now, Scribber. Can't we go in yet?' whined the slightly smaller one from under his dripping hood.

His companion had clearly heard this sort of thing many times before, for he didn't even bother to turn his head.

'Now what do *you* think?' he sighed wearily, dragging a leafy sleeve across his long and slightly twisted nose. 'You must be deaf or summat. It's still too soon.'

The whiner, or Wipp, as he was occasionally called, looked as if he was about to try his luck again, but he changed his mind just in time and instead sat quietly with his chin buried in his hands, sulking as he watched the last shreds of daylight gradually fade away. Fifteen minutes later, when even the bright red door to the house had turned a dull, lifeless grey, he shivered violently, shaking a miniature shower of raindrops from his cloak and hood. As soon as the shiver had passed, he tried to compose himself, then took a deep breath and gritted his teeth.

'Well, 'ow much longer *do* we 'ave to wait, then?' he asked bravely, gazing out across the garden with one eye, but watching his unpredictable leader from the corner of the other.

Scribber glared at the inexperienced youngster, trying to warn him silently, but Wipp was starting to feel that he'd had more than enough discomfort for one evening, and wanted to get back to their warm, dry cave and whatever was still simmering on the cooking fires. Rather unwisely, he persisted.

'Aw, come on! Surely most of 'em'll be in bed by now, after such a tirin' day an' everythin'.' He was trying to find room to straighten out a numb leg when he shivered even harder, making his stubby yellow teeth chatter noisily.

'Keep yer gob shut, or you'll 'ave the ruddy dog on us!' hissed Scribber, suddenly turning on him. '*I'll* say when it's time – got it?'

Before Wipp could lean away, a frighteningly strong, claw-like hand had gripped his upper arm, and five sharp fingernails were reminding him exactly who was in charge ... and who most certainly wasn't.

Two hours later, it was still raining hard, and with the temperature steadily falling, the rain was beginning to change to sleet. Long, wet strands of snot now hung precariously from the tips of the spriggans' cold, blue-tinged noses, or sometimes danced about in the gusty wind, but their hands were now jammed deep into their armpits, trying to find some last trace of warmth, and so the noses were left to drip – just like everything else around them. Then, just as the last bedroom light was finally switched off, snuffing out the invitingly warm glow from behind the curtains, a bedraggled owl hooted forlornly from in amongst the trees behind them. Scribber didn't even move, but Wipp gave a wide, disinterested yawn, and let his hood fall a little lower over his face ...

He was sure that he'd only just closed his eyes when a bony elbow jabbed him viciously in the ribs, making his chin snap up with a jerk and throwing his hood back onto his shoulders, but he was still trying to remember where he was and why he was there when Scribber's grating voice finished the task for him.

'Wake up, slug-slime, and follow me,' he croaked straight into Wipp's ear, deliberately startling him. He adjusted a bulging shoulder bag before carefully pulling a thorny branch aside for himself. 'And *try* to keep yer teef quiet,' he added with a sneer, ''less of course you want the dog tryin' out 'is ... in yer arse!'

A moment later, and with indescribable relief, the two of them were at last standing up straight and stretching, then running stiffly across the wet lawn, knees and ankles clicking and cracking on the way. They soon reached the nearest of several outbuildings, and with the strengthening wind starting to moan quietly on the rocking electricity wires somewhere above their heads, began to grope their way along one of its walls towards the farmhouse itself, up to their shoulders in dripping nettles. Despite the bad weather, Scribber was just thinking that their plan was proceeding reasonably well, when his sharp hearing picked up the ominous sound of gravel crunching underfoot, or worse still on this particular farm, underpaw. It stopped both of them instantly.

'Goblin-guts! Just what we don't need!' he snarled under his breath, hardly able to believe their bad luck, and already trying to decide whether to stay out of sight and hope for the best, or jump out and kill the reputedly ferocious farm dog before it discovered them and ruined their night's work.

He tugged a small dagger from his belt and pressed himself into the deeper shadows against the wall, dragging Wipp with him. Wipp's eyes were now wide open for the first time that evening, despite the rain driving straight into his face, and Scribber's fingers were tightening around the hilt of his dagger when an overweight ginger tomcat strolled casually around the corner of the building, on his way to nowhere in particular. A short, sharp hiss from amongst the nettles sent it screeching across the lawn as if the devil himself was just behind its tail.

'Huh! If *I'd* got 'old of 'im, 'e wouldn't 'ave lasted long,' boasted Wipp, as soon as the startled cat was safely out of sight.

He was now holding a dagger exactly like Scribber's. The gleaming, finely crafted weapon seemed quite out of place in his grubby little fist, but that didn't stop him from plunging it repeatedly into a fierce but completely imaginary cat somewhere just beside him. Scribber didn't trust himself to speak as he looked down disbelievingly at Wipp, but shook his head in despair as he pulled his cloak aside and sheathed his own dagger.

Forgetting nosy cats – and caution – they ran the

7

remaining twenty yards straight to the farmhouse, and were soon both pressing an ear up against the newly painted door, panting and listening for trouble. Apart from the rain, and the deep, hollow ticking of a large clock from somewhere inside the house, everything seemed quiet enough, and Scribber gently pushed the letterbox flap open with one finger before standing up on his toes to peer through it. The pleasant smells of wood smoke and home-cooking lingered in the warm air which drifted out into his face, a painful reminder that supper time had come and gone hours earlier. As he stretched higher still, he could just see a rug on the polished floorboards, a few pieces of dark, dreary furniture, and several doors leading off into other rooms. Light from a dying fire flickered past one of these, whilst steep, carpeted stairs melted into impenetrable shadows at the very back of the hall. There was no sign of the dog, which was encouraging, but it had started to rain even more heavily, which definitely wasn't.

'There's gotta be easier ways of makin' a livin' than this,' complained Wipp as he hopped from one foot to the other, trying to get some feeling back into his half-frozen toes.

There was a grunt of agreement from the letterbox before Scribber carefully extracted his nose and lowered the brass flap. He leant over and whispered into the filthy, pointed ear hovering close to his shoulder, 'You could 'ave somethin' there, lad – 'speshly when Redcap's payin'.' He turned and spat unceremoniously on the doorstep, as if the mere mention of the goblin's name tasted bitter in his mouth. 'But at least we gets to do our own little job, while 'e's rewardin' us 'andsomely for doin' one of 'is.' He tapped the side of his hood and winked knowingly at Wipp. 'Now, *that's* what I calls clever!'

Wipp broke into a toothy, dribbling grin as he remembered the small leather pouch which Redcap had dangled in front of their faces two days earlier, and the soft, irresistible rustle of the precious stones inside it. His eyes glazed over greedily as he imagined them, and for a few moments he even forgot about the water pouring from a broken gutter high above him, straight down onto his hood and cloak. Scribber waited, hands on hips, as Wipp drifted slowly back into the real world.

'It's all very well you grinnin' like some kind of 'arf-wit,' he whispered hoarsely, 'but if we don't find the soddin' key and get it back to 'im quick, Redcap'll be keepin' our earnin's and collectin' our blood in a barrel instead.' The master came nose-tip to nose-tip with his pupil, and leered at him with a crooked smile, doing his very best to frighten the young spriggan. 'Don't forget now, boy, goblins like 'im are always needin' gallons and gallons of the stuff!'

Wipp clearly had forgotten, for his grin vanished as he shuffled backwards to a slightly drier place and watched whilst his leader pulled a curiously bent wire from his bag. With the concentration and confidence born from a long and surprisingly successful life of crime, Scribber reached up and started to pick the lock with various expert twistings and fiddlings – most of them much noisier than Wipp would have liked. With tense pauses after several of the noisiest, three extremely long minutes ticked past on the unseen clock before the lock eventually clicked open. Smiling proudly, Scribber pushed the door ajar so that he could listen inside with one ear. The clock seemed much louder, but there were no unwelcome noises, and with Wipp suddenly right on his heels, he slipped through the doorway, out of the rain and into the dark but blissfully warm entrance hall.

High up in the wall of the old granary building, not far from the house, a pair of small pale eyes emerged from the gloom behind a window. A hand was pressed against the side of an odd little face, perhaps trying to catch a word or two from below, perhaps not – it was difficult to be sure. Unblinking, those eyes watched with great interest as the intruders crept into the house and closed the door silently behind them, then, a moment later, they retreated back into the darkness and disappeared.

Inside the farmhouse, the dripping spriggans tiptoed across the rug and looked around the half-open door to their left. The living room beyond it was in darkness, apart from a flame or two licking at the smouldering remains of a log in the fire grate. They almost expected to see the dog sprawled out asleep on the hearth rug, but nothing was moving apart from the huge shadows of two fireside armchairs, which leapt about silently on the patterned wallpaper like deformed, dancing phantoms. Seconds later, and without a word, both spriggans were scampering back across the hall and peering through the doorway opposite, wicked grins creeping steadily across their faces, and twitching fingers ready for action, brushing the hilts of their daggers. It was the kitchen, even warmer than the hall and still smelling temptingly of cooked food, but best of all, it was the room for which they were searching...

The warmth evidently came from a large cooking range with more oven doors than Wipp could even count. Two more cats were curled up contentedly against it, fast asleep. Some worryingly large muddy boots were there too, drying out beside the cats, whilst the feeble firelight from across the hall played on an assortment of brightly polished copper pots and pans which hung from the walls around the range. As their eyes became accustomed to the poor light, the spriggans also began to see a vast, wooden beam crossing the ceiling high above them. Just as Redcap had promised, a collection of old, handmade keys was proudly displayed along one side of it, hanging in a neat row. There were over thirty of them, all carefully arranged in order of size, and with the largest one looking as if it would have been perfectly at home in the front door of a cathedral.

With the tops of their heads just lower than the large pine table beside them, and suddenly wide-eyed with excitement, the spriggans craned their necks and gazed upwards. As they stood there silently with water still dripping from their cloaks, forming rings of tiny puddles around their boots, a sudden shower of driving hail rattled on the window behind the curtains, almost waking up the cats and making Wipp jump sideways into the table leg.

'Well, which one is it, then?' he whispered at once, wrapping his arms around himself and forcing out a false shiver which he hoped looked something like his embarrassing jump. 'You said it'd be easy.'

'It'd be a lot easier if y' shut it!' hissed Scribber, grasping a handful of Wipp's cloak and pulling him up against his chest. Wipp turned his head away from the stinking breath which blasted into his face. 'Why don't you do somethin' useful for a change, like gettin' over there and listenin' out for the dog?' He nodded towards the hall before shoving Wipp away so hard that the youngster staggered forwards and almost ended up on his knees. Scribber laughed under his breath before turning his attention back to the keys above him. 'Look ... for ... the ... fancy ... bronze ... shaft,' he muttered to himself, recalling Redcap's last instructions as he carefully studied each one in turn.

His eyes soon fastened onto the second largest of the keys. He was sure that it looked different from the others, but it was too high up for him to tell whether or not it was fancy, or even bronze, so he took a step back and in true spriggan fashion, grew rapidly upwards towards the ceiling. In a few seconds he was huge, close to eight feet tall, and looking down at a totally insignificant Wipp over by the door. With his hair now collecting cobwebs on the ceiling, the enormous spriggan brought his half-closed fist nearer to the keys, and a pale blue light suddenly spluttered into life behind his fingers, casting giant, darting shadows all around the kitchen. Wipp turned away from the hallway door and watched for a moment, fascinated, as his leader moved the eerie spriggan light around and inspected the second key more closely.

'Success!' hissed Scribber triumphantly, as he saw the intricate patterns worked into its bronzed shaft and large round handle. He took it down carefully, and after kissing it, slipped it safely inside his cloak. He was about to shrink back down again, but after a second thought, he moved the largest key of all along into the empty space, leaving one unused nail at the end of the row.

No point in makin' it too bleedin' obvious, he thought, grimly.

The strange light was snuffed out with a simple squeeze of his fist, and he shrank down to his smallest size even more quickly than he'd grown to his largest, patting the heavy key through his cloak as he did so, and clearly feeling pleased with himself for a job well done. Keeping one eye on the potentially troublesome cats, he crossed the kitchen and rejoined Wipp – almost slipping in one of his own puddles on the way. The youngster was watching the dark hall again, just as he'd been ordered to, but Scribber didn't trust anyone and leant over Wipp's shoulder to check for himself that the way was clear, making his feet squelch inside his wet boots.

'Well, that's you-know-who's business done with,' he muttered with some relief as Wipp looked up at him. 'Now let's get on with *ours*, while we still 'ave the chance!' He rubbed his hands together and his eyes lit up again, like a child's in a sweet shop.

They left the kitchen, crossed the hall once more and, side by side, began to climb the stairs. One ... two ... the third tread creaked loudly in spite of their light footsteps, stopping them both with one leather boot lifted high. Like two small leafy statues, they balanced there for five achingly long seconds, waiting and hoping, then, with a stretch and a heave, missed out the offending tread and carried on up. Remarkably, the others all behaved themselves and the intruders soon reached the top landing, but with their heartbeats now thudding in their ears and beads of cold sweat starting to trickle down their whiskery cheeks. Wipp, who was beginning to look distinctly pale, knew very well that the only way out was behind them, and even Scribber sensed that they were now in extreme danger. A long, narrow passageway lay in front of them, full of shadows, closed doors and dusty oil paintings of prize bulls or plough horses, but whatever the risks, they still knew exactly what they wanted. It was filling their minds as they came closer to it, almost oozing out of their pores with their sweat, for in one of the bedrooms, an innocent baby girl would be sleeping peacefully …

Trying not to breathe more than was necessary, they crept forwards using all their spriggan skills and cunning: listening, testing every footstep, watching each passing door handle for movement … ready to run. A young woman's cough came from one bedroom, stopping them yet again, and three steps later there were more anxious moments as the deep, muffled notes of a man humming to himself came from another, but they pressed onwards, utterly determined to finish their work. The last door would lead them to the child's room. After all, Redcap had personally guaranteed it.

With a final check over his shoulder, Scribber opened the door as quietly as he could and saw at once that the clever goblin had been quite right, as usual. The room was lit only by a small pink table lamp in a corner near the window, but the pretty wooden cot standing all alone in the middle of the floor was plain to see. The spriggans could barely contain their growing excitement as they crept towards it, up on their toes, but when they reached it they were still too short to see inside properly, and took a step back to grow a little taller.

'Ah! Ain't she sweet,' cooed Wipp a few seconds later, as they both gazed down adoringly at their so-called 'little job'.

She was breathtakingly beautiful – even the ugly spriggans knew that much – with unblemished skin, dark, curly hair, and tiny but perfectly formed rosebud lips sucking one of her thumbs noiselessly as she slept. With a nod of agreement and an evil smile of pure delight, Scribber reached into his bag, took out a small glass phial filled with a yellow liquid, and pulled the cork out with his brown and broken teeth. He tilted the phial above the baby's lips, and a few drops splashed onto them before running down her cheek and staining the white sheet below her. The spriggans were in their element now, leaning over their helpless prize and doing what they loved more than anything else.

'She'll sleep like a blinkin' log 'til we wake 'er up at the caves,' he whispered to Wipp elatedly as he pushed the cork back into the phial with his thumb. 'Yeah, we'll get no trouble from the brat now ... least not 'till we lock 'er in a cell and start gettin' 'er fattened up.'

Scribber tried to hold back a wicked laugh which had only managed to get as far up as his throat, and for a few moments he sounded like a peculiar, grunting pig. When he'd recovered sufficiently, he stared down hungrily at the child, grinning, and a thin trickle of dark saliva ran down from the corner of his mouth as he imagined her tender, roasted flesh falling from her bones and onto his plate. As he fought to drag his thoughts away from hot food and back into the dangerous world of large farmers and vicious guard dogs, his empty stomach rumbled so loudly that Wipp looked away, trying not to snigger.

'Let's leave our little gift and get off 'ome then, shall we?' suggested Scribber, still slightly distracted. Wipp clearly liked whatever was coming next, and nodded enthusiastically.

'Right then! Fair's fair, like you always says,' he chirped back, gleefully.

Scribber dug deeper into his bag and lifted out a shapeless bundle wrapped in a tatty cloth, which he started to unfold with great care. Inside was a large and exceptionally long-eared bat, and like the baby, it too was deeply asleep, drugged with the same yellow liquid so as not to give the spriggans away at a critical moment. Scribber chuckled to himself contentedly as he finished unwrapping the bat and thought of the others just like it, back at their caves.

Huh! Very 'andy things, these. They eat everythin' us lot leave, an' we gets to eat any of 'em what's stupid enough to get caught. Lovely!

He stroked its furry stomach with one fingernail, his head tilted slightly to one side and with a vacant expression which could almost have been confused with genuine affection.

Make good surprise presents, an' all!

He placed the unusual gift next to the child, but neither of them stirred. Then, from even deeper in his bag he finally produced a small leather pouch, and swore under his breath as his cold fingers fumbled with the long cords which tied it securely shut. It was soon open, though, and he held it out at arm's length to keep his nose away from the stinking contents. Wipp stepped back in disgust, pulling his hood across his face as Scribber dipped the tip of his dagger inside then brought it out with the very greatest of care, covered in something black and sticky.

Wipp thought it smelt like decaying fish, or vomit, or perhaps a mixture of both, but Scribber didn't seem to mind that much. Just like Wipp, he knew that it was the only substance in the world that would revive the bat, and he smeared some onto its lips with his dagger before bending a *little* closer and whispering to it, 'Wake up soon my repulsive little friend ... but not 'til we're well on our way 'ome, mind you.'

He arranged its leathery wings neatly, then turned to the baby girl and slid his long, damp fingers under her. As he started to lift her up, her knitted blankets fell away from her and covered the bat, which slept on as peacefully as if it was hanging from its favourite roost back at the caves.

*   *   *

The dog stood at the bottom of the stairs, cocking its head sleepily one way, then the other, as it tried to work out what or who had disturbed his pleasant dreams behind the door, in the darkest corner of the cosy living room. He'd already noticed that there was an unfamiliar and distinctly unpleasant smell in the air, which he sniffed at repeatedly, and the floorboards shouldn't have been wet either, he knew. His master always used the side door when it was raining.

A barely heard rumble began to grow from deep inside his chest, whilst a twitch of soft black lips briefly revealed two rows of white, neatly interlocking fangs, then suddenly he was wide awake and making his way up the stairs. There were no squeaking treads this time. He knew exactly where all the noisy ones were, so it was easy for him to follow the unwelcome smell without making a sound, padding his way wolf-like along the upstairs passageway and towards the last bedroom, where his special little friend Elspeth would be asleep in her cot. The smell led him all the way to her slightly open door, and he nudged it open wider with his snout before looking into the room.

He was surprised to see two rather unusual creatures standing with their backs to him. They smelt all wrong, *badly* wrong in fact, and they seemed to be more or less covered in wet leaves, which also puzzled him a great deal. He watched silently as the larger one lifted a limp and lifeless Elspeth out of her cot, and the smaller one looked on with an inane grin stretching across his dirty face from one pointed ear to the other. Like the first warnings of a distant thunderstorm, a much deeper rumble began to stir into life somewhere in the dog's throat, as he took a single step forward, then stopped, waiting for a reaction from the intruders.

Scribber was the first to realise that the ominous noise behind him had nothing to do with the bad weather outside. He stopped lifting Elspeth and looked over his shoulder. His face fell and he swallowed loudly ... the dog was filling the doorway, its teeth bared, and dark, unblinking eyes were staring fixedly in his direction. His mind raced through his list of options, but as lists went, it was miserably short, and Wipp was already looking up at him uselessly, expecting the usual masterly decisions.

Scribber carefully lowered the unconscious child back into her cot and turned to face the dog squarely. Then, with Wipp still watching him and copying his every move, the two of them grew rapidly taller. A moment later, their wet, matted hair was brushing against the ceiling, and their hands, now large and menacing, were easing their cloaks aside to reveal two daggers that had grown with their owners into long, slender swords. Relaxed now, and supremely confident, they looked at each other and smiled knowingly, but if their fear had gone, the dog certainly hadn't. His quiet rumbling had now become a continuous and louder growl, but the tall spriggans didn't care, and looked down at him with cruel amusement flickering in their eyes, convinced that he would back away at any moment.

Without any warning, but with a speed and ferocity which momentarily rooted both spriggans to the spot, the dog leapt into the room and sank his teeth into Wipp's thigh. The unfortunate youngster tried to hold back a howl and shake the dog off, but it was useless, and in the mayhem which followed he groped desperately for his sword. He tugged it awkwardly from his belt and began slashing feverishly at the brave dog, again and again, but either the sword had a mind of its own or the dog was far too clever, for the glittering blade missed its target every time. Scribber was already darting around them as they fought, waving his arms about like a shepherd with stubborn sheep, trying to distract the dog. But none of it worked. To begin with, Wipp cursed quietly under his breath, then more loudly through clenched teeth as his pain quickly grew and his swordplay became more frantic but even less accurate.

Wipp's sword did eventually hit *something*, though. Scribber made the serious mistake of getting a little too close to the fighting, and a second later Wipp was stabbing it neatly into his leader's leg, before letting go and leaving it rocking there like a carving knife stuck in a boiled ham. Scribber stopped abruptly and stared down at it in disbelief, then, with a tight-lipped roar of pain, he pulled it out and hurled it furiously across the room, not caring that everyone in the house must have heard him.

Amazingly, though, Wipp still hadn't given up, despite now being unarmed. With several vicious kicks followed by a brutal twisting action which would have dislodged a starving tiger, he managed to throw the dog off, sending it spinning heavily against Elspeth's wardrobe, whilst Scribber could only hop around the cot in agony, clutching his bleeding leg and snarling like a wounded bear. This all happened in less than one chaotic minute, but they could already hear a man's concerned voice calling out a girl's name.

There was no time to spare. They knew that they must escape at once, but also that there was no question of rushing back down the stairs, however big they both were. Even Scribber didn't relish the thought of an argument with a loaded shotgun. As the dog scrambled back up onto his paws and started to skid on the polished floorboards in his eagerness to attack again, Scribber suddenly threw his arms out to the side. His upturned palms immediately filled with an intense blue-white light which floodlit everything around him ... and stopped the dog exactly where it stood. In the same instant, the door slammed shut with a bang which rattled the pictures on the walls, and a powerful wind sprang up from nowhere, as if by magic. As it rapidly gathered energy, it began to race around the edge of the room, snatching up anything that was loose, and very soon, teddy bears, pictures, clothes and even the pink lamp were flying around in a tight circle, whilst the dog could do no more than lean into the wind and try to stay upright. The ceiling light and most of the curtains were ripped away next, to join the other flying objects, and all the time the noise kept growing and growing, easily masking the sound of running feet in the passageway.

Shielding his eyes from the blinding light, Wipp clung tightly to the cot in the relatively calm air near the centre of the bedroom, and stared, spellbound, as Scribber suddenly hurled the two balls of light straight at the window. They smashed cleanly through it and out into the night, lighting up the entire garden like an unnaturally long lightning flash, and the miniature whirlwind followed close behind them, at first snaking its way out past the jagged remains of the glass, but soon taking the whole window along with it. Splintered wood, shards of glass and lumps of painted plaster were soon joining several bedtime storybooks and tiny knitted cardigans, and together they were all blasted out into the dark, wet night.

The dog was thrown back to the floor with a yelp, but the spriggans ignored him and hopped across the room, each one holding a bleeding leg and shrinking as he went, then leapt through the gaping hole in the wall where Elspeth's window had just been. Still dazzled, they flew blindly downwards through the darkness, landing heavily on the lawn and rolling head over heels before ending up on their backs, staring up at a featureless night sky.

An unearthly silence followed as they lay there, bruised, winded and dazed, with the sleety rain lashing into their faces and most of poor Elspeth's belongings scattered around them on the grass. Several long, precious seconds passed by before they got up stiffly, like old men, and hobbled as quickly as they could across the lawn and into the relative cover of some leafless shrubs and bushes. They went quickly through these, then under the hedge they had recently been so pleased to crawl out of, and on into the trees, trying to run and not looking back. The dog was barking wildly by now, and the tattered remains of Elspeth's curtains flapped in the wind to either side of Farmer Featherstone as he leant out through the hole in the wall with his shotgun raised. It swung left and right as he searched in vain for a target, and suddenly there was a deafening blast as he shot into the trees, as a warning to whoever had managed to escape, if nothing else. Thirty yards away, the startled owl took off hurriedly and flew away to safety, but Wipp let out a shrill scream and fell flat onto his face, quite sure that he'd been hit ... the buckshot tore through the top branches, bringing a shower of twigs and autumn leaves down around him. Scribber stopped and looked back with a face which would have curdled milk.

'Gerrup, you fool!' he growled. 'Yer about as shot as I am.'

He limped away without another word, and a very miserable Wipp could do nothing more than drag himself to his feet and follow as closely as he dared – he was relieved to still be alive, but reeling from the thought that he'd just stabbed his own leader, and already dreading the inevitable and no doubt painful consequences. The two of them half ran and half limped down the muddy lane which led away from the farm, with the incessant barking becoming more distant with each step. Incredibly, it seemed that nobody was following them, but they didn't dare to stop and make sure. All they wanted was to get far away from Willow Garth Farm ... and quickly.

Three minutes later and almost exhausted, they ran blindly into a heavy metal gate across the lane and collapsed against it, panting. The lane behind them still seemed to be empty, and at first nothing was said as they allowed themselves a few moments' rest, but as they got their breath back, the wind suddenly found new energy, howling in amongst the bare trees, and the rain became heavier than ever, stinging their red faces and deepening the puddles around them. Wipp could feel Scribber's murderous glare burning into the side of his neck, but didn't dare to look at him as he examined his stab wound more closely.

'You ... you maggot!' snarled the furious spriggan between gasps for air, as he probed the gory slit in his thigh with one finger. 'You'll pay for this one day, when yer back's turned.'

He took another large lungful or two, and tried to put his weight on his injured leg. He wished that he hadn't, though, and Wipp flinched as several particularly unpleasant words flew past him, close to his hood.

21

'Great, ain't it,' groaned Scribber as the pain subsided a little. 'I 'ad a real nasty feelin' in me bowels when the others suggested I bring *you* along. I should've put me foot down ... foller'd me instincts like I norm'ly do.' He pulled a grimy rag out of a pocket and started to tie it tightly around his wound. 'Well, I shan't be makin' *that* mistake again. You can bet yer stinkin' boots on it!'

'But that dog was tryin' to eat me – I had to do summat!' wailed Wipp, still not looking up. He was picking slivers of glass out of his cloak, and clinging to the hope that his leader would be lenient with him.

But Scribber had seen and heard enough. According to his best reckoning, he was already wounded, tired, cold, wet and starving, but just to finish his day off perfectly, next month's special main course was nicely drugged and asleep ... and still in her warm bed. It was all far too much for him. Wipp had found all the glass he could and was checking his hands for cuts when a sweeping blow from a stiff arm knocked him cleanly off his feet and into a deep, mud-filled wheel rut. Scribber opened his mouth to shout out something too, but he couldn't be bothered any more. Instead, he dragged the heavy gate open with a struggle, then limped down the lane towards the relative safety of Lonmoor Woods, muttering various curses and shrinking down to his smallest size as he finally faded into the darkness.

Wipp got up and was wiping the worst of the mud from his backside when it dawned on him that he was all alone on the lane, with a ferocious dog and an armed farmer not so very far away. It seemed to be darker than ever, too, with danger lurking on all sides, and he knew that he had no choice but to follow Scribber yet again. With a final, anxious look around him, he did exactly that ... but at a safe distance.

*   *   *

Eighteen-year-old Annie Featherstone held Elspeth close to her chest as she paced up and down the upstairs passageway, rocking her unconscious baby sister. She was so, *so* close to tears, but trying desperately to stop them from breaking out in front of her other younger sister, Victoria, for that would be the very last thing that was needed. Although Victoria was nearly fifteen and fairly tough as far as girls went, Annie knew that she was completely devoted to Elspeth, and would be devastated knowing that their little sister had been harmed in some dreadful but inexplicable way.

Their father was standing at the end of the passageway, his shotgun resting against the wall and the acrid smoke from his shot still hanging around him in a spreading, hazy layer. Victoria's arms were locked tightly around his waist as she knelt next to him, in shock and crying inconsolably, but pleading with him between sobs to tell her what he'd been shooting at, and why Elspeth wouldn't wake up.

'Hush, Vicky. Hush now!' he urged, as he dropped down onto one knee beside her, his arm going around her shoulders and his big, farmer's hand pushing the hair back off her wet cheeks.

He glanced up at Annie as he knelt there, hoping for any encouraging news, but there was only a shake of her head and very, very tightly closed lips in reply.

'Victoria,' he said, speaking up and trying his best to sound unruffled. 'I want you to do what you can with our Annie while I get some more help. I need you to be really brave. Can you do that for me, lass?'

Despite his best efforts, he couldn't completely hide his growing alarm, and the last few words broke up slightly as his throat began to tighten. As he spoke to her, he looked down with dismay at the shattered young face pressing into his shoulder, and suddenly felt as if his mind was being torn in two. One part was fighting to keep control, to comfort his frightened family and retrieve some sort of order from the chaos which had engulfed them all, but the other part was already starting to spin, as his thoughts raced back to the death of his wife a year earlier, shortly after Elspeth was born. He'd been hopelessly in love with her: she'd been his whole world, his reason to live, and work, and laugh, and her sudden, mysterious death had shattered his life in every conceivable way. He wasn't sure how he could survive another catastrophe so soon after the last one ... or even *if* he could.

Victoria had now almost stopped crying, and she gazed up at him through the last of her tears. He rarely used her proper name, and so she realised that he really *did* need her to be brave – just like Annie. She nodded slowly, sucking in some deep breaths and wiping those tears away with the back of her shaking hand, then, with the sobs now nothing more than loud, wet sniffs, she left him and walked quickly to Elspeth's room, suddenly determined to make him proud of her. She pushed the door open and tried the light switch, but it didn't work, so she opened the door wider to let more light in. The room was a complete shambles. Rain was blowing in where the window had once been, soaking the walls and floor, and almost everything except the larger pieces of furniture had gone, somehow.

There were splashes of dark blood everywhere, some even running down the wet wallpaper, and she glanced up at five long, reddish-brown smudges across the ceiling where someone's bloody fingers had been. She shuddered at the sight of them, wondering briefly how anyone had managed to reach that high, then shut the wardrobe doors and picked up Elspeth's fallen chair, still fighting to keep her tears away. The discarded dagger lay under it, waiting ... With a prickle of fear on the back of her neck which she didn't expect, she picked it up and held it between a trembling thumb and finger, staring at it as it hung there, sticky with someone's blood. Confused and still frightened, she suddenly went to the missing window, held it out into the wind and rain, and dropped it into the garden. She didn't know exactly where, and she didn't care. She just wanted it out of her little sister's room forever. Finally, she walked up to the cot and ran her finger thoughtfully over the top edge of the headboard before starting to tidy Elspeth's blankets, quite unaware of what was lurking underneath them.

Wide awake and now free at last, the large bat flew up into her face, its wings beating powerfully but with barely a sound, and Victoria screamed. This was no spider-scream or tickle-scream, though. Long, shrill and piercing, it cut through the farmhouse like a sharpened axe through rotting wood, into every room and even out into the garden. She dropped the blankets and covered her face with her hands whilst the bat fluttered around the room at great speed, its long, paper-thin wings flicking her hair several times as it flashed past her. Annie and her father were running long before the scream had finished, and they burst into the bedroom together – just as the bat flew out through the remains of the window and away into the night. Victoria was left standing in the middle of the room, shocked into silence and unable to bring her hands down from her face.

Her father rushed to her, and once again he was down on one knee, holding her tightly. He stared at the mess in the room and pushed his other hand through his hair as a cold sweat began to break out all over him: he could feel his heartbeat throbbing in his neck as he tried to think quickly, but somehow he just couldn't. He did know, however, that he had to leave them all and get downstairs to the telephone. He simply *had* to.

Oh my God! There'll be snow on the top road by now – an ambulance will never make it. Should I get her in the Land Rover and take her myself? P'raps take Annie too...? Think straight, man! Think straight!

He got up and placed an unsteady hand on Elspeth's head as Annie held her in her arms.

Elspeth. My wonderful, perfect Elspeth. What's happened to you, my little love?

In some heartbreaking but wonderful way, she was the parting gift from his dead wife, and far more precious to him than any words of his could ever describe. With a brief, tortured look at each of the three remaining loves of his life, he turned and walked quickly out of the bedroom.

Fugitives and Friends

The wounded spriggans staggered through Lonmoor Woods as quickly as their injuries would allow them, for it certainly wasn't the sort of place to linger in. Mortals such as the Featherstones may have been blissfully unaware of what diabolical creatures actually lived there, but the spriggans knew very well indeed. Many a twisted tree root cleverly concealed the entrance to a stinking bogle or goblin den, whilst several of the muddy pools along the course of the stream were homes to even worse things, best not spoken of. As they picked their way between the trees, they tried not to think about who might be watching them pass by – or how they preferred their spriggans cooked.

As it happened, good fortune was still with them. They were reasonably familiar with Lonmoor's pathways, even at night, so they eventually arrived at a small gurgling stream just beyond the last of the trees, without once getting lost or attacked. It was now long past midnight and unusually dark because the moon had set early, but at least the infernal rain had stopped. They sat and rested on some boulders set into the bank of the stream, and scooped up a few handfuls of water to drink. Wipp kept yawning and despite what he'd done to Scribber's leg, complaining. All he could think about was getting back to the caves and devouring whatever was left of supper, followed by a long, deep sleep: a dangerous journey to Redcap's fortress without any meals in sight was the very last thing he wanted. Scribber was having none of it, though.

'Don't you *ever* listen?' he groaned. 'When are y' gonner get it through that thick skull o' yours? Redcap said bring the key *straight* back to 'im at Skelton tower! ... or did I get it wrong? P'raps me lug 'oles were a bit blocked.' He wriggled a finger vigorously in each ear, then stood up, crossed his arms and bowed his legs outwards, goblin fashion. Wipp knew exactly what was coming next, but there was no escape for him as the lecture continued.

'Oh, and by the way, please don't rush back. Absolutely not! In fact, have a few days' rest back at your caves first if you're feeling a bit tired, my dear friends,' said Scribber, giving a passable impersonation of Redcap. 'Is *that* what 'e said? I don't think so! Straight back means straight back, in my book, 'n' more than likely in 'is, too.'

Wipp had a sudden feeling that another swinging arm was coming his way, and so eased himself across his boulder to get a little further away from Scribber.

''Course, if *you* want to explain to 'im why we're a day late, then be my ruddy guest,' continued Scribber, without taking a breath, 'but do it when I'm somewhere else, right? *You* might be 'appy to rot away at the bottom of that escarpment of 'is, but –' the irritated spriggan jabbed his finger into his own chest far more firmly than he'd meant to '– there's no way *I'll* be joinin' you down there!'

Wipp was staring down at the rushing water, and didn't reply. He definitely didn't want to rot – down Redcap's horribly steep escarpment, or anywhere else come to that – but most of all, he knew that Scribber was going to get his own way as usual, whatever it took.

It was over seven miles to Redcap's tower at Skelton. The journey there was usually a difficult one, even in good weather, but they would have covered those miles quickly, moving as fast as young weasels late for their tea. This time, though, it was very different, for the ground was slippery and soft, and up to now each step had been agony for them. Wipp's thigh was swelling up around a neat square of four deep and bloody holes which exactly matched the dog's fangs, whilst Scribber's stab wound throbbed so much that he was sure he could hear it.

Just for a change, Wipp ended up getting his wish in the end, or at least part of it. No one could say exactly why they both fell asleep. Admittedly, they *were* injured and their escape *had* been exhausting – even frightening at times. Then perhaps it was their empty stomachs, or their natural love of sleeping whenever they weren't out stealing ... or just a yawningly good mixture of them all. Whatever the reason, sleep soon crept up on them, right there on the grassy banks of the stream, knocking them out without any more warning than a stretch and a rubbed eye or two. Even the steady *wop – wop – wop* of a sleek emergency helicopter as it raced along the far side of the valley did nothing more than make them roll over and pull their knees up under their cloaks.

* * *

Just as the church clock in the village struck one, a dazzling searchlight beam suddenly cut through the night sky and played over Willow Garth Farm. An air ambulance hovered noisily high above it. The bright circle of light soon found the lawn and stayed on it shakily as the aircraft made its way downwards, carefully avoiding the electricity wires and trees as it did so, then blasting away every fallen leaf from the garden and its hedges as it landed hesitantly on the grass.

The deafening scream of its turbine changed to a dying whine, and the rotors began to slow down. Then, as the pilot waited and watched, two men in green overalls jumped out clutching a bag each and, bending low, ran under the spinning rotors, across the lawn and straight through the open doorway of the farmhouse. A very anxious Robert Featherstone stepped aside before following them in. The rotors slowed down to a stop, then hung there, resting. Everything went quiet, and the light from an upstairs window showed that it was starting to snow lightly, but back on the banks of the stream, Wipp pulled his hood around his ears and began to snore.

Eight minutes went by before the red door opened again and bright light spilled out across the whitening grass. Little Elspeth, who was now wrapped up in metal foil to keep her warm, lay in the arms of one of the paramedics as he walked quickly back to the helicopter, trying to avoid the larger pieces of debris and her belongings which were still scattered across the lawn. The other man followed at his side, holding up a bottle of clear fluid connected to a tube which disappeared somewhere into that small but most precious of bundles. The farmer trailed along behind them in a sort of daze, leaving his dark footprints in the powdering of snow and, for a while at least, his entire familiar world behind him as he, too, climbed aboard. Annie and Victoria were left standing in the doorway, silhouetted in the light and trying not to cry, but this time failing. The family doctor was behind them with his hands on their shoulders, shouting something encouraging to them both, but it was drowned out as the turbine started up again. Its whine soon grew to a screaming howl as the rotors sped up, chopping powerfully through the falling snow and finally lifting the helicopter up and away from them.

*　　*　　*

The spriggans didn't stir. In fact, they slept through what was left of the night and long into the next cold, grey day.

Even breakfast time passed without them waking, and much of the dismal morning had gone by when they finally awoke, covered in a dusting of fine snow and under a disconcertingly high, but cool, hazy sun.

Wipp was first, disturbed by one of his own louder snores, but Scribber was close behind him – with the help of a carefully judged kick from Wipp's boot. Nothing was said as they got up and stretched their stiff, aching legs. Each one knew that they were equally at fault, but plenty of dark looks passed between them – albeit mostly in one direction. Needless to say, there was no hope of a late breakfast, and the pangs of hunger in their hollow stomachs soon merged into one continuous, gnawing grumble.

Now, although it hadn't been planned, they'd had a good rest if nothing else, and in some ways were as refreshed as they could be when they started to climb up the eastern slopes of Farndale, glad to be leaving Lonmoor and its unpleasant secrets far behind them. The lush, frosted grass under their boots soon gave way to brown bracken, dying off now in the winter chill but still high enough to force them both to grow a little taller than usual: Redcap was waiting, and they didn't have any time to waste by getting lost in amongst it. Their climb was hard and painful, but at least the cold wind kept it from being hot work, and they weren't even sweating when the bracken eventually turned to short, springy heather on the highest slopes. They made better time over this, and less than an hour later found themselves up on Blakey Ridge, trying to get their breath back as they stood close to the edge of the lonely road which runs north–south across the moors, but they could barely see it underneath its shallow covering of snow and slushy, indistinct puddles.

It was a depressing place to be, and as the icy wind blew their hoods back and threw their tangled hair around, they leant into it and let it tug at their cloaks. Even with their eyes streaming, they could see the whole of Rosedale valley in front of them: wide, deep and dotted at regular intervals with the farms of men, the moors melting away into a vague grey-blue horizon far beyond it. The last traces of the disused railway line snaked its way around the valley's edge, following every contour but remaining level as it twisted and turned, and over two miles away they could even see remnants of the ancient iron ore works scattered along its route, a dim reminder of past times when the valley had rung with the clamour of a thousand pickaxes down a dozen deep and extremely dangerous mines.

As Scribber stood there hunched and shivering, his thoughts slowly drifted back to the key inside his cloak.

If it's so blinkin' valuable to Redcap, there might be others who'd pay even more for it ... p'raps a lot more. Now there's a thing!'

Typically, his mind considered the possible rewards first, but the less agreeable details followed close behind them.

And anyways, what's the ruddy thing gonner unlock? And 'oo's to say 'ow many greedy swine already know we 'ave it? Hell's bloody bells. Some good-for-nothin' could be follerin' us right now! I must be soft in the 'ed standin' 'ere in the open for everyone and their dog to gawp at!

Not for the first time in his life, Scribber was torn between saving his skin and earning an easy income, but it was a difficult choice for him, and one he didn't feel ready to make ... not yet, anyway. He looked briefly all around, wondering if a murderous bogle was hiding in amongst the heather, preparing to leap on their backs and rearrange their throats with his knife. With a final glance up and down the deserted road – but not one word to Wipp – he splashed his way across it and set off eastwards towards Skelton, kicking the snow off the heather as he went. As ever, all Wipp could do was pull his hood tightly around his red, tingling ears and follow, with a heavy heart and a light stomach.

Making their way downhill, they passed close by the ancient burial mound at Kettle Howe, now nothing more than a thirty foot bump in the snowy heather, and eventually found themselves in the tall bracken again. They felt safer in amongst this, with only the tops of their heads showing as they weaved their way down, sometimes following old sheep tracks, sometimes making their own. Fifteen minutes later the land began to level out and the bracken surrendered to trees as they approached the lowest and wettest part of the valley. Scribber had explored this part of Rosedale many years before, but it was all new and unsettling to Wipp, who was now trying to keep one eye on his leader and the other on the trees around them.

Despite the level, easier going, Wipp was close to being worn out. He probably didn't have Scribber's stamina, and certainly not his wisdom (as Scribber often reminded him), for he decided to stop and empty the twigs out of his boots. Scribber carried on ahead as he leant against the smooth grey trunk of a large beech tree and struggled to pull off one of his boots. He'd barely started when a thin, hairy arm sprang out from a hole between the roots and a small but terrifyingly strong hand seized his ankle with a vice-like grip before tugging him downwards. In that same instant, the silence was shattered as Wipp squealed like a pig being dragged into a butcher's shed. Several of his worst nightmares seemed to be coming true for him all at once, as he imagined finding himself in a crowded den of half-crazed goblins, each one of them intent on devouring him alive, one limb at a time. Trying with all his strength to pull away, he groped frantically for his dagger, but his squeal leapt several notes higher when his fingers found only an empty scabbard. Raw terror quickly filled every nerve and fibre of his quivering body.

Now, Scribber wasn't in the habit of doing unpaid favours, particularly for lesser spriggans than himself, so it was quite out of character for him to turn back and help Wipp. If the truth were told, he was keen to stop all the noise quickly, before every little thug within five miles pricked up his pointed ears and set off to find an easy meal and some new boots. With Wipp in the throes of a bizarre version of tug of war in which his injured leg seemed to be the rope, Scribber returned with his dagger drawn. Without a word, or even a sideways glance, he walked straight up to Wipp and brought the blade sweeping down towards the hideous arm. It went through its wrist cleanly, pinning it to the tree and freeing Wipp in the same second, for he fell backwards, still screaming, and holding onto his leg as if it was about to be stolen from him. Not wishing to miss out on the chance of getting one up on a trapped goblin, Scribber gave the dagger several vicious twists before pulling it out of the tree, and the arm vanished even more quickly than it had appeared. There was nothing more than a blood-splattered leaf or two and some muffled whimpering from somewhere under the grass to say that anything unusual had happened there at all.

Scribber glared down at Wipp with an expression which left the wretched youngster in no doubt that his leader had very little respect for him – but basketfuls of contempt.

'You fool! You cretinous, half-baked fool!' he shouted, in amongst a spray of dark spit. He searched around uselessly for a few more appropriate words as he wiped his dagger on his cloak, but failed, and walked away in disgust.

Wipp stood up and brushed some wet leaves off his legs. He was feeling embarrassed and wishing desperately that he'd put up a braver defence, but he already knew that it was too late for all of that. As he ran to catch up, the awful truth dawned on him: Scribber would soon be enjoying telling the tale to everyone back at the caves, and his own miserable life there would become even more horrific than it usually was.

After ten minutes mostly spent tripping over the thorny briars which criss-crossed the ground, they heard running water ahead of them, and it wasn't long before they found themselves beside the River Seven, in the very bowels of Rosedale. It was swollen by the recent rains, and the two spriggans looked down doubtfully at the brown, surging water from the top of a steep bank of crumbling rock and slippery clay, with the sweet smell of damp, rotting vegetation filling the air. Scribber had a vague memory that this was the easiest place to cross, as impenetrable thickets of the dreadful briars lined the rest of the riverbanks in both directions for as far as they could see.

They slithered down the bank and eventually managed to cross the river on some of the larger boulders which showed just above its surface – with a wobble or two and a filled boot for Scribber halfway across, much to Wipp's private amusement. On the far bank was a small level area, also surrounded by briars, but thankfully the path was still plain to see, disappearing into the trees beyond. They hurried along, both wishing they had eyes in the backs of their hoods ... it was that kind of place.

As it happened, their instincts served them well, for they'd barely gone twenty yards when Scribber stopped and thrust his arm out in front of Wipp, nearly knocking him off his feet. They stood side by side, like two strange little bushes on legs, as the distant sound of tramping boots and chattering voices announced the end of their good luck. Wipp's glowing cheeks quickly turned pale, and even Scribber looked seriously worried, for he had no wish to meet any strangers whilst he had the bronze key on him. There was no escaping, though, with the river and its steep bank behind them and a dense wall of briars to either side of the narrow pathway.

'Oh, what joy,' groaned Scribber sarcastically before leaning towards Wipp and making it quite clear who was to blame for their predicament. 'It's 'ardly surprsin' they 'erd you back there with your goblin friend, is it? Come on, quick!' he ordered, before turning and heading back towards the river.

It was all there was time to say. Wipp soon caught up with him, but before he could ask what was happening, Scribber was gritting his teeth and pushing himself through the briars towards a thick layer of autumn leaves which had built up under them. A few seconds and several curses later, he was invisible, lying on his side amongst the leaves with his knees under his chin and his leafy cloak pulled up over him. Wipp watched, open-mouthed at first, but he came to his wits just before it was too late and did the same, not daring to utter a sound as the briars did their best to tear his hands to shreds. They had no choice but to wait and take their chances together, Scribber with his hand on his dagger, and Wipp once again bitterly regretting that he was unarmed.

The voices came closer, and all too soon they were right beside the spriggans as a large group of travellers came to a halt. Peering through a gap under his hood, Scribber watched with growing horror as a jumble of leather boots milled around less than a yard from the tip of his nose. He couldn't believe how quickly his luck had turned, and cursed the boots' owners, whoever they were, for choosing to stop exactly where he and Wipp were hiding, and not crossing the river at once. The key was digging into his side as tried to breathe without moving his ribs, and he cursed *it* as well – for getting him into this trouble in the first place.

But his heart sank even further when he suddenly realised that at least some of the travellers were goblins. He knew that if he and Wipp were captured by a large enough group of them, they could easily find themselves dangling over a red hot fire, perhaps to provide some light entertainment, but possibly for something much, much worse. From the sound of it, there was an argument going on, and Scribber began to notice some strange voices in amongst the general hubbub. These were completely new to him: deeper, but also smoother in a disturbing kind of way – definitely not the sort to trust, and best never heard again, he immediately decided.

Many of the group then began to talk at once. It appeared that they couldn't decide which way to go, for there was much said about crossing or not crossing rivers, or following someone upstream, or perhaps downstream – that sort of thing. They weren't the only ones with a dilemma, however. Curiosity was Scribber's second greatest weakness after greed, and he was now desperate to know who these unusual voices belonged to, although he knew that sneaking a look would be extremely dangerous. The chattering continued.

'I bet we missed them back in the bracken. They could have walked past us, right under our noses. Remember what crafty little scabs they are,' said one grating goblin voice.

He sniffed the air like a dog, as if a strange smell was worrying him. Lying there curled up, Scribber's nose was almost in his own armpit. He sniffed too ... and promised himself a plunge in a stream if he survived long enough to find one.

'If we missed them, then *you* fools are to blame,' snapped one of the deeper voices. 'You're supposed to be expert trackers – or so you assured us when you took our money – and nothing ever gets past you. What a joke! I doubt if you could even find your own stinking hovels on a summer's afternoon!'

This carried on for a while, with some pushing and

shoving thrown in for good measure, and everyone becoming steadily more agitated. Looking the other way, Scribber could just see Wipp – or a mound of leaves that he thought *might* be Wipp, but thankfully, the leafy mound wasn't stirring.

'P'raps there's a bit more to 'im than meets the eye, after all,' thought Scribber, mildly surprised.

Another one of the deep voices suddenly broke in over the general squabbling.

'Very well, then. If you can't decide which way they went, perhaps *this* will help you to think more clearly!'

There was a sudden metallic ring as a sword was drawn, and in the same second Scribber decided that he couldn't bear it any more and had to get a better view. Twisting his face sideways, he edged his hood into a new position using his cheek and tongue, and soon he could see six goblins as well as the lower halves of four much taller, slimmer figures. One of these was holding a long, curved sabre, its point only a few inches from the nose of an amazingly unconcerned goblin. Scribber stretched his neck – and his luck – to see a *tiny* bit more.

With a sudden excruciating feeling that most of his innards were doing their best to crawl up into his throat, he realised that the taller ones were dark elves. He'd heard stories about them around the cooking fires when he was young, but had been fortunate enough never to cross paths with a real live one. They fitted their description perfectly. Menacing, deep-set eyes were set a little too close together for comfort, and almost lost below dark, bushy eyebrows. Their hooked noses arched down to thin, cruel lips, whilst black wiry beards sprouted from the very ends of their pointed chins. They were dressed in black from head to toe and, as far as Scribber was concerned, looked entirely capable of living up to their extremely unpleasant reputation.

'We'd better be going, Malrin,' said one of the other dark elves politely, gazing through the trees to where the sun was setting. 'There's not much of the day left.'

'True enough. They must be further west of here,' replied the one with the drawn sabre. 'We couldn't have missed them the way we came – even with half-blind goblins as scouts.' He glared down towards the ugly specimen at the tip of his blade.

'And above all, we mustn't let the key slip away from us,' insisted a third one. 'We'll never have a better chance of getting it than now. If Redcap gets his greedy fingers on it first, things could get very difficult for us. Why, *bloodshed* might even be called for!'

The fourth elf, a particularly tall, repulsive creature with a thin white scar running from his ear to his chin, joined in.

'More than likely, I'm sure,' he chuckled, running a finger along his scar, 'but that rat of a hobgoblin seemed sure that the spriggans sent to steal it *must* come this way to get back to Redcap ... unless he was lying, of course – which would be nothing new. We have to find a good place to attack them.' He looked around, assessing the merits of where they stood.

'It's no good here,' broke in the third one again, as he eyed up the briars disapprovingly. 'Wait a minute. When we find them, what if they've swallowed the key?'

Scribber gulped quietly and grimaced. The news that they were hunting for him and Wipp was already twisting his bowels into a tight, painful knot.

'Huh! There's no problem there,' chirped the scarred one brightly. 'I'll just keep slicing bits off until I hit something hard.' He drew his sabre a few inches out of its scabbard and rattled it, grinning.

'Ingenious!' replied his leader, clearly impressed. 'But I think it might be less messy if we just burn them away to nothing in a roaring fire, then rake through the ashes for the key. That way we can even keep warm while we're waiting.'

Given the cold weather, this seemed to be a popular suggestion, and there was plenty of nodding going on as they discussed the finer but somewhat gruesome details. It didn't last for long, though, as a piercing, nasal voice interrupted their conversation.

'You didn't say anything about important keys when you hired us lot.'

The conversations stopped dead, and all eyes turned to the lowly goblin who had dared to speak. Incredibly, it was the one who was still looking up along the sabre. He was obviously stupid, as well as cheeky, thought Scribber.

Malrin looked at his lads and smiled, before moving the end of his sabre around in a circle close to the goblin's face, as if he was choosing a particular feature to permanently alter, or even remove.

'And what gave you the idea that we might want to discuss our private business with a bunch of festering *goblins*?' he asked, looking down along his nose and blade.

The dark elf watched, bemused, as the defiant goblin stuck his chin out another inch and crossed his arms.

'For a start, we like to know from the beginning exactly what's going on ... and if there are valuables involved, we usually get a share,' he replied confidently.

One or two of his colleagues shuffled their feet or glanced nervously at each other, but the goblin seemed determined to strike a fairer deal for himself and his friends, staring up at the dark elf boldly and still taking little notice of the razor sharp steel which had come to a stop in front of his left eye ... To everyone's amazement, and possibly one goblin's quiet relief, the elf chuckled and sheathed his weapon. Perhaps there *was* a kindly side to dark elves after all, guessed Scribber, as he watched and listened, fascinated. The elf started to turn away and the goblin just had time to grin proudly at the others before a gloved fist sprang at him from above and seized him by the throat. The grin vanished as Malrin's leather-covered fingers squeezed and lifted at the same time, effortlessly raising the goblin clear of the ground and half choking him for good measure.

Scribber realised that his guess had been horribly wrong, and the others all watched, shocked into silence and mesmerised, as the elf carried the wriggling goblin towards a large briar-wrapped tree and, ignoring the little boots trying frantically to kick their way to freedom, thrust the wretched creature through the briars and up against the trunk. By some black magic or other, he stuck there like a hat on a hook, and no amount of squirming would release him as the dark elf returned to the group, straight-faced, and turned to watch the results of his handiwork. The only sounds came from the goblin as he pulled feverishly at the thorny briars bare-handed ... and the splintering of living wood as a huge branch high up in the tree started to rock up and down violently. The dark elf stared up at it intently, willing it to break. No one else dared to move. With a series of deafening cracks the branch suddenly rotated downwards like a giant door knocker, crashing through the lesser branches, then smashing into the trunk and the screaming goblin with a sickening, squelchy thud.

Scribber couldn't see what was happening, but he heard the dreadful noise and even felt the power of it through the ground where he lay hidden, as the unfortunate goblin's last, pitiful screech was silenced mid note. A heavy, brooding silence followed, during which the shocked spriggan vowed to avoid dark elves at all costs, for as long as he lived.

It seemed that this particular elf was no longer interested

in having the remaining goblins along as scouts, company, or anything else, for he turned, drew and swung his sabre in one smooth movement, its curved blade sweeping in a wide arc and taking the two nearest goblin beards cleanly off their respective chins. Everyone else realised that necks could easily have been his target if he had so wished, and the remaining scouts needed no further encouragement to leave. With fleeting glances at each other just to confirm that they all agreed, they turned on their heels and fled along the path, back the way they'd come. The elf snorted under his breath and sheathed his sabre, clearly despising them for running off like cowards, but he didn't seem particularly surprised.

In amongst the fallen leaves, Scribber wondered if his luck had changed for the better at last. With their guides seeking safer work elsewhere, it was possible that the dark elves would now move on, and just for once, the news was good.

'Follow me, you lot,' ordered the leader, scowling, 'unless you want to spend the night here in the open, that is.'

Without waiting for a reply, he leapt from boulder to boulder across the water, not even wetting his boots, and was soon at the top of the steep bank on the other side. He stopped and looked back over his shoulder, before shouting down to the others.

'Come on, you layabouts. There's work to be done!'

With that, he promptly disappeared from view along the pathway towards Farndale, quite unaware that he'd just missed the perfect opportunity to catch his quarry.

Dusk was creeping up on them through the trees when the spriggans finally dared to crawl out from their hiding place, like two hedgehogs disturbed from their winter's sleep. After unhooking themselves from countless thorns, they stood up and shook the leaf litter and twigs from their hair and cloaks. Wipp was trying to get something out of his nose as he waited to hear what they were going to do next.

'It looks like we've got our dear 'ob to thank for all this,' grumbled Scribber through clenched teeth. 'He must 'ave seen us at the Featherstones' place, the nosey little ferret.'

'Prob'ly,' replied Wipp vaguely, as he tried a different finger.

'Hoy!' exclaimed Scribber. 'We seem to be makin' a habit of this, don't we?' He was glaring at Wipp, who snatched his hand down from his nose and hid it behind his back.

'Not that, you idiot – our luck. We've wormed our way out of trouble twice since last night. Somebody must love us after all!'

Wipp didn't answer. He was too tired and hungry, and he didn't know of anyone who even *liked* them, let alone loved them.

'Look, these 'ere dark elves are behind us now, ain't they?' went on Scribber, a little more optimistically, 'and gettin' further away by the minute, 'n' all. So our best plan is to get to the tower quick-like and finish our business with our goblin friend, agreed?'

Wipp look puzzled, and opened his mouth to ask about the 'friend' part, but, as ever, Scribber was stating a decision, not inviting a discussion, and he'd already sped off along the path. Wipp followed a few paces behind him, where he could at least finish sorting his nose out in peace, and as they hobbled along with their stomachs complaining more loudly than ever, Scribber thought about Redcap and the key again.

If these dark elves are tryin' so 'ard to find it, then it must be a right special key, that's for sure.

Predictably, his mind began to consider the possible treasures it might lead him to, and for some time he walked on humming to himself, wondering how best to proceed.

Okay, so I arn't completely sure what to do when we reach the tower, but that's my business and only mine. If Wipp only knew ... Gaud Almighty, I'd never hear the end of it!

Behind them, the entire western cloud-streaked sky grew steadily darker and redder, until a dazzling shaft of sunlight appeared unexpectedly from below the very lowest cloud, casting long, stretched shadows ahead of them and in-between the trees around them. The spriggans continued walking with the sunset glowing on the backs of their cloaks and hoods, happy in the knowledge that at least this *Malrin* and his dark elves were heading in the opposite direction.

*   *   *

Victoria slowly opened her eyes and stared absently at the rough, plastered wall at the far side of her bedroom, still half asleep as the first of the morning sunlight streamed through the trees beyond the garden and cast patterns of bright, moving spots across it. She watched them playing around one of her pictures, utterly lost in their constantly changing shape and motion. As she lay there, she became dimly aware of familiar noises coming from the yard outside, as old Tom, their underpaid but uncomplaining farmhand, urged the cows into the milking parlour, six at a time. The persistent hum of the milk cooler and pumps, the heavy, wooden door banging shut every ten minutes, and even the cows complaining in their usual, melancholic way – they were all sleepy, comforting sounds, almost tempting her back into her dreams.

But as she watched the spots of light and began to wake up properly, memories of that horrible night began to come back to her, in a trickle at first, but then smothering her under a tidal wave of sadness. She crossed her arms over her eyes and squeezed her fists tightly shut.

Oh, Elspeth. Poor Elspeth. Pleeeeease let her be all right. Why, oh why can't it all be a nightmare? At least I could cope with that.

She wished so hard that it might be, but of course it wasn't. It was all very real, and painful, too, as the vice-like ache of grief and despair already began to tighten in her throat. After a mental effort she even surprised herself with, she pushed most of her dismal thoughts aside, pulled on her dressing gown and shuffled along the passageway to find Annie, yawning as she went.

Annie was in her room, standing at the mirror with her head tilted to one side, and brushing her curly hair with short, strong strokes. Without turning, she smiled warmly at Victoria's reflection as her sister came in, but said nothing – which more or less said everything. Victoria managed to smile back sleepily before walking up to Elspeth's cot, which was now against Annie's wall. She ran her fingers across the small bare sheet, deep in thought.

'Will the nurses have tried to feed her yet?' she suddenly asked, unable to drag her eyes away from the cot. 'She must be so hungry by now, the poor little mite. If only she'd take some milk in her sleep, they could get rid of that drip thing, couldn't they? By the way, I'm sorry I didn't help downstairs this morning. I think I overslept.'

'I'm sure she's fine, and not in any danger,' said Annie reassuringly, amused at having to wait so long to get a word in. 'And stop worrying yourself about not helping. You're a *brilliant* help to me and Dad, you *know* you are. We couldn't manage without you.' Still brushing, she looked at Victoria over her shoulder. 'Dad rang earlier. He's leaving York hospital about now, and coming straight home.'

Victoria was about to ask something, but Annie already knew what, and stopped her with a touch of her lips.

45

'Don't worry, she's just the same as yesterday ... safe and comfortable. They'll soon sort her out, you'll see.' Annie did her best to sound confident and Victoria seemed satisfied with the latest news from York.

Lost in her own thoughts again, she left Annie's room and wandered away, only to soon find herself warmly dressed and out in the yard ... although not sure exactly how. The morning was bright and cool, her favourite sort of morning normally. A disgruntled whinny broke into her gloomy thoughts as her pony reminded her that he'd been ignored for too long. Victoria crossed the yard to the stable, and stroked his forehead whilst he looked out hopefully from over the door. They were pleased to see each other. Her best friend, Mark, had his own horse, too, and sometimes they trekked for miles together over the moors, but she wasn't in the mood for riding, and even those happy memories couldn't excite her now.

With her pony apparently satisfied that he hadn't been completely forgotten, she suddenly felt the urge to run to the far side of the lawn, from where she could see the whole valley. A few moments later she was standing by the low garden wall, and only a yard or two from the hedge where the spriggans had so recently hidden.

She took in the view slowly and deliberately, savouring everything in it. She'd grown up with this scenery. In some ways it was almost a part of her, and she'd often sought refuge in it when she'd been upset or miserable. She regarded each farm, copse, field and wall as old friends, and as she scanned the breathtaking panorama in front of her, she was pleased to meet each one of them yet again. To the north, the head of the valley was an indistinct blur, half lost in mist, but nearby, every detail was as clear as spring water. She could see the last few herds of cattle still not taken in for winter dotted about on the lower pastures, whilst on the higher grassland, scattered flocks of sheep were grazing as far up as the bracken-covered upper slopes. To the south, Lonmoor Woods stretched away from her, carpeting that part of the valley under a glorious muddle of trees determined to show off the very last of their vibrant autumn colours. In places, they swept downwards in wide, rolling swathes of ochre, gold and lush wine-red, right up to the river in the valley bottom, itself still engorged by the recent rainfall. She noticed some mist there, too, curling lazily around the trunks of the willows which grew along the banks, and suddenly wished that she could be in amongst them again, as she had been so many times before.

But with Elspeth so poorly, the magic of the view was spoiled, its sparkle all but snuffed out, and as hopelessness welled up uncontrollably in her again, her eyes began to fill with tears for the first time that day. She wasn't sure exactly how long she stayed there. Joyful memories and bleak daydreams tumbled together aimlessly through her mind as she leant on the wall with her chin in her hands, sometimes gazing out across the valley as far as she could see, and sometimes looking down, studying the moss and lichens on the stones near her elbows.

She was just thinking back to Elspeth's first birthday party, and smiling to herself as she recalled blowing out the candle on her cake for her, when she recognised the sound of her father's old Land Rover making its way up the lane towards the farm. She snapped back to reality in an instant, turning and running across the lawn to the end of the gravelled drive where the vehicle had already stopped. She tugged open the door before her Dad could even switch off the engine, and he'd hardly drawn a breath when Victoria reached in and pulled him out of his seat. He'd already guessed what was coming, and so wasn't surprised when two or three familiar questions hit him in rapid succession. It cheered him up straight away, and he chuckled as he held her by her shoulders at arm's length, waiting for her to calm down.

'She's absolutely *fine*, lass,' he said slowly and deliberately, hoping that the half-truth was convincing enough. 'They're still keeping her in a special room all of her own and watching her like hawks.'

Victoria opened her mouth to ask the obvious question but her father was too quick for her.

'She couldn't be in better hands, so don't you dare get thinking you have to go and sit with her all day long and half the night as well!'

She clung to each vital word and studied his face as he spoke, searching for white lies, but he must have done well, for she couldn't find a trace of any. She still wanted more information, though.

'Do they know what's wrong with her yet, Dad?'

'Not yet, half-pint,' he replied, using her favourite nickname. 'They still think she's in a sort of coma, but not like any they've seen before. There's not much more they can do apart from look after her, and wait and see.' He was relieved to be able to tell the whole truth this time.

'She must be starved if she's not eating anything,' said Victoria glumly, staring down at her boots. 'But Annie said she's not in real danger. Isn't that right?'

Her father was wiping some mud from his wing mirror as she looked up at him.

'Ay lass. *Exactly* right.'

He didn't risk looking back at her and giving away his innermost fears, but Victoria missed the sign, fortunately.

'That's great, Dad. Thank goodness!' She suddenly seemed much happier and turned to leave, her mind already elsewhere. She looked back over her shoulder at him. 'I think I'm off to the willows for a while, Dad. Is that okay?'

He looked up then, concerned. He was wishing that he'd

made a better job of reassuring her but, so far, he could see no end to the upheaval caused by the break-in, and actually could even have done with some reassurances himself.

''Course it is, love,' he answered more cheerfully. 'You get along. But don't be all day. I know what you're like when you get daydreaming down there.'

With a stretch upwards and a quick kiss of thanks, she left him and made her way down the farm lane, glad to be on the move with fresh air in her face. She felt as if she'd spent a month staring into space and wiping tears away, not just a day or two, and a few minutes later she found herself at the gate across the lane. Just like Scribber before her, she had trouble dragging it across the rough ground, and nearly trapped her toes under it as it juddered open. A short distance further on, she left the lane and took a well-worn pathway down through a copse of ancient oak trees. The ground around them was hidden under a thick blanket of autumn leaves of every colour, but they were too damp to make the rustling, crackly sound she was so fond of as she kicked large soggy clumps of them ahead of her.

She was approaching her beloved willows at last, when she heard music playing, and stopped to listen as it floated up to her. Her smile grew when she recognised the cheap mouth organ and a well-known tune being played pretty badly on it. It had to be Mark, no doubt in one of their favourite places, close to the water's edge. She ran ahead through the deep leaves with all traces of sadness temporarily banished, and crept up behind the unsuspecting musician as he sat playing on a fallen tree trunk. A fishing rod lay across it, abandoned. She was *so* pleased to see him, but she managed to control herself and stood close behind him in silence before quickly covering his eyes with her hands. The music stopped abruptly.

'Very funny,' drawled Mark casually, before returning to his tune with even more enthusiasm ... and volume.

'There's now't funny about bein' caught poachin' trout, young feller,' she bawled in her deepest, gruffest voice. He played a few more notes before grasping her wrists and pulling her hands away from his face, then looked at them with the mouth organ held tightly between his teeth.

'That's right enough,' he replied as well as he could with a full mouth, 'but it *is* funny when a gamekeeper's hands are as soft as a baby's bum ... *and* he wears perfume.' Mark spun around to face her and removed his mouth organ at the same time.

'My hands aren't *that* soft,' snapped Victoria, pretending to be put out and looking down at them for proof. 'And I *do* work around the place, as you know very well,' she protested, 'especially since Dad needed more help. Look! What's this then, Mister Clever?'

She held out her hand for him to see, and pointed to a small blister on it, clearly expecting an apology. Mark tried not to laugh. He guessed that she'd got it when she was last grooming her pony, and definitely not by pushing a stiff broom around a mucky cow shed, but he also noted the indirect reference to her mother's death, which brought him down a notch or two in about as many seconds.

'You should look after that, y' know. It might get infected.' He knew that he sounded a bit too concerned for his own good, but also that he was too late to save himself.

'Oh, don't you worry ... *I'll* be fine,' answered Victoria smugly. 'It's *you* who should be careful, sitting on things like that.' She looked down at the narrow trunk he was perched on rather precariously, and smiled innocently.

This sort of thing was all pleasantly familiar to Mark, and he took no offence as Victoria suddenly pushed him off it with both hands, nearly tipping him into the rushing water. He stayed on his back, propped up on one elbow and looking up at her, but she could see that he was annoyingly unruffled. She was pleased to see the face she knew so well, though, with its firm, dimpled jaw, ruddy cheeks, and that short pale scar cutting across an eyebrow, the legacy of a close encounter with a barbed wire fence when they were five or six.

'So, how's it going?' he asked, sitting up and becoming serious. 'It must be really weird not having Elspeth at home. Just ... I don't know, just *horrible* for everyone.' Victoria was studying her not-so-big blister whilst Mark searched around awkwardly for the right words.

'Look, Vicky. You *must* know I wanted to come over straight after the ... after that night.'

Victoria looked up, about to say something, but Mark wanted to try to finish what he'd started.

'It might seem to you like I didn't care much, but it really wasn't like that. Not one bit. I was worried, that's all. I thought I'd be in the way ... like I was sticking my nose in, or something.'

His cheeks were starting to flush an even deeper shade of red than usual as he drifted into slightly uncomfortable territory, but she smiled at him properly then, thankful for his concern and thoughtfulness. She sat down on the trunk and picked idly at the blister.

'It's *nice* that you've been worried. *Very* nice, actually. I guess it wasn't easy for you to keep away ... Huh, you know me – I'd have been 'round like a greyhound.' She chuckled quietly to herself at the thought of it, before pausing to think.

'*I'm* okay, I s'pose. A bit tired, that's all. Dad's been over at the hospital most of the time, and Annie went yesterday. They're *well* worn out, I can tell you. Dad even fell asleep sitting at the table once, before he'd finished eating.' Mark smiled, but immediately wished that he hadn't.

'I haven't been to York yet, worse luck,' added Victoria.

'D'you know? I think he's right.' She blurted the words out and her voice suddenly faltered. 'I couldn't stand to see her all wired up like that, with machines bleeping and everything. I ... I ...' Her words failed her as she fought against the despair which was threatening to well up and consume her yet again.

Mark had already noticed her slightly swollen eyes, and guessed that she'd been crying earlier. Distracted, he got to his feet, picked up a dead branch, and sent it spinning into the river. He was hoping that he wasn't about to upset her even more.

'Have you ... has *anyone* worked out exactly what happened yet? Who it was?'

He was desperate to be helpful somehow, but needed to get some answers first. Victoria didn't reply straight away, as his question rekindled some of the very memories she was fighting so hard to keep at bay. She slid off the trunk and turned away from him.

'Oh, hell! What's it to *you*, anyway?' she suddenly shrieked, as she gave up her battle and lost control of her emotions.

Mark's face dropped as her cruel words hit him head on. Here was a Victoria he didn't recognise at all, and suddenly he wasn't sure what to say or do. An awkward silence followed, broken only by the noisy water rushing past close beside them.

'Look, I'm sorry,' she said quietly at last, turning to face him. 'It can't be me talking. It's like I'm not in my body ... as if I'm watching myself from over there.' She nodded towards the nearest willow tree, before looking straight up at the clouds for inspiration. 'God, Mark. I don't know *what* I'm thinking any more.' Mark knew that she shouldn't be rushed, and waited. 'No one knows who it was. Not us, not the police, not anyone.' She muttered at first, her head down again, but then she flicked her hair back and spoke up as the gritty, Featherstone side of her broke through unexpectedly.

'Someone got in and went around the house. We know *that* much at least. Goodness only knows what they were after ... One of Mum's old keys is missing, but that's all, as far as we can tell. Now why on earth would they want *that*?' Mark could hear the frustration already growing in her voice again, but he let her carry on.

'I'm surprised Dad even noticed it was missing – he said it wasn't valuable or anything.' Her voice then fell to a dry whisper, as if she was talking to herself. 'Whoever it was went into Elspeth's room for some reason ...' Mark stepped a little closer to her. 'There was a huge bat in her cot and it flew up at me, then round and round the room.' She shuddered as she briefly relived the terror of it. 'And how did a bloody bat end up there, in her lovely little bed?'

Tears began to fill her eyes, and she put her hands up to her face, as if the bat had returned to taunt her. Her new-found courage seemed to be dissolving away and her voice started to tremble again.

'They say she's in some sort of coma, Mark, and that all we can do is w-wait ... *Wait?* It might be years and years. Just h-how the hell are we all meant to wait *that* long? Tell me that!'

Mark didn't have an answer for her, but he could tell from her flushed face and raised voice that she was still on an emotional rollercoaster, and perilously close to falling off it. He moved still closer to her and placed a finger on her lips. It was time for her to stop, he'd decided. Her head fell forwards onto his chest and stayed there whilst she took what comfort she could find, but Mark surprised himself. Pure, ice-cold anger appeared from nowhere and surged through him. He held her for a minute or more, letting her cry quietly as he fought with his own rage, then eased her away and held her by her shoulders. She didn't look up, but Mark could see tears falling from her cheeks and the tip of her nose, down into the grass between their feet.

'Vicky,' he said firmly, getting her attention by lifting her chin up. 'I'm not sure if I can, but I want to find out who it was, *and* why Elspeth won't wake up.' Victoria sniffed loudly and suddenly wished that she could cover up her blotchy face as Mark looked down at her. 'Yeah, I don't care if it even kills me. They just *can't* get away with it! I promise you, I'll find them.' He stopped, feeling self-conscious again, but also beginning to realise what Victoria was actually going through. 'I hate seeing you like this, you know,' he added, a little sheepishly.

Victoria pushed some wet hair out of her eyes and sniffed again, very ungracefully. Then she stared at Mark, long and deliberately, looking into his eyes for something. She didn't doubt his sincerity in any way, but was perhaps questioning his wisdom: she'd known for a very long time that Mark's heart always ruled his head.

'I hate *being* like this,' she finally answered apologetically, pulling her wrist across her tear-streaked cheeks and taking a deep breath. Mark wondered what was coming next. 'Shall we go and see Dad, then?' she asked, already knowing that they certainly would.

Traces of a thankful smile flickered at the corners of her mouth as they started their way back to Willow Garth, leaving the swollen river and its graceful willows behind them. A much happier Mark nearly forgot his rod, and he ran back for it, whistling. A few minutes later, as they approached the first of the oaks in the copse, Mark stopped and looked around.

'Listen!' he whispered. 'Did you hear that?'

Victoria stopped too, but her hands went straight on her hips.

'No!' she replied sternly. She'd already regained some of her composure and used her best schoolmistress voice, especially reserved for the times when Mark's imagination ran wild. 'I certainly did *not*!'

Ignoring him, she carried on up towards the farm and didn't look back, but Mark let her go and turned off the path towards the wide oak trees which were dotted all around him. It had been nothing more than the snap of a twig, or so he'd imagined, but it was enough to get his attention. Unseen by him, three figures were now pressing themselves tightly to the backs of three of those great oaks. They were tall and slim, heavily armed and dressed entirely in black. Close to invisible in the shadows, barely moving, but deadly if disturbed. As Mark approached, three hands went to three sabres and eased them an inch out of their scabbards. They were dark elves, malevolent in every conceivable way. The birds had even stopped singing.

'Come on, it's nothing,' shouted Victoria from further up the path.

Mark stopped again, still listening for something other than Victoria's voice, but she called out to him once more.

'Don't you think the intruder's got better things to do than hang around here listening to that racket you call music?'

The sabres slid another inch upwards as he unknowingly took a single pace towards the dark elves surrounding him – and certain, instant death. He peered up along the path towards Victoria, who was just disappearing from view, then all around him once more …

He knew that she was probably right, and promised himself he would find more time to practise on his mouth organ, as he ran to catch her up.

The dark elves sheathed their sabres silently. Their

business lay elsewhere, but they wouldn't have minded in the least if an unexpected killing had come their way.

The two young friends were soon approaching the farmhouse and its collection of stone outbuildings, and Mark looked up at the old clay roof tiles, blanketed with moss where the sun had never reached. Some had slipped from their nails and now lay askew in the rickety, cast-iron gutters. Just like at his parent's farm further along the valley, there was only enough money to carry out the most important repairs, and along with a lot of other things, those roofs would probably have to wait. The everyday clutter of a working dairy farm soon greeted them; a delightful mixture of order and chaos that had reigned for as long as both of them could remember. Victoria ran ahead to her father as he walked across the yard to meet them with a broom over his shoulder.

'Dad, look who's here. He wants to find the burglar!' The farmer was relieved to see a new enthusiasm and sparkle in his daughter's eyes.

'Does he, now?' he said, lowering his broom and smiling down at her. He also noticed Mark's determined expression, and knew at once that it would be unwise to treat the offer lightly. 'Well, that makes four of us then, I reckon.' It was just what Victoria wanted to hear, and she nodded quietly at Mark, officially confirming his new appointment. 'You'd better take Mark inside then, lass, and offer him a drink before he flakes out on us,' continued her father. Victoria seemed keen to oblige and turned to go, pulling Mark after her. 'And maybe show him upstairs?' he added. He was looking up towards Elspeth's boarded-up window, and wondering if it might help her to come to terms with what had happened if she confronted it all again, but with Mark along as company.

Victoria hesitated before agreeing, then, still pulling Mark along as if he didn't know the way, went into the house. Once in the kitchen, she nudged a dozing cat aside with her foot and set some water to boil on the range, whilst Mark stared at the long row of keys on the side of the beam. He saw the empty nail at one end, just as Victoria had described on their walk home.

'They must all be quite valuable, so why would they only take the biggest one? D'you know what it was for?' he asked, quite unaware that the largest key was actually still on the beam, just in a different place.

Victoria didn't answer him straight away. She was already pouring boiling water into a pretty teapot, then cutting a generous slice from a fruit-laden cake. She knew that it was Mark's favourite kind, and that he particularly looked forward to something just like it each Christmas Eve, which also happened to be his birthday. He got double rations then. As Mark watched Victoria placing the slice carefully on a plate, she suddenly reminded him of her mother, and his heart went out to her as he thought back to that sudden, tragic loss a year or so before. Victoria looked up at him and shrugged as she slid the plate across the table.

'Mum told us ages ago that the biggest key used to open the church door, or at least she thought it did. She said it had a new lock fitted when she was young, and that she got to keep the old key – well, something like that, anyway. Now tell me why anyone would want to steal *that*?'

Mark couldn't tell her, of course, but he did ask if he could see Elspeth's room, like her father had suggested. Victoria took him upstairs whilst the tea brewed and his slice of cake waited on the table.

The small and virtually empty bedroom was dark and forbidding with the window boarded up. The ceiling light still hadn't been repaired, and so Victoria lit a candle and took it in with them, making the room seem even more ominous.

'This bat really flew straight at you?' he asked, incredulously.

'Sure, right in my face. I tell you, I nearly died. It flew out of the window in the end – the burglar had smashed his way out through it. Poor Elspeth's stuff was all over the lawn!'

She stopped and gazed at the floor where the cot had been, so Mark quickly changed the subject.

'Did he leave anything behind? I don't know ... footprints? Fingerprints?'

'The police said there wasn't a single stranger's fingerprint anywhere – not even a smudged one. Must've had gloves on, they reckon.' Victoria held up the candle and moved it around to show Mark the rest of the room. 'No, he didn't leave anything ... except a lot of blood after Chopper had finished with him. I hope the bite gets infected and he dies from gangrene.'

She looked pleased at the thought of it, and was turning to leave when she stopped with her hand on the doorknob.

'Hey!' she exclaimed, thumping her own forehead and splashing melted candle wax onto the floor. 'Wait here a minute.'

Before Mark could say anything or stop her, she was pushing the candlestick into his hands, then sprinting along the passageway and rushing back down the stairs three at a time. He didn't have very long to wait before she was back with him again, breathless but excited, and holding out a little dagger between a finger and thumb, just as she'd done once before. Her hand was shaking.

'He left *this* behind. I threw it outside when I was tidying up the room, and it was still under the bushes. Christ, I'm such an airhead!' Mark looked at her with his head slightly tilted, as if to confirm her last statement, but she forgave him for his playful insult and just scowled back. 'It's only a toy, I reckon, but should we give it to the police, d'you think?' she added, lowering her voice.

Everything went quiet. Even the farmyard noises outside seemed to stop. Mark took the tiny weapon from her, then held it across the palm of his hand and studied it more closely in the light of the candle. He was intrigued by it. It was only six inches long from end to end, and it *looked* like a toy, he thought, but it didn't *feel* like one. Not one bit. Despite the poor light, he soon noticed the fine workmanship in it, too. The hilt, studded with red, blue and green gems that sparkled even in the candlelight, was carved from the blackest jet stone, polished as smooth as glass, and cold to his touch as he ran a finger across it. He moved it closer to the candle and saw that the blood-stained blade was covered with an intricate pattern of twisting, curling branches, each sprouting dozens of tiny but perfect leaves. Mystified, he looked up at Victoria, who could only shrug her shoulders again. He carefully touched the razor-sharp edge, expecting that to be cold as well, but for some reason it was warm, which puzzled him even more.

'Um ... I don't think we'll hand it over *just* yet,' said Mark, finally.

'Should we show it to Dad instead then, not the police?' asked Victoria. She was whispering now, although she wasn't sure why, and Mark thought carefully before replying.

'No ... I don't think so.' He tapped it in his palm, wondering to himself. 'Somehow, I think we need it more than they do.' Victoria nodded slowly. 'I've never seen anything like this before,' he added.

He dragged his eyes away from it and looked at Victoria. There were glowing embers of hope in her eyes which he badly wanted to fan into a bright flame, but he was reluctant to raise them over nothing and risk hurting her even more. In the end, though, he felt that he had to take that chance. It was just too hard for him to resist.

'If I can find out who owns this, I *might* be a bit closer to helping Elspeth, you know.' Victoria grinned, quite unexpectedly.

'What's all this "I" stuff? You mean "we", don't you?'

It was Mark's turn to smile then, realising that he should have known better.

'Are you *sure* you still want to help us?' she asked, although she knew very well what his answer would be: Mark never went back on his word, and his promise to her down at the willows was still reassuringly fresh in her mind.

'Now what do *you* think?' he answered, as he tried unsuccessfully to balance the dagger on the tip of one finger. 'But I'd like to start by helping you get rid of that cake first. Come on!'

Skelton Tower

The worn-out spriggans finally came to the edge of the high moor, just west of Newtondale, on the final part of their long and tiresome journey. The sun was setting fast as they left the last of the springy heather behind them and made their way down into the valley, keeping close to the field walls and hedges. Neither of them wanted to spend another freezing night curled up on the hard ground, and so they were secretly hoping that Redcap would offer them a roof over their heads, if nothing else. On the other hand, they were all too aware that he'd already been kept waiting a day longer than planned, and that there was no saying what kind of mood he'd be in when he eventually opened his door to them.

The spriggans breathed a quiet sigh of relief as the neighbouring farm to Skelton Tower come into view below them at last, with its freshly painted house, and barns filled to their roofs with bales of straw or hay, for they knew that they would indeed be standing on Redcap's doorstep before nightfall. The farmer there, a cantankerous old man called Kirby, generally kept himself to himself – much to the annoyance of the somewhat more genial Mrs Kirby – but his closest neighbour was even less sociable, and Scribber found it amusing that old Kirby was quite unaware of what unimaginable horror lived right next door to him. As far as the farmer was concerned, the tower was simply an unsightly, uninhabited ruin which spoiled his otherwise excellent views, but was of no real interest to him, or anyone else, most probably.

'We won't get offered any grub, that's for sure,' complained Scribber, his stomach now feeling as empty as a beggar's bowl. 'And anyways, I wouldn't eat anythin' Redcap threw on our plates, no matter 'ow 'ungry I got. There's no tellin' what it might be.' He spat far closer to Wipp's feet than he'd intended to, making the youngster dodge backwards. 'Gawd, I'm 'arf starved,' continued Scribber, rubbing his stomach with both hands. 'I think we've just got time for some nice eggs.' He suddenly had Wipp's full attention. 'I s'pose you'll be wantin' some?' he asked, looking down along his nose at Wipp's wet boot.

Wipp wasn't entirely sure where such luxuries as eggs were about to magically appear from, but he accepted his leader's kind (and rare) offer, nodding enthusiastically. 'Wait 'ere. I shan't be long,' ordered Scribber, as he slipped his bag from his shoulder and held it in his hand. 'And try yer best to keep out of sight,' he added with a sneer.

Wipp watched him roll between the bottom rails of a five-bar gate next to them, then scamper across a muddy orchard, making less noise than a leaf or two picked up by a puff of wind. Three of Kirby's fat sows were there, rooting about for the last remains of any rotting apples, but they didn't even raise a bristly eyebrow as he dodged around them and made his way to the rear of the dilapidated hen house he'd noticed from further up the hill. He checked all around him before trying to lift the rickety lid to the nesting boxes, but it was far too heavy and high for him. A few seconds later, however, and two feet taller, he lifted it easily and began to grope around inside.

An indignant hen must have objected to the unfamiliar fingers which appeared underneath her, because he soon snatched his arm out and dropped the lid with a bang.

After deciding to use less subtle methods, he unceremoniously grasped the hen by the neck and threw her out of the way over his shoulder. It wasn't long before four brown eggs were being rolled out of his bag and onto the grass in front of Wipp's knees.

Wipp wanted to know what had caused all the banging, but he'd only got two words out of his mouth when a warning look from Scribber shut it again smartly.

'What do we cook these in, then?' asked Wipp, changing the subject. He picked up two of the eggs and tossed them a few inches into the air, like a novice juggler.

'We don't have the ruddy time to cook 'em, do we?' snapped Scribber, exasperated. 'We suck 'em, that's what.'

Wipp watched curiously as his leader pulled out his dagger and used the tip of it to carefully make a small hole at each end of an egg, before sucking the contents out through one of them. With egg yolk dribbling down his chin, he signalled between slurps for Wipp to get on with his own, and Wipp's hand went inside his cloak for his own dagger. Once again it found only an empty scabbard, and the unfortunate young spriggan knew that there was no hiding the truth any longer, with his eggs nestling on the grass in front of him, waiting for his attention.

'It's gone ... me dagger's gone,' he mumbled, hoping that Scribber wouldn't hear him.

Scribber stopped sucking and crushed his half-sucked egg in his fist as he stared disbelievingly at the dejected youngster.

'It ... it must still be at the Featherstones' place,' confessed Wipp as Scribber's expression hardened, 'where you threw it, maybe,' he added bravely, but under his breath.

'You mean after you'd stuck it in me leg like only a stinkin' bogle would, is *that* what you mean?' hissed Scribber, daring Wipp to disagree with him.

Wipp hung his head in shame, and stared blankly at the eggs beside his knees. He didn't risk putting up a defence and so Scribber continued, spraying him with a sticky mixture of egg yolk and black spit for good measure.

'Yer rotten life won't be worth livin' when you get back to the caves ... *if* you get back, that is.' Wipp swallowed loudly and fiddled with his eggs as the volume increased. 'Why didn't you pick it up before we 'ad to leave? Don't you know how valuable them daggers are?' Scribber was trying to keep his voice down, but failing miserably.

Wipp actually knew very well, but that didn't stop Scribber from staying firmly astride his exceptionally high horse. The furious spriggan stuck out his long, knobbly tongue and struggled to scrape a piece of eggshell from it before giving Wipp the inevitable lecture.

'Six enchanted daggers, swiped from light elves after we killed 'em in the last great battle. Only six, mind you. Not twenty, or thirty – six! But now we've got just five. Fabulous! And tell me, my brainless little friend, what 'appens when them mortals find it, eh? ''Cos they're gonner, ain't they?'

Wipp shrugged his shoulders helplessly as Scribber's voice rose even further, to a slightly muted screech. 'Who can say what queer things it'll do to 'em?' Wipp shrugged again, but still didn't look up or speak. 'And worse than that, when they're 'oldin it, they'll be able to see us lot, ain't that right?'

Scribber finally ran out of patience – and words. He looked at the mess in his dripping hand and wondered how much more trouble might be coming his way on their return home. After all, he *was* meant to be in charge of Wipp. With his spirits sinking steadily lower, a queasy mixture began to stir itself around inside him: anger over the loss of the dagger, plus a creeping uneasiness about meeting Redcap more than one day late.

The sun had now set, bringing a bite to the evening breeze and reminding the spriggans that several hot fires would be crackling away merrily back at their caves. Scribber finished his other egg deep in thought, but didn't offer to help Wipp with his, unsurprisingly. He couldn't decide what to do about the key, as his natural greed for all things valuable was gnawing steadily into his mind. He dared not risk double-crossing Redcap by keeping it for himself – the likely consequences were too gory to even imagine – but he was sure that he'd been deceived when the theft from Willow Garth was planned. The swindling goblin had only described the bronze key as being 'of some interest', and nothing more, Scribber recalled bitterly. The dark elves were also all too fresh in his memory, and it suddenly seemed that everyone wanted exactly what he had tucked inside his cloak pocket.

For a few ridiculous moments, he toyed with the idea of gathering all interested parties together and offering the key to the highest bidder, but even *he* wasn't stupid enough to take *that* chance – he might as well throw the key through Redcap's window and slit his own throat at the same time, for that was more or less how things would turn out anyway. He was about to tell Wipp that there was nothing for it but to knock on the tower door and get the whole, dangerous business over with, when he caught a glimpse of someone moving quickly, close to the trees beyond Kirby's place.

'Hello, what's all this then?' he whispered, sitting bolt upright so quickly that he startled Wipp. 'Look – there! Someone's got a visitor ... and I'll bet it's not that old fool, Kirby, either!'

Scribber was quite right, for he and Wipp watched as the distant figure marched boldly down the slope and straight past Kirby's farm, heading for the tower. He was tall, slim, and dressed entirely in black, with long, dark hair tied back behind his neck. The end of a sabre protruded from below his cloak, and Scribber's skin prickled as he realised who it was. Any plans he may have had of going straight to Redcap disappeared from his head like chimney smoke in a gale. He now knew exactly what he had to do, and the thought of it made his stomach churn, raw eggs and all.

'Now there's a thing,' he whispered behind his hand. 'A dark elf sniffing around the tower just when we're 'ere. There's summat going on, and we needs to know about it – *before* we 'and the key over and collect our pay. Let's follow the black devil, agreed?'

Wipp didn't like the sound of this at all.

'Can't we just wait for 'im to finish what 'e's up to and *then* see Redcap?' he asked hopefully. He was running his finger around inside his collar, which suddenly felt uncomfortably warm.

'Now listen 'ere, lad,' replied Scribber, surprising Wipp with his kind, almost fatherly tones. 'It can't 'arm to find out what this pesky dark elf wants, can it now? If things go badly and we get caught, we can always act like we're daft in the 'ed – or even make a run for it. You'd do very well at either of 'em, I reckon.'

But Wipp wasn't so easily convinced. He was beginning to wish that he was somewhere else, *anywhere* else, actually, as long as it was a long, long way from Skelton Tower, but Scribber's mind was already made up, and he started to get up to follow the dark elf. Wipp didn't want to be left there alone with dark elves on the loose, and could only do likewise. As he got up he knelt on his lovely eggs, crushing them flat.

They made their way further downhill, still staying close to walls and hedges whenever possible, but keeping well behind the elf, and always out of sight. Redcap's late visitor, however, didn't seem at all concerned about being seen, for he strolled the last 50 paces up to the tower as calmly as you please, across an open area where the grass was kept short by a few grazing sheep.

Skelton Tower was the only surviving turret of a ruined castle, but it was still reasonably intact. Around it lay a scattering of large, half-buried stones, as well as the untidy remains of two tall and quite substantial walls. Inside the square tower itself, there climbed a steep, spiral staircase of solid stone, sealed off from the outside world by a wide entrance door, hung on long, iron hinges. Higher up were two rooms, one above the other, each with only a single slit window to allow in some natural light. As far as Scribber knew, Redcap wasn't in the habit of keeping company with dark elves, and from all accounts his only regular visitors were a parliament of noisy rooks which liked to nest in amongst the huge parapet stones, close to the roof.

Crouching behind some nearby gorse bushes, the spriggans watched, puzzled but fascinated, as the elf walked confidently up to the door and thumped on it with his fist. Scribber flinched, and thought that the elf was either extraordinarily brave, or equally foolish. Half a dozen startled rooks took off from the roof and flew towards the safety of the nearby trees, their dismal caw-cawing filling half the valley and echoing back from the buildings at Kirby's place. A minute went by and it seemed that the elf was growing tired of waiting, for he tried again, but even harder this time. Scribber dropped a little lower and decided that not even a dark elf could be *that* brave.

Then, the hinges squeaked loudly as the door swung open – so loudly that Wipp glanced back towards Kirby's farm, half expecting to see the old man heading their way. Without a trace of fear, the elf stepped through the doorway and into the darkness behind it, before the heavy door swung shut with a loud and ominously final clunk.

The spriggans stared at each other. Judging from the beads of sweat trickling down his face, Wipp was hoping for a last-minute change of plan, but those hopes were dashed when Scribber left the cover of the bushes and headed straight towards the tower. Clinging to his one remaining hope that Redcap was fully occupied with his visitor, Wipp followed close behind him, and together they ran across the open space as quickly as their sore legs would allow, then on towards one of the two walls which adjoined the tower, climbing upwards like a broken stairway to nowhere. Its jagged outline was now clearly silhouetted against the darkening sky, as were a pair of small cloaked figures as they clambered up its huge stones, towards the side of the forbidding tower itself.

In less than a minute they'd reached the top of the wall, and found themselves close to the slit window which opened into Redcap's lowest room. This was meant for firing arrows out of, not letting enemies in through – even skinny spriggans – and was never paid the least attention, so the unlikely spies pulled their cloaks tightly around them and settled down on their precarious perch like two scruffy owls, determined to learn what they could. There was only enough room for one of them to stand up and peer through the window, and there was no discussion about who *that* should be. Scribber was soon pressing his cheek against the cold stone wall and finding that the unusual, splayed window allowed him to see most of the gloomy room beyond it. Wipp could only sit next to him and watch out for trouble, as a solitary but very real owl hooted from the trees up at Kirby's farm.

*   *   *

The entrance door to the tower must have opened and closed itself by some goblin trickery or other, for once inside, the dark elf found that he was quite alone. He started to climb the winding steps, helped only by a glimmer of flickering candlelight from somewhere high above him. The damp walls felt as cold as death as he made his way up with care – each step had been worn smooth and curved from many centuries of use. At the top, his way was blocked by yet another door of thick, studded oak, and a single candle spluttered in a wall sconce next to it. He raised his fist once again, but this door swung open before he could even touch it, and with only the briefest of hesitations he stepped forwards into a poorly lit room.

The sight awaiting him inside Redcap's private sanctuary was an extraordinary one, even for a well-travelled elf, and he cocked an eyebrow in surprise as he looked around the candlelit room. It was small, with a bare, wooden floor and a high ceiling supported by a dozen thick beams. Green, slimy stains spreading down most of the walls showed that the roof was far from watertight, but there were one or two pitiful attempts at home comforts, none the less: a couple of chairs, a thread-bare rug in the centre of the floor, and even a tiny fireplace in which something was smouldering feebly. The fire obviously wasn't giving out any warmth, though, for the elf could see his breath on the cold air as he recovered from his steep climb.

The walls of the room were almost entirely covered with shelves, some of them sagging under the weight of a vast array of books and papers, maps, bottles and jars – some containing preserved animals, or parts of animals best not guessed at – countless skulls of all types and sizes, and other, smaller items of general goblin clutter which had been stuffed into the few remaining gaps. Given Redcap's reputation, the elf was surprised not to see any weapons, apart from a knife beside a crust of bread on a table near the fireplace, but he *did* notice a long row of identical cloth caps which hung from wooden pegs above the mantelpiece. Most were various shades of red, but two or three were a pale straw colour. Just like everyone else in his 'unseen' world, the dark elf knew of Redcap's habit of using fresh blood to dye his caps, and wondered briefly who his most recent victims might have been.

The small and somewhat dishevelled goblin stood at the far side of the room, close to another door which the elf presumed would lead to the room above them. Despite being half the size of his visitor, Redcap didn't seem particularly concerned by the arrival of the relatively well-dressed dark elf, who was now staring down at him menacingly, waiting for him to speak.

'What a pleasant surprise seeing *you* here after all this time, Malrin,' purred Redcap, perhaps a little more cordially than was called for. 'You are rather late for supper, I'm afraid, but there is a little left, I think. If you would care to ...?'

He ambled over to the fire and pulled a limb from a small, unidentifiable animal pierced on an iron rod over the coals and blackened from many hours of over-cooking. Outside the window, even a famished Scribber was relieved that he'd missed suppertime at the tower: he'd already seen three rats since arriving there.

Redcap sat down and ripped some of the dry meat from the bones with his sharp teeth, but the elf wisely declined the offer with a wave of his hand. The goblin wiped his greasy lips with his sleeve as he chewed, but never took his eyes from the tall figure in his doorway.

'Come in then, my friend. Shut the door and come in. Take a seat here,' he said with his mouth full, gesturing to a nearby chair.

For a few moments the elf seemed reluctant, perhaps at the thought of shutting off his only means of escape, but then he eased his cloak back on one shoulder so as to make his sabre more accessible and closed the door. Redcap seemed unconcerned by the gesture, and nibbled enthusiastically as he searched for more scraps of burnt meat. Malrin remained standing, watching him.

'It seems that we have some mutual acquaintances, Redcap,' said Malrin in a cool, business-like manner. 'A certain hobgoblin from Farndale, for instance?'

He expected a reaction, and got it, for Redcap stopped chewing at once. The goblin's eyes widened as his mind raced ahead, but fortunately they were now cast downwards and he managed to regain his composure quickly.

'Is that so?' he answered casually, leaning back and rubbing his fingers on his grimy red waistcoat. 'I've no doubt that our friends are rather few in number, and so it surprises me a great deal that we should have a *mutual* one. Well, fancy that! And when did you meet this, this *mutual* friend of ours?'

'If you *must* know, my lads and I came across him a few nights ago, in a cave,' replied Malrin. 'We only went in to take cover from a storm, but we heard him scuffling about at the back, trying to get away. He was nearly beside himself with fear, and started babbling something about finding a diary at a farm.'

Malrin watched Redcap closely. The miserable goblin's eyes were already giving away a great deal, even if his words weren't.

'He also had quite a lot to say about four keys,' continued the elf, deliberately exaggerating, 'And more than once he mentioned ... What was it, now? Ah, yes, a *hoard*, of all things. But he was reluctant to tell us much more, sadly.'

Redcap's shoulders dropped an inch with relief, but he tried to hide it.

'You see,' continued Malrin with a voice as smooth as

71

warm honey, 'he seemed extremely concerned about losing his other ear.'

Redcap looked up again at last and Malrin was delighted to see that his rosy cheeks had suddenly turned a sickly grey-green.

Even from outside, Scribber could see that Redcap was now seriously regretting allowing the dark elf into his stronghold, well armed and alarmingly well informed, but he hated the powerful goblin far too much to pity him.

'What do you m-mean, his *other* ear?' Redcap gulped noisily as a growing fear swelled in his throat and threatened to choke him, but Malrin persevered mercilessly.

'He said that *you* cut one off when you held him prisoner here. That's what I mean.'

Redcap didn't know what to say, and probably wouldn't have got the words out even if he did. Malrin stepped closer and leant down towards him.

'You had him brought here and you tried to get him to tell you everything. He refused, and so you thought you'd relieve him of his ear to encourage him. I think you should tell me what you know of this, and perhaps I'll consider working with you, rather than adding to your ear collection – with two of your own!'

Malrin decided to press his point home, and drew his sabre so quickly that Redcap barely had time to flinch, let alone jump clear. The razor-sharp blade was soon resting threateningly on the goblin's left shoulder. He tried to lick his lips, which had turned as dry as the stale bread on the table, and his eyes flitted everywhere: towards both doors, then momentarily to the bread knife.

'And how is it that you let me in here so readily, anyway?' demanded Malrin, suddenly curious. 'You did not know my business, and from all accounts you are not given to gossiping with passers-by. I could have been anyone.' He lifted the point of his sabre to within an inch of the goblin's large, pointed ear. 'I could have come for your head!'

'Actually, I … I thought that you were someone else … bringing … bringing me something,' spluttered the goblin before squeezing out the thinnest of smiles. 'But I saw *two* sp– I mean figures, come across from Kirby's place. Yes, I'm sure it was two,' he added, looking towards the window but with his mind obviously elsewhere.

At the window, Scribber was starting to enjoy himself, and grinned mischievously in the darkness.

Redcap had only just managed to stop himself from mentioning anything to do with keys or spriggans, and he swallowed loudly again as he searched the face of his tormentor for the slightest sign of a reprieve. There was none. The infamous goblin was paying the price for his disastrous error, and the last of his confidence began to ebb away as he watched the brightly polished steel hovering beside his face. His shoulders suddenly dropped again as he let out a long, tired breath.

'Let me think. Please let me think,' he murmured as he got up carefully, the sabre tip following him.

He eased himself towards the other chair, closer to the fire, and collapsed onto it before burying his face in his hands. He now looked old and exhausted, in every possible way.

'I'll tell you what I know,' he said wearily, without looking up, 'then you can decide whether to work with me or without me, as you put it. I can't be fairer than that now, can I?'

Out on the wall, Scribber had already heard more than he could have wished for, but his ears were now pricked up like a startled horse's, eager for more. He was finally going to hear all about the heavy key hanging inside his cloak, and he could barely wait. Wipp turned around and looked up at him sleepily, but Scribber signalled with a finger on a lip followed by a tightly squeezed fist for him to be quiet, or suffer the consequences. Wipp got the all-too-familiar message and looked back up at the moon as it rose above Kirby's place, far too worn out to care that he was spying outside the home of the most evil, devious goblin in existence.

'I cannot deny what you say,' muttered Redcap gloomily, as he struggled to gather his thoughts. 'Some time ago I heard a rumour that our ... *mutual* friend, this Farndale hob, had found something interesting. Apparently, he'd been sneaking about on a farm – hoping to steal some cream, knowing him – but he was disturbed, and given that the first rule of our world is that we *never* risk being seen, he had little choice but to hide in a barn.' He looked up at Malrin again, trying to gauge his level of interest. 'Whilst he was there, he found an old leather suitcase, covered in dust and pigeons' droppings. It hadn't been touched for years.'

Redcap paused and dabbed his forehead with a filthy rag he'd pulled from his waistcoat pocket. He was now sweating profusely, despite the cold room.

'Being a nosey hobgoblin, he had to look inside it, of course. He found some faded photographs, lots of family letters, too ... and an old diary.'

Almost imperceptibly, one of Malrin's eyebrows lifted.

'As far as I knew, he couldn't even read,' added Redcap as his lip curled upwards with contempt. 'He flicked through it, bored probably, but one page caught his eye and he tore it out. Later that morning, when the little pig was probably full of cream, he read it to himself.'

The elf lowered his sabre, but made it clear that he still meant business.

'Carry on. And don't even think about missing out a little fact here and there. For a start, where was this farm?'

Redcap decided to come straight out with the truth, just for a change.

'Why, I believe it was Willow Garth. Yes, the Featherstones' place.' Redcap's throat must have tightened further, for he was now massaging it with his long, thin fingers as he continued.

'The diary was written by a man called Witcher. He once owned every ironstone mine in Rosedale, and was very rich, or so they say, but he was mean, too, and kept his money to himself. It seems that the hob read of some treasure, a *hoard* as you call it. Witcher could have hidden it before he died, I suppose.' Redcap was hoping that he'd sounded sufficiently offhand, and risked glancing up again at Malrin. 'The hob couldn't keep his mouth shut, though, and soon he was saying too much to too many others ... Well, that was a *most* foolish thing to do. It soon came to the ears of those who would stop at nothing to see that page ... including me.'

The goblin reached out cautiously towards the remains of the fire, throwing the bare bones onto it and pulling off another unappetising morsel. Malrin's sabre point came up and followed him all the way.

'It is as well for you that you did not lie about the name of the farm, for I knew it already,' said the dark elf, who leant closer to Redcap and enveloped him in a steamy cloud of breath. 'The hob told us that he saw a couple of spriggans stealing a key there – a special key which had something to do with Witcher's hoard. We tried to find them, but unfortunately, we failed. Huh! Spriggans must be more tricky than I'd imagined ... or goblin guides more useless.'

He looked down his nose at Redcap, hoping that the insult had found its mark, before standing up and stretching his back. 'So, I thought it might be time to give you a little visit, to see if we could share some information. You know, *collaborate*.' Malrin managed an unconvincing grin for the goblin before lowering his sabre. 'So Witcher's hoard may be real after all. My, my, that *is* interesting. Half-forgotten rumours or children's stories tell of it, of course, but that is all. If this diary is genuine, then it would indeed be ...'

The elf's guard dropped further as his imagination took control and he stared straight through Redcap, temporarily lost in his own, greedy dreams. He could see the hoard clearly in his mind, a glittering pile of precious gems collected from deep inside the ironstone mines of Rosedale. He could almost touch them. Redcap stopped chewing and glanced at the door whilst the elf daydreamed, but there was no time to escape: the sabre was too close and too sharp to take the chance. Malrin finally snapped back to his senses, and tried to remember where he'd got to.

'The hob ... Ah yes, our little hob. He escaped from us at the cave. I made the rare, no, *unique* mistake of feeling sorry for a prisoner and didn't tie him up, but it won't happen again, be assured. After we'd given up looking for the spriggans, I sent some of my lads to Willow Garth to find out what they could. They came upon two mortals, a boy and a girl, and followed them for a while, but they could not find any trace of the hob, or his diary page.'

'You seem to be making a habit of losing people,' sniggered Redcap cheekily. 'It's likely that he was skulking somewhere dark and dusty, licking his wounds ... if his tongue reached far enough.' The goblin threw back his head and laughed out loud at his own cruel joke, giving the dark elf a good view of some well-chewed meat. 'You see, you are quite right, my dear Malrin. I *did* have him brought here, because I needed to question him – how shall I say – more *thoroughly*.'

A sadistic smile flickered across the goblin's greasy cheeks as he recalled the long and gruesome torture session.

'He told me most of what he'd read in the diary, all of it

useless drivel of course, but he refused to tell me what was on the important page, or where he'd hidden it, even when I roasted his bare toes in the fire coals.'

Malrin shook his head, pretending to be shocked. 'Tut-tut, Redcap. Whatever will you think of next?'

Redcap must have taken this as a compliment, for he leant back in his chair and suddenly appeared happy to be telling the tale.

'His tongue loosened quickly enough, though, when I got *that*.' With obvious pride, he nodded towards a glass jar on the mantelpiece, below his row of caps. A small, mutilated ear floated in liquid tinted pink with blood.

'Get to the point!' ordered Malrin, unimpressed. 'Where *is* this page?'

Malrin looked around the room. It was littered with books and papers of all shapes and sizes, and a single loose page could have been anywhere amongst them.

Redcap didn't answer, for an all-consuming greed was beginning to pull him apart, and a cold sweat was still breaking out across his pale forehead as Malrin advanced the sabre point once more, pushing it into the goblin's cheek and denting it, but not quite drawing blood.

'All right, all right! The page is just here,' sighed Redcap as he finally gave in, defeated. 'Look, I'll show you.'

Redcap reached out carefully towards a low shelf beside the fire hearth, and pulled a folded sheet of paper out from beneath a book.

'The little wretch thought I wouldn't find this.'

Incredibly, Redcap's warped sense of humour was still bubbling away somewhere under his dirty skin, and he chuckled to himself as he remembered the hobgoblin howling with pain and clutching his head where his ear had once been.

'He had it safely inside his boot all along.' Redcap stopped and became serious. 'It was a shame about his ear, really. If only he'd spoken up sooner, I could have saved him so much inconvenience.'

Malrin ignored the goblin's shallow lies and snatched the piece of paper from him, flicking it open with one hand. His eyes raced over it greedily. On one side, written in a firm, flowing hand, were some notes about Sir Henry Witcher's will – who might be getting what, and who wasn't. It was of little interest to Malrin. All that business was history, finished with a lifetime ago as far as he was concerned. As he turned the page over, however, his eyes widened. On the other side was a short verse, but not just any verse. He read it quickly to himself, and only once, but a deep yearning for the hoard smouldered so powerfully within him that every single word was etched into his memory ... forever.

The Witcher Keys

Dark bed, eternal,
Hard and cold,
The key of bronze
My blood shall hold.

Then silver, bright,
Close to my heart.
It pains me so,
That we must part.

Come, seek its home
Of oak, unseen
On mellow stone,
Yet iron between,

As large and strong
As Three Howes Gate.
So tarry not,
The Hoard awaits!

SKELTON TOWER

In tunnels black,
You may see light:
A guarded place,
Oh wondrous sight!

I warn you now,
The last is weak!
Take care, dear kin,
For others seek

What should be yours.
It waits there, still,
Hidden deep
Beneath my hill.

Sir Henry Reginald Witcher
10 September 1937

Two hundred yards from the tower, a large barn owl launched herself from an ash tree at Kirby's farm. Flying silently across open ground and towards Skelton Tower, where her keen eyesight had caught a glimpse of movement, she emerged from the darkness in a long, smooth, moonlit glide, her huge unblinking eyes fastened onto her intended prey, and the flight feathers at her wingtips twitching up, flicking down, steering her precisely to her next kill.

Wipp soon caught sight of her and watched her approaching, wondering if he'd be lucky and see her strike. Now *that* would be more interesting than the boring old moon, he thought. Then, suddenly, he was wide awake and sitting up straight. She was too high ... she was coming their way. He looked up and over his shoulder and saw Scribber, still engrossed with his spying. Then he peered down to the ground, but it was such a long way below him. The owl was very close now, rushing towards them with its legs reaching forward and its deadly talons spread wide, but in those last few seconds, Wipp realised that Scribber was its target ... and that his leader wouldn't know about the owl until it was on the back of his neck.

A great deal flashed through Wipp's simple mind then, much of it fleeting, jumbled-up memories of hardship, pain and bullying, with Scribber's ugly face or sharp nails mixed in amongst virtually every one of them. But there was something else in there, too. He wasn't sure what it was, because he didn't have time to work it out properly, but he knew, somehow, that it was important. After all, they *were* both spriggans.

As the owl swooped towards Scribber with its wings spread wide to slow itself down, Wipp leapt up and blocked its way. She veered aside at the last moment, startled to find that this particular meal was no rat, or rabbit – in fact, not anything that she was familiar with. Scribber heard the beating wings and spun around, grabbing wildly at the slit window as he did so and managing to steady himself, but Wipp slipped on the crumbling stonework and landed heavily on his chest with his legs dangling over the edge of the wall. He clawed frantically at the wall top, trying to find a firm hold, whilst Scribber watched incredulously, not daring to move or speak. The youngster stared up at him blankly for a few seconds, terrified and confused, then slid quietly over the edge and out of sight, tumbling down through the darkness and onto the unforgiving stones somewhere below him. There was a dull but ominous thud as Wipp hit them, and the voices from inside the tower stopped in the same instant. There wasn't another sound from Wipp. Not even a groan.

Scribber knew that he must get to safety, away from the window, and he scrambled back down the wall at once; as he did, more loose stones and dirt fell onto Wipp's crumpled body below him. As ever, Scribber was Scribber, through and through, and he was not in the least bit concerned for the fate of the young spriggan. Only frustration and anger filled him now, making his head throb as he leapt from one stone down to the next. He'd been *so* close to hearing everything he wanted to know – so very close.

From inside Redcap's room, the commotion outside was plain to hear, and everything happened quickly after that.

'Open the door now, or die,' snarled Malrin through tightly drawn lips, as he tried to watch the slit window with one eye.

Just like Redcap, he assumed that they'd been overheard and that someone was making their escape, probably knowing far more than was good for them.

Amazingly, the door lock clicked open at once and the dark elf went to leave, but he should have known better than to turn his back on a creature like Redcap. The reason behind the goblin's unexpected cooperation became very clear less than a second later. With new-found energy and quite remarkable agility, Redcap pounced from his chair like a young cat, towards the bread knife on the table. After all, it was his plan from the very start. He didn't give an owl's hoot that he'd handed over the diary page, or that the story of the hob had been told in full. None of it mattered to him in the least, because he'd never intended for the dark elf to leave Skelton Tower breathing.

As the treacherous goblin reached for the knife, however, Malrin sensed the danger and reacted with a speed and skill which no other living being could ever match, turning half back and bringing his sabre up and over his shoulder in a deadly, scything curve, down onto Redcap's groping fingers. Two of them were cut off cleanly and rolled across the tabletop, leaving a bloody trail as they went. Redcap leapt into the air screaming, the remains of his hand buried in his armpit. A great deal of blood, the severed fingers, his chair, the table and several piles of books and maps flew in all directions, before Redcap landed in a heap on the fire hearth, amongst it all.

Malrin stood over him with his sabre held high. The goblin stared up in agony at the victorious dark elf, then squeezed his eyes shut and waited to die.

'Know this, and know it well,' panted the furious dark elf, whose breath was now bursting from his mouth and nose in clouds, like a horse after a winter's gallop. 'I could have taken your whole hand, or arm, or even your ugly head if it had suited me, but I want you alive so that you can tell your festering boys to keep away from the dark elves and our business. They interfere at their peril. Let that be well understood!'

A genuinely surprised Redcap opened one eye only, and without another word, Malrin sheathed his sabre and quickly left the room. His feet barely touched the steps as he raced down the spiral stairs and out through the bottom door, into the night. He stopped and peered into the darkness with eyes which usually missed nothing, but there was no sign of anyone, and he was about to leave when his sensitive ears caught the sound of dust trickling down from the top of the ruined wall. He ran over to it at once, his beard twitching as he listened carefully again, and stared all around him, quite unaware that less than four paces away, Wipp lay covered with his leafy cloak and a sprinkling of dust, perfectly hidden.

Malrin had no time or patience for further delays. With a last look up at the tower, he strode away and was soon enveloped by the darkness. In any case, he thought, he now had the two things he needed most: Witcher's pathetic but precious verse, and a clear plan in his mind. Behind him, Redcap's pitiful groans drifted out of his window and across the top of the steep escarpment just beyond the tower, but few would have heard them, and even fewer would have cared if they had.

With Malrin gone, a cloaked figure appeared from behind the wall and went straight to the small, motionless body lying amongst the weeds and rubble. Scribber guessed at once that Wipp's neck was cleanly broken, for his was lying on his back but facing the ground at the same time. He stood up and grew three feet taller in as many seconds, before picking Wipp up as if he were a young child and throwing him over his shoulder. Scribber knew that Wipp's body mustn't be found there, close to the tower, or every goblin within ten miles would be baying for his blood when dawn came and Redcap discovered exactly who had been listening outside his window. With a final adjustment to his load, the angry spriggan left Skelton Tower and all its woes behind him.

After following the top of the escarpment for five minutes or more, with his wounded leg aching miserably and his energy fading rapidly away, he stopped and dumped Wipp's body unceremoniously onto the grass, close to the top of the steep slope. Scribber peered down it and shook his head, for somehow he'd always known that Wipp would eventually get himself into trouble that he couldn't get out of. Disrespectful to the very end, he kicked the limp corpse over the edge, sending it down to its final but most unpleasant resting place. Knowing Redcap as he did, he was sure that the decaying remains of many other unfortunate creatures would be somewhere down there, too, but it would have to do for silly Wipp.

'Would you believe it?' he mumbled, as he stretched his arms and shoulders. 'A ruddy spriggan what's lived in a cave full of rocks all 'is rotten life, but couldn't 'ang on to a few when it really counted.'

Without a trace of remorse, Scribber shrank back down

to his very smallest size and set off towards Kirby's place, for he knew that his business now lay with the dark elf, and that despite his earlier promise to himself under the briars, he mustn't lose track of him at any cost. Scribber was no ordinary spriggan, though, and in a few short minutes he'd caught sight of Malrin as he was making his way past Kirby's orchard, heading west. As Scribber jogged along in the darkness some distance behind him, the key thumping against his ribs, he smiled grimly as he clamped it tightly against his side. Its time was coming soon. He just *knew* it.

The Crypt

A small spider slipped downwards on its fine, silken thread and landed on Mark's forehead as he sat dozing against the dusty wall of the church belfry. He tried to remove the annoying itch with a flick of his hand, almost waking himself up.

It was late in the afternoon and the daylight had all but gone, engulfing the church and its large rambling graveyard in wintry shadows. Somewhere far below him a door creaked open and quick footsteps crossed the pretty tiled floor. They stopped at the base of the tower, directly below the belfry where Mark was sitting hidden from the entire world, and the peace was suddenly shattered as an agitated voice half called and half whispered his name.

'Mark? Are you in here?'

There was a short pause before the voice called out again, but this time there was a tired, impatient edge to it.

'Mark! Where the heck are you? *MARK!*'

The voice was now loud enough to break into his dreams and Mark awoke with a jump as he suddenly recognised whose it was – and its dangerous tone. Scrambling to his feet, he made his way around the single, enormous bell and over to the open hatchway in the floor, where the top few rungs of a long and distinctly wobbly ladder stuck up into the air. He peered downwards sheepishly at the familiar figure below him.

'Vicky? What's up?' he asked innocently.

'There's nothing up ... apart from you, by the look of it,' snapped Victoria, doing her best not to shout in church. 'You've been *ages*. You don't seriously think you'll find anything important up there, do you?'

Being Victoria, she was also taking care not to give the impression that she'd been worrying about him, and so was standing with her hands on her hips and her feet spaced well apart, craning her neck to see upwards. Mark noted her stance. She was obviously annoyed about something, and that usually meant he'd be getting the sharp end of her tongue for a little longer yet. He'd seen and heard it all countless times before, though, and knew exactly how to deal with it. Everything came back to him as he woke up properly ...

He and Victoria had assumed that the key stolen from Willow Garth was the largest one in the collection, which had always lived on the last nail, and also that it was the old one to the church. With that nail now empty, there was no better place to start their search ... or so they thought. They'd spent the best part of two afternoons searching the entire church and graveyard, not sure what they were looking for, but looking anyway, in the hope of finding some clue as to who the intruder might have been, or why they'd taken that particular key.

Late on the first day, they'd sat side by side on a wooden bench for over an hour, close to the grave of Victoria's mother, where freshly laid flowers adorned a long, low mound in the grass and its newly carved marble headstone. Many memories had come back to them as they'd talked of happier times a year earlier, and a few tears were shed despite Victoria's best attempts to hold them back. With a poor night's sleep behind her and rapidly losing heart, Victoria had decided that they were wasting their time and had gone home to see Annie and her father. She'd left Mark to his own devices, which suited him well enough. There were still one or two places he'd wanted to check out – all by himself.

'Look, I'm sorry, all right? I didn't know you'd been looking for me. I lost track of the time, I s'pose.' Mark looked at his watch for added effect and smiled down at her, hoping she wouldn't guess that he'd been napping. 'I've always wanted to have a good poke around up here, y' know, and now I have. By the way, the cobwebs are awesome.' He threw in an impish grin deliberately conjured up to tease her.

'I don't care *how* awesome they are!' she shrieked, as if she were scalding a naughty child, and obviously forgetting where she was for a moment.

Mark chuckled contentedly to himself: Victoria was clearly feeling more like her old self. She called up to him again, but far more quietly.

'I've been to your place to see if you'd come home yet – you hadn't.'

'Hadn't I?' sniggered Mark, pushing his luck a bit further than usual. Victoria ignored his attempt at a joke.

'Your Mum wants to know if you're coming home for tea, and if you are, to tell you to get a move on, before it all goes.' Victoria didn't wait for a reply and spaced her feet a little further apart. 'I told her that you don't deserve any if you can't even be bothered to show up on time, and what's more, she agreed with me.'

Mark kept quiet for as long as he dared to, mostly to unsettle her, but he was also thinking of the best way to respond. In the end he decided to make use of her greatest weakness – curiosity. He stirred it into life as only he could, for he knew her ways almost as well as he knew his own.

'Just forget tea for a minute. There's something up here you should see first. It's kinda spooky … but interesting, too.'

Victoria cocked her head sideways, but said nothing.

'Yeah. That's *just* how I'd describe it,' continued Mark. 'Shame if you don't see it really, after all our hunting around.'

There was still a stony silence from below, just as he'd expected. Victoria shook her head, partly in despair, but also to loosen up her aching neck, and with a final, exasperated look up at her dearest and oldest friend, walked out of the church, closing the heavy door behind her. Mark went to the belfry window and watched her as she walked away along the gravelled path, between the neatly cropped yew trees which flanked it. He was waiting for her curiosity to nibble away at her enough for her to react, and he was just starting to think that his plan might have failed miserably when she stopped just before the churchyard gate. She stood with her back to the church and her hands back on her hips as she wrestled with the possible consequences of giving in.

A minute later she was carefully climbing up the belfry ladder, and Mark, who was pleased with himself but gallant enough not to show it, helped her off at the top before welcoming her to the small and very dusty room. She was puffing after her climb, and trying to remove a long cobweb from her cheek and shoulder. Her face looked as if she'd just sucked on a lemon.

'This'd better be good, that's all I can say,' she panted. Mark knew that it was very unlikely to be *all* she had to say, and winked at her. 'Please don't tell me you actually like it up here,' she added. 'You must be out of your head.' She was rubbing her hands together, trying to warm them up, and looking around disapprovingly.

Mark ignored the harmless insults and ran his hand lovingly over the side of the bell, having decided that it was time to get her back on an even keel.

'I *do* like it up here, actually, it's cool.' He was smiling happily to himself as he followed some of the deep lettering on the bell – Y O R K A D 1 6 7 8 – with one of his fingers. 'I might even leave home and move in for good. You can visit me any time you like, though.' He couldn't resist teasing her just once more.

He went to the window again and squatted there, peering down into the graveyard. It was quickly filling with shadows and curling shreds of mist.

'Forget cool – I'd say it's more like bloody freezing,' said Victoria, hugging herself tightly. Mark didn't argue with her on that point, and pulled the collar on his jacket up a little higher.

'Look, it's just down here,' he said. 'Do you want to see it or not, then?' He dropped onto his knees and nodded towards the amazing view below.

Victoria suddenly looked tired and let out a quiet sigh of defeat as she edged her way around the bell and knelt down next to him. They both knew that there'd been more than enough talk of trivial things, and so they allowed the delicious peacefulness of the place to work its spell on them. A minute passed before Victoria answered.

'About just now, Mark. I'm ... I'm s–'

'Scared?' Mark interrupted her, looking concerned, but knowing very well what she'd been about to say. He was holding the mysterious little dagger and tapping the side of its blade against his palm.

'Me? Scared?' She laughed at him, but unconvincingly. 'No way! I'm ... Look, I guess I'm sorry, that's all. I know you're only trying to help.' She avoided looking at him, and slid the zip of her fleece up and down instead. 'I didn't mean it, okay? I'm just worn out,' she went on, finally turning to face him. 'What with losing Mum and now Elspeth being so poorly, I don't know if I'm coming or going.' She shuffled around, trying to get a little more comfortable on the hard floorboards. 'I shouldn't take it out on other people, should I?'

'You mean me? Oh, I don't mind,' said Mark. 'I'm thick-skinned enough.'

'Huh! Tell me about it,' replied Victoria. 'You should've been a rhino.'

She was quiet again for a few moments, trying to decide whether or not to say what was on her mind, and wondering if Mark might even be thinking the same thing, too.

'We're not getting anywhere, are we?' she finally asked. 'We've looked everywhere and it's just been a complete waste of time, hasn't it? Elspeth's stuck in York and we can't do a single bloody thing to help her.'

She let her head slump forwards onto the stone wall beside her, not caring about the cobwebs or pain, and Mark wished hard that he could say something inspiring, something that would lift her spirits as high as the spire somewhere up above them, but his heart told him it wouldn't be that easy. In the end, he kept it short and to the point as he put his hand on her shoulder.

'It's not like you to give up, Vicks. So don't, all right?' He changed the subject at once, before she could disagree with him.

'D'you know, it's weird, but ever since I've been carrying *this* around, everything seems a bit different. Sort of ... clear.' He spun the dagger on its tip. 'It's hard to describe ...' Victoria looked puzzled, and Mark tried again. 'Look, don't laugh, but before you came up here ... Well, I swear I felt this spider –' Victoria sat bolt upright. 'A *little* spider,' he added quickly, 'and get this – walking up the *outside* of my jeans. Now is that freaky, or what?'

'Your imagination always was wild,' she replied, shivering, before leaning forwards to try to get a better view of the graveyard.

She was unaware of it, but Mark watched her from the side, and for a few, brief seconds he saw her in a completely new light – familiar, but somehow surprising at the same time. He felt a blush creeping up the side of his neck.

Wow! Vicky's changing. Growing up. She's sort of ... pretty. Yeah, that's it. Definitely pretty.

He'd never noticed it before. She'd always been just his mate, the kid he'd grown up with. The feeling vanished as quickly as it had arrived – helped by Victoria's sharp intake of breath and a sudden stiffening of her body.

'What the heck's that?' she whispered breathlessly as she grasped Mark's wrist and brought her nose right up to the metal mesh which kept out the birds.

He leant forwards too, and stared down into the gloom. For a while he couldn't see anything unusual, but then he noticed something moving close to the hedge by the gate. It wasn't the usual munching rabbit or roaming cat. This was something larger ... something odd. They glanced at each other, silently agreeing to say nothing and keep watching – a cobweb even drifted onto Victoria's face, but was ignored.

The silence became almost deafening as they waited, hoping for another glimpse of whatever it was outside. Seconds turned into minutes and they were both beginning to blame their imaginations when they suddenly heard voices whispering to each other out there, high-pitched voices, but not particularly childlike, and urgent, too – as if there was trouble going on. Despite the distance, they were surprised that they could clearly hear the occasional word, including 'bronze' and 'spriggan', whatever that meant. They looked at each other again, mystified, and for some reason neither of them understood, just a little bit worried. But still they said nothing.

Then it was Mark's turn to grip Victoria's arm as he

caught his breath in surprise. Three small figures were heading for the line of yew trees bordering the gravel path to the church door. Victoria could see them too, as she clung onto Mark, and he gripped the dagger tightly.

With their eyes steadily widening, they stared in disbelief as the figures began to run from one tree to the next, pausing at each one. Dressed in black from head to toe and clearly not wishing to be seen, they checked left and right as they made their way steadily towards the church. Up in the belfry, a peculiar and inexplicable exhilaration suddenly surged through Mark and Victoria, dancing up and down their backs and arms in rapid, tingling waves and making their eyes water, for they both realised that despite their size, these were certainly not children. They didn't sound like them, and they didn't move or behave like them, either.

'No one, I mean *no one* will ever believe this,' whispered Mark incredulously. Victoria shook her head in agreement and shivered again, but not from the cold this time.

'I don't believe it myself yet,' she whispered back, unable to drag her eyes away from the strange sight below her. 'I thought they were just kids in fancy dress, up to no good. But they're not, are they?'

The black figures stopped just short of the church and gathered together in a circle as they discussed something heatedly. One of them jabbed a finger at a scrap of paper in his hand before they turned aside, still completely unaware that they were being watched from above, and ran towards a holly tree which stood nearby in amongst a jumble of old gravestones. Mark and Victoria knew the tree well, for they'd played around it often enough when they were much younger, sometimes scaring each other with stories of devils and witches. Just next to it, but partially hidden by the long grass, a set of steep stone steps disappeared a short distance into the ground, to an old but solidly built door. This was securely locked, and had been for as long as anyone could remember. As far as the village children were concerned, it was the start of a secret passage containing various unimaginable terrors, but in fact it was nothing more than the entrance to the long-forgotten Witcher family crypt. That family had once dominated most of Rosedale with their vast mining empire, and the Witcher coat of arms was still carved proudly into the oak door.

Directly above the crypt, and behind the holly tree, stood a tall monument of smooth grey granite. A low wall surrounded it, with handsome corner posts made from the same granite and supporting rusty, sagging chains. Inside the chains, unkempt grass and weeds grew around eight neglected tombstones, laid flat on their backs in two neat rows of four, like the start of a card game for giants. Each one bore the same coat of arms and even some family names, but most of them were so weathered or blanketed in moss that they were impossible to read.

The three little figures darted down the steps to the crypt. Above them in the belfry, and still holding onto each other and the dagger, Mark and Victoria could clearly hear them whispering to each other again and trying the door handle repeatedly, utterly confident that they were invisible and quite alone. They now seemed to be arguing amongst themselves, and Mark wondered if they'd managed to open the door and were trying to decide who should be the first to go in.

'Who can they be?' asked Victoria, pulling her collar more tightly around her neck. 'Not ghosts, surely.'

Mark shrugged. He hadn't any idea what ghosts looked like, but these little things didn't seem that ghostly to him … despite their surroundings. Unfortunately, though, Victoria's question wasn't asked as quietly as it could have been, and the chattering below them stopped abruptly –

she slapped her hand across her mouth as soon as she realised her mistake, but the silence continued whilst she and Mark wondered if they'd frightened them off or not. Down by the crypt door, the black figures were wondering, too. Had they heard something unwelcome, and if so should they go and find what caused it and silence it forever? Whatever else they were, they were certainly far, far from being frightened ...

'Shall we go down?' whispered Victoria anxiously, hoping that Mark would know what to do.

'I'll go. You wait here for a bit,' he replied, guessing that Victoria was more alarmed than she would like to admit.

In fact, he had a few nerves of his own, but nerves or no nerves, he was soon climbing down the ladder, and Victoria was too late to object to being left alone. She decided to give him a few minutes to himself and then follow: she didn't want to be the only one inside the church with goodness knows who or what lurking around just outside.

*　　*　　*

Unbeknown to the dark elves or their onlookers, the graveyard had another visitor that same evening. He was far more expert at keeping out of sight, though, for he was a spriggan. Scribber had followed Malrin for a whole day and a night, ever since they'd left Skelton Tower and its mutilated resident. He was cold and exhausted, caked in mud, and hadn't eaten a thing since his egg-sucking session with Wipp, but he was still determined to see what the dark elves were up to, even if it killed him. His hopes were rising as he crouched behind a gravestone and watched. He, too, had seen the dark elves run down the steps to the crypt entrance ... and come up again soon afterwards, empty-handed. Malrin spoke urgently as he huddled close to the others under the holly tree.

'This is the place alright,' he said, waggling the diary page under their noses. '"*Dark bed, eternal, hard and cold.*" Witcher's in there, all right, laughing in his coffin, knowing him, and waiting for someone just like us to pay a visit – and relieve him of his hoard!'

Scribber turned his head to catch their words, but he couldn't, no matter how hard he tried – he was too far away.

Malrin looked back down at the door to the crypt and sounded puzzled as he spoke again. 'For some reason, none of my powers will open that door, and believe me, I can open most things when I put my mind to it.' The other two nodded, frowning, before one of them spoke up more brightly.

'It would be a lot easier if we had the key.'

Malrin looked at him coldly, but somehow stopped himself from immediately reducing their little group to just two.

A moment later all three of them vanished – black figures swallowed up by an even blacker night. Scribber raised his head warily above the gravestone and rested his nose on its mossy top whilst he waited to make sure that the dark elves really had gone. Then it was *his* turn to dash across the grass towards the holly tree, dodging around headstones and between the yew trees by the path, his leafy cloak flying out behind him.

He raced down the steps to the crypt like a frightened rabbit and was soon wrestling with the door handle, but he was bitterly disappointed, just as the others had been before him. As he rested his forehead against the door, defeated, confused and wondering what to do next, he noticed the large keyhole next to the handle and immediately banged his head several times on the oak boards for being so stupid. He groped inside his cloak and found the key he'd carried around for so long, before poking it into the keyhole with a shaking hand. It fitted perfectly, and after two failed attempts in the rusty old lock, turned with a loud and encouraging click.

'So whatever Redcap wants so much is in 'ere, is it?' he muttered, as he pushed the heavy door inwards and took a step into the dark, musty room behind it. He smiled grimly to himself. 'It must be worth 'avin', if 'e cuts ears off to get 'is 'ands on it.'

At that same moment Mark opened the church door and, feeling unusually nervous, peered out into the graveyard. As far as he could tell there was no one around so, keeping close to the church wall, he made his way towards the holly tree, and was soon standing at the top of the steps beside it. He looked all around him, suddenly unsure about what he'd seen from up in the belfry and wondering if he and Victoria had imagined the whole thing after all – he ran his fingers through his hair as he struggled with indecision and a sudden, irrational fear of making a complete fool of himself. As he stood there, two bats flew past, making him jump.

'Come on. Get a grip, boy!' he whispered, annoyed with himself.

The thought of being in real danger hadn't entered his head, for the black figures, if they *were* real, seemed far too small to him to be dangerous. As a matter of fact, he'd just decided that the whole business was nothing more than a well-performed prank, and was turning to go back to Victoria when he noticed a dull blue light coming from somewhere down the steps. It stopped him instantly and sent a shiver down his spine. Staring down, he saw that the door was slightly ajar and that the blue light came from behind it. It was getting brighter, too. All of a sudden, he could feel his own hollow heartbeat in his chest as his hand went instinctively to his jacket pocket and lifted out the dagger – the blade felt warm again, just as it had the first time he'd held it in Elspeth's bedroom. He realised that it was no real weapon, but he felt the need for something sharp, and it was better than nothing, he decided. Gripping it tightly, he crept down the slippery steps.

With the dagger in his hand again, the blue light looked even brighter and colder, almost unnatural, and as he reached the door he saw the large key protruding from the keyhole – the light was throwing a stretched shadow of it across the door. Memories of the Featherstones' key collection flashed through his mind as he touched it lightly with his finger: it was still warm, fresh out of Scribber's inside pocket. Teeth tightly clenched, he pushed the door open a little further and peered around it into the crypt.

What he saw stayed with him for the rest of his days. Built into each of the four walls were two deep stone ledges, one above the other, each completely filled with a large marble coffin. Every coffin lid was carved with a life-sized effigy of the occupant, peacefully asleep on their back with their hands crossed on their chest, dressed either in their finest robes or full armour. The entire room was illuminated by an astonishing ball of iridescent blue light which floated close to the ceiling, bobbing about weightlessly amongst the cobwebs. A small hunched figure in a leafy coat stood in the centre of the crypt, sideways on to Mark, who watched, incredulously, as it cupped its dirty hands together and blew softly into them. They at once began to fill with a second ball of blue shimmering light, which was soon shining out in long, thin shafts from between its fingers. It released it upwards gently towards the ceiling, like a child releasing a captured butterfly, and there it stayed alongside the first one, bathing the crypt with even more light. Shadows played around the coffins as the lights drifted through the cobwebs or between the many dangling tree roots which had grown down between the stones of the vaulted roof in their search for life-giving soil.

The creature turned towards the coffins, and its cloak swung aside as it did so. It was enough for Mark to catch sight of something even more startling; tucked into its belt was a small dagger, just like the one in his own fist. Identical gems in the hilt caught the blue lights above them and blinked momentarily at him like stars on the clearest of frosty nights, and in the same, tingling instant Mark knew that he was with the Featherstones' intruder. There was no trace of doubt in his mind.

Scribber began to move from coffin to coffin, still wondering what Redcap was willing to pay so much for, and looking inquisitively around and over each one.

Mark was watching in disbelief when anger suddenly swept through him. It made his cheeks flush red and his heart pound even faster, but he was also afraid for the first time. He knew in his heart, however, that he must do something whilst he had the chance to fulfil his promise to Victoria, and so he pushed the door wide open and stood filling the doorway, waiting. Scribber heard the door move and swung around to face him.

For several long moments, the spriggan stared up at what he considered to be nothing more than a minor inconvenience – an impertinent young mortal, bathed in spriggan light and gripping a very familiar dagger. Scribber was curious as to how Wipp's dagger had ended up in Mark's hand, who had no business handling it, but also pleased that it had come back to its rightful owners without any effort on his part. He was not, however, in any way concerned with the threat presented by his unexpected company – or his newly acquired toy.

Slowly, *horribly* slowly, an evil grin crawled across

Scribber's face, striking a new and even deeper fear into Mark's heart, stabbing it with a knife of ice. Mark felt his knees begin to weaken and he steadied himself against the wall as the face behind the grin, then the whole body, began to grow larger ... and taller. Mark's eyes widened as they followed him upwards.

As the spriggan grew, Mark began to feel his own dagger getting heavier. He looked down and saw that it was growing, too, right there in his shaking hand: it was no longer a curious plaything but already a long, elegant sword, and Mark held it out in front of him, amazed. The bright, faultless blade and its gem-studded hilt almost made him forget where he was for a few seconds, but when he did look up again, Scribber was well over seven feet tall and some of the tree roots hanging around him were now touching his shoulders. The giant spriggan pushed his hood back, shook his hair loose and glared down at Mark, daring him to approach. The horrific sight made Mark reel, and he staggered again slightly as his breath seemed to be sucked out of his body.

The ugly spriggan had been awake for several days. His eyes were bloodshot and swollen. He was splattered with mud and blood and his lank hair hung in greasy strands across his face. His long, crooked nose – either blue with cold or lit from above – dripped steadily as he drew his sword from his belt and rested its point on the flagstoned floor.

'Oh dear me, it looks like I'm trapped,' he drawled sarcastically, and with alarming coolness. Then his face hardened, along with the tone of his voice. 'Gerrout of me way and I'll leave right now.' Mark stood his ground and placed his feet slightly further apart in reply. 'I might even spare yer miserable life!' added Scribber, lying without a second thought.

The words were distant and echoing in Mark's ears, as if they'd come from another place, or even another world, but he'd already made up his mind. He wasn't going anywhere just yet.

'It was you in the farmhouse, wasn't it?' He croaked out the words from a dry throat which didn't seem to want to work properly. 'What've you done to the little girl?'

He was doing his best to sound brave and confident, but he didn't recognise his own voice, which sounded strained and weak in his own ears. Scribber's grin widened, despite the disturbing fact that a mortal and a spriggan were facing each other, and what's more, *seeing* each other, for the very first time. It should have worried Scribber, but it didn't. He was sure of himself in every way, and showed it, for he had no intention of leaving a live witness behind to tell the tale. The rules of his own, normally unseen world wouldn't be broken ... not by him at least.

'We came mostly for that key, not the brat,' he hissed, nodding towards the door. 'Their dog ruined our plans to take 'er. She was gonner be our tender little mid-winter treat,' he whined, suddenly brimming with hate. 'We always take babies when we gets the chance!' His mouth started to water uncontrollably as he thought of it, making him dribble, and he wiped his arm across his wet chin.

Along with his fear, Mark was now fighting to control a growing rage. His jaw began to ache as he clenched his teeth together, and his knuckles turned white around the hilt of the sword as he thought about trying to use it. At last, he spoke up, trying to steady his slightly trembling voice as he did so.

'She's in a coma, you ... you animal! What've you done to her?'

The spriggan laughed out loud and threw his head back, baring his stained teeth and black, knobbly tongue.

'She only needs a little bit of this,' he sniggered, as the echoes of his laugh died away. 'Why don't you come and get some?'

He was holding out a tiny leather pouch in his open hand and beckoning to Mark with a curling middle finger at the same time.

'Here boy, take it ... If y' dare!'

Then, as Mark stared at the little pouch, his jaw slowly relaxed and he felt his fear draining out of him, right down to his feet and out through his toes, into the flagstones, although he had no idea why. Then, incredibly, it was gone.

In its place came certainty. He knew that he must fight – fight for Elspeth – but more importantly, he knew that he *would* fight, whatever was about to happen to him. He drew a deep breath and lifted his sword to point it straight at the living nightmare towering above him, but almost at once the tip of the heavy blade began to wander about, bringing a snort of contempt from his colossal opponent. They stood facing each other for several more seconds, Scribber waiting, Mark praying, then, as if by some silent but mutual agreement, they rushed forwards with their swords held high, and clashed together noisily.

The creature's strength was terrifying. Mark felt like he'd run into a tree, and grunted as his breath was smashed out of him, but he managed to push himself away as its foul breath blasted down into his face. A second later, Scribber was slashing at him with strong, sweeping strokes, but although Mark had no real skills with a sword, he surprised himself by somehow managing to block each one of them, albeit awkwardly.

Then, strangely, everything seemed to be slowing down for Mark, and he began to feel his sword making its own decisions, irrespective of his own feeble efforts – it was twitching and jerking in his hand of its own accord, and seemed to know just what to do to deflect each potentially lethal blow. Despite this, his opponent drove him steadily backwards towards the door, and Mark was eventually thrown against the wall by a vicious blow aimed at his neck. Yet again, Scribber's sword was deflected away by his own ... *just*, although it sliced through Mark's jacket and cut deeply into the shoulder of his sword arm.

A brief look of surprise flashed across the spriggan's face. He wasn't expecting such a spirited defence, and continued his attack with renewed energy and venom.

Mark swapped his sword to his other hand and managed to protect himself from two more powerful blows as he backed further away from Scribber. Behind him on the floor and almost hidden in the shadows lay a long, stone coffin with an effigy of a heavily armed knight carved into its massive lid. Mark didn't see it, and suddenly he was tumbling backwards over it, with the spriggan's sword slicing uselessly through the air where his head had just been. He fell into the dark, narrow gap between the coffin and the wall, and found himself trapped on his back, looking up into Scribber's hideous but victorious face. The spriggan leapt up onto the coffin lid and held his sword up high in both hands, with the tip pointing down at Mark's chest.

In that moment, Mark could only think of two things as he lay there, trapped and barely able to move ... the crypt was a horrible, lonely place to die in, and if it was locked up afterwards, his body would probably never even be found. As the sword plunged down towards his chest, he could do nothing more than shout out a simple, final but defiant word.

'NO!'

As the word left his lips he felt his own sword move again. Still in his peculiar snail's-pace world, he watched his sword turn the driven blade slightly to one side, so that it missed his chest and stabbed downwards through the gap near his armpit, before striking the stone floor beneath him. By some good fortune, or more magic, its point jammed between two flagstones. Mark waited for the pain to come ... but there was none, and a sweet but short-lived relief coursed through him.

The furious spriggan above him roared and pulled upwards on his sword with all of his considerable strength, but it was stuck firmly, almost as though it had decided to change owners for itself.

*   *   *

Victoria had waited for as long as she could bear to before following Mark down the belfry ladder and out into the graveyard. As the cold night air hit her, she was shocked to hear the dreadful noise coming from near the holly tree and ran to the top of the steps, which were still dimly lit by the blue light. She knew at once that something was very wrong and an inexplicable dread came over her as she screamed out Mark's name.

Inside the crypt, Scribber, who was now down on one knee and wondering if he could strangle Mark from on top of the coffin, heard the shrill scream and turned to face the open door. He could see Victoria at the top of the steps, with blue-washed evening mist drifting around her. He tilted his head to one side, questioningly, unsure who this pretty young mortal was, but in doing so he took his eyes off his prey for a moment too long. Mark summoned what little strength he had left and managed to lift his own sword up above the coffin before bringing it around in a rattling sweep across the stone lid. It found the unsuspecting spriggan's ankle, cutting cleanly through his leather boot and into the dirty flesh inside it. Scribber roared out again – in pain, this time – shaking his head from side to side in anger before dropping onto both knees with bloodied spit streaming from his gaping mouth. He stared down hatefully at Mark, who lay helplessly behind the coffin, one sword in his hand and another rocking gently to and fro from his armpit.

'We 'aven't finished this yet,' he snarled, before leaping from the coffin and launching himself through the doorway towards Victoria.

With the blue light weakening quickly and Victoria's scream still ringing in his ears, Mark struggled desperately to get up and follow, but a searing pain shot through his injured shoulder and he felt himself slipping into an altogether different kind of darkness, one he was utterly powerless to avoid. With Victoria's safety swamping his tortured mind, that darkness grew and completely engulfed him as he slumped back down to the cold, unforgiving floor, unconscious.

Ignoring his wounds, Scribber ran up the steps three at a time and charged headlong at Victoria as she stood waiting for Mark to answer her. She no longer had any contact with the dagger, and so never saw or heard her attacker: he was in his own world, quite separate from hers for as long as he wished it so. It was just as well that she had no warning of him, though, for it would have needed a far braver heart than hers to survive the shock of it. Scribber was now unarmed, otherwise a young and innocent life would have ended there and then.

Halfway up the steps his sensitive ears caught the patter of leather boots on the lane and he made the quickest decision of his life. He knew that the dark elves would soon be upon him, with their sabres drawn and his blood near the top of their wish list, and so in the end Victoria escaped lightly, with nothing more than a brutal, glancing blow from his thick arm and shoulder as he barged past her. She was tossed aside into the tall grass under the holly tree, like a young child being knocked over by a clumsy adult, before rolling down a short grassy slope and coming to rest against the side of an ancient tomb. She lay there in the darkness, dazed and alone, the wind and sense knocked clean out of her.

Scribber had no time to lose. He hobbled across the graveyard towards the rear gate, usually used only by the gardener, weaving around headstones and virtually destroying the flower arrangements on several graves. He was shrinking down to his normal size as he went, when he suddenly stopped and patted his cloak. His face dropped even faster than the rest of him. He turned around, ready to race back and lock the crypt door, but he could already hear the main gate swinging open. There was no time left and so, still unable to believe his own stupidity, he spun around on his one good heel and headed for freedom once more. He'd no time for fiddling with latches and leapt over the rear gate in one painful bound, before disappearing into the mist.

Mark and Victoria were now both lost to the world, and only the fading blue light seeping past the crypt door hinted at any sign of life in that silent, desolate place, itself so full of death and stillness.

* * *

The peace ended as suddenly as it had begun when a gate latch fell noisily and three dark elves, lead by Malrin, entered the graveyard for the second time that evening. Defeated by the crypt door, they had headed out of the village, walking behind a hedge at the side of the lane so as to avoid any unwanted company. But even at that distance, the sounds of the struggle had immediately caught their attention. Before the swords in the crypt had clattered against each other four times, they were through the hedge, in the lane, and on their way back to the graveyard at a run. There had been no need to discuss any details. There was trouble back near the church, violent trouble, and they wanted to be part of it. Now they ran straight to the top of the crypt steps and stopped, silhouetted against the dying light below them. Victoria lay only a short distance away, completely hidden.

'Spriggan light!' panted Malrin as he peered down at the door, trying unsuccessfully to control his growing rage. 'If the thieving rats have beaten us to it, somebody will be paying dearly. *Very* dearly!'

He pulled his sabre from its scabbard and glanced at the other two elves. They knew from bitter experience that it was unwise to be anywhere near Malrin at times like this, when heads often ended up separated from shoulders, and they gulped as they fiddled with the cloak fastenings against their throats, which suddenly felt exposed and vulnerable. Malrin ignored them and went down the steps with his sabre in his hand, expecting them to follow. They did, but a little reluctantly, and they also kept well behind him, despite the possibility of a large spriggan or two jumping on them from above at any moment.

Malrin pushed the crypt door further open with the point of his sabre, but even as it swung inwards, Scribber's sword, which was still jammed into the floor, quickly shrank to become a small dagger once again. It loosened and fell onto Mark's chest as he lay there unconscious, but only just in time. Malrin walked into the crypt and looked around.

'Come out, spriggan filth, if you know what's good for you,' he cried, wondering if a spriggan could fit behind or under one of the many coffins. There was no reply, which didn't really surprise him. He strolled past the lower ledges, which were level with his shoulders. Each of the coffins was raised up on short legs, and Malrin stabbed his sabre into the dark spaces below and between them. There were none of the screams he was hoping for, even when the other two joined in enthusiastically, but the rattle of the sabres below the coffins did start to stir somebody.

A very confused Mark gradually drifted all the way back to the living hell he had so recently left behind him, but he had the good sense to keep as still as the coffin next to him, and perfectly hidden, as he tried to work out what was happening. As the fog cleared from his mind, he twisted his neck and looked out from under the coffin – it stood clear of the ground just like all the others – and found himself watching the legs and boots of what appeared to be the very same figures he'd seen from up in the belfry earlier. He strained to see more, but the slight movement made his shoulder throb like a beaten drum and he almost fainted again: he touched it lightly, but it was sticky with blood and the pain made him wish that he hadn't. Thankfully, the black figures had stopped their searching and were now standing by the open door.

Malrin leant back against the wall near the door and chuckled to the others as he looked down at the bronze key, still in its keyhole.

'All that business in the woods with our "expert" guides, searching for the spriggans and their precious key. We needn't have bothered.' He sheathed his sabre smoothly. 'But then the damn fools didn't even know what it was for, did they?'

Malrin waved the diary page in the air and was obviously cheering up, much to the relief of the other two.

'Do you know,' he went on, 'I didn't realise that spriggans were so gracious, doing our work for us. Please remind me to kill my next one quickly instead of cutting his arms off first.'

The others nodded and laughed back at him, but they were thin, nervous laughs. Malrin was as unpredictable as April weather, and could change from being mildly agreeable to diabolically violent in the time it took to draw his sabre. Caught up in his own, greedy excitement, he barely paused to take a breath.

'In Witcher's verse it says that the second key, the silver one, is close to his heart. Hah! And there I was, beginning to think that he was just particularly fond of silver. I'll wager it's a lot simpler than that, my friends! Those Witchers never trusted a soul, and Sir Henry was no different from the rest of them. It wouldn't surprise me if he swallowed it for safe keeping.' The dark elf's lip curled up at the gory but pleasurable thought of retrieving it from inside the corpse. 'Let's find him and get what we came for, before those gormless spriggans work out what we're up to and come back.'

He spat venomously onto the floor. Perhaps it was just the dust they'd all stirred up in the back of his throat, but more likely it was his deep, aching hatred of the Witcher family – every last one of them. The fact that Sir Henry had made such a good job of hiding the hoard was eating away at Malrin's twisted mind like an open sore: he would *never* forgive him or any of his kind for that single, selfish and most inconvenient act.

The dark elves were now confident that they were alone, and so worked their way along the coffins looking for Sir Henry, the last and most formidable of all the Witchers. Fixed to the ledge below each coffin was a small brass plate bearing the name of the body above it, and Malrin rubbed the dull surface of each one with his elbow before studying the lettering closely – the crypt was becoming gloomier by the second now, and he had to get closer and closer to the engravings to read them. One of the others suddenly shouted out.

'I've got it, I've got it!' he exclaimed, like a child finding a lost toy.

Malrin was next to him before he'd finished the second 'got', pushing him aside so that he could see for himself. He would have made a good Witcher, for just like them, he didn't trust a soul.

'Why, you're absolutely right! What are we waiting for, then?'

He leapt up onto the coffin, then down into the narrow space behind it. The others stood below and watched, for they knew what was coming next, and that their leader didn't need or want any help from them. With a determined grimace, Malrin held his hands just above the massive lid and let out a long, quiet hiss from between his teeth as his head fell forwards and his eyelids fluttered then closed. He was biting his lip in total concentration, making his beard jerk back and forth.

Nothing happened at first, but after some more hissing and beard-jerking the lid suddenly started to edge its way across the base, marble grating on marble, and cobwebs stretching then parting as the coffin was slowly opened for the first time in seventy years. Malrin followed the lid with his hands, but never touched it as it slid along noisily. The magic came naturally to him and he was well practised, for he'd often used it to unblock cave entrances – usually to kill and eat whoever was cowering inside – and many more times still to ruin field and garden walls, just to show off or be destructive. When the coffin was open far enough, he gazed excitedly into its dark, fusty interior, as if a surprise present was waiting there.

Below him lay the mortal remains of the very last Witcher to control that family's extensive mining empire in Rosedale. He'd been a great man in his living days, although most of the unfortunate men or boys who'd toiled for a few pennies a day in his deep caves and long, stifling tunnels would probably have disagreed. In his coffin, however, he was just the same as every other man who'd lived and died: bones, dust, and nothing more. His lonely corpse lay with its empty eye sockets staring blankly upwards, and its lower jaw fallen down onto its neck in an everlasting but silent scream. Its arms were crossed over its chest, which was partially covered in the tattered remains of a best suit. Several bare ribs now showed through it, whilst a silver watch chain hung from a buttonhole and disappeared down towards a long-forgotten watch.

'Look! He doesn't want to let go of it, even after all this time,' laughed Malrin out loud, looking at Sir Henry's fist and finally realising the meaning of part of the verse.

The dark elf had as much respect for the dead as he had for the living – absolutely none. He took a deep breath and leant into the coffin, before lifting the clenched hand from its resting place and prizing the fingers open. Sir Henry's hand came to pieces at once, its bones rolling across his waistcoat and falling with a soft clatter down into the coffin, like a cupful of badly thrown dice. There, right in front of Malrin's nose, was the bright little key, lying on what was left of Sir Henry's waistcoat. It may have been small, but it was worth a king's ransom to the dark elf, and he lifted it to his lips before kissing it lovingly.

> *'Then silver, bright,*
> *Close to my heart.*
> *It pains me so,*
> *That we must part.'*

With unbelievable difficulty, Mark wormed his way a few painful inches across the unforgiving flagstones to try to see more of what was happening, and watched as Malrin jumped down to join the others. The blue spriggan light had almost gone as the jubilant elf tossed the key up and caught it like a lucky coin, before pushing the others in front of him and running out through the door.

Now Mark was all alone, and he took in his first proper breath. He was still gripping his own weapon, but it was only a small dagger which now lay on his chest, just where it had toppled over. He peered down at a large bloodstain which covered his shoulder, and let go of his sword to try to sit up, but the pain was too much for him and he slumped back to the ground, defeated. He shook his head, fighting to stay conscious, but was unable to stop himself from drifting gently away into a strange, dark dream which seemed so very real to him. Or maybe it wasn't. He just couldn't tell any more.

The Court Elves

It was quite out of character for him, but just for once, Malrin was in a reasonably good mood. In fact, from the moment he'd run out of the crypt with the silver key held tightly in his fist, he'd barely stopped smiling. For the two dark elves following somewhat less happily at his heels, it was a rare treat indeed, and they wouldn't even have been surprised if he'd broken into a song, or at least hummed something to himself as he ran along, punching the air with delight. But song or no song, they made their way along the lane and away from the churchyard at a good pace, keeping one eye out for any spriggans who may have had their own plans for the silver key's future.

'*Now* we're in business, my lucky lads,' he puffed, as they jogged along in the dusk.

The others didn't answer. To start with, they thought that being described as lucky was ridiculous: he may as well have called them handsome or compassionate whilst he was at it. Lucky or not, they weren't under any illusions, either. If there were any profits to be made from the key, they knew from long and bitter experience that these were extremely unlikely to be coming in *their* direction – their leader would make quite sure of that. Malrin chattered happily as he ran, oblivious to the misgivings of his two 'not-quite-so-lucky' lads.

'It was just where ... he said it would be ... right on his mouldy chest. He couldn't bear the thought ... of giving it to anyone else ... to look after!' He spat into the hedge for good measure, venting his intense hatred of every Witcher who'd ever lived.

Half an hour later and almost out of breath, they arrived back at their temporary home: a small, derelict barn at the edge of a field. They were far from their true home, deep in the West Riding of Yorkshire, a journey which on foot would have taken them many days or even a week to make.

Inside the barn, five or six more dark elves had dozed away the time since Malrin and the other two had left to find the crypt earlier that day. They'd soon found some bales of straw which had been split open and scattered along a wall under one of the more watertight parts of the leaky roof, and were making good use of them.

Malrin kicked open the door as loudly as he could, knowing exactly what would be going on inside, and walked in. A meagre fire was smouldering in the centre of the earthen floor, its smoke drifting idly upwards and out through one of the many gaping holes above them. Hovering high in it was a large ball of dull red light. Dark elf-light. This was casting hazy, swirling shadows on the whitewashed walls as the smoke curled up and around it, on its way to freedom.

There was plenty of rustling straw and a few sheepish looks as the elves emerged from their itchy nests, but they were amazed when they failed to receive the traditional painful treatment reserved for such occasions. Instead, Malrin was swinging a dead rabbit alongside his knee, and seemed far more interested in eating than shouting. The rabbit was soon over a revived fire, and as they waited for it to cook he surprised everyone even more by reading to them from the page he'd snatched from Redcap's hand ... a line here, a line there, but not all of it, needless to say.

Part of it had told of the bronze key – the key to the crypt. Malrin explained to the ugly, upturned faces around

113

him that although it was the last key Sir Henry had had to deal with, for anyone trying to find his hoard it of course had to be the first, the starting point. The others sat cross-legged in a circle around the fire, happily breathing in the smell of burning fur as they listened to the last words of a dying man some seventy years earlier. Malrin imitated Sir Henry surprisingly well … for a dark elf, that is.

'To my beloved daughter, Edith, I shall leave twenty guineas and ask that she looks after the key to the family vault. The dear girl is blessed with fair looks but, I am sad to say, the wits of a ewe, and so the key will be safest with her, I feel sure.'

> *'The key of bronze*
> *My blood shall hold.'*

Malrin noticed a grin of approval from some of his audience and decided to continue. He was even starting to enjoy himself.

'I shall, upon my arrival there, be acquiring the very last space in that hallowed room. There will not, therefore, be further need for any other person or persons to disturb my slumber. My descendants must argue amongst themselves for the remaining plots of earth above me, under God's open sky … or be damned.'

The dark elf stuck out his stomach, poked his thumbs into his jacket pockets, and laughed out in a deep voice, as Sir Henry might once have done.

Edith's story could have ended right there, with everyone, including Malrin, none the wiser. Like countless others, it was soon lost in Farndale's murky history, and only rekindled when a greedy hobgoblin with a particular fondness for fresh cream came across an old diary in an even older suitcase … and on the very farm he was so familiar with, amazingly.

He'd been living close to Willow Garth for many years, and he knew everything that went on there. He knew exactly what had become of simple Edith and her key, because he could clearly remember both of them. He'd always known that the bronze key was important, and that two clever thieves had recently stolen it, for he'd watched them from high up in a granary close to the back door as they'd picked the lock in the pouring rain. But they hadn't been the first to try to take it from its place on the beam. No, not by any means. There'd been another visitor before them, sneaking in under the cover of darkness and thinking that no one would know, but the hob had seen *him*, too. Nothing ever escaped his notice at Willow Garth. After all, it was as much his home as it was anyone's, as far as he was concerned.

One of the dark elves by the fire let his head fall forward as he began to doze off, but Malrin brought it straight back up with a snap of his fingers.

'This Witcher girl, Edith. She must have added a line or two of her own in the diary, long after the old man died. Hey! She sounds even more stupid than Sir Henry–' Malrin spat towards the fire as soon as the name left his lips '–thought she was. According to this, years later she had no idea where the bronze key even came from!'

There was some general shaking of heads as the others showed their disapproval, then his eyes darted down the page, double-checking what he would read out and what he would not.

'Let me see, where are we now … Ah, yes. This Edith got married – she did well to find anyone, in my opinion.' He looked up expectantly, and laughter rippled around the little circle again. 'Then she leased a farm using Witcher's twenty guineas –' some more spit flew into the fire and sizzled noisily '– and it seems that they had a daughter called … called …' He was now holding the page sideways and studying a family tree someone had drawn in the corner of it. 'Called Laura. Right, then. This Laura girl grew up, then married a Robert Featherstone and had three brats of her own – all girls. How sweet! Ah, here it is. It says she added the old key to her collection, the one her mother gave her.'

Malrin stopped and thought to himself, then reached towards the fire and turned the rabbit over on its stick. The others watched him, waiting, as he pushed a smouldering branch back into place with his boot.

'So these Featherstone girls, it appears that they are ...' he counted on his fingers as he worked it out properly, ' ... the *great-grandchildren* of Sir Henry.'

The others dipped their heads, expecting to get wet, but their leader continued without a pause.

'They probably don't even know it! But then, what does it matter? There's no sign of any family fortune, is there? For a start, that farm of theirs is falling to pieces.'

The stick through the rabbit had almost burned away at one end, and it finally snapped, dropping their supper into the ashes – twelve hands darted forwards to save it, and three minutes later only a few bones and four singed paws remained.

The diary readings and various one-sided arguments about what was to be done and where they should go next had continued long into the night. Then they'd slept, and slept surprisingly well, with a strange mixture of very pleasant treasure-hunting and not nearly so pleasant life-and-death swordfights forming their dreams. Actually, they slept long into the next morning, and so when Malrin eventually woke up, his mood wasn't quite as merry as it had been the previous evening.

The elves were not alone in their draughty barn. In a dark corner, almost lost in the shadows, lay a hound. Not any hound, though. This was a hellhound, an enormous and truly terrifying beast of a dog, and one of a pack bred specially by dark elves and a few of their nastier associates. Two more of them were somewhere outside, either asleep or gnawing on the remains of an unfortunate sheep or goat. The dark elves held them in high regard, whether riding on them at night at great speed, or using them as a living weapon against their enemies: they stood shoulder high to their masters, were packed with tight, rippling muscles and covered in short, white, wiry hair. Their jaws were wide and powerful, their teeth long and deadly, but these were as nothing compared to their huge, staring eyes, which never blinked and were as red as freshly spilled blood. Those dreadful eyes could see clearly in the pitch dark of a moonless night, enabling the hounds to run at breakneck speed through dense forests, with two or three dark elves on their backs, holding on as if their lives depended on it ... which they often did.

Malrin got up from his straw bed, stretched his legs and wandered over to the corner where the hound lay with his eyes wide open. He nudged a well-gnawed bone closer to its nose, wisely keeping his distance, but the hound moved nothing more than one eyebrow and so Malrin left him and went outside. The other two were there, curled up against the wall of the barn and enjoying the bright morning sun. He chose a place that wasn't too close to them and sat down, leaning against the wall himself and half closing his eyes as the sun began to warm him up a little. It was just the place for making plans, he thought, as he squinted at the climbing sun through his bushy eyebrows.

*   *   *

Mark wasn't sure whether he was alive or dead. He could quite easily be dead, for the place in which he now found himself was as terrifying as he imagined hell might be: a vast, dark cave, with eight living skeletons encircling him as they performed a bizarre, rattling dance. Each of them carried a long, rusting sword, which was thrust towards him over and over again in short, brutal jabs, and he could only stand there, hopelessly trapped in the middle of the circle, trying his best to dodge each one of them.

If he was alive, however, then he was in the middle of the very worst kind of nightmare and he longed to wake up from it, before his tormentors stopped merely taunting him and actually cut into his tired, aching body. As he turned and turned, frantically trying to watch all eight skeletons and their swords at once, he was forced to shield his eyes from the glaring beams of light which shone out from their empty eye sockets. The lights were there one moment and gone the next, as the skeletons faced him or turned away – some were so bright they temporarily blinded him, whilst others were only a pale orange glow through the backs of hollow skulls. As he turned faster and faster, the lights began to merge together to become one writhing, continuous circle surrounding him, but without any order or pattern, and Mark began to feel giddy as more and more of the dreadful swords almost found their target.

Then, with immense relief, he suddenly felt that he'd stopped spinning and was lying motionless on his back, although he dared not open his eyes for fear of what he might see. At least the skeletons had apparently given up and gone away, but the bright lights still darted about somewhere above him, and it seemed as if he was now seeing them through his closed eyelids, for they'd become a fiery, red-orange colour. Perhaps he really *was* alive after all, he hoped, for despite the bone-aching coldness of the crypt floor being all too fresh in his memory, he now felt warm for the first time in what seemed a week. Best of all, he realised, he was even comfortable. Whatever he was lying on was soft and yielding – almost as good as his own bed at home, he decided. As he lay there, gradually relaxing, his fear and confusion began to dissolve away, like early morning mist in the first warmth of the day, and soon he felt compelled to open his eyes.

Little by little, he cracked open his eyelids as he watched the bright lights jiggling around above him, and they grew brighter still, making him squint again, until at last he could see what they really were. There wasn't a single skull in sight. There were no swords or any pain, either, only the delightfully warm sun on his face as it shone in amongst the highest branches of a tall Scot's pine. The tree appeared to be bursting out of the ground somewhere close to his head, before soaring up into a faultless, arching sweep of the purest blue sky he'd ever seen.

He couldn't remember ever having been so thankful for anything in all his life: to be alive *and* to be lying in that remarkable place, watching a breathtaking display by nature at its very best. It was ridiculous, he knew, but he almost felt as if he was drinking in the glorious sight above him, like cupped handfuls of cool spring water on a hot day, and he lifted a hand to shade his eyes from the bright, life-giving sun as he took his fill of it. Without sitting up, he then looked around him as all of his senses came back in a wonderful rush of sights, sounds and smells.

He was lying on lush grass, laced with fallen pine needles, and their pungent aroma was filling his nose and lungs refreshingly, washing away the last traces of the musty crypt and its rotting occupants. He saw, too, that he was at the edge of a circular, sun-filled glade, itself completely surrounded by the majestic pine trees. To his intense relief, Victoria was lying on her back close beside him, but covered from her neck downwards with a most peculiar cloth of countless shimmering colours. She seemed to be deeply asleep. He could see her breathing

119

gently and instinctively knew that she hadn't come to any harm back at the church, but he couldn't work out why she was there, or come to that, why *he* was there.

He looked down at his feet and saw the shape of them under another thin cloth similar to the one covering Victoria. It, too, seemed to have no single colour, but every colour imaginable, for each time he moved, they swirled across it in rippling waves, like wind crossing a field of ripe wheat. It also seemed to be virtually weightless, and yet he felt warm under it: he could feel the morning breeze on his face and knew that it was a cold day in spite of the strong sun and clear, blue sky.

Lying neatly on the grass between him and Victoria were two identical daggers, very much like the one with which he was now so familiar. Then Mark suddenly recalled the creature in the crypt, the weapon he had used, and his own wounded shoulder, as memories of the violent struggle returned with a shock. His other hand moved under the cloth and went to his shoulder ... carefully. He could feel hard, dried blood on his jacket, but there was no pain, not even any tenderness, and that puzzled him. Easing the cloth down, he peered at the gash in his jacket, before lifting his arm and moving it around, cautiously at first but then more easily, and wondering all the time why it didn't hurt.

Then he reached out towards the daggers. They were alike in every way, down to the last twinkling, ruby-red gem, but as he touched one of them something made him jump, and he pulled his hand away quickly. He'd caught a fleeting glimpse of several figures sitting around him on the grass, or at least he *thought* he had, and his pulse raced as he propped himself up on one elbow and looked around the glade uneasily.

There was only peace and quietness around him, and the perfect beauty of the place made it difficult to believe that danger could also exist there, so he sucked in a deep breath between his teeth, moved his hand back to one of the daggers and this time grasped it firmly. The figures instantly appeared again and he sat bolt upright, letting the cloth fall onto his legs. He was about to jump towards Victoria to protect her and was gripping the dagger tightly, ready to use it.

'Please wait, Mark,' said one of the figures.

The palms of his hands were turned upwards to show that he was unarmed, and those three calm and composed words stopped Mark in a heartbeat.

'You have no need to fear us,' he continued. 'We brought you both here and have watched over you through the night.'

He gestured towards the two others, who were sitting on either side of him. As he did so, Mark noticed that there were several more just like them, scattered around the edge of the glade, standing quietly with their arms crossed. They were difficult to see clearly, almost ghostly, but they were definitely there, even after Mark rubbed his eyes.

He couldn't stop staring, for they were all quite unlike anyone he'd ever seen before. They were shorter than he was, he guessed, but not by much, and they wore cloaks made from the same strange cloth which still covered Victoria. The colour of their shoulder-length hair varied from burnt gold to silvery-grey, whilst their fair faces were young and yet somehow wise at the same time. But their eyes were even more remarkable. These were a vivid green, alive almost – much like the trees above them – and filled with sparkling joy, as if their owners were about to break into heart-warming laughter at any moment.

'Who are y- *you*?' asked Mark hesitantly. 'I ... I don't get it. How did we end up here?' The figures looked straight at him in silence, but there was only kindness and concern in their handsome faces.

'In your speech we are called light elves,' continued the middle one. 'You might think that your eyes and ears are playing tricks on you, or even that you are in a dream, but we *are* real, I can assure you.' He paused to give Mark time to understand what was happening. 'We brought both of you here and we will not harm you. That is not our way. Although you cannot know it yet, you are in need of help ... and help that perhaps only we can give!'

'What do you mean, help?' asked Mark, alarmed. 'Are we in danger here?'

The elf held up his hand to stop Mark's mind from going too far in the wrong direction.

'No, not here, but to begin with, we carried you and Victoria from the churchyard to this place, to rest ... and also to be healed.'

He looked towards Mark's shoulder and Mark touched it again.

'Wow!' muttered Mark. 'Look ... thanks, all of you, it's fantastic, but how come it's not hurting any more?' he asked, bewildered.

The elf smiled at him patiently, his green eyes radiant in the bright sunlight.

'You are full of questions, but that is only natural,' laughed the elf. 'You will have many more of them, I am sure, before this day is very much older. As for your shoulder, this kept you warm through the night and helped to take the pain from your wound.'

The elf took hold of the cloth which still covered Mark's legs and felt it between his fingers.

'You are the first mortal ever to have touched cloth such as this, but we felt that you deserved special treatment.'

He paused again and his companions nodded in agreement. He knew that there was a great deal for Mark to take in and that it would be unfair if he was rushed.

'What do you mean, *mortal*? Look, this can't be real. I

must still be asleep,' insisted Mark, as he studied the dagger in his hand. 'But there were those little black creatures at the church. Yeah, that's right ... and I had a fight with that, that giant in the crypt.' He locked his hands behind his neck and looked upwards, searching for an answer. 'Ah – I know. He killed me and this is heaven, isn't it?'

'No, not heaven,' chuckled the elf, looking around him, 'but close to it ... particularly today.'

'Then it's got to be a dream,' declared Mark. 'I'm not here at all. I'm ... I'm still asleep in the belfry.' He gave himself a sharp slap on the back of the neck, but instantly regretted it.

'Not the church either, Mark,' laughed the elf sitting to the right. 'So please don't try to wake yourself up any more ... Watch!'

He leapt lightly to his feet and before Mark could move had grasped the lad's wrist. Mark immediately shrank back in alarm. He was still confused and even the warm hand on his arm didn't convince him that he was really awake, or that he and Victoria weren't still in some kind of danger. He looked across at her again, but the elf beside him guessed his thoughts before he could speak.

'Don't worry, she is unharmed. Let her rest a little longer. Her cloth is healing her bruises and giving her strength, just as yours did for you.'

He let go of Mark's arm and returned to the others. Mark shook his head and looked around, still trying to understand what he was seeing and hearing, but it wasn't easy, given what had happened over the last few hours. Questions raced though his mind.

How do they know my name ... and Victoria's? And how long have we been here? It's morning now, so we've been out all night, I reckon. Christ! Everyone at home'll be having a fit.

'Look, I don't want to be rude or anything,' said Mark

as politely as he could, 'but we really must be getting back home. They'll be *right* upset, I can tell you!' Mark pushed the cloth away and started to get up.

The middle elf leant back on his hands and broke into a long, hearty laugh which seemed to completely fill the glade.

'Ah, yes, of course,' he said, trying to compose himself. 'You needn't worry yourself about such things whilst you are with us, in our world. An hour for us is but a fleeting second of your mortal time, and so your families will not be missing you yet, I promise you. And in any case, there is a great deal that we must speak of, and it will take up a good part of this wonderful morning, I expect.' He looked around him appreciatively and took in a deep breath through his nose.

'Trust us ... and try to relax!'

Mark, who was still on one knee, was relieved to hear that at least he and Victoria weren't being missed ... apparently. He closed his eyes and decided to try to do as he'd been asked.

'Your world and ours are *both* real,' continued the light elf patiently. 'They exist alongside each other, but separately – most of the time. That is how it is now, and how it has always been. We elves exist in the same world as the creatures you came across at the church, but we are not like them in any other way, you may be quite sure of that.'

He stopped again, as he studied Mark's face and tried to gauge whether the young mortal had started to accept what was happening. Mark opened his eyes and sat back down, no longer quite as anxious, but more determined to try and understand.

'All right then, carry on,' he said a little more cheerfully, wondering what else was still to come. 'But I warn you now. If I can't get my head around all this business and start laughing, you'll just have to forgive me.'

He placed the dagger on the grass beside him and looked up. The figures had vanished, but a voice spoke out from the view in front of him as Mark looked around anxiously.

'You can only see us whilst you have the dagger, Mark. You are in our world, the unseen world, when it is with you. Please keep hold of it.'

Almost reluctantly, Mark picked up the dagger again and the three figures reappeared at once, still sitting cross-legged in exactly the same places. Mark shook his head in disbelief and looked down in awe at the tiny weapon in his hand.

'We found this at Victoria's home, after it was burgled. That giant in the crypt had the other one, I think.' Mark was about to explain further but the elf interrupted him.

'The creature in the crypt was visible to you only because you held a dagger then, just as you do now. Had you disturbed him without it, you would probably have never left that place alive. As for the daggers, we know all about them. They are very precious to us ... in fact, valuable beyond words. They have never been far from our thoughts, not since they were taken from us many, many years ago.'

The elf looked briefly at his two companions, but the joyful sparkle had almost left their eyes as he continued.

'These are freyals, enchanted swords taken from the bodies of our fallen brothers after the last great battle against an army of the evil ones.' He lowered his voice to a whisper. 'A Sluagh, as we call them. There are six freyals in all. Up until last night all six had been lost to us since that most sorrowful of days, stolen by thieving spriggans from the bodies of our dead comrades.'

The last hint of a sparkle in the elf's eyes died away, and they hardened as he spoke, focused on nothing. He seemed to be reliving the horror of that battle, and even its pain, for several long seconds passed by before he snapped back to the present and managed a brave smile for Mark.

'I am so sorry, Mark. I am telling the tale too quickly for you, and there is so much that you do not know about our world and the beings in it – spriggans included. Please forgive me.'

'Don't worry about that ... there's nothing to forgive,' said Mark more confidently, 'but I can hardly believe all of this.' He was now staring at the dagger again. 'If it's true, what you said about these ... er ... these freyals, then they must be really important to you. I'd like to give them back to you right now, but you'd probably disappear and I'd be talking to myself again.' It was his turn to smile then.

Pleased that Mark was starting to relax, the elf to the left stood up and came close to him, before dropping down onto one knee. Mark tried not to shy away as the elf held out a wide leather strap, which he quickly fastened around Mark's wrist. It was made of the thinnest, softest hide, and set into its honey-coloured surface were six small but perfect green gems – just like those on the hilts of the daggers. They were equally spaced so that at least two were always visible, and they glinted in the sunlight as Mark mumbled his thanks, but he didn't know why he'd been given such an unusual gift and couldn't hide his growing bewilderment.

'Wear this and you will be in *both* of our worlds, whether you have a freyal with you or not. There is one for Victoria, too. It is beside her on the grass.'

Mark put his dagger down beside the other one, as the elf stepped back and joined the others ... without disappearing.

'You see, Mark, many centuries ago, when all this open moor was thickly forested – long before men came here to live, even – our ancestors forged each freyal with hard labour and incredible skills. They are imbued with all of the magic that we are able to give to such things, and they will protect the life of anyone wielding them, in any way they are able to, but only if that person is of a good and worthy heart. I expect that the dagger grew for you and guided your arm in the crypt, but any evil creature trying to use one would find it a far more difficult and unpredictable weapon. It would certainly surprise them from time to time.'

'D'you know, I *thought* it was trying to help me,' agreed Mark incredulously. 'So my heart can't be all bad then, can it?'

The elf chuckled, for he was glad to see that Mark's sense of humour was beginning to show itself.

'No, not *all* bad, but a little distrustful at times,' he replied light-heartedly. 'Yes, the spriggans took all six freyals and have kept them under close guard in their filthy caves ever since. Unlike us, spriggans have the power to grow very large whenever they wish, and we are no match for them, one to one. Also, the entrances to the caves are virtually impossible to find. If we do find one, it will be blocked the next day and it is very dangerous for us to search around up there for new ones. We have tried to retrieve our freyals many times, but we have always failed, and countless good elves have lost their lives as a result.' The elf suddenly looked dejected and he stared blankly at the grass in front of him as he continued. 'Without them we are far less able to counter the wickedness of the evil ones.'

Mark looked at the daggers which lay in the sun next to him and admired their beauty again, just as he had done the first time he'd seen one in Elspeth's bedroom. He would never have guessed that they were so special, and he suddenly felt privileged just to have handled one, let alone to have fought for his life with it. The middle elf suddenly slapped his knees and jumped up, startling Mark.

'Enough of this gloomy talk! Today at least is a fine day, and in many ways, too. The sun is warm on our backs, and two freyals have returned to us, wonder of wonders! *And* you two are fully recovered,' he looked at Victoria as she slept, 'well, almost. Come, Mark, I think we should walk. There are legs to stretch and sights to see. In fact, there is something I would like you to see right now, and in any case, the day is far too perfect to spend it under the shade of these trees, pretty though they are.' The elf took another deep breath and gazed up at the arching canopy of blue above their heads. 'By the way, my name is Roall and I am the court elf of meadows.'

Mark thought that he was well named, for his flowing hair was the colour of sun-dried hay. He did, however, briefly wonder what *court* meant, as the elf continued.

'This is Stirran, court elf of rocks, and please meet Planiss, court elf of springs.'

They both stood up and joined Roall, before the three of them bowed courteously, and as they did so, Mark noticed that each of them had an unusual pair of slender, curved sticks, hinged together at one end and slung across his back on thin cords. He couldn't guess what they might be as he stood up too and returned the compliment, although not quite as gracefully. He suddenly felt himself beginning to relax in the company of the elves, which surprised him a great deal, but they were simply too kind and thoughtful for him to be fearful or suspicious of them any longer. Planiss and Stirran came close to where Victoria still lay, and sat down beside her. They shook their hair free and turned their faces up to the sky, closing their eyes and leaning back on their hands to take in the warmth of the morning sun.

Mark left them and, still feeling as if he was in a pleasant dream of some kind, followed Roall to the edge of the glade and into the pine trees. The elf's footsteps were silent, but Mark could hear him humming a tune quietly to himself as he came towards the edge of the knoll upon which the glade and its thick ring of trees neatly sat. The trees soon came to an end, but beyond them the bright sky and an uninterrupted view waited to be admired. Mark ran the last few paces to catch up with Roall, and together they stepped out of the shadows and into the full sunlight.

*   *   *

Almost a mile away, Malrin was still sitting up against the wall of the barn near the two hellhounds, his tired eyes half closed after his midnight storytelling. He was just drifting into a dream in which blood-red rubies were dropping from a heavily laden ruby tree and pattering onto his head and shoulders as he tried uselessly to catch every one, when he thought he saw something very strange, far away to the north. His head jerked up as the dream ended abruptly and his eyes opened properly. At first it was just a flicker of movement from high up on a knoll, in amongst the tall trees there. A buzzard, maybe – there were plenty about. As he stared, though, he saw something else, something once seen but never forgotten. A light elf – his sworn enemy – had emerged from the trees and was standing there for the entire unseen world to see. That in itself was rare enough, but a moment later he was followed by a young mortal. Malrin sat bolt upright. One of the hellhounds lifted his heavy head, disturbed by his master's sudden movement, but he found nothing to concern him and it was soon resting on his front paws again.

Malrin dared not move, fearing that the figures on the knoll might see him just as easily as he could see them, and for several tense minutes he watched with unblinking eyes and wondered to himself. He'd sent a scout over in that direction earlier, but hadn't heard a thing from him since –

he guessed that he'd probably taken liberties with his brief freedom and was asleep against a tree somewhere. He mulled it over, until the truth of it all began to dawn on him.

Malrin knew as well as anyone else in his world that elves and mortals *never* mix: the two of them up there on the knoll had clearly forged some kind of alliance, for the mortal could no doubt see the light elf standing beside him, and was probably even talking to him. Any alliance between the unseen world and that of mortals, however insignificant, would be unique in his experience, and so there was surely some kind of trickery in the wind. He could almost smell it as his mind began to race ahead:

The silver key's been out of the crypt for less than a day and suddenly light elves are making friends with mortals – scheming together, making plans. I should have known it!

His mouth went dry and his skin started to prickle as he broke out in a sweat, a sweat born purely of greed.

They want the silver key. Of course they do – the key and the priceless hoard it could lead them to … My hoard! I must make a plan, too. Yes, right now. Kill them, perhaps, or torture them first to find out what they know? Let me think… Let me think!

Hellhounds

Mark and Roall were standing together at the top of a steep, grassy slope which swept down from the knoll towards a small lake far below them. Mark thought that he recognised the lake and its central, rather overgrown island, although he remembered it as being more like a large, stagnant pond. An unblemished sky and soaring valley sides were reflected in the surface of the beautiful lake which now lay before him. He could even see a few birds swooping down to feed close to its surface ... a surface which was alive and sparkling in the sunlight, as if a sack of diamonds had been cast carelessly across it.

The elf wrapped his arm around the tree next to him and stared into the far distance, shielding his eyes from the sun with his other hand. The ring of tall pines, as well as the peaceful glade where the others waited, also seemed familiar to Mark, but again it wasn't quite how he remembered it. It was as if his memory was playing games with him or he'd perhaps dreamt of it once, when he was very young.

'I think I know this place, but it seems different, somehow,' said Mark, puzzled.

Roall dragged his eyes from the breathtaking view and turned to Mark, smiling knowingly. He was thrilled to be able to speak face to face with a mortal, the first one he'd ever met properly, and was also enjoying the business of introducing him to the ways of his own world.

'I am quite certain that you *have* been here before, and more than once, probably. After all, we are not that far from your home,' replied the elf, 'but you are seeing it differently this time, with *us* here.' He swept his arm across in front of them, as if he was introducing the view to Mark, like an old friend. 'This is how it *really* is, good and bad. Before today, I expect that you would hardly have noticed the finer details. In our world, everything is plain to see, or hear, or even feel. More *obvious*, if you like. A new leaf is greener and softer in spring, whilst the sting of a hailstone on your cheek is keener ... does that make sense?'

Mark *thought* that he understood, but he was struggling for words as he gazed out across the wide expanse in front of him. It really did seem fresher and clearer. He could see a thin wisp of smoke drifting up from a chimney many miles away at the southern end of the valley, and far up on the western ridge he noticed several buzzards soaring above a rocky outcrop which must have warmed up a little in the sun.

'Up there, above Lonmoor Woods, do you see that deep gully?' asked Roall, not taking his eyes from it. 'That is close to where the spriggans have their caves.' He turned back to Mark, and saw the question in his eyes. 'Spriggans? Oh yes, spriggans. You have already had the pleasure of one's company, although you could not have known it. It was a spriggan you fought with in the crypt. You were indeed fortunate to survive where so many others have perished.'

Mark looked up at the distant gully, amazed to think that such creatures could live so close to the farms he new so well, dotted along the edge of the valley, and yet never be glimpsed or even heard of, as far as he was aware.

As they stood there together, with both of their worlds laid out before them, Roall went on to talk more of spriggans and their vile, greedy ways, and Mark soon realised that he was indeed fortunate to have survived the fight in the crypt, as he learnt of their formidable strength and their ability to grow to a gigantic size whenever it suited them. Much of the morning passed by as they talked, but for Mark it came and went in the blink of a blackbird's eye – although an occasional rumble from his stomach reminded him that he hadn't eaten anything for over a day.

On the far side of the glade from where they stood, a stray breeze rippled briefly through the branches of the pines, but to a watchful light elf standing guard nearby it was far more than that. Perhaps it whispered to him in some secret way, for he turned and stared into the trees nearest him. He studied each of them closely, and listened as the same unnatural breeze moved his hair off his shoulders and brought two or three pine needles down from the tree above him, to join the others strewn around his feet.

There was something wrong, but he didn't know what. He left the warming sunlight and lush grass and walked into the cool shade below the trees, then, after ten careful steps he stopped, still almost invisible in his cloak, turned and waited ... and listened again, watching. But still there was nothing. He was now close to a fine, tall tree, with his back to it. Behind the tree and not even breathing, a black form lurked; an extension of the shadow, but more dangerous than any shadow. He was following Malrin's orders, observing the comings and goings within that area, just as he'd done since dawn. But now he'd been disturbed, and he was annoyed at that ... He hated light elves more than anything else in creation, and so his decision to forget any orders and attack was a simple one.

In one swift movement, the malignant shadow became a deadly killer. A weighted cord flew out from behind the trunk, across the light elf's neck and back to its murderous owner. Half a second later, the cord snapped tight and the light elf was dragged three feet backwards, up against the tree and unable to call for help, the life already being squeezed out of him. He dropped his bow and clutched at the cord around his throat, trying to get his fingers behind it but failing. The cord tightened even more, cutting into his flesh, and the strength started to seep from the arms and hands of that fair elf, his face turning red and his mouth gasping, fishlike, at nothing. The dark elf, now with a knee up against the tree for added effect, twisted the cords in his fists as he tugged and tugged again, his black tongue just showing between his teeth and his cheeks pulled back in a grin borne of undiluted evil pleasure.

Then, when all seemed utterly lost, the expression on his face suddenly turned from glee to surprise. The cord dropped from his fingers a second later, and the half-dead light elf sank to his knees. Behind the tree stood another cloaked figure, still grasping a small but beautiful sword which was now buried deep in-between the ribs of the dark elf. It was Stirran. He pulled the sword out of the body and watched without emotion as it slumped to the ground and lay there, motionless.

'Just as good as it ever was,' muttered the court elf, as he held the bloodied sword up and it shrank to become a small, clean dagger again. He went to the injured light elf and helped him to his feet, then together they returned to the sunlit glade, where Stirran handed over his shaken comrade to several others who had now run up to them. He then quickly crossed over to where Roall and Mark were still talking, and interrupted the elf by whispering into his ear. Roall's features hardened as he heard the news.

'Your stomach tells me that it is well past your breakfast time, so you and Victoria should be getting back to your families,' he said, turning to Mark. He was relaxed and chuckling, despite what he'd just been told. 'But there is something that I would ask you to do first.'

'Sure ... if I can,' replied Mark, who was keen to be of any help.

'Will you come back here alone, later today, before dusk falls? Get Victoria home safely first, but say nothing of what has happened this morning to her – not yet, at least. There are some important matters which we need to discuss with you, but somewhere where it is a little safer to do so.' Roall looked around him, concerned that the dark elf had not been working alone. 'You will be interested in what we have to say, I am sure, but it is up to you whether you come.' He glanced sideways at Stirran. 'What do you think, Mark?'

Mark didn't need to consider Roall's offer for long, as two things were already very clear in his mind. The elves had shown Victoria and himself great kindness by bringing them to the glade and healing their wounds in some magical way. He felt hugely indebted to them for this, of course, but he was also afraid that once he left, he would never set eyes on a light elf again. The promise of a future meeting was more than he could ever have wished for.

'Oh, I'll be back all right – there's now't I'd miss it for,' he replied excitedly, 'except for a huge breakfast, or is it lunch, or p'raps both!'

Roall was pleased and nodded, knowing that Mark had made the right decision.

'Very well, then. We have other business to attend to, but we shall be waiting here for you after the sun has dropped below the ridge road. Keep the bracer on your arm, remember, or you will not be able to see us.'

'Bracer?' asked Mark, looking down at the wristband on his arm.

'You shall see,' laughed Roall. 'Go to her now and wake

135

her gently.' He looked over to where Victoria was still lying. 'You will have much to talk about, no doubt.'

'No doubt at all,' said Mark, who was already imagining her barrage of questions.

With a last look at the two elves, and a fleeting, secret wish that he really would see them again, he left, suddenly eager to get back to Victoria. As he broke through the trees and jogged across the glade, Planiss, who was still watching over her, jumped to his feet and took a few steps back: the strange cloths were now folded neatly across his arm, but Victoria didn't stir. Roall and Stirran watched from the trees as Mark undid his bracer and knelt down close to her, then Planiss left them to join his friends. Together they watched happily as Victoria began to wake up. As soon as she moved, the three of them turned away and seemed to melt into the trees, leaving the two young mortals and the peaceful glade behind them.

Mark led a very confused Victoria back to Willow Garth. Just as Roall had said, it wasn't very far at all from the knoll, but more remarkable still, Victoria appeared none the worse for her encounter with the fleeing spriggan near the crypt. Mark could only assume that the strange cloth had worked its magic on her just as it had for him. She wanted to know all the details, just as he'd expected, particularly regarding the crypt and what she'd heard going on down there, but Mark assured her that all was well and that he'd explain everything to her when the time was right. She pleaded with him not to keep her waiting, but Mark kept his word to Roall. He was sure that there would be a good reason for his request, and he already trusted him enough not to question it.

As the elves had predicted, no one seemed to have missed Mark at home. In fact, it was as if he hadn't been away at all. This was very strange, and something which he didn't understand in the slightest, but he was thankful for it in any case. Much later that afternoon, Mark asked his parents if he could have some more time to himself, away from the farm, and was relieved when his parents agreed, although his father did suggest – between several violent sneezes – that he took a warm jacket and hat.

The lad wasn't one to ignore good advice. With his hat on and the collar of his thick jacket turned up, he was as warm as roasted chestnuts as he made his way out of the village and back past the church, avoiding looking over the graveyard wall and towards the crypt. He was lost deep in his own thoughts, and so before he knew it he was climbing up the side of the knoll towards the copse. The bracers were safely in his jacket pocket. He knew that wearing one would make the light elves and their world visible to him, but he decided not to until the last moment, for fear that other, far less friendly things might start appearing all around him.

It was four o'clock, but the late November sun was already slipping rapidly down towards the high western ridge as Mark climbed the steep footpath back up to the pine trees. He could barely wait to meet the elves again, and as he went higher he recalled each word spoken to him earlier that day, including their mention of 'help': he wasn't sure if they were referring to what had happened to Elspeth or not, but he intended to soon find out. As he puffed his way up towards the first of the trees, nagging doubts about all that had happened at the glade began to fill his mind, but with an effort he managed to push them aside as he scrambled up the last and steepest part of the pathway and finally arrived at a fence by the edge of the copse itself.

The trees seemed a little less awe-inspiring to Mark than when he'd awoken from his dancing skeletons earlier that day, but they were still a pleasure to see. He stopped to catch his breath, and looked up at the tips of them as they all nodded together in the fresh breeze. There was always a price to pay for a bright, sun-filled day in November, and this occasion was no different, he thought, as the cold evening air made his cheeks glow and tingle. The sun finally dipped behind the ridge and the vivid colours around him instantly lost their keen edge as dusk started to settle gently on the valley. Mark blew out his breath to try and make a cloud, but the breeze took it away as he climbed over a rickety stile which straddled the barbed wire fence. A minute later, he was standing in the centre of the glade again.

It was deserted, and horribly quiet, too – not at all like it had been earlier, when it basked in the sunlight and the chatter and laughter of the marvellous elves had filled all his senses. He could see two flattened patches of grass where he and Victoria had laid, and was somehow relieved to see proof that he really had been there earlier that day. He stood quite still and listened out for any signs of life. The sound of a nail being hammered home on some distant farm drifted up to him through the trees, but that was all.

'Aren't you forgetting something?' said a quiet voice just behind him. He jumped and spun around, but there was no one there.

'Roall?' whispered Mark breathlessly. 'Is that you?' He clenched his fists and hoped that he was right.

Suddenly, his hand went into his pocket. The bracers were there, and if he could have, he would have kicked his own backside for forgetting about them as he pulled one out and struggled to strap it onto his wrist. He soon discovered that it wasn't a one-handed job for a novice, as he fumbled with the thin straps. With it on at last he looked around expectantly and was delighted to find two of his new friends close behind him, their arms folded and wide grins across their faces. It was Planiss and

Stirran, their cloaks open at the front and their hoods down on their shoulders. Each of them had a bow at their side, too.

'You are very punctual ... for a mortal,' said Planiss, but in a most inoffensive way.

'We were just going to have a practice whilst we waited for you, but the wait was rather short-lived,' added Stirran, who was tossing his bow a few inches into the air and catching it again idly.

'Look, er, please carry on ... yes, do – unless we have to talk right away,' said Mark hesitantly, worried that he'd spoiled their plans. Like most young lads, he was quite interested in archery, and was secretly hoping that the elves would continue despite being interrupted.

'We *do* have a few minutes before we are all wanted, so thank you, we shall,' replied Planiss with a steadily growing smile.

Mark then watched, enthralled, as the elves stepped forward and eased their cloaks back over their shoulders. Side by side, they took their positions, raised their slender bows and drew the bowstrings back with the ease and confidence gained from a lifetime of experience. Mark couldn't see any arrows, though, and wondered what was going to happen as the elves held the bowstrings back effortlessly, at full draw.

Only then did two incredible arrows appear from nowhere: first their bright silvery tips, nuzzling against the sides of the bows, followed immediately by gleaming white shafts which grew rapidly from the tips and back towards the bowstrings. When they reached them, there was a brief glimpse of fletchings made from perfect white feathers before the arrows were loosed. The strings hummed as the arrows sped down the length of the glade, passing cleanly through two pine cones which dangled from the tip of a branch. The shots were expertly aimed, and the cones were shattered into tiny fragments before the elves lowered their bows and rested the ends on the grass.

Mark was just wondering why the elves made no move to retrieve their arrows, when he noticed that both of them were wearing wrist straps identical to his own. He looked down at his, realising that it was exactly the sort of thing an archer would wear. Then, the elves put their bows across their knees as if they intended to break them in two, but instead simply folded them in half and slipped them over their shoulders by their strings. Mark now recognised them from earlier, but his bewilderment must still have been obvious to Planiss.

'Yet another wonder for you to see today,' announced the elf proudly. 'We have no need to carry arrows with us, for our bows always produce a good and true one whenever they are drawn ... and however many times we draw them. It is an extremely useful bit of elf magic which we have always used, but you should also know that our bows will only produce an arrow if they are well aimed *and* with a just cause. No enemy of ours could seize one and use it against us. It would be useless to them!'

He shook his cloak down again and lifted his hood up over his long, silver-grey hair before speaking up.

'The time has come for us to go to the others, Mark. Roall suspects that even this lovely glade is being watched by our enemies for much of the time, and so he is waiting for us at a place where we shall not be overheard. Are you ready?'

'As ready as I'll ever be ... I think,' answered Mark, with a peculiar mixture of excitement and nervousness beginning to stir around inside him.

The elves led him across the glade and between the pine trees, towards the place where he and Roall had stood earlier that day. With his bracer now on, Mark could see, hear and feel everything around him perfectly. He thought back to the tiny spider climbing up his jeans in the church tower and smiled as he finally understood why he'd felt it – and why his footsteps on the soft pine needles now seemed so noisy. He could even hear a squirrel scampering along a branch somewhere above him, and the breeze seemed colder than ever around his red ears, bringing a shiver down his back.

Beyond the trees, a narrow path fell towards the lake below them, and the elves began to make their way steadily down it. Mark followed them and soon discovered that the unusual shimmering cloth of their cloaks had yet another magical quality. The elves were becoming increasingly difficult to see ... bracer or no bracer. Their cloaks seemed to blend in with everything around them, and Mark soon found himself focusing on their boots more than anything else. Far away and below him he could clearly see the small lake, its little island covered in thick undergrowth and one or two spindly trees, but the water seemed dark and uninviting now that the sun had set, and as they approached it the wind swept over its surface, making strange, fan-like patterns which came and went in almost the same instant.

Soon, the three of them were standing together again, close to the water's edge. Mark wondered where this 'safer' meeting place could be, and looked around for any sign of Roall, or anyone else. There was no one to be seen. A sudden gust of biting wind told Mark that the weather was turning for the worse and he thrust his hands deep into his jacket pockets before shrugging his shoulders together in a futile attempt to keep any warmth he still had left in him. His father had been right, yet again. The banks of the lake were mostly lost behind thick tufts of reeds, sedge grass and other half-drowned plants which grew out of the water or the green mud that seemed to be almost everywhere. Mark decided that he didn't like the place after all, and was curious as to why the elves had stopped there.

'Which way is it now?' he asked, hoping that it would prompt them to move on. He had lowered his voice, although he wasn't sure why, and Planiss didn't answer, but turned to Mark with concern in his eyes and a finger at his lips, urging him to be silent. Both elves seemed to be listening out for something, but Mark assumed that they would soon skirt around the lake and carry on up the valley, given that the island was impossible to reach. He'd tried it several times before, but below the deeper water was a sticky, boot-sucking bed of putrid mud. As far as he could remember, nobody had ever managed to get across, and in any case, the overgrown island had never looked worth the effort. Suddenly, Stirran gave an urgent, half-whispered warning and pointed to the west.

'Listen! Beware!'

Mark spun around and stared into the dusk-filled meadows which stretched from the lake to halfway up the sides of the valley. They were empty and lifeless – even the bats had decided that it was too cold and windy to be out feeding. Nothing moved, and nor did he, although he suddenly felt exposed and vulnerable standing there in the open, wishing that he was somewhere else. A few seconds passed before Planiss suddenly grasped Mark by the arm and pulled him back toward a tree they had just passed. They got behind it quickly and pressed themselves against its trunk, but Stirran stayed where he was, dropping down onto one knee and snapping his bow together in one smooth movement. He looked back over his shoulder towards Planiss.

'I could use some help here, you know.'

Stirran looked desperate, but Planiss was used to his friend's little jokes and took no notice. Try as he might, Stirran couldn't keep a straight face for very long, though, and despite the threat of danger he was soon doing his best to smother a mischievous grin.

'You're a better shot than me. I'll guard Mark,' shouted Planiss back to him.

Stirran shook his head and returned to the job in hand. He knew Planiss as he would his own brother, and didn't mind doing the dangerous work. In any case, he was fairly sure that it was his turn.

As Stirran waited and watched, Mark suddenly heard a soft *whoosh*, and two arrows thudded into the ground close to where he'd been standing only a moment before. They stood at a drunken angle, quivering ominously, and were fletched with feathers as black as midnight. Mark let out a low whistle as he realised how close he'd come to being hit, but the whole valley still seemed unnaturally quiet.

Stirran continued to stare into the gloom for a little longer, until he was satisfied, then brought up his bow and drew it fully, his back arched and his bow arm pointing high into the evening sky. Mark watched as another of his startling arrows appeared from thin air and immediately streaked upwards, before it was lost from sight and fell towards its target – whatever that was. There was another long pause, and for a while all Mark could hear was his own heartbeat pounding in his ears, then the hairs on his neck stood on end as an unearthly howl drifted towards them from across the fields. Mark had never heard anything so deep or pitiful before, but it left no doubt in his mind. Stirran's arrow had found its mark.

*   *   *

Malrin had spent the rest of that day in a dark, restless mood. Since seeing the light elf and mortal talking together, different schemes had come and gone in his evil mind, as bloodlust, greed and curiosity jostled for supremacy. He'd avoided the company of the other dark elves, which suited them admirably: they were a little puzzled by their leader's long, distracted afternoon, but they were thankful not to be on the receiving end of his boot or tongue for a few blissful hours. As the afternoon turned to evening, however, Malrin got his second surprise of the day, and his fruitless search for a plan of action was finished for him.

He now watched, incredulously, as *two* light elves and, as far as he could tell, the same mortal made their way down from the high knoll towards the lake below them. In that same second, all his previous reasoning was forgotten, and he sprang to his feet.

Yes, kill them all at once and be done with it. If a bunch of light elves and some scheming mortal think they can interfere with me and my key ... Well, they can think again.

With his mind made up at last, he rushed into the barn and roused the others with the back of his hand and a torrent of shouted orders. Sleep was still being rubbed out of many eyes whilst bows and quivers were plucked from the corner near the hellhound. There was plenty of grumbling, too, all of which was ignored, and as Mark and the light elves approached the island and dusk crept further into the valley, Malrin and the others crouched behind a field wall and gleefully fired their black arrows high up into the darkening sky.

They were thoroughly enjoying themselves for a while, seeing their distant targets darting this way and that – even hiding behind a tree – but less than a minute later Stirran's bright arrow came down amongst them without a sound, not even a whisper, and plunged into the body of one of the great hounds as he sat waiting excitedly for some new sport. Not realising what had happened to him, he looked around inquisitively before letting out a long, mournful howl with his snout held high, and collapsing sideways in a large untidy heap. The arrow's shaft was half buried in the beast's chest, and blood was trickling along it, staining the white feathers a deep crimson. The dark elves abandoned their entertainment and walked up to the dead hound in stunned silence, watching as the white arrow faded away in front of their eyes. They stood in a circle around the body, looking disbelievingly at each other, for they had ridden the hounds into the most horrific battles, and invariably rode them out again afterwards – unharmed. Malrin left the others, and started to walk towards the lake.

'Follow me!' he snarled through his teeth. He didn't trust himself to say very much more.

*   *   *

'Quickly, to the water!' shouted Planiss, as he prepared to run. 'Follow us, Mark!' he urged. 'The others are waiting for us. We must warn them!'

With that, Planiss left the cover of the tree and ran straight towards the lake. Mark stared as the elf sped between the decaying stumps of two long-dead willow trees close to the water's edge and took a mighty leap out over the mud and reeds towards the dark water beyond. He opened his mouth to shout a warning, but there was no need: Planiss splashed down onto the surface a long way short of the island, but only as if he was running through puddles on a farm track. Onwards he went, through water which only seemed ankle deep. Mark watched, completely mystified, as he reached the island and scrambled up its banks into the safety of the bushes. Stirran wasn't far behind him, barely wetting his legs.

Mark suddenly found himself sheltering behind the tree alone, wondering how he could possibly follow the elves. It was a crazy end to a crazy day, and it didn't really surprise him that running on water was yet another of their many skills. Well, it certainly wasn't one of *his*, he reminded himself, and his childhood memories of the foul mud which waited to trap anyone who tried, persuaded him to stay exactly where he was ... on firm ground. Stirran's urgent words from the bushes interrupted his thoughts.

'Come on, Mark! Do what we did ... all will be well, you'll see. Come quickly – before more black arrows do!'

Stirran sounded confident, but unfortunately, Mark wasn't. He stepped out from behind the tree and took a few paces towards the lake, but stopped as fresh doubts plagued him again. He was about to shout across to the elves in the hope of getting some kind of explanation when another black arrow buried itself in the ground close to his feet. Another two then bit deep into the tree he'd just left. It was all the convincing he needed, and a moment later he was sprinting towards the water, between the two willow stumps and leaping for all he was worth over the reeds and towards the uninviting water.

As he jumped, he shut his eyes and let out a defiant shout to no one in particular, waiting for the shock of the water closing in around him. The shock came, but it wasn't the one he'd expected, for he landed awkwardly on some kind of walkway hidden just below the surface of the water. He only just managed to keep on his feet as he slipped and staggered across it, his arms flailing wildly to keep his balance, but in a frenzy of splashing water, slipping boots and grasping hands he somehow reached the island and threw himself thankfully onto the bank. He looked up rather sheepishly and found himself nose to nose with Stirran, whose green eyes twinkled with delight as he pulled Mark up into the bushes.

'How long has *that* been there?' gasped Mark, amazed that he'd never heard talk of it amongst his friends.

'Not as long as *we've* been around ... but a pretty long time,' replied Stirran cheerfully, relieved that the three of them were together again and unharmed. 'I told you that all would be well. Now quickly – follow me!'

Mark could tell that Stirran was impressed with his brave leap out into the lake, but a near soaking plus a shower of black arrows had left him in a far less enthusiastic mood than his new friends. Stirran had disappeared on his knees through the undergrowth, and Mark could do nothing more than crawl after him as quickly as he could, hardly able to see where he was going in the failing light, and not knowing what he'd find when he got there. He did, however, allow himself a thin smile as he wondered what trouble he was getting himself steadily deeper into, but nobody saw it.

His fingers squelched down into cold mud and he knelt painfully on several sharp stones as he crawled along, trying not to get poked in the eye by a forest of twigs and broken branches, but there wasn't a single sound from the elves up ahead of him. He was even starting to think that he'd taken a wrong turn when he saw a pale green light in front of him and soon afterwards he burst into a small clearing, with both eyes intact. He stopped and stared, still on his knees. Squatting in front of him were no less than five light elves, with their cloaks on and hoods up. All at once, several hands were lifting and pulling him into the middle of the group, and he immediately recognised Roall, Stirran and Planiss, but not the two others. In amongst the lowest branches above them floated a shimmering ball of watery green light, which had turned the elves' cloaks a swirling, golden copper-green, and their concerned faces a sickly shade of ochre.

'Down, Mark, down!' urged Planiss, as he pushed the startled lad closer to the ground. 'The enemy is upon us and we are in great danger. Keep low!'

There was a sudden clatter of branches and leaves as an arrow raced towards them, and a muted thud as it sank deep into the trunk of a tree just above their heads. Two more quickly followed, tearing straight through the bushes and across the clearing without hitting anything substantial. Six heads dipped a little lower, then Roall whispered urgently to Mark, with no hint of his familiar smile: 'It seems that there is nowhere safe for us to meet. We cannot stay here any longer. Dark elves must have seen us come onto the island and they will not give up until we are all slain. Stay close to me, Mark, and if we all get away from here alive, come to us once more, tomorrow morning, in the glade. We must take our chances with who may or may not be spying on us, but if you do not come, a great deal will be lost ... by you and by us.'

Roall turned to the two elves Mark didn't know.

'Agoriff – take to the trees and see what can be done. Flinnor – we shall surely need your help, too. Follow me, my friends!'

At that exact moment, and without any warning, yet another black arrow flew into the clearing and hit Stirran squarely in the back. He was thrown forwards onto the ground by the force of it. Mark started to rush towards him, but the elf rolled over and got up, apparently unharmed. Mark was dumbfounded.

'Our cloaks!' whispered Planiss. 'They will turn most arrows aside, and a great deal more if they have to!'

Without further explanation, the remaining elves disappeared into the bushes and Mark dived in after them, crawling once again for all he was worth. Somewhere up above him, Agoriff had already climbed one of the taller trees and was hidden amongst branches which looked far too slender to take his weight. It didn't seem to concern him in the slightest. The wind was blowing in the face of the court elf of trees, pushing his hair back, and he was perfectly at home up there. He fancied that he could actually smell the dark elves and their remaining hellhounds as they approached a stone wall less than two hundred paces away and took cover behind it. Agoriff slipped his bow from his back, snapped its limbs together and prepared to defend his friends as well as he could.

Behind the stone wall, Malrin and the others had put the loss of their hound behind them and were now enjoying their favourite pastime. As far as they were concerned, their prey was trapped helplessly on the island and it would only be a matter of time before every one of them was dead, face down in mud or water.

Mark caught up with the others at the edge of the island just as Agoriff was choosing his first target. Two dark elves had stood up to use their bows when a shining white arrow streaked over the water and the field beyond it, straight towards them. One let out a strangled scream, dropped his bow and fell onto his back, straight and stiff. The arrow had passed cleanly through his neck and its fletchings were up against his bleeding throat. The second dark elf dipped his head down just as a second white arrow clipped the top of the wall, glanced off it and finally vanished as it flew over the barn behind him.

Then it was Flinnor's turn. Mark watched as the court elf of the sky stepped out onto the water close to the end of the submerged walkway and darted around the edge of the island. His feet hardly touched the rippling surface, as if he weighed nothing at all, and Roall noticed Mark's expression.

'Flinnor often surprises us, too, but in other ways,' he whispered. 'He has a habit of disappearing and turning up where you would least expect him, but that is what sky elves are like. Watch!'

Roall and Mark leant out over the water to keep sight of Flinnor, and saw that he was already on the far bank, crouching in amongst the reeds. Two black arrows were cutting through the air just above his head as he prepared to draw more fire from the enemy, lifting his bow ...

'Now!' ordered Roall. 'Flinnor has their attention. To the water!'

Despite the poor light, the two old willow stumps were still plain enough to see on the far side of the water, and Mark felt his way onto the submerged walkway with his feet. Then, with the icy water lapping at his boots, he ran straight towards the stumps, with the elves close behind. They could hear Agoriff's bowstring singing out again and again somewhere behind and above them as they splashed their way across the water, and with a well-judged leap they found themselves back on firm ground. Flinnor was crouching there, waiting for them, and true to form he was thirty yards from where he'd been only seconds earlier. They all huddled together for a few moments, knowing that a lucky arrow might find an unprotected leg or throat at any moment.

'Run, Mark, you must run!' panted Roall, who was hoping that Mark was as good at running as he was at jumping. The others had their bows partly drawn, ready to defend the group.

'We shall meet tomorrow, then,' he added, before dropping his voice and leaning closer to Mark. 'The cure for the sleeping child is not so far from us!'

It was all Mark needed to hear. With no more than a nod to each of the elves, he sprinted away from them, into the dusk. Down a farm track he went, the shortest route back to the village, with his jacket flying out behind him as he ran for his life. He could see the lights in the distant cottages surprisingly well, for the bracer on his arm still gave him that power, but it also let him hear very well, too... There was something barking far behind him, something large and ferocious.

The hellhounds had seen him. Their blood-red eyes missed nothing. Mark had only run a dozen or so paces when one of the two surviving animals stood up and leapt on top of the wall beside Malrin. Drool flew from its gaping jaws and long pink tongue as it barked and barked again – a deep, resonating sound so terrifying that once heard it could never be forgotten. It could hardly wait for Malrin to let it go, its eyes fixed excitedly on the fleeing lad one moment and Malrin the next, straining as if held by an invisible leash. Loose stones from the wall tumbled from under its powerful legs and lion-like paws as it prepared to leap forward. It barked again and Malrin smiled at it. The slightest nod of its master's head in Mark's direction was all that it wanted, and the hound sprang from the wall, almost demolishing part of it, before speeding across the open ground which separated it from a rare treat: an evening meal.

With long, easy bounds it crossed the field of short winter wheat in a few seconds and was soon on the track behind Mark, who now heard the fast, soft beat of paws behind him, getting louder all the time. He didn't dare to look back over his shoulder. The village was three minutes' hard run away and that was all he thought about. He had no idea of what was chasing him and he didn't care. He just *had* to reach the village.

Virtually invisible in their cloaks, and oblivious to the dangers of being out in the open, three court elves now knelt side by side, near the banks of the lake. A fourth knelt behind them, facing the opposite way and protecting their backs. Their hoods were cast back and their fingers were at their bowstrings, ready. Each of them instinctively knew that the hellhound would soon be at Mark's heels, and so they quickly drew their bows together. The hound was fading in the gloom as it raced away from them, and they'd already lost sight of Mark somewhere beyond it, despite their sharp eyesight. Stirran's arrow appeared first and he let it free at once, but it flew just over the running hound and disappeared. Yet more black arrows hissed over their heads, and Roall, at the rear, returned the fire as well as he could. Flinnor and Planiss shot next, their arrows speeding along beside each other and arcing down onto a now very distant target, but the hound didn't alter his pace and there was no howl of pain to tell of success.

Stirran was drawing his bow again for a final, desperate shot when he noticed that Flinnor was no longer at his side. The sky elf had decided to get a little closer to his target, and Stirran watched as he raced down the track in his own special way, leaning forwards in a long glide with his arms and bow held out to the side, before floating to a stop and standing quite still in the middle of it. For several long, precious moments he peered into the distance towards something, then brought up his bow and drew it. By now it was too dark for the others to see him clearly, but they all heard Flinnor's bowstring and four seconds later the hound had collapsed into a rolling, tangled mass of legs, ears and tail. The arrow had only found its back leg, and so it would probably live to hunt and kill again, but at least it wouldn't be gnawing on Mark's bones that night.

On Pine Needles

Despite his exhausting run from the lake, Mark hardly slept that night. His head was buzzing with everything he'd seen and heard that day, along with at least a dozen questions he would like answers to. Tired or not, he was still out of bed well before dawn, though. It was his father's turn to do the early milking at Hill Garth Farm, but Mark had too much on his mind to stay in his warm bed for much longer than usual. There was even a spring in his step and a whistled tune on his lips as he got dressed and went downstairs, for he was unable to stop thinking about Roall's hints of finding a cure for Elspeth. At the same time, he couldn't deny that the prospect of meeting the elves again was an exciting one: he was still struggling somehow to accept that they were real, and more than once during his sleepless night he'd convinced himself that the whole thing was simply one long, weird dream. He longed to be back with Roall and the others, if only to prove to himself that it certainly wasn't.

Putting his doubts aside, he knew that he mustn't delay explaining everything to Victoria for very much longer. After all, she was in the middle of a drawn-out, living nightmare, as were the rest of her family, and the sooner they heard some good news, the better. All of these things drifted in and out of his head as he finally pulled his boots on, laced them up, and stepped out onto the front doorstep. He was strangely pleased to feel that the boots were still cold and damp from their soaking in the lake the previous evening, and he wriggled his toes inside them uncomfortably before setting off through the sleepy village. Frightening but unlikely memories of black arrows and howling dogs came back to plague him as he walked briskly down the lane, and he whistled a little louder to push them to the back of his mind.

There were few signs of life in the village at that time of day, apart from a smoking chimney at the milkman's house and the cries of a hungry baby from one of the cottages close to the pub, but it was a time of day that he'd always enjoyed, and a familiar one for him, too. He did a lot of the early milking at the farm, and liked the thought of being one of the first people to see what the new day had in store. He soon passed by the last few straggling cottages and the village trailed away behind him as he marched along the lane. He'd intended to go straight to the glade, but five minutes' walk brought him to the rough track leading up to Willow Garth. He stopped there, close to the flaking, painted sign he knew so well. He was still undecided as to whether or not he should go and see Victoria when he started to shiver. It wasn't the ideal morning to be standing around doing nothing for very long, with wisps of cold mist moving through the hedgerows like the remnants of banished ghosts. A heavy dew covered the ground, too, and if it had been any colder, there would have been a sharp frost. He stamped his feet, wishing now that his boots were warm and dry, and made his decision.

Half an hour later, and still whistling, he was toiling his way up the steep pathway towards the glade, just as he had the previous evening. He eventually came to the sagging barbed wire fence and the stile which crossed it, and offered his hand to Victoria as she climbed over warily. They chattered to each other as they walked between the tall pine trees, and Victoria was brimming with questions, just as

Mark knew she would be. He'd been carefully recounting everything that had happened to him since he'd left her alone up in the church belfry two days earlier, but she made quite sure that nothing was missed out.

Mark knew that she could easily have laughed in his face, of course, particularly at tales of sword fights in crypts, and strange beings with magical daggers and bows, but fortunately she had very real memories of hearing the commotion down in the crypt, and of waking up in the very same glade they were now approaching. In fact, she suspected that his story was all true, even though it was incredible: she always knew when Mark was teasing her, and her heart told her that this wasn't one of those times. She'd stopped him as they walked down the track from her home, and looked straight into his eyes as he described the creature sliding the lid off the stone coffin in the crypt. She knew for sure then. His eyes never lied to her, even if *he* sometimes tried to.

They walked into the glade side by side, Mark literally holding his breath in anticipation. It was deserted. The disappointment was etched onto his face as he looked all around, peering in amongst the nearest of the trees. He even glanced down at their wrists, wondering for a moment if they'd forgotten to wear the bracers, then ran his fingers reassuringly across the soft hide of his own, feeling the hard, green gems under his fingertips.

He dreaded to think what was going through Victoria's head, and looked briefly at her, unsure if he should apologise or try to laugh it off. But Victoria didn't give him a chance to speak. As it became obvious that they really were alone, she turned to him, took his face in her hands – just like his mother used to when he was young – and broke into one of her reassuring, cheeky laughs. Her smile alone could easily have said it all, but she had to make completely sure.

'Relax Mark, for God's sake! They'll soon be here, you'll see, then you can introduce us, can't you?' Mark waited eagerly for more. 'And anyway, I was right next to you in that belfry, remember? We both saw them ... *and* I remember waking up over there yesterday.' She nodded towards the two patches of grass which were still flattened. 'I'm sure they'll come ... even if you're not.' As she took her hands away, she gave him a friendly slap on both cheeks with her fingers. 'Come on, let's talk some more before they get here,' she added.

Warm relief flowed through Mark, and much to Victoria's amusement, he even let out a sigh and dropped his shoulders as he finally relaxed. They walked slowly around the edge of the glade together, until Victoria decided to sit down on the soft, dry, pine needles which lay everywhere beneath the trees. Mark joined her, and there they stayed for another hour or so, deep in pleasant, easy conversation. He took Victoria at her word, and was no longer worried that she might ridicule him as they drifted back into their old, familiar and comfortable ways – it felt to them like putting on slippers which had been warmed up in front of the fire, and their chattering voices or occasional laughter soon filled the empty glade.

In fact, they almost forgot where they were, and didn't even notice their cold fingers and red, tingling ears. Mark was so pleased to see the Victoria he remembered from a few weeks before, particularly after he'd told her about Roall's hints of a cure for Elspeth, although he wondered if he was wise to raise her hopes too soon. But it was worth it in the end, just to see her like that again – happy and full of hope. It was as if she'd been hauled out of a cruel, unforgiving sea of grief and torment, just as she was about to drown in it, and he was thrilled to watch the little dimples in her cheeks coming and going with each smile or giggle. The real Victoria had well and truly returned to him, he decided. The morning was slipping past, though, with the last traces of mist sent marching by a steadily strengthening breeze, and there were brief glimpses of a hazy sun somewhere behind the cold, unbroken clouds.

The light elves surprised both of them in the end. Not that they meant to, but the two youngsters were utterly absorbed in each other's company and so it was easy for a large but silent group of them to creep into the glade unseen. Many of them dispersed around the edges again, or in amongst the trees to stand guard, but the court elves themselves, all five of them, finally approached the pair from behind. Roall came first and stopped a few paces away, aware that they'd be more surprised than was good for them if he came any closer unannounced. He was reluctant to interrupt them, but had to of course, out of good manners if nothing else.

'We meet at last,' he said quietly, stepping around them and facing them both.

'Bloody hell!' shrieked Victoria, who leapt up and stumbled backwards at the same time.

Astonishment obliterated manners as her eyebrows shot up and her mouth fell open, but Mark's face positively lit up. He was unashamedly delighted, but much to his surprise, Victoria was completely unprepared: she couldn't believe what she was seeing and was quite lost for words ... for once. Mark laughed and got to his feet too, rubbing the pine needles from his hands then lifting Victoria's sagging chin with one finger. She barely noticed.

'We've been waiting for ages. I mean, well ... quite a while, anyway,' said Mark awkwardly. 'We ... er ... we weren't sure when you'd come.'

Roall smiled at him, guessing that 'if' would have been nearer the mark than 'when', but he didn't seem to mind in the least. He then turned to Victoria and introduced himself and the others. Stirran and Planiss seemed to be rather shy, for they fiddled with their bracers and looked downwards as they stepped forward. Agoriff and Flinnor were quite the opposite. They went up to her eagerly and bowed so low that their bows nearly slipped forwards off their backs. Just like their fellow elves, it was the first time either of them had personally met a mortal girl, and they seemed determined to enjoy the occasion. Victoria, however, still couldn't find any suitable words. Her mouth moved around uselessly as she tried to, and she didn't know who to look at next.

Mark was trying hard not to laugh at her when Agoriff leapt upwards and grasped a bough of the tree above them, before pulling himself effortlessly up onto it. He was a happy elf by nature, but he was always at his happiest in a tree, and he straddled the bough with his arms crossed and his legs swinging free, as he grinned at everyone below him. Mark spoke up again, as Victoria still hadn't found her tongue.

'Look ... last night, down at the lake ... Thanks a lot for what you did – whatever it was. I think some kind of wild dog was chasing me up the lane, but something stopped it.'

He looked at each of the elves around him, and even the one above him, but he wasn't expecting anyone to admit to anything, and no one did.

'The dark elves are always trouble for us,' answered Roall, 'sometimes deadly trouble. It is because of them that we have been unable to talk to you safely until today. Last night we kept them busy for some time after you made your escape. Why, Agoriff here says he almost tired out his bow arm!' Up in his tree, Agoriff heroically circled a 'stiff' arm, with a pained expression. 'I think the dark elves will need a few reinforcements before they can get up to any more of their tricks,' added Roall, with obvious satisfaction.

'They'll be walking for a while, too, not riding,' added Planiss cheerfully, knowing that two of the three hellhounds were now useless to their masters.

Mark looked as if he was about to ask for an explanation, but changed his mind: he didn't know what Planiss was referring to, and perhaps it was better that way. No one knew what to say next and there was an awkward silence. Then three of them started to speak together, although they only managed to get one word out each. They all stopped, and after a gracious wave from Roall, Victoria continued, having recovered a little, at last.

'I'm not sure what to say.' She whispered at first, but then coughed and tried to speak up. 'Mark warned me about you, of course, how I'd be in for a shock and everything, but ... but ... it's amazing. Awesome!'

She looked at the slim, graceful elves standing around her in a half circle and shook her head, as if trying to wake herself up.

The elves smiled at each other, clearly amused and even a little flattered. Victoria suddenly hoped that she hadn't offended them, and so she greeted each of them properly – and somehow remembered all their names, which seemed to impress them a great deal.

'Mark told me what happened last night. You could easily have been killed down there by the lake ... any of you.' The last few words were under her breath as she glanced sideways at Mark.

The elves mumbled their thanks for her concern, one or two of them still not sure how to deal with this pretty young mortal. But Flinnor wasn't quite so reluctant to speak up, and Victoria jumped as she suddenly found him by her side. He was hovering just above the ground, as if he would float away in the next gust of wind.

'It is good of you to worry like that, but you really should not,' he said kindly. 'We are very good at looking after others – if they deserve it, of course – but we usually manage to keep ourselves out of harm's way, too.'

Victoria tried to ignore the strange fluttering sensations in her stomach and managed an understanding nod in return. She turned to Roall and forced herself to look straight into his face. A question was burning inside her.

'I know you've been through a lot already, I really do, and Mark has told me there could be a lot more danger still to come.' She glanced at Mark, who nodded. 'I'm sorry, but Mark ...' She was reluctant to ask the selfish question which was now right on her lips, but she took a deep breath and blurted it out anyway. 'Mark said you might be able to help my sister, Elspeth. Is that true?'

Roall rubbed his cold hands together and looked along the unbroken circle of elves standing guard around the edge of the glade, seeking the best answer. Just like Mark, he didn't want to raise any false hopes in her.

'It is true that we *might* be able to help her ... if luck is on our side,' he said, choosing his words carefully.

He sat down beside them on the thick carpet of needles, and the other court elves quietly joined him – apart from Agoriff, who remained in his beloved tree, his thoughts seemingly elsewhere. Mark and Victoria dropped back onto their knees and Roall now faced Victoria, but a cool hardness in his green eyes told her that the time for pleasant chatter and compliments had passed.

'We know exactly what has happened to your sister!'

Victoria caught her breath and she saw Mark stiffen next to her as Roall explained.

'Two expert thieves from our world – we call them spriggans – came into your home, Victoria. They wanted an old key, but they wanted your baby sister, too. Sadly, that is their way.' He watched Victoria as he spoke, unsure

160

of how she would cope with such startling news. 'We keep a close watch on all that goes on in these valleys, especially if there are spriggans or dark elves involved. We do what we can to lessen or even prevent the damage and pain they cause – that is our sole mission in life, but we only have so much power, and in recent years it has often been too little, alas. At Willow Garth our task was a simple one, for we only had to wake up your dog. We left the rest to him.'

Victoria looked at the figures sitting around her. It seemed that she already had a great deal more to thank them for than she'd realised.

'You know why Elspeth won't wake up then?' asked Mark incredulously. He was just as astonished as Victoria.

'Oh yes, we know all too well,' sighed Roall. 'She was drugged by those spriggans, and won't wake up until she is given some of the vile stuff they use to revive their victims. I am afraid to say that without it she will sleep on, perhaps for a month or more, before ... before ...'

'Before what?' croaked Victoria, hardly daring to ask. Roall couldn't bring himself to finish the sentence.

'You must get this "cure" for her by some means. In fact, by *any* means. Without it she can never again be the wonderful child you once knew.'

Victoria buried her face in her hands as the awful truth hit her like a runaway horse.

'It now seems that we both need something from the spriggans,' continued Roall as he came closer to them and dropped his voice to a whisper, ever mindful of enemy ears. He pulled a freyal out from his belt and tossed it lightly in his hand.

'Elspeth's cure for you ... and four more of these for us! We dared not tell you any of this until we were as sure as we could be that we would not be overheard. If the spriggans had the slightest idea that anyone planned to visit them, they would be ready and waiting. Nothing would be gained, and lives would most certainly be lost. Mostly *our* lives.'

Mark recalled the terrifying spriggan offering him something just before they fought in the crypt, and suddenly felt sick.

Oh no! It must have been the cure for Elspeth. If only I'd made a grab for it when I had the chance.

Bitterly annoyed with himself, he ran his hands through his hair and blew out a long breath as he tried to grasp what he hoped were the facts, but he was still unsure about too many things. Roall seemed to sense his frustration and looked at him, waiting, so Mark spoke up.

'You say that there are six of these daggers, I mean freyals, one for each court elf, but there are only five of you. Is there someone else we still haven't met?'

He hoped that he wasn't being too inquisitive, for Roall glanced at the others before answering, and suddenly seemed unsettled.

'I'll try to explain. Yesterday, after you awoke in this lovely place, I spoke of a Sluagh. It is best thought of as an event, an occurrence if you like, but the very worst kind imaginable. The beings that create it are known as the Unseelie Court, however, what they are called is of no importance here. It is what they *are* that should concern you a great deal more.'

Roall suddenly looked even more uncomfortable, as if the mere mention of a Sluagh was enough to bring him physical pain. He gazed down distractedly at the ground in front of him, then picked up a few small fir cones and threw them aside one at a time as he continued his story.

'They are a foul, depraved host. A gathering of the most wicked beings in creation ... goblins, dark elves, sometimes bogles ... or others I will not even speak of in this place.' His voice fell again as he looked at Mark and Victoria. 'I only pray that you never see them, or innocently stray into their path.' Roall could see that he'd already shocked the youngsters, but knew that he must finish what he'd begun. 'They have been amongst us since time began, and they are still with us, like a festering wound that can never heal. When the mood takes them, they go about under the cloak of darkness and bring misery to many folk, whoever they may be, mortal or immortal. At times they prowl silently in the shadows, but at others they will fly – if there is no moon. They are led by enormous white hounds with red, staring eyes, or ride on them when they have need of great speed. It is a sight which would strike fear and dread into even the bravest heart.'

The elf stared into space as horrific memories hurled themselves at him, but somehow he wrestled his mind away from them.

'We few light elves do our best to retaliate against their wickedness, and the freyals were our greatest weapons. There are some other good souls in our world who assist us as and when they can, but they are not equipped or trained to take up arms against a Sluagh, and so we usually find ourselves in battle alone.'

He sounded tired now, as if his energy had ebbed out of him whilst those unwelcome memories had seeped in.

'The five of us before you are part of the Seelie Court, and we are solemnly sworn to oppose the Unseelie Court and all their works. And so, you see, we are court elves. You could, if you wish, say that we are the leaders of the light elves ... well, five of them, at least.'

Mark looked at them with renewed wonder, and felt even more privileged to be in their company. Roall turned to him and smiled grimly as he guessed his thoughts. 'Yes, you are right, Mark. There are six freyals,' and his voiced faltered slightly, 'but only five of us. The sixth court elf has been taken from us ... forever.' Victoria suddenly looked up, concerned and confused. 'His name was Trifillo, and he fell in battle some years ago, at an entrance to the spriggan caves. We were attempting to find an unguarded way in, but dozens of spriggans suddenly leapt out from everywhere: it was as if they had expected us, and given how many enemies we have in these valleys, such a thing is always a real possibility. Before we could gather our thoughts or draw a bow, they grew gigantic and heaved boulders down onto us, then whisked up whirlwinds which flung even more rocks about, like autumn leaves in a storm. Trifillo was hit by one and we never saw him again. We were hopelessly overpowered and forced to withdraw, having only killed two or three of those beasts. We miss him dearly. He was the court elf of fire, and believe me, he was a very good master of it.'

Roall chuckled to himself as he remembered his old friend and the crafty tricks he would get up to with something as simple as a candle flame.

'He rarely stopped joking, either. My goodness, he brought a smile to many a face, day and night, good times and bad.' Roall's expression hardened. 'He did have a less funny side to him, though. He was easily the most skilled amongst us with a sword, as many a goblin would tell you, if they still had heads to talk with, that is.'

'I'm sorry he's gone,' replied Mark. 'It's so unfair that someone like him should be killed, especially by spriggans.' Roall put his hand on Mark's shoulder and spoke earnestly, even passionately.

'I feel that it is time for the light elves to enter those caves again, to try once more to get back what is rightfully ours.' Mark nodded slowly, but wasn't fully prepared for Roall's next words. 'You must go there too, Mark. You have a just cause, and no one else can help the sleeping child!' The court elf avoided looking at Victoria, for he would never suggest that she was deliberately taken into such a dangerous place. 'We could help each other, I am sure of it,' he added, trying to sweeten the bitterness of the pill he was offering.

Mark had half suspected that something like this was coming, and he only needed a moment or two before answering..

'I know you could help me, but how could I help you? I'm no warrior. I'm not even brave. The spriggan in the crypt nearly killed me, and there was only one of him. What use would I be against a whole cave-full?

'Ah, that remains to be seen,' said Stirran, who had been waiting patiently for a chance to speak. 'You may yet have skills and strengths of which you are unaware. We know that you certainly have a brave heart, despite what you say. Most mortals would have died of fright in the crypt, well before any sword found its mark. We would be proud to have you fighting at our sides – if it comes to that.'

'But I don't have any weapons, and even if I did, I wouldn't know how to use them properly,' answered Mark, feeling completely useless. Planiss stood up and came over to stand in front of him.

'You have *this*, if you will take it,' said the court elf of springs, dropping onto one knee.

Across his upturned hands, Planiss held a folded bow much like his own. It was beautifully made, with tips of burnished gold and lines of tiny green jewels sunk into its smooth and slender limbs. Mark didn't know how to thank Planiss. He took the strange bow from the elf and held it in his hands gingerly, wondering what use it could ever be to him. A voice suddenly broke in.

'Before you all go any further, *I'd* like to say something,' announced Victoria boldly.

They all stared at her, slightly taken aback and wondering what was coming next, but she didn't leave them guessing for very long.

'If you lot think I'm going to be left out of this plan, then you're all on another planet ... especially you, Mark Walker!'

She glared at her lifelong friend as an unearthly silence descended on the glade, and Mark's cheeks flushed red: she had her hands on her hips and was talking to him as if he was a greedy little boy caught with his hand in the biscuit tin. The elves glanced at each other, amused, but not rude enough to show it.

'I may be a girl,' she continued with hardly a breath, 'and you might think that being a girl is enough reason for me to trot off home quietly and leave you all to go to these, these *spriggan* caves and get what we need to make Elspeth better ... and even find your stolen daggers, too.' She tried to slow herself down, to no avail. 'This is *my* just cause as much as it's yours – even more than it's yours, if you *must* know. After all, she's *my* sister. If you go–' she looked at the fair faces around her, then at Mark, who was now an even deeper shade of red '–then I go, too. And that, I'm afraid to say, is that!'

She didn't expect any arguments, and in the end there weren't any. Everyone there could see that she meant what she said and wasn't the least bit interested in having her mind changed.

At that exact moment, there was a hushed but urgent *'Shush!'* from above their heads. Looking upwards, they saw Agoriff with a finger at his lips. He was sitting up straight and studying something on the far side of the glade, something which the others couldn't see. Each of the court elves either moved their hands towards the bowstrings on their shoulders, or eased a cloak away from a freyal. Agoriff was already holding his empty bow across his knees, his fingertips curled tightly around the string. He was now leaning forwards as far as he dared, staring into the trees beyond the glade, then moving his head left and right, as if trying to find something he'd lost. Clearly, none of the elves guarding the perimeter was aware of any problem, for no alarm had been raised, and the group below Agoriff could only wait anxiously. Victoria tried not to think about what might be lurking in amongst the trees, and the others wondered if the dark elves had somehow managed to steal up on them yet again, to eavesdrop on their hopes, fears and secret plans.

Suddenly, Agoriff locked his legs tightly under the bough and drew his bow. A gleaming white arrow materialised at once then sped across the glade, hitting something with a dull *whack*. There was a shrill squeal, which judging from its tone was one of annoyance rather than pain, followed by silence. Agoriff slid down from his perch and started to run towards his quarry as soon as his feet touched the ground. The others were behind him a second later, with Flinnor quickly pulling ahead of the others and his boots just catching the highest tufts of grass. It was Agoriff who disappeared into the trees first, though, and he was soon with his prey.

It was no dark elf. The arrow had passed through a hood of coarse cloth and was now pinning a short, chubby figure to the trunk of a tree. It was twisting and turning like a half-landed trout, getting itself wrapped up in its own cloak and making a great deal of noise about it, too. The others all soon caught up and formed a circle around Agoriff and his captive, wondering what it was that the elf had snared with his well-aimed shot.

'Will it be enough for lunch?' asked Stirran at once.

Mark and Victoria guessed that the elves already knew exactly who they'd captured, as they showed no trace of fear, or even concern, but the little figure struggled even more vigorously following Stirran's question: it clearly didn't want to be lunch, or any other meal, come to that.

As the arrow faded away and the strange creature was freed, it was grabbed by two of the elves, which only made it spit and snarl even more.

'There isn't much meat on it, is there?' groaned a very disappointed Planiss.

'No, and we can't live on just skin and bones,' said Stirran, adding to the misery of the captive, who couldn't see the mischievous glint in the elf's eyes, or the knowing looks passing between the others.

'Do you know, I think it's a hob!' exclaimed Roall in mock surprise, joining in with the slightly cruel but playful sport. 'Now, why would a hobgoblin be spying on us, all the way up here?'

Victoria was lost for words again, as she watched Planiss pull the hob's hood down onto his shoulders. His hair was a tangled, dirty mess, like a long-deserted raven's nest, and his eyes darted about like a cornered animal's. He licked his lips with a long, dark tongue, which sprang in and out from between two uneven rows of jagged, brown teeth. He even tried to bite Planiss twice, but the elf was far too quick for him.

It was just then that he recognised Victoria. The Farndale hob had watched her grow up over the years at Willow Garth, and knew her as well as he knew anyone else. He was obviously surprised to see her in the glade, though, and particularly so with light elves as company, for he stopped his wriggling for a few seconds and looked at her questioningly, his head cocked slightly to one side. Roall and Planiss kept a good grip on his arms – but out of biting range – and the hob began to realise that there was no hope of escape. He gradually stopped his squirming around and finally stood there, dejected and clearly feeling sorry for himself.

'Exactly how long have you been watching us here, hob? If you lie, we will know, so beware!' Roall brought his face close to the hob's, and obviously meant business. 'Don't be tempted.'

The hob started to splutter and mutter in an uncontrolled swirl of panic and fright, but stopped after Planiss did his best to calm him down. He let go of the hob's arm and straightened his cloak for him, which was twisted around from back to front. The suddenly indignant hob snatched his cloak out of the elf's hands, before glaring up at him and trying to speak again.

'I weren't spying on you, I just 'erd voices, that's all,' he whined. 'There's no 'arm in that, is there?' The hob looked around him hopefully, but his knees were shaking and his voice wasn't far behind them. Roall moved even closer to him, ignoring the unpleasant smell which drifted up to his nose.

'We know who you are, hob, *and* where you live. It is indeed a strange coincidence that you are here with us today, just when these mortals are.' Roall glanced up at Victoria. 'If you do not tell us what your business here is, we might make new arrangements for lunch after all. It *is* getting near that time.' He looked up to where the sun was hiding, trying to judge whether midday had arrived yet. Without meaning any real harm, he prodded the wretched hob's protruding stomach with the point of his freyal, and eyed him up and down enthusiastically, as if he was a freshly skinned rabbit.

'I ... I've been watchin' what's goin' on, that's all,' cried the hobgoblin anxiously. 'I see'd you all by the lake last night, fightin' and flittin' about. I even see'd that great 'ound chasin' yonder lad.' He looked up at Mark before stumbling on. 'I ... I knows summat you might like to know, that's all, so I do. But I w-won't tell you nuffin' for now't!' he added more boldly, considering his rather precarious situation.

'Oh, we may give you something all right, if you speak

169

up quickly,' replied Planiss, smiling. 'A year or two longer to live – how does that appeal?' He had now drawn his freyal, too, and was having a harmless poke at the hobgoblin, licking his lips hungrily. The hob struggled violently again, determined to escape, but the grip on his arms tightened at once.

'All right, all right!' he groaned, sounding tired and beaten. 'The devil deserves all 'e gets, anyways.'

The elves were puzzled. Two freyals jabbing a little more firmly into the hob's exceedingly tight jerkin made it clear that more details were needed.

'Deserves it 'e does, seein' as 'e did this, so 'e did.'

The hob lifted up his tangled hair to reveal a large, raw wound where his ear had been cut off. The others all took a step backwards. It was clear that the unfortunate hob must have suffered abominably, and suddenly everyone felt sorrier for the scruffy little creature. Another, somewhat gentler jab from Roall's freyal prompted him to continue.

'I don't care what 'e does if 'e knows I've blabbed, I'm damned if I do! A swine 'e is … a … a wicked pig. I 'ope somebody locks 'im in 'is stinking tower and throws away the key, so I do.'

The hob paused, still not sure if he was saying more than he ought to, and wondering if any pointy-eared good-for-nothings were nearby, listening and all too ready to report him. His voice fell to a whisper, just in case.

'Redcap did this, just to make me tell 'im about the little book I found.' He turned his head for all to see the grizzly sight. 'But 'e's done worse than this, for sure … a lot worse.'

He gazed up at Victoria and she felt his stare upon her. She shivered and looked at Mark, unsure of what was coming next, but had a nasty, empty feeling in her stomach that it would somehow involve her. She tried to speak, but her voice wavered as an inexplicable dread slowly crept over her.

'What d'you mean ... worse?' she asked in a dry whisper.

No one else made a sound, and the hob looked straight at her, as if they were quite alone. He knew that he was about to unleash indescribable pain upon the young girl he'd lived so close to for many years: in a strange, secretive way, he felt that they were both part of the same family, as far as he was concerned. Family or not, it was against his hobbish nature to be wilfully cruel, and so he took in a deep breath and screwed his face up slightly before saying what had to be said.

'I see'd them spriggans come to your place and swipe the big key. They were lucky to get out in one piece, that's wot I say. Very lucky indeed, so they were.' He licked his lips again and looked around at everyone briefly, almost apologetically.

'But p'raps a year ago, someone else came in t'night to try to take it ...'

The hob was struggling now, and looked at the faces around him for help. He swallowed hard, trying to watch all of them at once.

'That devil, Redcap!' The hob put his hand up to his missing ear. 'Your mother 'eard him and came down to see wot was goin' on. That ol' dog of yours were fast asleep ... Redcap made sure enough of that wiv some goblin trickery or other.' He gulped again, and wished that he hadn't started at all.

'Redcap weren't really trapped, though, not one bit. She couldn't even see 'im, poor woman. He could've left 'er ... but 'e didn't. A redcap 'e is. Scum, so 'e is. There's now't worse than a redcap.'

The hob paused and looked down, unable to look at Victoria as he spoke the last few appalling words under his breath.

'Struck 'er down where she stood, so 'e did. Struck 'er down dead withou' as much as a second thought!'

An even deeper and longer silence then fell upon the glade and everyone in it. Mark stared at Victoria in pity and disbelief, and as he went to her side he saw her face crumple and distort as despair swept through her. She sank to her knees, Mark supporting one of her limp arms and easing her down as she sobbed uncontrollably, lost in her own private, heart-wrenching grief.

*   *   *

An hour later, the two youngsters were still sitting under the trees together, away from the group. Mark felt pretty useless, but he also knew that he could probably help his friend more than anyone else, and so he tried his best to do just that. The news that her mother had been murdered by a creature from the elves' world was totally abhorrent to Victoria, but from deep inside she somehow found the inner strength to begin to bear it. She had to, of course. There was no other real choice. After all, she might never have found out what actually happened on that night long ago, but now she had, and little by little the pain of knowing how her mother had been taken away was tempered by a surprising and fierce determination to seek revenge. She knew at once that it was wrong, but she craved it, and although she tried and tried, she couldn't make the feeling go away. The same thoughts kept running through her tortured mind.

I don't know why it's turned out like this, but I'm sitting here with creatures from the same world as this maniac, Redcap. It must be fate. Yes, that's what it is, and perhaps there's some chance, even a tiny, tiny chance that I could find ...

Whilst Victoria was running out of tears and trying to come to terms with what she'd heard, the court elves found out all that they needed to know. They took the hob aside and treated him well enough, so he willingly told them the story of the diary he'd accidentally found, what it had contained, and how he'd lost the most important page from it, and his left ear, in almost the same breath at Skelton Tower. They also discovered that Redcap had soon learned every word on that page by heart, even though the dark elf Malrin had relieved him of it shortly afterwards.

The hob proved to be well informed regarding the fate of the precious page, just as any nosy hob worth his salt would be. He'd made it his business to find and follow the dark elves from the moment he'd escaped from the tower, less one ear and his favourite pair of boots. He'd also overheard all of Malrin's late-night scheming and storytelling in the old barn, where his greatest problem had been avoiding the three dozing hellhounds. It was there, lying on the roof close to a large hole and half choking in the fire smoke, that he'd discovered that Malrin had the second key and was already making plans to get the third. He also heard exactly what the dark elf intended to do that very day in order to achieve those plans, and knew in his heart that the light elves should at least hear of it. In fact, it was his only reason for being at the glade: he was a rascal, and he freely admitted it, but even rascals can have a sense of fair play, or so he assured the five court elves surrounding him.

Roall came over to Mark and Victoria. They were sitting on a fallen bough under a vast natural canopy of deep-green, and they asked the elf to join them. He knelt down beside Victoria and his heart ached for her when he saw her red, swollen eyes, but there were decisions to be made quickly and he couldn't afford to give her any more time to recover.

'We must talk,' he said, apologetically.

The youngsters nodded. They, too, realised that time was slipping past, and what remained of it was becoming more and more precious. They were both keen to hear what Roall had to say.

'The hob has quite a story to tell, although we already knew most of the less sorrowful parts fairly well.' Roall was choosing his words with care. 'You two must take each other's counsel and decide what is best for you. As for us, we have little choice. The dark elves have a small but rather important key and the hob tells us that this very evening they intend to use it in Hoarfrost Hall, where they hope to take a giant step closer to a treasure which they desire above all things in our worlds. This hob is a scoundrel, just like all of his kind, but he has nothing to gain by lying to us and so we believe what he has to say. It is our duty to also be at the hall tonight, whoever lives there now, for the dark ones are certain to cause havoc, and we must try to spoil their plans, whatever they are. What do you think *you* should do?' Roall was hoping for a particular answer, but wasn't entirely sure that he would get it.

'We know what we *want* to do, but we don't know if we can,' replied Mark, looking at Victoria for confirmation. 'The only important thing for us is finding Elspeth's cure. We *must* try to get it from the spriggans. Vicky and her family couldn't bear another tragedy ... especially after what this Redcap character did.'

Mark glanced at Victoria again, hoping that she would forgive him for mentioning that name again so soon.

'The trouble is,' he went on, 'we don't know how to get the cure. If we came with you now, we'd probably get in the way, wouldn't we Vicks?' Victoria nodded silently as she stared across the glade, exhausted in every way. 'D'you think that's what we should do?'

Roall smiled and got up on one knee. Pity filled him again as he saw Victoria's young, shattered face, but the way forward was now clear to him at last.

'This is for you then, Victoria,' he said, as he held out a neatly folded garment, which she touched lightly.

She noticed that it was made of the same material as the elves' cloaks, and recalled that, according to Mark, she'd spent a whole night under something very much like it only two days before, being gently healed by its magic. Agoriff then approached them, smiling, and handed Victoria a fine thumb stick, with skilfully carved patterns cut into its polished wood. The tips at the forked end were each capped in silver, and finished with a small but perfect sapphire of the very deepest blue.

'Good for walking with,' said the tree elf, who had a natural love of all things wooden, 'and who knows, perhaps useful in other ways, too.'

Agoriff knew perfectly well that there was a large dose of freyal magic within the fine stick, and that Victoria would discover that fact for herself, given time.

'Thanks a lot – both of you,' she replied hesitantly.

She didn't know what else to say as she took the light, silky cloth and let it spill out into the shape of another cloak and hood. Roall wanted to redirect her thoughts from the past to the future, and knew just what she was thinking as she tried to weigh it in her hands.

'It is made from spider's silk, which only we light elves can weave. In its own way it is far stronger than steel and will turn an arrow aside if you are unlucky enough to stop one.' Roall watched her feeling how thin it was between her fingers. 'Don't worry, it will also keep you warmer than you imagine, and make you all but invisible to most creatures – from both of our worlds. I hope that you find it useful on your short journey.'

He waited for his last words to sink in, then Victoria managed an awkward smile as at last she knew that she would indeed be going with them.

'There is one here for you too, Mark. That old coat of

yours looks just right for chasing cattle around fields in, but you will be a great deal safer with this on your back.'

The elf gestured towards another neatly folded cloak lying on the grass behind him, and Mark mumbled his thanks for yet another incredible gift.

'However,' added Roall, cutting short Mark's embarrassment, 'your path and ours must be different ones when we leave this place.' The court elf's whole manner now filled them with confidence and they both listened eagerly. 'I must go at once to the great house of Douthwaite Dale – Hoarfrost Hall. The dark elves are most probably on their way there as we speak, from what the hob has told us.'

He stood up, making it clear that time was running out, but stepped closer.

'It seems that whatever happens, you two must find a way into the spriggan caves. I warn you now that this is a task which is almost certainly beyond you, and you could easily die in the attempt, just as many brave elves have before you. You have to understand what it is that you are attempting. Remember Trifillo, if nothing else!' Roall left them in no doubt as to what the outcome might be. 'Well, do you understand?' He was studying their faces intently.

Mark and Victoria looked at each other, but not for long. They couldn't see anything in each other's eyes that hinted at fear or indecision, only determination mixed in with the last trace of a tear or two. They understood each other perfectly, as usual.

'We understand,' said Victoria, answering for both of them. 'Point us in the right direction and we'll try our best.'

Roall laughed under his breath. He was impressed by their resolve, but also amused by their innocent presumption that they would be travelling alone.

'Only Stirran and Flinnor shall come with me to meet

the evil ones at the hall. You shall have two friends with you – unless you would rather go alone, that is?' Roall gestured towards Planiss and Agoriff, who were still standing on each side of the hob, holding onto him.

'I think we'd like them with us, if that's all right with you,' joked Victoria, who was actually delighted and relieved at the same time. Suddenly the hob spoke up.

'Hey, take me, too! I can squeeze into places what none of you lot ever could.'

Stirran looked doubtfully at the hob's paunch, the result of too many feasts of thick cream, and shook his head in disapproval. The hob was almost certainly exaggerating his abilities, but he was keen to make up for the distress he had caused Victoria and wanted to go wherever she went … for now, at least. The elves let go of their prisoner and tried to keep straight faces as he made a pathetic attempt to tidy himself up and stand as tall and as straight as he could, apparently ready for anything the unseen world could throw at him.

'We could come to yonder caves by t'old railway tracks. Them spriggans won't be expectin' any visitors from that way,' suggested the hob confidently. 'No one ever uses it much …'

Mark had a feeling that the hob hadn't quite finished what he was saying, but it passed quickly. The elves looked at each other, remembering what had happened to the sixth court elf on the usual approaches to the caves, and wondering if the hob's suggestion was indeed a worthwhile one. Besides, they felt that he'd been through more than enough recently, and it couldn't be denied that he knew a great deal about the area. Each elf knew that he could be extremely useful to them all.

'Then it is decided,' said Roall. 'We shall come back to join you as soon as our business at the hall is finished – unless it finishes us first, that is.' He smiled at Mark and

Victoria. 'May all the good spirits on these moors be guarding your backs.'

With that, he turned and left them, with Stirran and Flinnor following. The hob, who was pleased to be in more pleasant company than he was generally accustomed to, adjusted his cloak and pushed his untidy hair back under his hood. He looked up beside him at Agoriff.

'Well, I'm right glad you only aimed for me 'ood!' He sounded genuinely grateful, but Agoriff looked down at him and made a very good job of being surprised.

'I aimed for your *neck*, hob. It was my weakest shot this month.'

The hob swallowed noisily and rubbed the back of his neck with his hand, relieved that it was still intact.

A minute later the glade was empty and peaceful once again. The only movement came from the highest tips of the great pines, as they rocked gently towards the dipping afternoon sun, with a gentle easterly breeze in their dark green needles.

Hoarfrost Hall

The journey from the glade to Hoarfrost Hall was a far from pleasant one for the three court elves. Luckily, they were reasonably familiar with the countryside, for Douthwaite Dale starts where the southern tip of Farndale ends, but it didn't help them much. There was every chance that the dark elves were using the lanes, and so they were forced off them into awkward territory, with many streams to cross and hedges to squeeze through. At least the River Dove helped by showing them the way. They only had to follow it until it rushed through the narrow, rocky gorge where Farndale came to an end, before tumbling on downwards to Lowslack Mill. There, it could at last slow down and rest as it made its way sedately past the remains of the mill's old waterwheel and under the ancient stone bridge just beyond it.

This was indeed a damp and lonely place. Its closest neighbour was the great hall itself, another half mile to the south, but nobody, including elves, ever went to that mill unless they had good reason to. It was once haunted by the ghost of a young girl who drowned in the millpond over two hundred years earlier, and it might still be, as far as Roall and the others knew.

Flinnor was restless, for he could have flown the eight miles to the hall in as many minutes. As court elf of the sky, he alone amongst them could take to it – as long as there was some daylight remaining. Up there, he was in his true element, as happy as a child peeking into a Christmas stocking – even when he was in a hurry. This time, however, he had company, and so there was no question of him flying very far ahead, only speeding along just above the ground, stopping frequently and urging the others to keep up with him as well as they could.

Like the River Dove, the elves eventually burst out of the narrow gorge and soon found themselves crossing the flat meadows close to the mill. The river almost slowed to a halt here, in a series of long meanders which snaked their way drunkenly across the bottom of the valley. The tired elves avoided crossing the river at the old bridge and chose a shallow place further downstream: they weren't overly concerned about the ghosts of young girls, but time was short, and they were wise enough not to go looking for unwanted trouble.

What little remained of the daylight had retreated behind the high valley sides to the west as the elves forced their aching legs to run across the wet meadows beyond the mill. Its tumbledown collection of stone buildings, house and all, were covered in a thick blanket of sodden, green moss. It had spread over every roof and even the tops of each stone making up the field walls, like strange, dark snow – it was as if the sun had never once managed to dry it out properly. The mill's reputation for being the dampest place for miles around was well deserved indeed.

As he ran onwards, Roall's mind returned to the hob as he'd stood surrounded in the glade, recalling the words from the diary: it had told of the silver key, a key which might be used at the great hall, and the others listened with great interest to those few words:

'Come, seek its home
Of oak, unseen
On mellow stone,
Yet iron between'

Malrin's devious mind was well practised at solving puzzles and so he'd soon worked out that the silver key must be taken back to Sir Henry's ancestral home for it to be of any use – the dark elf would soon be at the hall and would stop at nothing to get what he wanted.

The court elves didn't have a minute to lose. The moss-covered buildings at the mill were soon lost in the gloom behind them, and up ahead they began to see dim lights showing from one or two windows at the hall. The vast, rambling house lay tucked hard against the eastern valley edge, well protected by a steep, wooded slope on that side, and its own elegant gardens and grounds on the other. Tall, bare trees lined the long, curving entrance driveway, whilst many others were dotted around the hall's sweeping parkland, sometimes trapped inside small protective squares of timber fencing.

The light elves were soon at the start of the driveway, but they took to the parkland instead and ran from tree to tree, keeping out of sight as much as possible. Not for the first time, Roall found himself wondering how much longer either world would have to suffer the antics of the dark elves. It seemed as though he'd spent his entire life running here, there and everywhere, attempting to put right what the Unseelie Court had harmed or destroyed, or even meeting them in battle, one to one. As he dodged from tree to tree, he tried yet again to imagine how his life would perhaps have been without the sharp stones inside his boot that were Malrin and his loathsome followers. Because of them, he knew that there must have been countless opportunities for joy and contentment which had slipped away from him and the other light elves for ever. He surprised himself then, for he felt tears of pure frustration coming to his eyes as he ran: he was annoyed with himself and wiped them away with his sleeve as the next tree emerged from the gloom in front of him.

181

With their cloaks around them, the elves were now little more than indistinct, fleeting shadows, but there was a grim determination in the set of their jaws and a rarely seen blaze in their green eyes as two of them gripped their freyals with white-knuckled fists and the third slipped his bow from his back.

As they approached the house, Stirran fancied that he could see the deadly flicker of flames in amongst the dark outbuildings, spurring him on to even greater speed. The other two noticed his change of pace at once, and matched it. A few seconds later, the firelight was plain for them to see, and as they ran onwards, ever faster, the pop and crackle of fire reached their ears. Then, with the hall looming up and beginning to fill their view, they suddenly felt the icy kiss of snowflakes on their cheeks – one or two quickly became many, clinging to their hair and cloaks or going into their eyes as other noises came to them: a whinny from a frightened horse, then the clatter of hooves on cobbles. With snowflakes suddenly filling the air and driving into their faces, the elves now peered ahead through half-closed eyes. They could see a mare near the stables, a fine hunter from the look of her, but she was loose, terrified by the flames and searching desperately for a way out. She eventually panicked and jumped awkwardly over a five-rail fence, slipping on the wet cobbles as she did so, before cantering into the darkening parkland, shaking her head and mane and still whinnying in distress. It was all too clear that the dark elves had arrived before them, and had not been idle.

Without a word, the court elves split up as they ran. Flinnor peeled off to the right towards the fleeing horse, whilst Roall continued straight ahead at a breakneck sprint, heading for the rear of the hall. Stirran veered to the left, towards the fire which now burned more brightly than ever inside the stable block. He soon heard more frightened whinnying from inside it, and several of the stable doors shuddered on their hinges as the trapped animals threw themselves repeatedly against them.

Stirran, court elf of rocks, already knew what he must do. He saw two men bursting out from the back entrance of the house, with a woman following close behind them. They were shouting to each other as they ran towards the stables, gathering buckets which stood by a water trough as they went, and one of the men carried a large red fire extinguisher. Stirran paid them no attention. He knew that they wouldn't notice him, and in any case, he didn't have any time to spare. He ran past the end of the stables and was soon scrambling up the steep bank behind them.

Up he went, weaving through the trees with great speed and expertly avoiding the exposed roots and tangled briars which would have tripped up any other being before they'd taken three steps. Half a minute later and far up the slope, he dropped to his knees out of breath and placed his hands against a boulder almost as large as himself. It immediately succumbed to his will and, without being pushed, started to slide slowly across the ground, inch after inch, piling up a mound of earth and grass in front of it as it went. A few moments later, water suddenly appeared from underneath it and the earth quickly turned to mud around its base, becoming a thick, gurgling mush. As the boulder slid further along, more water bubbled up from the ground behind it and became a flood, then the slope finally tore itself open as the pent-up spring water gushed out, free to flow at last. Stirran stood up and watched with satisfaction as the surging water gathered speed and rushed down towards the stable block below him. Even Planiss would have been proud of him, he thought, still panting.

The stables were built into the side of the bank, and so their back windows were level with the ground. With a shattering of glass, the torrent crashed its way in through them, and the greedy flames were soon being quenched by a deluge of brown water which rushed across the cobbled floors in every direction, then out through the open doors at the front. Looking down, Stirran could see the men leading two more hunters away from the building. They kept rearing up in fright and the men had to dodge their flailing hooves several times. The woman led two foals away, too, frightened and straining at their halters. Inside, the flames faltered and spluttered, then died away, and a minute later all that remained was a smoking, hissing mess.

*   *   *

Flinnor was now alone in the parkland, and so felt no guilt in taking to the air at last, whilst there was still a glimmer of daylight remaining. In any case, he couldn't hope to catch a bolting horse without using his special skills to some extent. He slipped easily from a run into a smooth glide, his arms stretched out to the side and his cloak fluttering along his back like a flag in a storm. He swept around two ancient beech trees which came out of the deepening dusk from nowhere, then, with the snow stinging his face, he sped across the open ground towards the steady thudding of the runaway's hooves on the turf. The sound grew louder, and soon the elf could see the mare up ahead, still cantering in a straight line across the park, towards Lowslack Mill. He came up from behind her, out of sight, and slipped onto her back before she'd realised what was happening, but the surprised horse bucked violently and Flinnor soon found himself lying on his back in the wet grass, looking up at falling snowflakes as they materialised from out of the dark sky.

'Shhhh ... it!' he whispered, closing his eyes ... and thankful that he didn't have an audience.

He shook his head in disgust, but was actually enjoying the serious challenge and sprang up for another attempt. In seconds he was airborne again and swooping down onto the horse from behind once more. This time he clung determinedly to her mane with one hand, bringing his mouth up close to her ear and whispering to her in his own tongue, soothing her as only a light elf could, and running his other hand down her rigid, straining neck.

'Mollenti, mas difaro. Mollenti.'

The wild stare in her eyes gradually disappeared, and she slowed to a trot, then a walk, with the snowflakes melting on her steaming coat and Flinnor still talking to her quietly, repeating the same few words again and again. Her fear had left her, and soon the magnificent animal was walking calmly back towards the distant house and stables. Flinnor was pleased with his work. It wasn't often that he had the chance of a horse-ride in the snow, either, he reminded himself.

*   *   *

Roall dared not think what might be happening behind the house. He had run as quickly as his tired legs would allow, invisibly and silently, straight past the mortals as they'd dashed for the buckets. He knew exactly what Flinnor and Stirran would be trying to achieve and was content for them to get on with their own tasks: he had little doubt that they would be successful, each in their own way.

He raced along the side of the hall, bounding over two garden walls and around several bare rose bushes before coming to the back of the house. It was almost in total darkness, but a bright shaft of light shone out from a closed window. Roall ran up to it at once, fighting for his breath, and after wiping some snow from the glass looked in over the high windowsill. There was no one inside the small room, only a lot of shelves laden with vases and flower pots, above a huge earthenware sink. He looked around him, exasperated and squinting in the snow, then noticed that the next window along was open slightly – the snow on the sill had also been recently disturbed and so Roall went towards it.

He had no warning of what happened next. The window slid up another foot and before he could back away, three black figures were rolling out of it one after the other, slim and familiar figures which sent his hand straight to the freyal at his hip.

The court elf shrank back into the shadows against the wall and pressed himself into the ivy which covered it, holding his breath ... the shadows were deep, but not *that* deep. Had the figures been human, there would have been no question: his cloak and elf cunning would have hidden him completely. However, these were dark elves, equally as skilled, or even more so, but with pure evil coursing through their veins, tainting their every thought or act, fuelling them in their relentless quest to bring pain and chaos to all living things. Roall tensed himself and waited, his fingers just touching the large, solitary gem at the tip of the freyal's cold hilt.

One by one, the figures dropped noiselessly to the ground – shapeless, black forms on an even blacker night – and then they left, leaving barely a footprint in the shallow snow. Five seconds later the last of them had vanished into a hedge, and Roall dared to let out his breath.

He'd done nothing to give himself away, and so it could only have been some sixth sense which made the last dark elf suddenly stop. The first two were already part of the night, making their escape, but the third one paused, turned, and Roall watched in horror as he stepped out of the hedge and stared back towards the ivy-covered wall. A quiet hiss, almost one of exhilaration, escaped from the dark elf's lips.

Even Roall's cloak couldn't hide him from those all-seeing eyes, and he knew at once that he was discovered. He gripped his freyal firmly, but it stayed under his cloak as he clung to the hope that the dark elf didn't want to be delayed and would turn away. That hope was shattered in a fleeting second as the hiss stopped, only to be followed by two more from the deeper shadows. Out of those shadows came the others. They were in no hurry and felt no fear, and all three of them soon stood together, side by side. Malrin stepped forward and drew his sabre in one easy movement ...

Roall finally took a deep breath in, but wondered if it was to be one of his last as he stepped away from the wall and faced his enemies in the falling snow. He understood exactly how dark elves thought, and knew that there was no way out of his situation other than to face it head on. Stirran and Flinnor were out of earshot and would have problems of their own, he guessed, even if they were less dire than his. It was to be one against three, and nothing else. They all stood silently for a few moments before Malrin spoke.

'A court elf ... My, my, we *are* honoured!' The sarcasm was spread thickly and Roall ignored it. 'And if I am not mistaken in this poor light, do we keep company with Roall, their brave and illustrious leader, sticking his pretty nose into someone else's business as usual?'

Malrin brought his hand to his brow and peered towards the light elf, who was still partly hidden in the shadows of the hall.

'You know very well that it is me, Malrin. You are fortunate to catch me alone.' As far as Roall was concerned, this was *his* fight, and only his. 'Did you find what you came for?' he added, boldly.

'You'll never know that – not in this life, anyway,' sneered Malrin from under a curled lip.

The other two didn't move as Malrin took a single step towards Roall, then charged forwards without warning. His venomous hate was vented in a sigh of sadistic pleasure as light and dark elf clashed together. Roall brought his freyal up above his head, holding it in both hands. It was now a fabulous sword, and even in the gloom its green jewels glittered defiantly as the dark elf's sabre cut downwards in a slicing sweep.

The swords rang out three, four, five times, as the freyal protected the court elf from the lethal weapon in Malrin's hands. Six, seven. It moved at lightning speed, now attacking back. Eight, and nine. It stopped Malrin, then drove him backwards step by step, and hope stirred again in Roall's heart, although he knew that even a freyal could fail him at any moment. That hope grew as Malrin staggered back another step into the darkness, but Roall realised his mistake and paid the price for it in the same instant. There had been no retreat by the dark elf, only trickery and deceit as he had drawn Roall towards the hedge where the other two still lurked. A ferocious, scything blow came from nowhere, and Roall took it fully on his side, the power of it taking him off his feet and throwing him cleanly over a garden bench and the low wall behind it.

Everything went quiet, and the dark elves looked at each other with joy and pride in their black eyes, convinced that their adversary of many years was slain at last. As a window slid open high above them and a man's voice called out, they sheathed their sabres neatly, then, happy in the knowledge that Roall was cut wide open and would never trouble them again, they turned and left Hoarfrost Hall. Their hellhound was close by, where he had been left tethered, waiting patiently to carry his masters towards their next mischief.

188

At last, some form of peace descended on the hall again. There were no sounds from the horses, or the fire, or even from the other two light elves. Nothing moved, and a minute ticked past on the tall grandfather clocks inside the house whilst the gods played their games of fate, and Roall's destiny was decided upon ...

*   *   *

The court elf of meadows pulled himself painfully up onto the low wall and was surprised to find himself breathing – although it hurt like the devil when he did. The pain told him he was definitely alive, though, which was encouraging, and the freyal, now just a dagger once again, was also safe in his hand. For that he was equally grateful. He stood up with difficulty and peered at the long gash in the side of his cloak. Roall then knew just how close he'd come to leaving his friends forever: he'd never seen his cloak pierced, let alone slashed open like a rotten sack.

A long, low howl drifted up to Roall from across the parkland, a sign that the dark elves would soon be far away, carried off by their great white hound, but there was no point in pursuing them. Even if he had the energy, which he didn't, he was far from being in good shape and had no hope of gathering the others together in time. Holding his side, he hobbled stiffly to the open window and pulled the curtains aside, revealing what used to be Sir Henry Witcher's private study. Roall recalled the words of the hobgoblin again, and how a silver key might unlock a secret door somewhere within it.

'Come, seek its home
Of oak, unseen'

Behind that door would lie the third Witcher key. Large, strong, forged from iron, its size and strength would let it turn the rusting works of a lock in an even stronger and larger door: Three Howes Gate, the entrance to a vast network of abandoned tunnels once owned by Sir Henry himself. The ironstone mines of Rosedale.

'As large and strong
As Three Howes Gate.'

Roall tried to ignore the shooting pains in his side as he climbed up onto the windowsill and dropped awkwardly into the study. He was too late to foil the dark elves' plan, knowing very well that the iron key would be in a pocket and on its way to Rosedale by now, but for some reason, perhaps just his deeply ingrained distrust of the dark elves and all their ways, he was compelled to see for himself. A tiny door was still hanging open in the middle of an oak-panelled wall. He walked around a large leather-topped desk and up to it, closing and opening it again with one finger, and wishing that he didn't feel so much like a burglar. Then he held his hand up, allowing a small sphere of green light to grow in his palm, and looked into the cupboard hidden behind. At the back of it, Roall could see the honey-coloured stone of which the house was built.

' … unseen
On mellow stone'

Nestling up against it was a smart, wooden box. The lid was open, and the inside was lined with padded, red velvet cloth into which was pressed the shape of a very large key with an unusual square handle.

'Yet iron between
As large and strong ...'

The key was missing, just as he'd expected, but Roall could see something else next to the box. He left the ball of green light hovering above the door and lifted it out. It was the skeletal frame of a folded bat's wing, and from quite a large bat, judging by the size of it. He took a step back and spread it out gently, then looked down as he felt something crunching under his feet. In the light he saw the rest of the skeleton, its bones strewn all over the carpet as if they'd been thrown down in anger.

This is very strange indeed, he thought. *How could a bat get in there and die ... unless ... unless a spriggan had left it there!*

It all came to him clearly then, as his mind raced ahead.

Spriggans must have taken the iron key long ago, years probably, leaving their customary gift in its place. They would have had no need for little silver keys. They could pick any lock given enough time and no interruptions. A hidden cupboard in the study of a rich man ... perhaps an open window on a summer's evening ... they could not have resisted it.

He shook his head in wonder and whispered to himself, 'So the dark elves didn't find what they came for, after all.' He thought back to them as they'd spilled out of the study window.

Huh! No excited chatter. No thieving grins on their ugly faces. Not even a gloating word or two before the fight. It would have been just like Malrin to have the iron key spinning on his finger ... if he had it.

He picked up the bones and put them back into their resting place, before closing the secret door. The silver key was still in its keyhole and so he turned it, perhaps locking the cupboard for the very last time. He looked at the insignificant little key between his fingers and smiled.

191

All the trouble this has caused ... and now it is discarded, useless to the dark elves and anyone else.

Slipping it into his pocket, Roall reached up to the green light and closed his fingers around it to snuff it out, then, with several grimaces as his side throbbed, he climbed out of the window and back into the cold night air, before sliding the window down behind him. It was snowing heavily now, with large flakes filling the air like cherry blossom in a spring gale – he looked up at the sky but it was a lifeless, impenetrable grey-black, and the snow fell into his eyes, making him blink.

He made his way to the front of the house and found the other two court elves standing there together beside a broad, leafless elm tree at the start of the driveway. The runaway horse stood contentedly at the fence it had so recently jumped in a panic, whilst a few wisps of steam drifted out from the open stable doors. Nearby, the two men and the woman were pointing in different directions and shrugging their shoulders at they talked amongst themselves, bewildered and totally unaware of their unusual company.

The light elves didn't speak as they looked at one another, the snow already settling on their heads and shoulders. Each had borne his own cross at the hall, and Roall's was by far the heaviest, but there was no rivalry or competition between them, and Roall made sure that the gash in his cloak stayed out of sight, at least for now. They all knew that they must leave at once, and return quickly to the northern end of Farndale to catch up with the others. Any tales of one-sided swordfights and uncooperative horses would have to wait. They also guessed that the hob and the others would be somewhere along the disused railway track by then, and with any luck well on their way to the caves. The sooner they were all together again, the better. Roall needed no reminding that with dark elves prowling in the area, and unsatisfied ones at that, danger would be waiting everywhere for the young mortals and their guides.

With a final look back at the hall, they turned and started their return journey. They were soon lost from sight, and lost in their own dismal thoughts as they sped across the lonely parkland and meadows of Douthwaite Dale in the deepening snow.

Jack-in-irons

Long before a single snowflake had settled on the mossy roof of Lowslack Mill, an unusual party was toiling its way up a steep, winding lane at the opposite end of Farndale, not far from the village. The strange sight would have raised an eyebrow extremely quickly, if anyone had been observant enough to see them, that is: two teenagers, with a pair of light elves and a hobgoblin for company, and most of them close to invisible. The hob was at the rear of the group. As he was only half the size of the others, he took two steps to each of theirs and still had to put in a short sprint now and again just to keep up. At the front, Planiss and Agoriff were making light work of the heavy-going, wrapped in their cloaks but with their hoods back on their shoulders and their long hair swinging free. In-between came Mark and Victoria. They were now more thankful than ever for their surprisingly warm gifts, as the temperature was falling quickly and a lively wind hinted at worse to come. Unlike the hardy elves, however, their hoods were most certainly up, and only their breath on the cold air could have given them away as the five of them all but melted into the countryside, like half-formed spirits.

The lane wound its way from close by the village church up to the high road on Blakey Ridge. It reached that lonely place not far from the Lion Inn, an isolated but welcoming haven of warmth and refreshment for weary travellers passing by, but sadly deemed too far away and too steep a climb on foot for even the thirstiest villager. The valley sides were very steep in that area and so the lane snaked its way up at a lazy angle, even turning back on itself once or twice as it tried to find the easiest way up the unforgiving slope. Despite this, it was so steep in a few places that the two youngsters were forced to help their aching legs with their hands, pushing down on their knees. They persevered, though, not wanting to fall too far behind their more energetic leaders and so delay them in any way.

Halfway up, as they made their way around a particularly tight bend, the elves stopped and waited patiently for the others to catch them up. They were soon all together again, and as the less fit amongst them found their breath, the whole group looked back the way they'd come and were dismayed to see that it looked considerably shorter than it felt. Worse still, far away to the south a dark, forbidding wall of cloud was moving steadily up the valley towards them, and the light began to fail in front of their eyes as they watched the sky turn a heavy, old-saucepan grey. Victoria soon recovered enough to speak, as she rested her chin in the forked end of her stick.

'These presents are brilliant! The cloak's as warm as fresh toast, and this stick …' she lifted her chin and tapped the end of it on the ground, 'it's just the right length for me. How did you manage that?'

Agoriff just smiled. He knew that the stick would always be just right for her, whatever it was used for.

'We are in for some snow before very long, by the look of it,' said Planiss, as he eyed the approaching cloud apprehensively.

The others guessed that he was right: they'd all grown up in Farndale and knew the signs well enough. In a few minutes it would reach them. They could even smell its clean freshness, like approaching rain. Turning away, they looked up the lane ahead of them, but the ridge still seemed a long way up and was now almost lost in low, threatening clouds. Victoria and Mark were thinking about the same thing, as usual. They were both weary, but not so exhausted that they could ignore a growing concern about what they were steadily getting themselves into. A cave full of spriggans was fast becoming the very last place either of them wanted to try to find.

'We'd better get going,' shouted Mark, the wind now buffeting his hood and taking his words away as they left his lips.

He wasn't sure what plans the elves had for finding shelter, or even if they had any plans at all, but the thought of a wet night out in the open, even wearing an elf cloak, was just too miserable to think about. Mark was quite right, of course, about pushing on. They had no choice but to move on and up, snow or no snow, aching legs or not. Planiss spoke then, shouting against the ever strengthening wind. He had their full attention as they huddled together around him.

'Do not worry,' he yelled, guessing their concerns. 'Believe it or not, we have a choice of where to take shelter, but we have to see what the weather is doing at the top before we can decide. There is the inn, of course, which has plenty of outbuildings where we shall not be noticed, particularly on a night like this, or the old miners' store by the disused railway line. I am sure that we could find some room in there amongst the junk ... if we must. Let's go!'

He pulled his hood up at last and set off uphill again, the others falling in behind him quickly and silently – Mark felt that any choice of shelter was better than none, and he was keen to get the climb behind him as the first few snowflakes arrived, flying almost horizontally. The hob followed last of all, still determined to keep up with everyone, but those last few minutes before the snowfall set in passed all too quickly, and with a suddenness which even surprised the elves, it was upon them. The lane turned white in front of their half-closed eyes as the large flakes raced in every direction, driven wild by wind which had lost its way close to the ground. After only a minute, the youngsters' boots were crunching or sliding on an inch or more of it. Mark moved towards the edge of the lane to get more grip on the grass and heather there, and Victoria followed him, her hooded head bowed downwards and her stick becoming more useful with each exhausting step.

They already felt as if they'd been climbing for hours. The extra steepness of the top half of the lane, combined with the icy air which they sucked in by the lungful, sapped their energy with alarming speed. There was no longer any conversation, only a gritty resolve to get to the top and take cover from the blizzard. The snow and wind seemed intent on finding their way through any gap in their clothing, especially around their necks, and they tried to hold their hoods tightly shut around their faces: it didn't help very much and soon turned their exposed fingers blue and numb. Just as Victoria's legs were getting ready to give up and turn to jelly, they came to the very top part of the lane, just below the ridge road itself. It levelled off a little there, and the going became easier, much to their relief. The hob, who was still trailing well behind, despite the best efforts of his short legs, found a hidden reserve of energy and put in a very respectable burst of speed, catching the others up just as they reached the place where the railway line had once crossed the lane.

Planiss beckoned to the others to gather around him, but he still had to shout to be heard above the din. Their cloaks flapped like the sails of a turning yacht as they strained to hear him.

'The ridge road is only a little further on, but the inn is almost a mile north of here!' he shouted.

The others all knew this very well, and weren't keen to

be reminded of it. They nodded back, hoping that Planiss was going to choose the less painful option.

'It would be madness to go there in these conditions. We will go to the old store and take what shelter it has to offer. Are we agreed?'

He received silent but much more enthusiastic nods from everyone, and shortly afterwards they were standing on the ridge road itself with their backs to the wind. The snow had been falling for much longer on that higher ground. It was also blowing straight across the road, not bothering to stop and cover it, but the verges were already buried under deepening drifts. They crossed it in a silent line, the wind pulling ever more ferociously at their cloaks and hoods as they were exposed to its full power. On the other side of the road, and with Rosedale somewhere in front of them if only they could see it, was the course of the disused railway track. Their journey would usually have been an easy, level stroll along crunching cinders, but now it promised to be a back-breaking trek through deep snow.

The wind was now blowing straight into their faces and they had to lean into it to make progress: all heads were down and hoods up, the elves' included. Victoria was at the rear, still putting her stick to good use as she struggled bravely along. The hob, despite often being buried up to his thighs, was relieved to be walking on level ground again, and would probably have skipped along if he could have. Several times, though, he stopped and looked back into the blizzard behind them. The first time, Mark, who was immediately behind him, imagined that the hob was checking on him and Victoria – being thoughtful. After the second time, Mark wasn't so sure. It seemed like the hob was looking further back, well past them. Mark checked for himself then, but apart from Victoria doing her best to step into his footprints, there was nothing unusual to be seen. In the end, he decided that there was enough to worry about ahead, let alone behind, and so he ignored the hob and his silly games.

After ten minutes of this gruelling effort, Agoriff spotted the roof of the building they were seeking, not much more than an indistinct blur twenty yards ahead of him: he turned and urged the others onwards, pointing up ahead and shouting something which none of them could hear. As they finally approached the old store, they were forced to wallow through the deep drifts which had built up around it. These were above Mark's knees and the bottom of his cloak rested on them as he fought his way to the only door and tried the handle. The others stood close by, cold and dejected, and could do nothing more than hope that the door would open soon and allow them to get under cover. Needless to say, the handle didn't work, and Mark threw himself against the stout door desperately, again and again. He soon had to stop, sore and exhausted, but also annoyed that the door seemed to be the only part of the building which wasn't falling to pieces. He tried to get his breath back as he leant against it, defeated. Agoriff nudged him aside. He was holding Victoria's thumb stick, but Mark wondered what he could do with it, apart from knocking on the door to see if anyone was at home.

The elf placed the end of it against the door, and then Victoria saw that her new gift was even more special than she'd imagined, for it was growing fatter, right there in front of them all, and was soon as thick and strong as a fence post. She looked at Mark, who could only shrug and watch the tree elf at work ... he was starting to get used to their little surprises. Agoriff steadied himself in the snow drift, then swung the heavy stick hard against the door. It was now a small but very effective battering ram, and the door shuddered on its hinges with each blow, but no door could withstand that sort of treatment for very long, and after several powerful blows it suddenly burst inwards. The whole group surged forwards and tumbled though the doorway.

Inside, what little light there was seeped in through two grimy windows, each covered in metal mesh designed to keep vandals out, and dusty, fly-filled cobwebs in, by the look of them. Fine snow had blown in under the door and was sprayed across the old floorboards like a large but delicate lace fan – most of the clutter close to the door had a covering of the same powdery snow, too. Perhaps best of all, though, it was relatively quiet, compared to the racket outside. As Planiss forced the damaged door shut and propped it closed with a broken shovel, it became quieter still and the blizzard was temporarily locked outside.

The group stood in a dripping circle, stamping their boots and lowering their hoods, and there was even a smile on one or two bright red faces, still tingling cold and adorned with clumps of wet hair. There were piles of old gear everywhere, long since discarded by railwaymen and miners alike. Steel ropes lay coiled in rusting, toppling heaps, whilst worm-eaten timbers and broken tools, buckets of huge bolts and nuts, plus a vast array of rusted, unlabelled tins filled with goodness-knows-what surrounded them.

'Luxury!' sighed Mark, running his finger through some filthy cobwebs on the wall next to him, then watching the hob jump up and down in an attempt to warm up. Victoria's thoughts went back to the church belfry and she decided that her suspicions were correct, after all: Mark must have spider's blood running in his veins.

'I sh'pose you'd like to move in *here*, too,' she said carefully – her chin was so cold that it didn't move very easily and made her sound a little drunk. Mark knew just what she was referring to, and rocked his head as if he was seriously considering it, just to annoy her. Seeing her standing in that dismal place, shivering, with melting snow dripping from her cloak and hair, but still with a remarkably cheerful look in her eyes, reminded him that she was unique, a rare and special person he was very proud to know. Above all, everyone there now knew that she was certainly prepared to put up with anything in order to help Elspeth.

'Well, it's not *quite* as cosy as one of the stables at The Lion ... but I've seen worse ... I think,' said Planiss, interrupting his thoughts.

The others weren't too convinced of his last point, but didn't really care any more, now that they were inside and not outside.

'At least we are going in the right direction for the caves,' he continued, 'isn't that correct, master hob?' Not for the first time that day, the hob's mind was elsewhere and he didn't answer at once. The elf repeated the question, reaching down and tapping him on the shoulder to get his attention.

'Well, this *is* a good way to get to the caves, isn't it?'

The elf knew the area reasonably well, but not as well as the hob did. He certainly wasn't aware of another route which would bring them this high up the side of the valley, well above the normal cave entrances. The hob looked up at him, but unwillingly, like a pet dog that had been up to mischief, and knew it.

'What? Oh, aye, it's a good 'un, all right,' he replied. ''ardly no one comes this way any more – the odd shepherd p'raps, but now't else.'

Planiss peered down at the hob, as he still wasn't getting the full attention he wanted. The others noticed the same brief hesitation, and Mark was even tempted to ask the hob a thing or two himself. In the end, though, he deferred to the wisdom of the light elf: Planiss and the hob were from the same world, after all, and no doubt understood each other's ways well enough. Agoriff broke the silence, if silence there could ever really be with such a storm raging outside – the wind was making the roof tiles rattle overhead, whilst the gap around the door whistled like a young lad on his way to a sweetshop.

'We should get some rest,' he said, trying to sound positive: it wasn't the best place for a rest, even if a summer breeze had been wafting sleepily through it. 'I know that it is not ideal–' there was a *humpph* from someone, but the elf persevered '–however, when this storm passes, we shall have a weary journey in front of us, probably through deep snow.'

Agoriff cupped his hands together and blew softly into them. Victoria thought that he was warming them up, but a green light soon spluttered into life and shone out from between his fingers. He cast a glowing sphere gently towards the ceiling, where it hovered and gave out its useful but rather eerie light. The others knew that Agoriff was quite right about resting, and Victoria was the first to find a place which seemed slightly less atrocious than the rest. She sat on the floor and leant back against a wall, tugging her cloak tightly around her. The others did their best too, with Mark perching himself like a strange hen on several rolls of fencing wire over which he'd thrown the remains of a few old sacks. Victoria watched him, shuddering to think what might be living in amongst their half-rotted remains, but Mark was Mark, and she knew that he wouldn't care one little bit.

The two elves sat cross-legged in the centre of the floor, just beyond the fan of snow in front of the door – dozens of slushy footprints had now ruined its pretty patterns. The hob made the most fuss of settling down, searching here, searching there – just about everywhere, in fact. Victoria opened one eye and watched him tiredly as he moved some timbers aside and tried to judge if the dark space behind them was large enough for him to squeeze into. For a while she wondered why he seemed to be trying to find a hiding place more than a resting place, but she was worn out, and her eyelid drooped back down as exhaustion finally caught up with her. A minute later she was dreaming of her warm, soft bed back at Willow Garth, puzzled as to why the usually familiar patchwork quilt covering it now seemed to be six dirty old sacks, sewn together with orange baling string.

The elves sat motionless, their green eyes half open but still resting, as was their way. The occasional flick of their hair when a particularly strong gust of wind found its way in under the door was the only clue that they were alive, and not statues skilfully carved from some rare and colourful stone. Despite the conditions, sleep did eventually come to all of them: fitful sleep, but sleep never-the-less, and the hob must also have found the dark place he'd been so keen to discover, for he was nowhere to be seen. The door remained firmly shut, and so he was certainly in there somewhere: a long life, much of it spent hiding from someone or other, had moulded him into a true expert. He might even have held his own against a spriggan – on a good day.

*   *   *

The indescribable horror came upon them an hour before dawn, but without any warning. Not even a second. Nothing. The destruction of an entire corner of the roof was instantaneous. One moment there was only the whistling door singing to them in their restless dreams. The next, a fist the size of a prize ham was being punched down through the roof with incredible power by a long, hairy arm the thickness of a telegraph pole. With a deafening crash, the roof tiles, splintered timbers, dust and snow cascaded downwards. Time all but stopped in that instant, perhaps shocked into slow motion by the explosive energy of the arm, and in the next long fraction of a second everyone inside the store was wrenched from their dreams into a mind-spinning, nightmarish reality. Even as Mark tried to leap up from his uncomfortable nest, a heavy, nail-laden roof timber rotated downwards and hit him across the shoulder, spinning him slowly around and down onto the floor. Strangely, the pain he waited for didn't come, but he had too much on his mind to realise that his cloak had already saved him from serious injury. He did wonder why his legs seemed to belong to someone else, though, for they felt lifeless and leaden as he tried to stand up and get to Victoria.

He fought to move more quickly, watching helplessly as the fist above them opened and its thick, leathery fingers spread out hideously into something all-grasping, all-crushing. Debris flew into his staring eyes and wide-open, shouting mouth, but he heard no shout, only a deep, vibrating jumble of meaningless noise which sounded like he was trying to speak underwater. He saw the elves turning and standing up in one achingly long movement, their hands reaching for the bows on their backs as they prepared to face their attacker.

Victoria happened to be the closest to the destruction above them, and suddenly those vast fingers were groping down into the room, reaching out for her through the billowing dust and snow which had already engulfed her. She grabbed her stick from the floor just as the fingers closed around her shoulder and chest, but the cruel thumb was around her neck with two fingers locked under her armpit, squeezing tight, before Mark could even take one useless pace towards her. As a pair of bows snapped into shape and the fingers of Planiss and Agoriff moved towards their bowstrings, the arm started to haul the hand back upwards. Victoria dangled from it like a live doll, her legs pedalling in the air, one hand pulling desperately at the huge thumb which was almost choking her, pressing the life out of her as she was snatched away.

As she went up, her precious thumb stick – still laced with the magic of the light elves – instantly grew to become a short, stout spear. Its polished wood gleamed in the failing green light above them and that same light, even through the dust, was suddenly reflected in the bright metal of a pointed spearhead. Whether it was by that same magic, or because Victoria found some hidden strength of which even she was unaware, the spear in her hand moved quickly across her chest, jabbing upwards with surprising force. With their bowstrings now fully drawn, the elves let out a long cry of defiant rage as their arrows slowly formed and the spear point sank into the hairy arm, through its tough, dirty skin. The blood from the wound sprayed across Victoria's shoulder and one side of her face, but the arm didn't stop. The hand didn't open. There was no roar of pain from whatever it was out there, and up, slowly up, she went, as the snow came down through the gaping hole in the roof.

As Mark took his second step, he reached for an iron bar close to him, but his arm was disobedient, too, just like his legs, and would only move slowly. He couldn't understand his limbs any more, and although his shout was still coming from his mouth, long and deep, it was still unfamiliar to him. He saw the elves' arrows grow on their drawn bowstrings and spring from them at last, greedy for their targets.

Deep into the thick wrist went one, and into the mighty forearm went the other. Then there was a pause ... but only one of surprise. For what seemed an eternity, but in fact was no more than two seconds, Victoria hung from the fist with her legs now kicking wildly in every direction, still clutching her short but apparently useless spear. Then the spent arrows melted away and she was gone. Only the jagged hole in the roof proved that it wasn't another bad dream – that and the blood-stained snow and rubble where Victoria had been sitting asleep all of seven seconds earlier.

As time tried to find itself again, Mark's shout gradually became his own, rising in pitch and at last bellowing out defiantly, filling the small room. There'd been no chance to use the iron bar and he let it drop to the floor with a clatter as he lunged for the door. Agoriff was already there, kicking the shovel aside and pulling the door open violently. He looked back at Mark for a moment, driven snow quickly sticking to him and flying crazily around the room. He shouted above the storm and his words were filled with dismay. Mark would never forget them.

'Jack-in-irons!' Then his voice dropped to a hoarse whisper which only Mark was close enough to hear.

'Jack has Victoria. He's taken her!'

Without another word, he plunged out into the blizzard and was gone. Planiss darted forward to stop him, but he was too late. Jack-in-irons was never one to refuse a gift horse, or a gift elf, come to that, and although Planiss shouted desperately for his dear, brave friend to return, it was pointless: Agoriff was scooped up like an over-adventurous toddler running away from its parents. He was utterly powerless in Jack's enormous hand, from which he was now hanging by his legs, upside down: his cloak hung below his head whilst he hit out at the fat fingers around his thighs ... with absolutely no effect.

Jack-in-irons, Jack the Giant, the most feared creature on the moors and an enemy to all – whichever world they inhabited – blundered his way through the snowstorm, following the route of the old railway line, and heading in the direction the others would have taken come daybreak. Thick chains slung around his waist and over his back chinked and clanked against each other as he strode away, his bare, hairy feet leaving long scars of bare heather in the deep snow.

From his chains hung many strange, round objects, some of them hairy, some not. They were the decapitated heads of victims long past ... or not so long past. The stiff flesh of his most recent kills, now dried and shrunken, was pulled back tight across their twisted faces, baring their teeth and shrivelled tongues in a permanent, grotesque smile of death. Jack had hunted once more, and with great success.

A shocked silence fell upon the three lucky ones who were still inside the building, and the green light above them began to fade away, turning everything below it a deathly grey. Planiss wasn't sure what to do about the others outside, but he did know that his first task was to stop Mark from rushing out after them and becoming the third of Jack's victims in as many minutes. He'd slammed the door shut and was keeping it that way with his back and arms pressed against it as Mark stood before him, hardly able to restrain himself and covering his eyes with his hands as if he was trying to block out everything around him, telling himself that it couldn't be true.

'We cannot leave yet, Mark. You know he will get us too. You must understand that, surely!' Planiss spoke wisely and with total authority, for he knew that clear leadership was needed. 'Find your brave heart, Mark, just as you did in the crypt!' he shouted, not moving from the door.

He waited for Mark to regain control of himself and take his hands down from his face, but when he did, his eyes were filled with horror and helplessness as they finally met the elf's.

'We will soon follow and see what can be done,' said Planiss as reassuringly as he could, and a little more calmly.

The elf slowly lowered his arms as a hint of panic even

started to nibble at the edge of *his* mind, too, but he fought to keep it at bay as he looked around the room, hoping for inspiration. Then, in the corner furthest from the damaged roof, he saw the lid of a large wooden box start to lift up, and eight small, well-chewed fingers appear from under it. The hob had obviously chosen his resting place well, but as far as Planiss was concerned there had been more hiding going on than resting, as if the hob had been expecting trouble from the very start. He ran at once to the box and lifted the lid, pulling the startled hob out by his hood and throwing him unceremoniously onto the floor, before kneeling on his chest. It didn't take the hob long to start squealing like a lost piglet.

'I ... I can explain ... Don't kill me. Please, don't kill me! I can help you ... I really can.'

With memories of the hob's strange behaviour outside rushing through his mind, Mark watched Planiss lift the hob by his collar as if he was about to knock his head on the floorboards.

'We don't have time now, but let us hope that we all live to hear your story, hobgoblin. Get up! Stay close and do not even think of leaving us or you will feel the wrath of a court elf ... between your scrawny shoulderblades.' Planiss touched the end of his bow.

His grovelling apparently successful, the hob wormed his way out from under the elf and staggered to his feet. He straightened his cloak and waited for further orders, but Planiss turned to Mark.

'*Now* we can go after our friends. May the good spirits be with us ... and them!'

With that, he dragged the door open one last time and the three of them stepped out into the blinding snow. The blizzard had lost none of its energy. With an effort, they pushed their way through a new, deep drift which had already built up close to the door, and turned to follow the huge but rapidly fading footprints which disappeared off to the south, along the railway track. The hob trailed after the elf as well as he could, wallowing through the deepest drifts as if he was drowning in them, whilst Mark brought up the rear, where he could at least make sure that the hob behaved himself.

As they battled their way forwards in the near darkness, Mark wondered if the hob really had known that the giant was in the area and likely to attack them. It was hard to believe, for it could so easily have been the hob who was snatched away, not Victoria, but it didn't occupy his mind for long. The thought of what Victoria might be enduring at that very moment, or even if she was still alive, was slowly exploding inside his head, and unwanted tears of pure desperation were beginning to fill his eyes as Planiss broke into his gloomy thoughts. The elf had stopped suddenly and was slipping his bow from his back. Mark reached for his own at once, although he doubted if he could do anything useful with it, and peered into the storm.

'What is it? Can you see them?' shouted Mark eagerly above the howling wind, just before it snatched his hood from his head and flattened it out across his shoulders.

He ran up to the elf and fumbled with his bow, trying to unfold it, but Planiss reached out and gripped Mark's arm, stopping him. The court elf of springs turned to face the high ridge he knew was somewhere above them to the west and raised his bow, drawing it fully and aiming high. There was no white arrow this time. Mark stared as a deep-red shaft appeared close to his bow hand and grew quickly backwards, then three crimson feathers took shape and finally touched the bowstring. Even in the poor light, Mark could see that the feathers were wet, and seconds later he knew why. Blood ran from them and onto the fingers of the elf, trickling across the back of his hand and down his straining wrist. Planiss let it go and it sped away, lost instantly in the myriad of snowflakes around them, then he lowered the bow and looked at Mark and the hob who was close behind him, trying to shelter from the snow.

'It is a blood-arrow ... an urgent call for help,' shouted the elf tiredly, as if firing it had drained what little strength remained in him. 'It will find the others. They will know that we need them now more than we have ever needed them!'

He said nothing more, but looked straight at Mark. His green eyes were bright and clear, asking Mark to trust him. Mark started to ask something, looking through the snow and gloom towards the ridge, and wondering how Planiss could be sure of his aim, but before he could speak the elf had folded his bow away and was moving onwards again, following the disturbed snow. Mark leant into the wind, and with the hob sandwiched safely between them once again, followed close behind.

The blood-arrow flew and flew, over the hidden ridge at first, then far across the full breadth of Farndale. The magic within it gave it the long life and huge range it needed, as only a blood-arrow of the court elves can possess. It soared upwards, reached its dizzy peak, than dipped downwards, gathering terrible speed as it raced through the blizzard to an unseen target far below. Somewhere down there, three tired court elves were making their way up the valley at speed, quite unaware of the disaster which had unfolded up at the miners' store. The blood-arrow would find them, though. There was no doubt of that.

Sheriff's Pit

With his long strides, Jack-in-irons was soon far away from the miners' store and the annoying little darts which the light elves had dared to fire his way. As he loped along, with his spike-covered club slung over his shoulder and his bare toes pushing the snow into piles with each gigantic step, he grinned. It was a nasty grin, from an even nastier face. His lips were flabby and drooping, and saliva was streaming from them and dripping off the end of his chin. A short, flat nose was flanked by cavernous nostrils which flared wide open as he marched along, and his breath puffed out from them in cloudy bursts – like an angry bull's. His bloodshot eyes, which were the size of dinner plates and so far apart that he could almost see his own ears, gazed unblinkingly, straight ahead. He had no fear of being followed, not him. Jack feared no one in either of his worlds – that of mortals, or the unseen one of elves and hobgoblins – for he existed in a murky place somewhere between them both, and was happy to find his supper in either, whoever it might be.

As the blood-arrow of Planiss soared up into the night sky, Jack was already half a mile along the disused railway track, in the thick of the snowstorm. His fists were full and their grip was all-powerful. Victoria was close to unconscious, and being thrown about like a soft toy as the giant's unusually long arms swung back and forwards relentlessly. Her only remaining thought was to keep awake, to live and somehow help Elspeth, but it required a mental effort that was almost beyond her as the monstrous fingers squeezed the breath from her lungs and half strangled her at the same time. She couldn't feel her right arm at all, as those fingers had dug cruelly into her armpit for far too long and stopped her blood from flowing to it. Her other arm seemed to be working normally, though, and so she concentrated on keeping a tight hold of her thumb stick. However, it was now nothing more than a pretty walking stick, of no use to her or anyone else.

Still clinging to the edge of consciousness, she caught an occasional glimpse of Agoriff swinging about on the end of the other hairy arm. He was still upside down, but she couldn't tell if he was alive or dead as his cloak hung around his head and shoulders. The chains around Jack's waist and over his shoulders still rattled and clanked, whilst the shrivelled heads strung out along them bounced about crazily. In a strange, almost grotesque way they reminded Victoria of one of Elspeth's toys – pretty balls on a string fastened across her pram for her to play with – but it was a ridiculous thought, she knew, probably conjured up in her tortured mind to lessen the horror of what they really were. She closed her eyes, thought of her baby sister, and tried to find a little more determination from somewhere, anywhere, so that she might see her again one day.

She hadn't screamed once. She didn't have the breath, the strength, or the will to, and in any case, she was certain that no one would hear her. Instead, she clamped her teeth together and squeezed her lips shut against the pain as Jack suddenly stumbled over a snow-covered boulder and jolted her aching body.

No one can help me now. Not Mark, or even an army of elves. Oh, Mark. Where are you? We never said goodbye ... I'm going to die, I just know I am.

212

She surprised herself with her own calm acceptance of that fact, seeing both of her sisters in her mind as she did so, and her father too, as they all played in the garden together at Willow Garth. She was so very sorry for what she was about to bring to them all. More sorrow. First her mother, then Elspeth ... and now her, lost forever without a trace, somewhere out on the moors in a snow storm.

As her grim thoughts drifted back to the painful present, she realised that she was far less frightened than she should have been, and was more worried about the others back at the miners' store. After all, there was still hope for *them*. Images of mangled bodies lying scattered across the floor of that miserable little place were just beginning to fill her aching mind when she started to slide out of the giant's grasp. He soon put that right, throwing her up and grabbing her by the waist instead. The pain of the violent jerk almost made her pass out, but at least she could breathe properly at last, as the pressure came off her bruised ribs.

Only a few minutes later, and with the storm still howling in their ears, Jack and his two latest victims approached an old and much-repaired barrier of barbed wire, posts and rails. Most of the rails were rotten and in various stages of falling off, whilst the equally decrepit posts leant drunkenly in different directions, with snow steadily piling up against them. The giant stood still for a moment and took his first quick glance behind him before casually casting his booty over the fence and into the drifts on the other side, as if they were nothing more than two freshly killed lambs. They landed with a dull *crump*, face down in the snow and close to each other, dazed ... or dead.

The ground sloped steeply there, and Victoria, who was now coming to her senses with the help of the snow down the back of her neck and in her ears, felt herself sliding as soon as she tried to get up. She dug her toes in quickly and lifted her head to look around. Despite the poor visibility, she could see that the fence was part of a large square, perhaps thirty feet long on each side. Inside it, the ground fell towards a low, central area, where a few thin gorse bushes were being shaken about by the wind. She lifted her head higher still and saw that those bushes were literally clinging to life around the edge of a wide hole or depression of some kind, which she couldn't see into.

On the outside of the fence, a well-worn, painted sign swung in the wind on its last remaining nail. It read:

SHERIFF'S PIT
DANGER
KEEP OU
By order of the Witcher Mining Co.

The missing **T** made no difference to Victoria. She couldn't see the sign from where she was, and perhaps that was just as well. Sheriff's Pit was all that remained of a long-abandoned lift – a straight, dark shaft which plunged hundreds of feet down to the abandoned ironstone mines which burrowed their way into the bowels of the hill somewhere underneath her. It was as dangerous a place as any could be, the final resting place for many overly inquisitive sheep, and probably other creatures, besides. Victoria stretched up to see Agoriff more clearly, and shouted his name out above all the noise. His head was under his cloak, and Victoria was extremely relieved when it finally moved – she reached out for his arm, but immediately started to slip down the slope again. She let out a short cry before ramming the end of her stick into the snow to try to stop herself, and hanging on to it grimly. Then Agoriff started to slide too, and the awful realisation that they were both in extreme danger hit him as he finally regained consciousness: in one frantic movement he threw his cloak back over his shoulders and made a grab for Victoria's stick. He already knew that it was their only hope.

The two of them slid inexorably towards the greedy hole in the ground. The stick gouged a line through the snow and grass, leaving a green trail, but it couldn't stop them – the slope was too steep and too icy. A moment later they were sliding past the little gorse bushes. Ignoring the sharp thorns, Agoriff grasped at one within reach of his spare hand, but it came straight out of the ground. They were beyond any help now. As their feet came to the edge of the pit's gaping mouth and Victoria saw what was about to happen, she screamed for the first time.

Then, in that final second, when all seemed lost, the thumb stick reacted. Agoriff, court elf of trees and master of all things wooden, was gripping it tightly, and this may have helped a great deal. As they fell helplessly over the edge, the stick quickly lengthened in their hands, suddenly spanning the eight-foot-wide hole like a makeshift bridge, but sagging ominously as their fall was stopped with an arm-wrenching jolt. They hung on. They didn't know how, but they did, as they bounced up and down and their feet pedalled uselessly above the blackness of the shaft below them. Victoria stared at Agoriff. There was cold terror in her wide, staring eyes, a terror which made her stomach curl up tight and her feeble hold on the stick steadily weaken as the strength started to drain out of her bare, numb fingers. She shouted out, her voice rising to a shriek.

'I ... can't ... hold ... on. *I ... can't ... do ... it!*'

Agoriff was devastated.

'Hold tight!' he shouted back. 'Be brave and be strong!'

As Victoria's grip continued to fail, the stick reacted again. It started to shorten! Victoria watched, horrified, as

215

the ends of it moved inch by inch, steadily inwards towards the edge of the hole. She couldn't understand it.

Oh my God! It's trying to kill us quickly, to get it over with. We're finished!

She was wrong, though. She and Agoriff started to slip downwards, but with the incredible stick now bent like a huge bow and its ends scraping down the sides of the shaft. Victoria's last thoughts before they disappeared into the ground were of Agoriff's words. She held on as bravely as she could, and as tightly as she could, but she was utterly terrified.

They endured it together, drawing on each other's determination to live, jerking about like misused puppets as the stick bumped its way down, and further down, with them dangling below it. Soil and stones broke away from the sides of the shaft and disappeared noiselessly below them, and Agoriff's hold was even broken once, leaving him swinging by one hand, but countless years of tree climbing helped him regain it quickly. And still they bumped their way deeper and deeper, down into the hill. The light soon faded away and turned to grey. Then black. Then blackest black, where eyes are pointless and only demons see. The appalling descent seemed to take an eternity, and the two brave things suffering it knew that the stick could break or slip at any time. Loose stones from above continued to fall down on them, or past them – one large one even hit the stick between their hands. But they still hung on.

Then, without any warning in that inky darkness, it was all over. They landed on something soft and wet, before falling against the damp sides of the shaft with the choking reek of decay filling their nostrils and lungs in an instant, almost overpowering them. It was absolutely silent, too, once the last trickle of soil from up above them had died away. Victoria stared into the darkness and rubbed her eyes, but she couldn't see a thing, not even her fingers. She even thought that she might be dead, and tried to push herself up, but a searing pain in her shoulder made her catch her breath.

Then, joy of joys, a green elf light spluttered into life and grew stronger. As the small, glowing sphere floated away from Agoriff's shaking hands and drifted a short way up the shaft, they were greeted with a sickening and horrific sight. They were squatting in a thick soup of mud, stones and rotting sheep. The remains of their curly fleeces, now flat and shapeless without flesh to fill them out, formed a decomposing woolly carpet. Half-bare, eyeless skulls lay all around them, some with gaping, bare-bone jaws and rows of ugly worn-out teeth, now all tinted green in the hovering light.

They stared at each other, speechless ... and smiled. Their smiles widened. Then, in that most gruesome of places and in defiance of almost certain death, they burst into laughter. Their laughs raced up and down the shaft, echoing, until it seemed that they were back with all their friends and family again, enjoying themselves. They'd survived when all the odds were stacked high against them, survived where previously every living thing had died instantly. The thumb stick was lying at Victoria's feet, short once more, insignificant even. Its skilful magic was completed, and would probably never be surpassed.

Back up in the world of light and fresh air, high above those two laughing souls, the blizzard raced unheedingly across the top of Sheriff's Pit. Three figures stood huddled against the old fence and its warning sign. They looked all around them, shielding their eyes from the snow with the sides of their hoods, but puzzled as to why the enormous footprints had stopped and turned away. It was only good luck – of which there had been very little that day – that stopped them as they turned to follow Jack's tracks down into the valley. On the other side of the fence, five yards away, a spindly gorse bush lay flattened and covered with only a thin layer of fresh snow. It was enough.

They turned back into the wind and followed the line of the fence, with Mark lifting his knees high to get through the deepening drifts. The hob, who had his arms wrapped tightly around his body as he jumped up and down to warm up, stayed behind one of the thicker corner posts, where he'd managed to find some protection from the wind. The drifts were up to his chest, and he wouldn't get through them without a ridiculous struggle. The other two soon saw the place where Jack's captives had obviously been thrown and, with dread rising in his throat, Mark scrambled over the fence at once, before steadying himself and peering towards the ominous pit. Planiss knew of its reputation for taking lives with impunity, and shouted to him.

'Don't move, or you could be down there with them!'

His tone didn't invite any further discussion. Mark stepped back to the fence and held onto it, as Planiss slipped between the rails and joined him – his boots barely sank into the snow and he showed little sign of sliding on the treacherous slope. With a wave of his arm, he signalled to Mark to stay where he was, and started to approach the pit himself, stepping sideways and taking the very greatest care. He was soon kneeling at the very edge of the gaping hole, and saw the marks left by Victoria, Agoriff ... and their stick.

'They were here!' he yelled back at Mark, but this time with a trace of hope in his voice. 'Tie this to the post and make sure it stays there.'

Planiss made his way back up to Mark, pulling at something on his cloak as he went, then making peculiar movements with his hands in the air – Mark wondered if it was part of a ritual, or some kind of elfish magic. The elf reached him and held something out for him to take, and only then did Mark understand, as he saw the fine silken thread between his outstretched fingers. The wind snatched it away and threw it around – it was the spider's silk from which the cloaks were woven, thinner than thin, but stronger than steel. After several failed attempts, Mark finally captured it and wound it around the post a dozen times, before wrapping his arms around it too, and bracing himself. Planiss leant towards him and shouted into his ear.

'I'm going down. Be prepared, Mark. They may be dead.' Mark's face fell. 'But they may not be. The stick was with them, and it may have helped them to survive. It looks like they were alive when they got here, and that, at least, is something! Either way, I must go to them at once.' He tugged at the thread, to test it. 'It is very deep, so watch my rope.'

'You call this a rope?' shouted Mark back, eager to cling to the flicker of hope in the elf's face and words. 'Will it hold you?' he added, incredulously.

'Me, plus you as well, if it had to. But I need you here. Keep a good hold of it, and watch out for the others. The blood-arrow will bring them to us.' Planiss turned to go, but added an afterthought, and not as loudly. 'Watch the hob. I don't trust him. He seemed to know what would happen to us up here. Beware!'

The elf plucked the tight thread with his fingers just as the first glimmer of dawn threatened to show itself at last.

'If I don't come back, you must tell them what has happened. Even if I fall, there may still be hope for Victoria and Agoriff.'

With that, the brave elf made his way back to the pit, walking backwards and pulling the thread from his cloak as he did so. He was soon standing at the edge of it, then slipping his bow from his back and circling the thread twice around one of its smooth limbs. Finally, he looked up into the sky, perhaps for the last time, and walked backwards into the void: the thread suddenly tightened, and Mark held on even more determinedly whilst the wind sang on it like a boiling kettle. Twenty feet away, the hob was motionless against his post – frozen stiff perhaps, wondered Mark – and so, more or less alone, he prayed that somehow his dearest Victoria was still alive. He suddenly felt sick and light-headed at the thought of losing her. It would all be his fault, and he'd have a long, sad life to grieve for her, and wonder how that life might have turned out if she had been a part of it.

Planiss slipped down his thread, like the largest and strangest of spiders. One hand gripped his bow, which slowed his descent and stopped the thread from cutting straight through his fingers, whilst the other grasped the edge of his cloak, as the thread was steadily pulled from it. He stared down anxiously into the darkness as he went, kicking himself clear of the side each time he came too close to it, but he could see nothing below him and was even starting to lose hope. Then, after several frightening minutes, those hopes were rekindled as he imagined that he could see something glowing, something green, way down there. Then it was real, without any doubt, and hope turned to sweet relief, then joy. If Agoriff was alive, then Victoria might be also, and he shouted her name downwards. His words were deafening in the quiet shaft, as echoes ricocheted back to him again and again, but they were mixed with a chorus of other words bouncing back up … and not his own.

'Mark-ark-ark! … Is that you-ou-ou? … We're down here-ere-ere … We're okay-kay-kay … Be careful-ful-ful!'

Victoria heaved herself up onto her feet, cradling her aching shoulder and arm with her good one, and craning her neck to stare upwards. Planiss' feet suddenly emerged from the blackness above the green light, quickly followed by the rest of him, before he landed softly on the woolly mess. Victoria couldn't hide her delight in seeing him, Mark or no Mark, and the three of them clasped each other tightly as they stood there for long seconds in total silence, in the cold, wet filth, breathing in the stench, but so thankful that they were together again, and still alive.

*   *   *

Over a mile from where Mark stood patiently waiting for any news from the depths of the pit, and far, far below him in the valley bottom, the blood-arrow also waited. The court elves rarely used them, and Planiss, who had just fired it across the valley, had done so only once before in his long and eventful life. On that day, Trifillo had been taken from them all, but even the scores of light elves who'd rushed to their assistance couldn't bring the court elf of fire back to them.

This arrow stood almost upright in shallow snow, close to the lane where it passed by the village church – in fact, just where it was intended to be, and a neat circle of snow was stained red around its partly buried shaft. The court elves would find it there, but no one else in creation would, not even a dark elf, for it was conjured up from within the very soul of a court elf. Only after it was found and interpreted, would it disappear forever, its work done.

Flinnor came upon it first. He was ahead of the others, as usual, but not as far ahead as he would have wished. Since the first hint of daylight, he'd been flying for short distances in-between the frustrating times when he could only wait for the others, willing them to catch him up. It was annoying for the other two elves as well, particularly Roall, whose ribs ached miserably and left him in poor shape for a long, fast run. Still, he fully understood Flinnor's impatience, and did his best to keep up.

Flinnor flew up to the blood-arrow in a smooth glide which had started two hundred yards earlier. It was like a beacon to him. He could feel its energy and urgency growing as he came closer to it, despite the falling snow which had hidden it from him to begin with. At last the sky elf understood why he'd felt that something was amiss for the previous hour or more. He was kneeling beside it, but not touching it, as Roall and Stirran came jogging around the bend in the lane. They knew at once what was waiting for them, for the same uneasiness had crept into their minds as they'd run along in the pale gloom before a hidden dawn.

'Where are they?' panted Roall, as he ran up to Flinnor.

It was all that he needed to know. Just like the others, his instincts had already told him who'd sent it, and when. Flinnor pushed the stained snow out of the way and looked closely at the arrow, noting the angle of it, and how far it had buried itself into the ground. He looked up at Roall, alarmed, as he touched the shaft lightly.

'They are close to the old track beyond the ridge road,' he said, confirming the thoughts of the other two.

'It is from Planiss ... and Agoriff is in great peril!' Flinnor ran his fingers slowly through the bloodied feathers of the fletchings, but his companions knew that there was more to come. The sky elf's voice dropped as the enormity of the arrow's message became horribly clear.

'Victoria, too,' he whispered under his breath.

There was no worse news for them than this. Their whole being, their very reason for existing, was to protect the innocent from the wicked, and suddenly they knew that they may have failed this time. Flinnor stood up, and together the three of them turned silently to face the eastern slopes of the valley – if only they could have seen further than twenty paces away. Snow had started to settle on their cloaks before anyone said anything.

'You must fly ahead Flinnor,' urged Roall. 'Get to them quickly and do what you can! We shall follow on foot, alas.'

The climb would be a steep one for them – straight up the side of the valley – and a slow one, too, even for elves in a hurry. Flinnor nodded and took a few paces forward before slipping into another glide, but now with a different purpose and vigour. He soared away from them, curving upwards and sideways as he judged where his destination lay, and was soon out of sight, enveloped by the falling snow. Roall and Stirran left the lane, cutting across the edge of the church graveyard and running past the very gravestone which Scribber had hidden behind with the bronze key warm in his pocket. The ground started to rise as the lower slopes of the hillside eventually greeted them, and up they went, climbing over gates or darting through the less dense hedgerows, on a direct course for the place from where the blood-arrow had been fired.

*   *   *

At the bottom of Sheriff's Pit, Planiss did what he could to retrieve some kind of order from the chaos. He comforted Victoria, whose injuries were already easing as her cloak worked its healing powers on her, and told her that Mark was somewhere high above them, safe and unharmed. Dried blood from Jack-in-irons was splattered across her face and cloak and smeared on her cheek after her attempts to wipe it off, but at least the blood wasn't hers. In the green elf light, Agoriff examined their foul prison and soon discovered the only signs of openings in the curved stone walls. He could see the top part of a large door, presumably through which generations of brave miners had once come and gone, and realised that the rest of it was buried beneath the debris he was standing on.

Sadly, the door had also been bricked up, and bricked up well. Close to their feet he could also see a small square opening. It might have been just large enough to squeeze through, if it wasn't for the iron bars which crossed it. Agoriff dropped to his knees and pulled at them, with his nose uncomfortably close to the stinking floor, but they were solid, set into a strong timber frame and fastened with a bolt on the far side which he couldn't reach, however hard he tried.

Through the bars, there was only more pitch darkness and silence, although there was a faint waft of warmer air drifting in, tainted with a stench which surpassed even the one under his nose. He looked back up at the others, ill at ease despite Planiss now being with them: Jack would have had a good reason for throwing his victims down here, but those reasons were best not talked about yet, he decided. His voice was tense, but there was no trace of panic as he spoke.

'I can't see anything out there ... but I don't like the look of what I can see just *here!*'

He was now examining the edges of the barred opening, and even in the feeble light he could easily see bloodstains and many deep gouges in the timber frame, presumably where countless dead creatures had been dragged out of the pit to become someone's meal.

'I do not know how to get out of here, but we must get out quickly, that much I *do* know!,' he said, standing up and stretching his legs ... much relieved to have his nose further from the floor.

'Can you get us up the same way you came down?' He looked hopefully at Planiss, but the tree elf should have known better.

Planiss was expecting the question and there could be no avoiding the truth just for Victoria's benefit.

'I came down like a spider, my friend, but none of us

224

have the strength to climb three hundred feet back up like one. We need to be pulled up on a rope, unless we can all sprout wings in the next few minutes. First, I must let Mark know that you are safe, Victoria. Cover your ears!'

Planiss looked up the shaft, and whilst the others did as he'd asked, he let out a shrill, piercing call which seemed to race up and down the entire length of it. Far above, Mark jumped as he heard the elf's thin but clear words come to him above the noise of the wind ... even the hob's head came up with a snap.

'We are all unharmed, Mark, but we need a long rope ... a *very* long rope. We do not know how long we have ... Please, hurry!'

Mark's heart almost skipped a beat with joy as he learnt that everyone was alive down there, but he didn't know what he could do to help. Any ropes which had been in the old store would be rotten and far too short, and although he had an ideal one back at the farm it would take hours to go and fetch it in these conditions. As his newfound happiness quickly evaporated and alarm crept up to tap him on the shoulder, he felt himself breaking out in a cold sweat, despite already being nearly frozen.

*   *   *

Flinnor's timing was immaculate. He emerged from the blizzard, fast and low, his arms spread wide and his wet hair streaming behind him. When Mark turned around to see what the faint rustle was, Flinnor was already standing there with his face aglow, shaking the snow out of his hair and cloak. Mark quickly told him everything – sparing him the details, but letting him know that no one had been killed so far, amazingly. Flinnor sucked in a sharp breath when he heard that Jack was behind all of this, but the relief was plain to see on his face as Mark repeated the words which had just floated up from the depths of Sheriff's Pit. He looked up at Mark as he brushed some ice from his legs.

'I could fly and find your rope at the farm, but I am sure that it would be too heavy for me to fly back with. I must return to Roall and see if he can think of something. I …'

He was interrupted as the hob stepped out from behind Mark, where he'd been trying to find some better shelter than that on offer at the fence post.

'I knows a way … if yer interested,' he yelled up at them.

The hob paused, as if he had sudden doubts about getting more deeply involved and being responsible for what might happen next. He banged his arms around his body, waiting for inspiration.

'It were my idea to come this way in't first place,' he finally mumbled, 'along past this 'ere pit.' He could see that the others could barely hear him, so he spoke up. 'What I 'ave in mind – it's, well, it's a secret way to the bottom of Sheriff's pit through the back part of them spriggan caves … if you be brave enough to try it, that is.' He stopped again, suddenly wishing that he hadn't started at all.

'To get to your friends quick we *could* risk it. It'll sound too dangerous to you by 'arf, I knows, but it'll be faster than runnin' around t'valley like 'eadless chickens, tryin' to find ropes which'd more 'n likely be no good anyways!'

He had their full attention now, and was pleased with himself for it. Some unfinished business of his still burned in his mind, but he wasn't about to tell them about that – not yet, anyway. It was bright and clear to him, though, as he closed his eyes and saw Redcap's laughing face and the bread knife in his hand.

Oh yes, I'll be there when that pig sticks 'is snout out a bit too far, and take it off for him. Tit for blinkin' tat, I says. An ear for a nose. I'll teach him what's what, even if it's wiv me last breath!

Up above them, the weather was improving. The sun was gaining strength somewhere far above the clouds as the wind and snow below them gradually lost theirs. What had been impenetrable cloud cover was now fragmenting into wisps and streaks, with even a hint of icy blue briefly peeping through here and there. Mark and Flinnor bent down lower to hear what the hob had to say, but it couldn't have been good, for Flinnor's head dropped even further as he heard the details. Soon the hob had finished, and Mark looked into Flinnor's eyes, seeking approval. There was no real choice for them, and speed was of the essence if any lives were to be saved. A reluctant nod from the elf showed that he agreed, for the hob's plan was probably the only plan that could possibly work.

Mark watched as Flinnor floated up from the ground, his arms outstretched and the wind trying its best to pull off his cloak. He was soon over the fence and edging steadily towards the top of the terrifying shaft, then he was above it, hovering like a giant dragonfly over a black pond, looking down to where he knew their friends were hopelessly stranded. Frustration filled him, for he knew that he couldn't fly into the pit without falling: he needed daylight to fly, even a glimmer would do, but light couldn't enter this pit quite as easily as everything else apparently could. He put his hands around his mouth and called downwards in high, warbling notes which, to Mark, sounded like a peculiar mixture of words and musical notes. Whatever they were, he hoped that anyone down there would at least know that someone was trying to help them. With that, Flinnor soared effortlessly up and away from the pit before disappearing towards the valley hidden somewhere below him.

Roall and Stirran had progressed surprisingly well with their exhausting scramble up the hillside when Flinnor suddenly appeared out of the storm and was standing with them again. The two other elves, seldom tired by any task thrown their way, were very happy to stop and rest. They heard Flinnor's news with great delight and much back-slapping, thankful beyond words that in this case the blood-arrow hadn't foretold of a complete disaster, only the threat of one, and five minutes later they all watched as Mark and the hobgoblin slipped their way down the slope to join them. It was not a merry meeting. The hob's plan was soon explained again, bringing a shiver down several spines which had nothing to do with the bitter wind whistling around their ears.

They listened as the hob told them how, at a safe distance, he'd once overheard two spriggans talking of the 'old way' into their caves, a tunnel which for some obscure reason was now hardly ever used. He thought that this might be their only chance of quickly getting to the bottom of Sheriff's Pit, which backed onto a part of the spriggans' vast cave system, – assuming, of course, that the way wasn't blocked by a rock fall, or flooded out. Whatever else it was, it sounded fast, and it was speed they needed now, above anything else.

The Old Way

As the storm abated and some semblance of calm descended on Farndale once more, a small group of figures careered down the steep valley side below Sheriff's Pit. Three elves, one hobgoblin and a teenager were each fired with that rare energy born from desperation, fear and determination, all rolled into one bundle of pure resolve.

They had to reach the banks of the River Seven quickly, almost half a mile away from them in the bottom of the valley, and then follow the vague directions offered by the wretched hob – a doubtful business in itself given their steadily growing distrust of him and all his ways. They leapt ditches and scrambled through or over hedges and fences, heedless of thorns, snow drifts and the crunchy, part-frozen mud in various fields and gateways. Thoughts of the plight of Victoria and the two elves at the bottom of Sheriff's Pit fuelled them perfectly, carrying them downwards with even greater speed.

And so they soon found themselves standing in the sunlight on the banks of the river, tired out and breathless, as its flooding waters rushed past them in a brown, swirling mess, carrying all kinds of rubbish along with it, even large branches and old timbers from gates and fences which had slipped into the torrent. The group paused, momentarily unsure of where to go or what to do next, until the hob stepped towards the very edge of the bank, looking first upstream, then downstream as he tried to get his bearings.

He was quite certain of what he said next, and the others had very little time and even less energy to argue.

'Follow me! The entrance is some place on this 'ere west bank. I *knows* it is.' He was staring upstream now, his hand shielding his eyes from the bright glare of the snow.

Without waiting for any remarks, he darted off in that direction, keeping close to the water's edge. The others were close behind. Several fallen trees blocked their way, but the little hob was under them in a flash and the others over them almost as quickly. Flinnor somehow resisted his instinct to fly on ahead, knowing that it would be pointless to do so, and kept his feet on the ground like the others. The hob, meanwhile, kept stopping to peer over the edge of the bank, clearly looking for something known only to him, and after five minutes of his stop-start antics, a wide smile across his chubby cheeks told everyone that he'd found it, under a large, overhanging willow tree and partially hidden in amongst drowned reeds.

There, buried in the side of the bank, was a rusty iron grating. Water from the swollen river rushed through its bars and disappeared into the darkness of a spillway or some kind of underground stream just behind it, although the bars were almost blocked with branches and other clutter which had been washed downstream. Before the others could even move, the hob was down on his stomach in the mud and snow, trying to pull the tangled mess away with his bare hands. He shouted to the others as he worked.

'We 'ave to move this thing! From what them spriggans said, this is the start of the old way ... an' now 'tis *our* way.'

The elves looked dubiously at the grating, the cold, filthy water, and the hole it was disappearing into. More or less the same thoughts crossed all of their minds.

Surely this is some kind of a prank, one of the hob's tricks. What would be the point of dying somewhere down there? That would not help anyone in the pit.

'We are elves and a lad, not salmon and otters! Even *we* can't go down *there*,' gasped Stirran as he stared down at the hob incredulously.

The elf wasn't fearful of very much in his world, or even Mark's, but he was convinced that anyone going into the spillway would be drowned in a few seconds – if their neck wasn't broken first. It would be a needless waste of life and nothing more, as far as he could see. The hob looked back up over his shoulder at Stirran.

'I'll agree with 'e that it don't look too good, an' admit that them spriggans talked as if it were dry when they jumped down 'ere … but we can't be stood 'ere gossipin' about it like old dears at a blinkin' garden party.' His voice got a little louder. 'Do we try it or don't we? There's no other way we can get to that pit quick-like … an' you all knows that well enough!'

What he said was undeniably true, but not quite what the others wanted to hear. Fed up with talking, the hob returned to his task of clearing the grating, but this time he was quickly joined by the others. After a short struggle and several skinned knuckles, they pulled the heavy grating from its muddy home and up onto the bank: the water seemed pleased to be unrestricted at last, and poured happily into the forbidding hole which was now clear for all to see. They looked at each other silently, not voicing the obvious question.

'I'll go first,' piped up Mark decisively, answering it for them.

He was beginning to worry that they would be too late to help the others and he wanted to get on with it. The elves had not forgotten his bravery in the crypt and admired him for showing the same courage now.

'Very well,' replied Roall, 'but if you go down first, we

must all follow quickly, so that we can help each other out ... if need be. Agreed?' He looked down at the hob, who he thought might be the one in the group to show some reluctance.

'Count me in!' said the hobgoblin with surprising pluckiness. 'I'll go second if you wants,' he added, looking up at Mark, 'and these 'ere elves can follow on when they feels up to it.'

The cheeky words of the hob were meant light-heartedly and taken so, for all their lives were undoubtedly at risk, and no one wanted to spend what might be their last few moments alive arguing.

'It is agreed, then,' concluded Roall. 'May the good spirits be with each of us ... and especially with our brave hob here.'

Mark looked down into the gushing spillway apprehensively. He pinched his nose, wrapped his other arm around his body, wished that he'd gone to church more often recently, and jumped down it without even a splash. The hob followed immediately, just as he said he would, and four seconds later the three elves had all joined them. The riverbank was suddenly deserted, and five brave souls were gambling with their lives once more, but for the very best of reasons. The water still raced down the spillway as if nothing unusual had happened, whilst a few, straggling snowflakes instantly melted as they landed on the grating which now lay discarded amongst dozens of slushy footprints in the snow.

* * *

Deep inside a hill, and far, far from the little gathering who had risked everything at the riverbank, Jack-in-irons lay in his cavern. It was a depressing place in every way ... not that he cared, though. He wasn't interested in home comforts or pleasantries, only killing and eating, and usually (but not always) in that order, with only a short pause between the two. His home was a damp, badly lit rock chamber, a remnant of the great mining days in the valley. Its entrance door was a vast oak affair, now hanging on the sole remaining hinge-pin near its top, and set deep into the stonework. Only Jack had the strength to drag that heavy door open and shut, and so he was unlikely to be disturbed by anyone stupid or nosy enough to come visiting.

Having thrown his next snack down Sheriff's Pit, as he sometimes did to save carrying it the long way around, he'd decided to have a short doze until his appetite demanded more attention. He'd devoured a whole calf earlier that night, up near the inn on Blakey Ridge, and it was only the irresistible smell of human flesh in the miners' store which had prompted him to line up his next meal so soon after his last. He lay there now, awake again, on his back with his hands behind his head, staring up at the glow-worms on the rocky ceiling and trying to decide how long to wait before collecting his fresh food. After all, he thought, the bodies would be stiffening up before long and he *was* partial to his meat warm and still soft.

He eased himself up onto one elbow and wiped his slobbering mouth with the back of his hand before getting up and scratching his ribs with what little remained of his fingernails, his mind apparently made up. For good measure he let out a long, resonating belch, which filled the whole chamber with the putrid reek of partially digested calf, but he felt better for it. Jack left his home by the back way. Stooping to avoid the low ceiling, he began to make his way towards the ruined lift shaft where his very special breakfast of girl and elf awaited him.

*   *   *

233

It was hard to say what shocked Mark more: the freezing water which immediately soaked him to the skin, or the fact that he wasn't instantly drowned. The water from the river poured down a steep, naturally formed spillway which was just wide enough for his shoulders and just high enough to not immediately break his neck. Usually it was dry, and the spriggans who used it long ago would have had to slither down its rough floor on their backsides. Now, though, with the flood water emptying itself into the hill's innards, the journey down was at least a little easier on the buttocks, if numbingly cold.

To start with, he could see nothing. That was easily the worst part of it – not knowing what he might be about to hit at bone-snapping speed, but thankfully, that horror was short-lived. He was soon made all too aware of the hob close behind him, who wailed like a demented banshee most of the way down, and then came the wonderfully reassuring glow of bobbing green lights somewhere behind him, as the three elves each lit their way downwards. The spillway turned left then right, then left again as it snaked its way deep into the hill. It was a long way, too: Mark even had time to wonder what would be waiting for them at the bottom.

A dead end, a bottomless hole, or what? Heck, if we survive this, how do we ever climb back up? If it was dry, it would be almost impossible. But with all this water? There's no bloody chance!

He put those worries aside as he tried his best to stay upright and prepared to hold his breath, quite sure that he was about to be drowned. Then, without any warning, it was all over. With an enormous splash, he plunged feet first into a large but fairly shallow pool. It was stony-bottomed and as cold as death. He was pitched forward onto his chest by his own speed, and before he could get up the hob landed heavily and painfully on the backs of his legs. As he struggled, wide-eyed and tight-lipped, to get his head up above the surface and take a breath, he saw blurred green light and black shadows darting about on the stone walls around the pool as the elves arrived and proceeded to land one by one on top of him and the hob.

With a struggle, Mark fought his way out from under them all and eventually managed to get to his feet before coughing up a lot of water, whilst the elves untangled themselves and stood up too, thigh deep in the mucky water. They looked at each other, half-drowned rats that they were, and wanted to shout out for joy, but they were wary of what might be down there with them ... hiding and waiting. They smiled and coughed some more, though, as Mark punched the air with delight, momentarily forgetting the dire situation they now found themselves in. Bathed in green light, they made their way to the edge of the water and stood shivering amongst the boulders and driftwood there, dripping wet and unsure what their next move should be.

Stirran already had his bow in his hands and his fingers at its string, whilst Roall grasped his freyal tightly and stared hard into the dark corners which the elf light couldn't reach. They could see a pathway along the edge of the pool, albeit a rough and rock-strewn one. The hob nodded towards it, shrugging, as if he wished he could offer them something better, and so they turned and started to make their way forward, stepping over the larger boulders and scattering the frogs which seemed to be everywhere. There was really nowhere else for them to go.

The cold water lapped gently at the path's edge and its sleepy notes echoed from the rock walls which surrounded them, blending together into one continuous and somehow disquieting tune. Mixed in amongst it all was the constant plink-plink of water dripping from an unseen roof somewhere above, like the very start of a heavy rainstorm. Unfortunately, it would all perfectly mask the sound of anyone who might be following them, or waiting up ahead in some dark recess, but it couldn't be helped.

Actually, apart from the frogs, there was no living thing in those uninviting waters. Nothing more substantial could surive there, for it was a pool one week and a mud hole the next, littered with a thousand slippery rocks and little else – devoid of food, warmth and light.

Life there was not, but death there most certainly was, or more precisely, half-death. *She* was in it somewhere. She was part of it, and in many ways she was even the same as it: chilled to the marrow, inert but threatening. Always devious.

The Powler Hag existed in the same indistinct world as Jack-in-irons, who even then was striding down his passageway with food on his mind, on his way to the bottom of Sheriff's Pit. She, too, was half in the world of men and half outside it, one moment real enough to be standing on the deserted ridge road on a warm summer's evening, breathing in the honey scent of the heather, the next, nothing more than an unexpected shiver down a spine, or perhaps a wisp of evening mist down by the river.

As the pool spread further into the hillside it became gradually deeper ... and stiller. The lapping waves died away to nothing more than an occasional ripple, and even the incessant dripping stopped, leaving the surface calm and lifeless, like black glass. Powler much preferred this part of her realm. Even from deep in the water she could easily see the distant green lights bobbing their way along her path, and hear the clattering as rock fell against rock under the stumbling feet of her clumsy visitors. She'd been aware of them from the moment they'd entered her world, for she was mistress of it in every respect, as many a doomed spriggan had learnt over the years – seconds before they drowned in her arms. It annoyed her that they were too cowardly to use this way any more, and as she swam along at the bottom of the pool, just above the dark mud and its deserted wormholes, she thought to herself in her unhurried, calculating way.

They've got no guts, not a single one of them. No sense of sport. Boring, so very boring … But there's some hope of sport today, it seems!

Her tattered rags and long, knotted hair were intertwined and swirled behind her as she swam, whilst her unblinking eyes moved independently, like a pike's, as they followed the murky lights up above her. Her mouth gaped wide open, lined with pointed, broken teeth as green as the slime covering the rocks around her. Up she came from her lurking place, swimming to shallower parts where she could see the five figures on the path more clearly. She already knew just what they were, every last one of them.

Elves are too fleshless, men too heavy, she thought, considering her menu with an evil composure. *The hobgoblin's for me. Oh, yes … light, tender, meaty, all in one.*

Further up she came, quite invisible to them all, not causing the slightest ripple on the surface. They were now approaching her favourite striking place, where the water was deep, even close to the pathway, and where a particularly awkward rock or two would hold their attention. Her thin, bony arm reached out in front of her and she ran her tongue hungrily between her jagged teeth as she swept up towards the surface. She only had eyes for the hobgoblin now.

There was very little to see from up above the surface in those last few seconds. Before he knew what was happening, a grey, gnarled hand with hideously long fingernails slipped out of the water, grasped the hob's ankle and pulled him into the pool in one smooth but lethal movement. It was so fast that he didn't even call out. There was nothing more than a quiet splash and he was gone. He'd been at the back of the group, and the others spun around at once, but there was nothing for them to see.

For almost half a minute they looked at each other or at the place where the hob had been, shocked and frightened, with only the croaking of a distant frog to break the interminable silence, then Mark called out as loudly as he dared. The others joined in, their voices echoing from distant, hidden walls as they stood there with bows half drawn, looking for a target or any sign that he was still there. But as the minutes passed, it became clear that the hob wouldn't be crawling out of the water, soaked to the skin and embarrassed, and the others could do little more than watch several perfect rings grow and spread out across the water from around the pathway, before disappearing into the darkness ... just as the hobgoblin had.

Even more precious time slipped past as Mark walked back along the path, leaving the elves to search amongst the rocks at the water's edge. Their search was in vain. The hob had gone, along with his plan ... and gone forever. They eventually accepted that this was so, and although it was difficult, they made the decision to give up the search and continue their way further into the hillside. In truth, they all felt that something far from accidental had happened, although they had no idea what it could have been, and didn't really want to discuss any of the more disturbing possibilities. They could only move on quickly, before someone else suffered the same fate.

Wet through and numb from the penetrating cold, they continued to pick their way along the pathway, still secretly hoping that the hob would suddenly surprise them all and climb out of the water, coughing and spluttering. Flinnor was unable to take to the air in the darkness, from where he could have searched further, but in any case, being on the path seemed far more preferable to him than being over the sinister water. Instead, they all kept close together, wishing for more light to see by, but fearful of what or who it might draw towards them if they used it.

Roall, who was still at the front and now the only one with a light, at last saw the rear wall emerging from the darkness ahead. He ran towards it, half tripping but not really caring any more, such was his eagerness to leave the dreadful pool behind and find a way to higher and drier places. He waited for the others to catch up, shivering as he held up his light. The wall was sheer, rising straight from the deepest part of the pool, and there was no sign of the pathway continuing past this point, where it had widened out into what appeared to be a small, rocky beach. They could see the remains of a wooden jetty, partly on dry ground where some of the walkway survived, and partly in the water, where what was left of the supporting posts showed only as a line of waterlogged, rotting stumps just above surface.

Roall lifted his arm higher still and at last his elf light became much brighter, enlarging the space around them, but making them feel small and vulnerable as they dared to take in more of their surroundings. Near the top of the rear wall they could see a huge iron wheel with a chain still hanging from its rusting rim: an equally large iron bucket – less its bottom – was still attached to the end of the chain. Once, it might have lifted water from the pool and up into the vast mine system which overran the hills for miles in every direction, but now only spriggans and bats lived up there. Those infested caves were now far less productive ... and infinitely more dangerous.

In the brighter light they soon discovered a doorway set into the rear wall. It was tall and wide – no doubt meant for use by large miners – but now it was partially blocked by fallen rocks, and the remains of the door itself lay flat on the ground, almost buried beneath them. The group gathered together beside it and Roall thrust the light into the space behind, where they could see well-worn stone steps rising steeply from the rock fall and curving steadily around to the right: the rocks had come mostly from a collapsed roof there, leaving the steps intact. Mark wondered what might be waiting up them, just out of sight around the curved walls. The elves had similar fears, and Stirran lowered his bow to say what was on his mind. As it happened, he was speaking for all of them.

'I do not know what happened to the hob back there, and I would rather not know, really.' He stared out across the water and shook his head sadly. 'There is no other way out of here that I can see, so we must take this one – the others must be desperate for help in the pit by now. Which of us is going first?'

Mark stepped forward.

'It's got to be my turn, if you can light it up a bit for me.' He started to climb over the rubble to get to the steps beyond.

'Hold on there!' interrupted Stirran, who knew very well that apart from being his usual brave self, Mark was impatient to get to Victoria. If he were to lead, he might rush on ahead, perhaps straight into a group of spriggans.

'Thank you for your kind offer, Mark, but I think that this is elf work,' he said politely. 'We are slightly smaller targets, and quieter, too.' Mark stopped and looked back at Stirran over his shoulder. 'We don't know what we'll find up there, do we?' added the elf. 'And by the way, as far as taking turns is concerned, who jumped down that spillway first?'

Stirran hoped that he hadn't offended the lad. Mark seemed disappointed to have to stand back, but he knew that Stirran was right. Befittingly, the court elf of rocks led the way, thrilled to be leaving the water behind him and getting in amongst dry, predictable stone. Roall followed, then Mark, with Flinnor bringing up the rear. He glanced behind him as they started to climb, still hoping that the hob would step out of the shadows and surprise them, dripping wet and ready for anything.

*   *   *

In Sheriff's Pit, three despondent figures squatted with their backs to the wall. Their knees were drawn up high and their arms were wrapped around them for a little extra warmth, but they kept their backsides well up from the floor. Victoria's cloak was over her knees, whilst the two elves had their bows across theirs. They had allowed their elf light to die down to no more than a glimmer, for fear of what may be living on the other side of their prison walls, and they were silent. Now and again a trickle of soil or a few small stones fell amongst them, or on them, but there was no other sound. Not to begin with, anyway.

It began so indistinctly that it was more like a feeling than a sound: in their minds, but not their ears. They didn't even look up at first, but simply sat and wondered idly about it. It was growing, though. Very, very slowly ... but growing for sure. Plannis was the first to lift his head and listen properly. The other two heard him move and they looked across at him, waiting for a nod or a shake of his head, but before they received either they, too, suddenly felt the slight vibration in the middle of their backs, coming from the stone wall. It was weak, but it was regular, and it was still growing.

Thump ... Thump ... Thump ... Thump ... It didn't miss a beat and it now had their full attention as they pushed themselves off the wall and listened hard. Planiss stood his bow against the wall and moved his cloak aside to find his freyal. He pulled it from his belt and the others saw that it was already a small sword. His fingers curled and uncurled around the smooth grip a few times, before he slowly stood up. The other two watched him but didn't move. The noises kept coming. Soon they were clear to hear, and soon after that they were terrifyingly loud. They knew it had to be Jack-in-irons, and they also knew that they were trapped like rats down a very long drainpipe, but worst of all, they knew in their hearts that any rescue attempts by the others were going to be too late for them. Their 'luck' had finally deserted them.

Victoria and Agoriff stood up then as well, and the three of them pressed themselves against the wall, trying to get as far as possible from the barred opening. Victoria's thumb stick was by her side, but it seemed to know that danger was close by, for it had already grown a little longer and thicker. Still the noises grew and grew, echoing up and down the shaft above them, filling it entirely. They could now hear great bursts of exhaled breath too, and began to sense the power of the giant even through the solid rock of the pit walls. More earth was shaken down into their hair from higher up the shaft, then, quite suddenly, the noise stopped and there was silence. It was even worse than the noise, for it let their imaginations run free, and they held their breath as terrifying visions of what might happen next came to them.

The silence was short-lived, for it was shattered by a bull-like snort from just outside the opening at their feet, a snort of surprise and annoyance in equal measure. The hint of green light coming from the pit told Jack that all was not as it should be, but it hardly worried him, for food was food, after all. However, this was *his* food, and he wanted it *now*. A bolt slid across and the barred door swung open. There a pause, just long enough for everyone in the pit to look at each other helplessly, before an enormous hand – and a horribly familiar one to Victoria – thrust its way in towards them. It was almost too large to fit through, but it did, and it was soon groping around on the rotting fleeces, feeling for the corpses which Jack assumed were there somewhere, waiting for him.

Instinctively, Victoria and the elves slid sideways to where they felt the safest part of the wall was – close to the hole, but to the side of it, and not *too* close. They forced themselves against it, wishing that they could melt into it as the gigantic hand felt around, like someone trying to find a light switch in the dark. In its search, it came across a sheep's skull, which it picked up and rolled between a huge finger and thumb ... then suddenly crushed like an eggshell. Another hot grunt blasted in through the opening, but now it was a grunt of raw rage, and the three prisoners reeled at the stench of his foul breath and dirty, sweating skin.

They couldn't remain undetected for long. No one could have. After a few more seconds of frantic groping by the hand, one of its fingers brushed Victoria's leg and the next moment all those fingers opened to grasp her for the second time that day. Planiss was ready, though, and he had no hesitation in bringing his freyal down with all his strength onto the thick wrist. At the same time, Victoria raised her stick above her head. It had become a spear again, but this time with a long, thin point of bright steel. Using both arms and forgetting her injured shoulder, she thrust it into the back of the hand with all her strength, as she recalled the terrible pain that same hand had inflicted on her whilst she'd been carried along in the blizzard.

It hurt Jack's hand a great deal more than he had hurt her, and a deafening roar made their eardrums ring: it was a roar of agony and uncontrolled anger, the like of which they had never heard. For good measure, Agoriff leapt to one side and drew his bow. An arrow formed at once, but Agoriff held his fire as the arm writhed about, seeking revenge, and he followed it with his aim. The arrow flew from the bow, all of two paces, and under the nail of Jack's fat thumb. It went in deeply, but was immediately snapped off as the hand was snatched out through the opening with another roar, then another, shaking the walls over and over again.

Spriggans and Bats

Stirran led the others warily up the stone steps, away from the dreadful pool. As they climbed they felt the cold and dampness behind them being gradually replaced by warmer, drier air ahead. To begin with it only smelt stale and old, but as they climbed higher it became steadily fouler, then rancid in the backs of their throats, making them want to gag. Mark pulled his hood around his mouth, dreading to think what they would find when the steps ended, but it didn't help.

The elves moved easily and silently, and Mark tried hard to, but he couldn't match their natural stealth and cunning. At last, the bobbing light ahead of him stopped and went out, but Mark wasn't sure whether to be relieved or terrified. Encouraged by Flinnor's hand in the small of his back, he felt his way up the last dozen steps and soon found the others, huddled together at the very top. They were keeping back in the deeper shadows of the stairway, from where they could gaze at the dim scene before them in relative safety.

It was a vast, almost cathedral-like space. This was no man-made mine or hall, but a natural cave, stumbled upon by miners more than a century before. It soared upwards so far that the roof was all but lost from sight, despite the light from six or seven flaming torches which flickered in their wall brackets close to the ground. Long, thin stalactites hung precariously down from it, glistening wet and alarmingly pointed, and in amongst them three large spheres of pale blue light drifted about – spriggan lights, without a doubt, but larger than any the elves had ever seen, and enormous compared to the one Mark remembered from the crypt. He watched, mesmerised, as one or other of them occasionally touched a wall or stalactite, before bouncing softly off it like a child's lost balloon and continuing on its haphazard journey. Although they could just hear some kind of shouting or arguing from a long way off, there wasn't a single spriggan to be seen in the huge cave ... but there were plenty of bats. The upper levels were teaming with them. There were roosting bats, hanging row by row, and flying bats, reeling and diving with barely a rustle from their long webbed wings. Their droppings were heaped up in tall piles below their favourite roosts, and it was these which stank. One of them was so high that it almost buried two particularly hefty stalactites which had fallen down centuries before and lay broken, one across the other.

As their eyes became used to the poor light, the group also began to notice many large nets high above their heads, slung from rock to rock, or stalactite to stalactite. Most of the bats were managing to fly clear of them and so avoid becoming spriggan supper, but Mark could see one or two careless creatures helplessly caught up in them and no doubt destined for the cooking pots.

'Which way?' he whispered. He couldn't stop thinking about Victoria and was keen to keep on the move.

'We've never been here before,' answered Stirran behind his hand. 'We have tried to get to this place many times but failed, and now we *are* here we don't know which way to go, or where to start looking for ...'

Mark guessed what was on Stirran's mind, but didn't blame him for it. He realised that the stolen freyals were very much in the thoughts of all three elves, along with

Elspeth's cure and Victoria's rescue, and fully understood what those daggers meant to them. He also remembered that many of their kind had perished whilst trying to retrieve them from the spriggans. Stirran looked embarrassed but Mark quickly helped him out.

'Don't worry, Stirran. When Vicky and the others are safe, we're bound to have time for finding other valuables. I've got one in mind myself, remember.'

He smiled reassuringly at the rock elf, but felt his own skin suddenly prickle as the enormity of the tasks in front of them reared up and temporarily overwhelmed him. They crouched there, waiting and wondering, before Mark's gloomy thoughts were finally pushed aside as he noticed the gash in Roall's cloak. He touched it inquisitively.

'I thought these were indestructible.'

Roall looked down at it. Flinnor and Stirran looked too, still unaware of what Roall had been through at Hoarfrost Hall.

'Almost so,' he replied, 'but a dark elf's sabre would test anything to its limits.' He stood up and adjusted the bow on his back. 'Follow me and watch out ... for all our sakes!'

Mark wondered exactly how close Roall had come to being killed, but any further questions would have to wait as he entered the enormous cave, staying close to the steep wall behind Roall and Stirran. Flinnor, whose neck was starting to ache from walking along looking backwards, came last yet again. As they crept along, some of the more inquisitive bats came very close, and Mark noticed that a few of them were truly gigantic. The thought of one of those furry brutes attaching itself to his head sent a crawling shiver down his spine, and he realised how terrifying it must have been for Victoria when she tangled with one in Elspeth's bedroom. It now seemed like a lifetime ago, though.

They passed two closed doors set into the walls. These were both covered in undisturbed cobwebs and locked, and so were ignored. In many places, large heaps of foul-smelling bracken had been piled up or squashed down flat – presumably forming spriggan beds – and everywhere they looked, iron pots and cauldrons, plates and knives, bottles and chewed bones lay thrown around after their last use. The group had no choice but to pick their way carefully through it all, trying not to make any noise, but it was unpleasant and difficult work.

After far too much of this, and with each of them beginning to wonder how large the cave could really be, they eventually found themselves at the entrances to two identical narrow tunnels, nestling side by side in a smooth, sheer wall. They'd also reached the very rear of the cave at last, and they now stood there in silence, waiting for someone to suggest a plan. Each of the tunnels was a little higher than Mark, but barely wide enough for two men to pass each other. Cold air was drifting out from one, and warm, stale air from the other, but otherwise, both offered only pitch darkness and unknown dangers to anyone daring to enter them. However hard they all looked, there was not a single clue as to where they might lead, but there were still no signs of any spriggans, for which they were thankful.

'We could be anywhere,' whispered Flinnor as loudly as he dared, rotating his stiff neck. 'Do we choose one of these or go back along the other side?'

Mark was crossing his fingers and hoping for a change in their luck when they heard something, or felt it through their boots. It was hard to say which. It was a deep, distant rumbling coming from the cooler of the two tunnels, and it instantly solved their dilemma. Mark and Roall disappeared into the darkness of that tunnel at once, a green light already growing brighter in Roall's fist. The others were right behind them and running.

The ground under their feet was earthy, smooth and also disturbingly well trodden, but they didn't care: they'd crept along like burglars for far too long, and now they ran hard. The freyal in Roall's free hand was long and menacing as he pulled ahead of the others, his sore ribs temporarily forgotten. Bows came to hand too, and even Mark slipped his own from his shoulders as he ran and snapped it together, having decided that it was time to put his bracer to its full and proper use, beginner or no beginner.

The tunnel had started off level, but further in it began to slope downwards and they ran all the faster for it. In fact, their speed and determination was so great that it seemed nothing could stop them – until Roall's light suddenly changed from a steady jerk-jerk-jerk to a wild swerve. The others slid to a halt and found themselves standing close to the edge of a deep and deadly chasm, stretching across the full width of the tunnel. It was a twelve-foot leap to reach its far side, but amazingly, Roall was standing on that far side, looking back at them. Unlike the others, he hadn't had any warning, and so was forced to jump before he could think. Fortunately, a youth largely misspent leaping over every thing and anything had prepared him very well, but the others, who didn't have that natural advantage, looked down nervously. Everything below the first six feet was lost in blackness, and Stirran's face fell as he kicked some stones into it but heard nothing back. They looked at each other briefly and shrugged, before turning and walking back the way they'd come.

'Now just hold on!' shouted Roall.

Twenty paces back up the tunnel, however, the others turned and sprinted downhill once more together, but even faster than before. They leapt across, one after the other, and as they did so, each of them let out an uncontrollable shout, a do-or-die shout, if ever there was one. 'Die' was, in fact, a realistic possibility, but the dice of mistress luck fell for them, not against, and so in the end 'do' it was. They all cleared the gap well enough, with a bit of scrabbling about on landing and a few more falling stones, courtesy of Flinnor. He wasn't quite so light on his feet in the dark, and he expected to hear much more about it from the others later – if there *was* a later.

'You didn't really think ...?' chuckled Stirran, but Roall was already running again and didn't hear him.

The ominous noise ahead of them was much louder now, bouncing off the walls and throbbing in their ears, whilst a most peculiar mixture of fear and hope that it might be Jack-in-irons stirred around in each of them. They reached the end of the tunnel in less than a minute. The first they knew of it was when they nearly collided with a pair of doors which filled the tunnel from side to side, both half open and well past their best, like everything else in that godforsaken place. Everyone had managed to stop just in time, and now they looked anxiously through the gap between them from the relative safety of the darkness behind. In front of them, the tunnel opened out to become much wider and higher, and two torches burned brightly there, filling the space with flickering yellow light.

Jack was there, too. The giant was sitting up against a side wall, close to one of the torches he'd lit, and next to the entrance to yet another, wider tunnel. He'd given up hitting the ground angrily with his club and was holding his enormous hairy arm up to the light, studying his wrist from different angles, but paying particular attention to the dark blood which dribbled from a long cut across the back of it. As he studied his injuries he moaned quietly under his breath – a continuous, whimpering sort of moan which sounded almost child-like and pathetic. Mark was even more surprised when he thought he saw a tear or two in the corners of the giant's eyes, as the light from the torches caught them.

Just behind Jack was the small, barred opening into Sheriff's Pit. Jack had hastily bolted it shut again after he'd received his painful injury, but out from it came something wonderful. Soft, green light. A thin shaft of it cut through the dust-filled air, casting a twisted, striped square on the ground close to the giant's feet. In an instant, it lifted the hopes of three elves and one young lad, for it told them that they were at the right place and perhaps even in time: someone was still alive in Sheriff's Pit and strong enough to put up a spirited defence, by the look of Jack's wrist.

Mark could barely contain his excitement at the thought of seeing Victoria again. Sensing this, Roall kept a steadying hand on his shoulder to stop him from rushing out to meet Jack-in-irons one to one. The giant was still whining pitifully and trying to squeeze something he couldn't see out of his thumb, as Mark whispered to the elves.

'We must do something! He'll attack them again any minute ... he's bound to, isn't he?'

'I fear there is not much that we can do,' replied Roall, and Mark's heart fell like a rock into the pit of his stomach, 'apart from take him on **now**, all of us together!' added the elf through his teeth.

Mark surprised himself then. He was actually delighted at the prospect of attacking an angry, wounded giant well over three times taller than he was, and probably twenty times stronger, but then he *was* fired with a steely determination to win ... and the certainty that he would soon free his friends in the bottom of the pit, or die in the attempt. He put his arm around Roall and unfortunately squeezed just hard enough to make Roall flinch. Despite the healing powers of his cloak, the huge bruise across his ribs was determined not to be forgotten just yet.

'Sorry,' whispered Mark apologetically. 'I'm really on your side, you know.'

'It is my *side* that I am worried about,' replied Roall, unsure whether to quietly laugh or cry.

The meadow elf's spirits were now rising, too, and one giant wasn't *that* much to tackle after all, he told himself. He tucked his freyal back into his belt and slipped his bow from his shoulder.

'We all fire at once, agreed?' There were three nods in reply. 'Oh, and be ready to run,' he added, somewhat unnecessarily.

Mark took his place alongside the elves, still tucked into the shadows behind the doors and with his bow ready, just like them. He was suddenly convinced that it wouldn't work for him, but it was too late to worry about that now: the others surely would, and they would get Jack's attention quickly enough. Roall checked that they were all ready and received three slightly more nervous nods.

On his silent command they all sprang out, side by side through the double doors, drawing their bows as they went. Jack looked up at the sudden movement and leant forward slightly, but he didn't get up. He didn't have time to. Three arrows, so white that they gleamed, flew from the bows and hit Jack in the shoulder and chest, throwing him back heavily against the wall. Mark aimed too, but badly ... his arrow came later than the others as his bow waited for its aim to be true. It soon followed the others, though, finding a home in the giant's fat stomach after passing cleanly through a link of the thick chain which hung around it.

Jack's bellow shook the walls and half the hill, too, by the feel of it, as he sprang to his feet with surprising speed and reached for the spiked club which stood next to him. Then he *really* roared out, and a bolt of fear and doubt momentarily stunned his attackers, for his gaping mouth was as large as an empty beer barrel and filled from cheek to cheek with broken, stumpy teeth of every colour from yellow to decaying black. As his thick tongue shook like a pink milk jelly in the back of his throat, the elves retreated a step or two in shock, taking Mark with them. The giant squared up to his attackers with his back to Sheriff's Pit, and with another ear-splitting roar of blind rage, took the weight of his club in his unwounded hand, preparing to scatter the puny elves and their cheeky mortal companion with one simple sweep of his arm.

But a second volley of arrows was already on its way. One found his throat, one his chest, and another his thigh. The fourth hit one of his chains and shattered uselessly into splinters just before it vanished in a shower of dazzling sparks. The onslaught was not enough to kill him, but it was just enough to make the startled giant take a single step backwards. He wasn't used to walking backwards – it was totally against his nature – and halfway through that step he tripped over his own large feet and sat back down against the wall with a shuddering thud which even brought down a few stones from the roof and walls of the tunnel.

He stared down at his chest, hurt and bewildered, and rubbed the painful place where one of the arrows had hit him and then so annoyingly disappeared. Confused or not, he was furious that any creatures as small and insignificant as these would dare to attack *him*, the most powerful being on the moors or beyond, but with his breath knocked out of him, he stayed against the wall for a few seconds longer than he should have, and so his final surprise that day came from where he least expected it.

Inside the pit, Victoria and the two elves had held their breath, and each other, as the dreadful racket outside filled their little prison and made their ears ring. They had knelt side by side near the bars on a decomposing fleece, peering into the room beyond and watching helplessly as the giant stood up and faced his assailants. They could have cheered as he fell back against their spyhole, and when Victoria saw the thick, hairy neck pressing against the iron bars, she grasped her stick and leapt to her feet without a second thought. It was still a spear, and ready for use as one. Whether she was trying to help the others outside, or was simply desperate to clear their only way out of the pit as quickly as she could, no one could say, for as the elves jumped clear, she thrust the spearhead between the bars and into the back of that neck – with two hands and all of her strength. Jack's bushy eyebrows shot up, but he didn't even shout out this time. With nothing more than a surprised 'Huh?' followed by a glimpse of two wide open, bloodshot eyes for the others outside, his head fell forwards onto his chest and stayed there.

The only sound was the clatter of the spear as it was wrenched out of Jack's tree trunk of a neck and fell to the ground. The elves were stunned into silence, unable to believe that the brute slumped forwards in front of them, defeated, really was Jack-in-irons. A second or two later, they realised that Jack could stir again at any moment, and badly wounded giants in confined spaces were probably best avoided. Everyone moved quickly.

Unable to restrain himself any longer and ignoring the very real dangers, Mark leapt forward and climbed up onto Jack's broad back in order to peer through the barred opening. He was instantly greeted by a very familiar face. It was framed in the opening, blood-smeared and filthy, but Mark beamed as he gazed at the delightful picture in front of him. As Victoria scowled back, he reached through the bars and gave her cheeks a friendly slap with his fingers, just as she'd done to him at the glade.

'*Now* who likes hanging around in grot-holes?' he asked

cheekily, hardly able to hide his relief and joy in finding her alive and well.

'Don't just stand there poking fun at us,' she snapped. 'Make this bloody hole bigger before he wakes up – unless you fancy another fight with him, hand to hand!'

Mark got the point and a few seconds later he had picked up Victoria's spear and was using it to lever out some loose bricks below the bars. A few became many, and soon a large piece of wall was coming to pieces and falling out onto Jack's shoulders. Dammed up behind the bricks was a deep, oozing mass of putrefying rubbish. Mark began dragging it out with his bare hands and pushing it down onto Jack's back without any concern for his own safety. He wanted everyone out of the pit, and quickly.

Stirran and Flinnor rushed forward and helped, whilst Roall stood close to Jack's slumped head with his freyal held high, ready for the slightest movement. The sickening contents of Sheriff's Pit now burst out unaided, like dark, congealed porridge laced with flesh, bones and rocks. The barred opening soon came out along with it, as did Victoria, Agoriff and last of all Planiss, freyal still in hand and a wide smile across his grimy face as he slithered down to join the others. They were all covered in muck from head to toe, but they were free, and that was all that mattered to them.

The time had come for them to make their escape, but it could only be from a bad place to an even worse one. Each one of them still had unfinished and unpleasant business to attend to, and so, sadly, there was no question of them fleeing down the passageway which beckoned to them invitingly just next to one of Jack's flaming torches. They could even feel cool air coming from it, and relatively fresh air at that, after the stench of everything else around them. They wondered if it might even lead them to the crisp, clean air of the valley, for which they now all longed.

It was difficult for them to turn away and walk back to the caves, but none of the group hesitated in following Roall as he entered the tunnel which had brought them to the pit. This time, the short journey would be a tiring uphill slog, not a downhill sprint, but they were all clear in their minds where their duties now lay. For the elves, the four missing freyals were calling to them after fifty years or more in the hands of spriggan robbers. As for Victoria, she knew exactly where her little sister would be at that precise moment: in a lonely hospital bed. There was one thing in her mind now, and it would only be found in the caves. She was the last to leave that place, and had almost done so when she turned and ran back to the giant. She scooped up her thumb stick from beside him and gave him a hard kick in the ankle as a parting gift. She left quickly then, knowing that at least he was far too large to follow her up the narrow tunnel back to the caves. He *looked* dead, but ...

They jogged up the steady incline together, unable to hold back smiles as they glanced at each other and wondered who was the dirtiest. For the time being, they seemed oblivious to the danger which surrounded them, and Victoria came up alongside Mark as they made their way steadily upwards.

'Where's the hob got to?' she asked, between jolting breaths. Mark felt it wasn't the time or place for too many details.

'He was with us nearly all the way ... but he never made it.'

Mark watched for a reaction from her, unsure if she had already formed some kind of attachment to the little creature who'd watched her grow up at Willow Garth. Her silence told him that she probably had.

They soon arrived back at the gaping chasm across the tunnel floor, and it was obvious that none of them, including Roall, would manage the huge leap when it was combined with an uphill run. Agoriff came to their rescue as he took the thumb stick, which, with the help of some softly spoken but unintelligible words, obliged him by growing into a long, slender pole. The others watched as he toppled it across the gap to form a bridge. Well, a bridge of sorts. He stood to one side and politely offered the others the chance of being first across the terrifyingly narrow walkway, although they all knew very well that he was quite happy to be that person himself. The elves all went over, as they were lightest on their feet and so best able to show the youngsters how easy it really was. Victoria showed Mark up by going before him and making an admirable job of it, too. Mark went last of all, but to everyone's alarm, he stopped and wobbled horribly at the halfway point where the pole sagged the most, his arms flying around as the pole twitched violently from side to side. No one knew how, but he somehow recovered his balance and half ran, half dived the last few feet to safety. The others cheered and slapped him on the back. He was thankful for their praise, which was genuine, and his extremely good luck, which he felt sure must soon run out.

A few tiring minutes later they arrived, puffing, back at the start of the tunnel. It wasn't long before several bats were fluttering close by to investigate their unwelcome visitors, who were now once again bathed in the cool blue light of the vast cave. Victoria had to summon even more courage than she'd found when facing Jack, as memories of what had happened in Elspeth's room resurfaced. She grasped Mark's arm in alarm, but he quickly assured her that bats weren't interested in anything larger than moths, and certainly nothing as large as her.

They could hear the occasional echoes of distant shouting from somewhere in another part of the mine, but the brave group had not yet been discovered, which was all that really mattered. Less encouragingly, they still had no idea which direction they should go in, as so far, they hadn't seen any sign of where the spriggans might store their more valuable possessions. Roall poked his head around the corner and into the cave, before peering all around him.

'There is still no one about ... but I have a bad feeling. It is far too quiet around here.'

He strained to listen to the distant sounds again, but even his sensitive ears couldn't pick out any words which might give some clue as to what was happening. With a growing feeling that he was getting too close to the edge of a very steep cliff, he stepped out into the enormous open space. Just beside him was the entrance to the second tunnel, which didn't smell any better than the last time he'd stood there. He walked a short way into it whilst the others stayed safely out of sight, then held out his hand and risked a little of his own light, revealing the first five or six yards. Several doorways stood on his right-hand side, with shadowy hints of others disappearing into the darkness. He stepped towards the first of them. There was no door, only steel bars and a frame, fastened with a chain and padlock which he lifted up and examined. Hungry spiders rushed out onto their webs as the chain moved for the first time in months or years, but the padlock was securely locked, and Roall wondered what or who could deserve to be shut away in such a miserable, lonely place. He checked around him and listened again before passing his fist between the bars and lighting up the room beyond them.

Despite a long, hard life filled with countless horrors, the court elf was utterly devastated by the sight waiting for him there. It was no room, but a small, cramped cell – only five feet square, at the most. The dusty floor was bare, apart from two bowls which lay upside-down, a discarded wooden spoon, and a thin layer of dried-out bracken against the rear wall. Roall held his light a little higher, and fought to control his rage and disgust as he saw the skeletons of two young children, probably no more than two years old when they'd met their ghastly and untimely death. The tattered remains of their dirty clothes – clearly human, not spriggan – were draped over their bare bones, and they were both curled up tightly as if they were still trying to keep warm, even in death.

His dark thoughts were suddenly interrupted. The others were coming after him, wondering what it was that had made him stop and stare. Roall pulled his hand back and cast the cell into darkness as Victoria stepped into the circle of green light around him.

'This one is empty,' he lied. 'Let us see if they all are.'

Still shocked, and without another word, he moved further into the tunnel and came to the next door. It, too, was barred and locked. The group followed him, quite unaware of the horrors which lay within the first cell, but Roall signalled for them to stay back whilst he lit up the second cell and peered into it. This wasn't empty, either. It was similar in every way to the first one: stinking, unlit, bare and cold, with only a meagre layer of dead bracken in one rear corner. A bowl on the floor held a few spoonfuls of dark, unappetising liquid, and there were many small bones nearby which seemed to be mostly of bats – although he noticed a rat's skeleton lying amongst them. A bedraggled creature was curled up in the corner like a scared animal, partly covered with a rough sack. It had long, ginger fur, and seemed to be dead. Roall let the others came forward then, and they looked through the bars silently, each one sickened by the stench of death which hung heavily in the air. Roall had seen enough and he walked on towards the third door.

It was then that they heard something coming from the second cell. It was so quiet that it was almost missed, but it was just enough to stop them instantly and make them listen again. As they waited, it came to them once more, but it was now a little louder – 'Help!' Everyone rushed back to the bars, amazed that whoever was there, they were alive and could manage to speak. Roall thrust the elf light back through the bars and the occupant lifted its head tiredly, letting its tangled hair – not fur – fall aside to reveal its face. The features weren't clear, as they were caked in dirt and hidden in the shadows, but one thing *was* clear and it made the elves gasp as they strained to get a better view. Its eyes were green. They glittered feebly in the light which Roall quickly held high and allowed to brighten.

No one was sure to begin with, or they couldn't find their tongues despite their soaring hopes, but it was Planiss who spoke first. His voice was faltering and hoarse, for he desperately wanted to believe that he was right.

'Trifillo? Is it ... is it really you?'

It was all that he could say before his emotions took any further words away from him. The prisoner looked up then, straight at them, and pulled his hair aside with an emaciated arm which was covered in open sores. The effect was instant, and electrifying. Suddenly, five incredulous elves were grasping the bars, or the elf next to him, as they looked down at their dear friend, the friend they believed had died years earlier on the rocky slopes outside, and who they'd missed so very much. The chains and padlock were tugged at by most of them in turn, as the joy of their discovery quickly turned into a frantic effort to free Trifillo from his prison. Planiss thrust the tip of his freyal into the padlock and did his best to prise it open, throwing in several magical commands and a few rather less polite words for good measure, whilst the others shook the bars. The clamour soon subsided once it became clear that the bars and lock were indeed secure, and they all tried to calm down as Trifillo sat up as well as he could and peered up at them tiredly.

'Roall, Stirran, all of you,' he said in a thin, rasping whisper. 'My wonderful, beloved elves.' He licked his parched, swollen lips with an even drier tongue and tried to swallow. 'Not only am I found by light elves, but by the very ones I have missed so much. I have waited so long ... So *very* long!'

His voice failed him as he fought with emotions which pulled him in several directions at once. As he tried uselessly to moisten his lips again, the other court elves felt tortured by their helplessness, unable to offer him even a few drops of clean water, but Trifillo battled on determinedly. He'd waited years for this day and had rehearsed it a thousand times in his head.

'They hardly ever come in here any more, the spriggans ... no, not after they gave up trying to get secrets from me. I used to sing to myself just to annoy them, but I stopped that two years ago, I think.' He paused, trying to remember the unimportant detail. 'They throw me a scrap or two to eat sometimes, but I never did like raw bat very much,' he added, with a quiet grunt.

The court elf of fire even managed a grin of sorts, but it was only a trace of one, and was missed by the others.

'The key to my little home will be in the next room. I hear them go in and out sometimes, and they always went in there first before coming in here and ...'

His words faded away as appalling memories of long and fruitless torture sessions rushed back to him. He tried to speak again, but it was clear to everyone outside the bars that he was exhausted and perhaps close to death.

'Be careful!' was all that Trifillo could finally mutter before his head fell back against the unforgiving wall and his eyes slowly shut.

The others sprang into action. With Trifillo's last words still echoing in his ears, Roall ordered Victoria and Agoriff to stand at the entrance to the tunnel and watch out for trouble. Stirran and Flinnor were posted at the bars to Trifillo's cell, whilst he, Mark and Planiss approached the third doorway. There were no bars this time, only a closed, heavy door, boasting not one but three large keyholes one above the other: they felt the bitter pill of failure sticking in their throats as they saw the locks and realised that their hopes of freeing Trifillo were already in tatters.

But as they stood there, silent and dejected, a torch on the wall opposite spluttered into life and grew to a steady, bright flame. Everyone was bathed in its welcome light, but more than this, the elves were heartened to know that Trifillo, even locked away and in such low spirits, could still manage to work a little of his magic in order to help them.

The door to the third room was now lit up and plain to see. It had no handle, but the bright flames showed something much more interesting. It wasn't properly shut. Mark was the first to notice the tiny gap, and he pulled at the door gently. It opened a little more, without even a squeak, and so Mark pulled it again, with Roall and Planiss now holding their freyals tightly. Mark kept pulling until the gap was wide enough to get his head in, then, not daring to breathe, he peered through it. The two elves were impatient for news but they got it soon enough when Mark withdrew his head and eased the door back shut as far and as quietly as he could.

'Er, I don't think you wanna go in there,' he whispered to the elves, who were looking up at him expectantly.

'But we have to,' whispered Roall with a note of frustration in his voice. 'So stand aside!'

Mark did as he was told, reluctantly, and now it was Roall's turn to look. A few moments later he, too, was gently shutting the door.

'You are right, Mark,' he whispered. 'Planiss ... *you* go.' Roall hadn't the least intention of putting his own safety before anyone else's, but his playful words at least eased the tension which now almost crackled in the air.

The door to the room wasn't locked, because it needed no locks. Roall stopped Planiss stepping forward and eased the door open again himself, whispering his thanks to the spirits that it moved silently, then they could all see that the contents of the room were protected by something far more effective than any number of sturdy locks. Tethered to a chain which ran from wall to wall, halfway into the room, was a truly immense hellhound. The elves were sure that it was twice as large as others they'd dealt with, and very powerfully built – the ultimate guard dog. But there was some good news, too. It was sleeping – a hellhound's favourite pastime – with the well-chewed thigh bone of a horse or cow nestling safely under its massive paws.

How it was that such a terrifying servant of the dark elves came to be in that particular place, even the court elves couldn't begin to imagine. They knew all too well that the spriggans, with their passion for stealing, wouldn't have hesitated in taking it from the dark elves, given the opportunity, but the journey back to the caves with it must have been interesting, to say the least. Mark was amazed by its size and dormant power. Several bulging muscles in its shoulders and back legs were twitching in its sleep, and a hairy eyebrow moved left and right, perhaps following its dreamed-up prey. Mark stared at it and gulped.

At the far end of the room, a finely carved chest stood against the wall. No doubt it would once have had pride of place in the entrance hall of an elegant house, before thieving spriggans took a liking to it, that is, and it now looked absurdly out of place in its new home. Smart, brass straps and hinges adorned it, and two padlocks hung idly from the lid. They weren't fastened; as far as the spriggans were concerned, the hound was more than enough protection for the handsome chest and its contents.

Roall pushed the door shut once more and drew the others close to him. He was considering their options, and the risks each one would bring, but none of them were even remotely pleasant, and most involved the hellhound receiving a large and unexpected meal of raw elf. After a great deal of whispering and a few well-meant disagreements, a plan was finally agreed.

There were one or two clear rules. Victoria wouldn't go in at any cost, and would keep watch at the end of the tunnel. Flinnor would go in, as he was the lightest and fastest on his feet, accompanied by Planiss, who was the most skilled with a freyal should the fearsome beast wake up. Mark insisted on joining them, both as Victoria's representative and a slightly larger opponent for the hound if it came to a fight (the elves weren't convinced on this point, but conceded in the end). The other elves would stand by with their bows, ready to protect the others if they could.

The door was then pulled wide open and three courageous figures crept into the room, with Flinnor leading. Planiss took his place within striking distance of the slumbering hound and gripped his freyal tightly: the torchlight from the passageway danced along its long blade as it rested on his shoulder, waiting for work. Behind him, in the doorway, Roall, Agoriff and Stirran stood side by side with their bows fully drawn. Three arrows already waited as the elves held their fire, mindful that this particular hellhound would take a lot of stopping, if it came to that.

Mark and Flinnor dropped close to the ground and slipped well below the chain which stretched across the room, before creeping towards the chest up on their toes. As he passed by the hellhound, Mark wondered how fast he could get out of the room if it woke up, and decided that it would be *extremely* fast, chain or no chain. Side by side they went, both still keeping one eye firmly on the hound, then lifted the lid together, slowly at first to check for squeaks, then quickly. Light from Trifillo's flames cast sharp shadows of themselves on the wall above the chest, and larger, indistinct ones of the elves in the doorway as the two amateur thieves looked down and at last saw exactly what the hound was guarding.

The contents had obviously been thrown in with little regard for their value or importance; three golden wine goblets studded with rubies had been cast idly into one corner like worthless trinkets. In another, lay several small leather pouches, each one tied up tightly with a long cord.

'Wow!' mouthed Mark silently, as his thoughts leapt back to the crypt and a spriggan holding out an identical pouch, tempting him with it. With a trembling hand, he picked up one of them and put the cord over his head and around his neck, as a heady jumble of joy, pride and relief rushed through him. Flinnor, who knew exactly what Mark had just achieved, smiled and patted him on the shoulder, but neither of them dared to even whisper.

It was the elf's turn next, as he reached in and picked up something far more precious to him than even a thousand golden goblets. A single freyal was now growing in his hand and he heard a low whistle from someone at the door as he ran his finger along its faultless blade. He held it up proudly for the others to see, the familiar green and red jewels in its hilt sparkling in the light of the flaming torch – or perhaps it was simply with the pure delight of being held by a court elf once again.

One more interesting item lay in the chest amongst some spriggan clutter. It was a large steel ring onto which were threaded at least twenty keys. Some were small, and some large, but Flinnor hoped that one of them would release his beloved friend from years of torment in the cell next door.

He lifted it out as quietly as he could, but the keys clinked together despite his very best efforts, and he stopped with the ring halfway out of the chest. The hellhound licked his drooling jowls in his sleep and crossed his paws the other way, but his gory dreams continued uninterrupted as Flinnor and Mark turned and started to leave – holding their breath for longer than was good for them, judging by the colour of their faces. The tip of Mark's bow touched the chain as they slipped underneath it again, making it rock gently, but a few moments later they were back with the others, and taking in some very slow, deep breaths.

Only when the two of them had reached the door did Planiss dare to lower his freyal and tiptoe to safety. As he did, he saw something familiar hanging on the wall. It was covered with thick dust, but Planiss would still have recognised it anywhere. It was a silken elf cloak. He lifted it from its peg, knowing that its rightful owner would be pleased to see it again after all this time, but shuddered as he saw several leather straps covered with sharp metal studs hanging on the next peg, and wondered how Trifillo had managed to survive those endless days of beatings and torture.

They were soon all back at Trifillo's cell, with Flinnor trying each key on the steel ring in turn. He was almost unable to contain his excitement, and the faster he went, the more he fumbled, but after a few more attempts, and one excellent catch after he nearly dropped the whole bunch on the floor, the padlock clicked open. Roall stood back from the rush and watched happily as the others carefully helped poor Trifillo to his feet and hugged him affectionately. The chatter was non-stop, but still hushed, and in those few moments as he waited patiently for the cell to empty, Roall's fingers played with the bunch of keys which Flinnor had thrust into his hands.

It was then that he felt the unusual, square handle of one particularly large key, and in the same instant knew that he was holding what Malrin would happily have killed him for at Hoarfrost Hall, and that the spriggans had indeed beaten the dark elf to the third key, probably by many years. Roall thought that it would be a shame to leave it behind with the spriggans, out of sight and out of mind, but also lost forever to anyone who might rightly make use of it. He tugged the ring open and took the key off, before slipping it inside his cloak.

Then, at last, it was his turn to put his arms around the elf he thought he would never see again, as Trifillo hobbled out of the cell, his old, dusty cloak already thrown untidily over his shoulders. Stirran and Agoriff supported him, one on each side, and the happy group rejoined Victoria as she ran back to meet them. Never one to forget his manners, Roall introduced Trifillo to Mark and Victoria before they all stepped into the cave again. The bats became curious at once, and were soon filling the air around them as they stood there close together, like lost children.

It didn't matter, though. They had rich pickings indeed, in fact, more than they could ever have imagined possible. Trifillo was reunited with them, and a freyal had come back to its true owners. As for Mark, Roall had bravely sniffed the foul-smelling contents of the little pouch and was now confident that the cure for Elspeth was really theirs.

As the group prepared to move on, one or two of the bats came a little too close for Victoria's comfort, and she threw her arms around Mark. She buried her head in his cloak for a few seconds for protection, but soon pulled it away and looked up at him, her face screwed up.

'Phew! Was that you?' she asked, stepping back and covering her nose with her hand. Mark looked indignant, but was trying not to laugh as he pulled at the cord around his neck before dangling the leather pouch in front of her.

'Certainly not!' he exclaimed. 'It's this.'

She hugged him again, but quite differently this time ... and didn't say another word.

The Seven Calls

'At least things can only getter better from now on,' said Mark cheerily as they began to make their way back across the cave and, if their luck held out, towards daylight and fresh air again.

They'd only gone a few yards when an exceptionally large bat wheeled past them, nearly knocking Flinnor over and making Victoria jump sideways. As it fluttered away silently into the blue-blackness a noise came to them from the tunnel they had just left. It was a sinister noise, a deep and distant rumble, a pained, angry groan ... but with a familiar tone to it. It could only have been Jack-in-irons.

Perhaps it was the penetrating depth of that moan, or the brooding resentment which tainted it, but the soundly sleeping hellhound opened one eye, then both. Next, it cocked one ear, then both. Exactly three seconds later, it sprang up onto its paws, wide awake, and leapt wildly towards the closed door, as only a ferocious dog could. The leash and chain brought it to a neck-breaking halt which it barely noticed, and it immediately let out a torrent of barks and howls which would have woken Satan himself. The chain snapped tight again and again, and the brackets at each end of it began to loosen as the hound tugged like a beast possessed. In fact, it was exactly that.

Mark looked around at the others. 'Okay, so I could have been wrong,' he said, pulling Victoria closer to him.

It was all he had time to say. A moment later they were moving as quickly as they could along the edge of the cave, slowed down only by Trifillo, who could muster little more than a steady walk, even with helping arms supporting him. The poor fire elf played what part he could, though, and each unlit torch they came to flickered into life and gave them better light to go by. They weaved around all kinds of spriggan gear and mess, and once or twice slipped in something disgusting on the hard floor, or even ended up on their hands and knees amongst it all. None of them needed any encouragement to flee, and their freyals and half-drawn bows were ready in their hands. The noise behind showed no signs of stopping, and those at the rear, helping Trifillo, kept looking backwards, expecting either a white, living nightmare of a dog, or a crazed giant, or even both, to be coming after them at any moment.

It seemed more like an hour, but only five minutes later they arrived back at the top of the steps which had brought four of them up from the pool, and they all slid to a stop on the stone floor, polished smooth by a million hobnail boots. It was a brief stop, no longer than was needed to catch their breath and be sure in their minds that there was no point in considering those steps as a way out. The pool held only uncertainty and fear for them, whilst the chances of successfully climbing back up the dreadful spill-way beyond it, with cascades of freezing water driving them back downwards the whole time, were thinner than slim.

They waited and listened out. It now seemed quieter behind them at last, but they could still hear those distant, raised voices coming from somewhere ahead. Roall's bruised ribs ached miserably and he bent forwards to ease the pain, but he was still very much in charge as he straightened himself up, well, almost, and looked around him.

'We have terrors behind us, more terrors below us, and

for all we know, terrors in front, too!' He sighed and looked at Mark and Victoria.

'You two have done yourselves proud. It seems that we can only go forward, and there may be trouble – or worse than trouble, by the sound of it. We must stay together, no matter what happens. Do you agree?' The two youngsters nodded and tried not to look anxious as Roall continued. 'We have come too far to be stopped by a few angry spriggans on their own front doorstep, so be brave, and we will soon be taking a pleasant stroll with the sun on our backs and clean snow under our boots.'

They were all appreciative of his efforts to lift their spirits: Trifillo even raised his head and peered out through the matted ginger hair which hung across his drawn face. He tried to speak, but no words came as his lips moved uselessly.

'Hold on, friend,' whispered Agoriff in his ear. 'We might even give you a freyal to swing around if things get difficult.'

Trifillo gave up trying to speak but he did manage a nod. *If only I was stronger,* he thought grimly to himself. *I could have shown them a trick or two with a sword, but ... Another day, perhaps.*

They finally left the vast cave and its bats, before entering a much narrower, lower one which stretched away from them into the distance. The going became steadily more difficult, though, as they came across more abandoned cooking fires and tall piles of stinking bracken bedding. These were very difficult to climb over, and smelt even worse than the contents of Sheriff's Pit, decided Flinnor, as he waded, thigh deep, through a particularly well-used specimen. Just as Mark and Victoria were treading their way carefully over the dubious contents of an upturned cauldron, a new noise came to them all. Everyone stopped just where they were. It sounded like someone drumming their fingers on a table, but getting more agitated as they did so, for it was getting steadily louder.

The all looked at each other, hoping that their guesses were wrong, but Roall had already moved Victoria behind him and his fingers were on his bowstring. The other elves did the same as they stared back into the half-light behind them, waiting for something to come out of the impenetrable darkness at the far end of the cave. Suddenly, Trifillo was looking up, then half lifting his arm, and every torch in the place was bursting into flames: those closest to them first, but soon followed by all the others along the length of the low cave, and even into the main cave itself. Trifillo grunted under his breath, pleased that he could help again.

Now they could see everything – including the hell-hound running down the length of the main cave and straight towards them. Even from that distance, they could see its huge red eyes, standing out like bloodstains on its white fur, and it was running hard, with a purpose. Its legs were moving with a smooth, powerful rhythm that would soon take it to its prey, and nothing they could do was likely to stop it.

Those who could, stood side by side with their bows drawn. The target was too far from them really, but the five of them knew that only a miraculous shot would stop the brute and the sooner they attempted it the better. The hellhound was set on killing ... and devouring.

Five white arrows flew down the length of the low cave. Considering the distance, each of the shots was good, and two even hit the hound ... but they had no apparent effect. A second volley was loosed close behind the first, but the hellhound swerved around some cooking fires at just the wrong moment, and so only one arrow found its mark, sinking into its shoulder. The others missed and clattered against the stone walls far behind it. There was no sign of it slowing down as another five arrows formed in the bows, and Mark moved in front of Victoria too, alongside Roall, wondering what on earth he could do to protect her if the elves' efforts failed. If anything, the hellhound had sped up, and it was now barking as it ran. It was a terrifying, heart-stopping bark, as a bloodlust surged through it and it entered the lower cave where they all stood. Victoria could now hear each of its breaths as they were sucked in and blown out. Her hand found Mark's and squeezed it hard ... There could only be one more attempt.

The arrows flew towards it with great energy and accuracy now that it was so close, and four hit it, sinking into its neck, chest and shoulders. It did not fall, though, or even pause. There was nothing more than a shake of its great white head, as if a persistent fly was annoying it, and still it charged ahead, directly towards them. Roall's head fell as he lowered his bow, defeated, and Mark's heart raced as he felt Victoria stiffen behind him.

As those last five arrows had raced away, Trifillo somehow found the strength to take hold of a freyal which Stirran had put aside. He was far too weak to lift it, and the point of it scraped across the floor as he pulled it to him, but actually, that was exactly where he wanted it. A moment later, a flame appeared at the tip and flared up at once, before it darted across the floor and away from him. The court elf of fire watched with a twisted grin as the line of fire rapidly grew longer and longer, before racing into the flattened piles of bracken which filled the tunnel from side to side. These were tinder dry, and the fire spread through them almost instantly, no doubt helped by more of Trifillo's magic. With a sudden roar, a wall of hot, crackling flames leapt upwards and sideways, filling the tunnel in seconds, and the hellhound behind it disappeared from view. Even that monstrous beast couldn't cross such a barrier: the searing heat was skintighteningly hot, and even thirty paces away, the group stepped back and held up their hands to protect their faces. Mark leant towards the court elf of fire and shouted to him over the roar of the flames.

'Thanks, Trifillo. I think you saved all our skins with that trick.'

The elf turned to him and Mark saw, close up, just how bad a state he was in as he licked his cracked and swollen lips before answering with difficulty.

'If that white devil finds a gap in the flames, we'll need more than tricks just to keep them. Let's get out of here!'

Together they turned and started their final bid for freedom. The cave narrowed even more after a short distance, and the bats had all but disappeared, but there was still mess everywhere, and one or two smouldering fires, as if the whole area had been suddenly abandoned. The large blue lights which had been bobbing about in the main cave were nowhere to be seen, and now there was only an occasional smaller version tucked into the furthest corners of the rocky roof above them.

On they went, feeling increasingly exposed and vulnerable as daylight seeped towards them from somewhere ahead, growing stronger all the time, and the uproar ahead was becoming louder, too, but a distant howl from behind was a stark reminder that the only way out was forwards, whatever was happening there. Their cloaks came into their own once again, now that they had dried out from their soaking in the pool, and the group were little more than half-formed ghosts against the walls as they stumbled ahead.

They finally edged their way cautiously around the last corner. There, before them, was the entrance cave. More nets hung from its roof, and dazzling sunlight beckoned from beyond a wide opening at its far side. Shouts and bellows came from beyond it, mixed in with the constant clatter of rock on rock, and the rattle of spent arrows against stone, but they crept further forwards, holding Trifillo up and keeping close to the wall. They'd soon crossed the empty cave and were tantalisingly close to their only way out – the cave faced eastwards, and outside, the morning sun was lighting up the entire western side of Rosedale valley. The group moved forwards again, right up to the massive door stones which had been dragged aside at the entrance itself, and crouched in the shadows beside them. Then, at last, they could see what was happening.

Victoria gripped Mark's arm and pressed herself against the door stone. Outside, an army of at least twenty spriggans had grown to their very tallest and most powerful. They had their backs to the cave entrance and many were picking up and throwing large rocks down the slope. Others launched long spears, grunting with the effort, and raising their fists in victory when one of them hit its target. Whoever their visitors were, they'd stepped into something far worse than they could ever have imagined, and were certainly paying a high price for their foolishness. The spriggans were in such a rage that they seemed indifferent to the countless arrows which streaked up the slopes towards them, but as the group watched, a particularly ugly specimen with two arrows already in his thigh took another in his eye and keeled over backwards, like a felled tree. Several more dead spriggans lay crumpled amongst the rocks whilst another wounded one was bellowing like a bull as he pulled at one of several arrows in his chest. The arrows were all black.

* * *

Malrin had spent a busy night gathering a fair-sized band of his most blood-thirsty followers together, after his failure to find the iron key at Hoarfrost Hall. The bat's skeleton in

Sir Henry's secret little cupboard had told him exactly who'd taken it and where it would be, and so the rest was relatively easy. Of course, it had meant extra work and some delay, not to mention the hastily arranged recruitment of willing fighters, so he was in the very worst of moods, and those around him wisely kept their distance. His temper became worse still when he was finally forced to resort to offers of payment, for most of his troops weren't keen to take on a whole herd of aggravated spriggans without promise of a considerable reward. There were treasures untold, or so he assured them all, sitting there in the caves just for the picking – once the spriggan scum guarding them were 'dealt with' and their strong-rooms broken open, that is. The guarantee of a plentiful booty certainly helped settle the matter.

There were now more than sixty dark elves scattered across the lower slopes outside the cave entrance, and they were firing a constant barrage of arrows, in-between taking cover as rocks and spears flew past their heads and bounced down into the valley. Mark and the others then watched incredulously as a large, writhing cone of twisting wind, laden with all kinds of debris, worked its way from deep in the bottom of the valley steadily upwards, towards them. Conjured up at will by the spriggans, and horribly unstoppable, it would soon be in amongst their opponents and adding very nicely to the turmoil. Agoriff urged Mark and Victoria to keep back, whilst an exhausted Trifillo could do nothing more than sink to his knees and sit quietly in the shadows, unable to help further, and completely in the hands of his rescuers.

'I had been hoping that we could slip out without saying farewell,' whispered Planiss, always one to get humorous when the going was at its toughest. 'Any ideas, anyone?'

He looked around the group, not really expecting anything inspirational, but still optimistic.

'We could make our way back to the pool ... if we have to.'

Mark said it, but immediately wished that he hadn't, for he dreaded the prospect of fighting against the floodwater in the long spillway. They all looked at Trifillo then, and knew that he could scarcely walk, let alone climb and swim at the same time. That unpleasant option was still out of the question, thankfully.

'Look, if you all wait here, I'll sneak back and see if I can find another way out, if you like. It'll be less risky than all of us hunting around, won't it?'

The elves stared at Victoria, then at each other, slightly taken aback. Stirran smiled and slowly shook his head in disbelief.

'Are all young mortals like you two?' asked Roall. 'It's a shame you're not elves. I would have been proud to fight alongside either of you in many battles I can recall.'

He paused and thought for a moment whilst Victoria blushed and waited. Mark held his breath and hoped that he wasn't about to find himself trying to talk Victoria out of her plan.

'I think that we should stay together and *all* go back,' announced Roall. 'If we get split up here, it could be forever!'

Everyone seemed to agree, even Victoria. There were no objections and no other suggestions, and so Stirran and Agoriff helped Trifillo up again. As Trifillo did his best to stand up straight, Mark suddenly felt uneasy about something and turned to stare back into the caves, trying to see anything at all after the brightness of the sunlight just around the corner. As his eyes re-adjusted to the gloom, they opened even wider when he saw six spriggans striding towards them. They were all at their largest, too, clearly expecting trouble, and judging from the amount of shoving and yawning going on, extremely annoyed at having been woken up.

'I think we need another plan,' whispered Mark to the others, who still had their backs to the new danger.

They followed his eyes, but soon wished that they hadn't. Three of the spriggans had axes resting on their shoulders, whilst the others each carried a beautiful sword. The last three stolen freyals were still being put to evil use, and the unfortunate crowd at the door had nowhere to go. They were trapped. Spriggans in front, spriggans behind – and Mark felt like kicking himself for believing that he could bring Victoria into such a dangerous place and yet leave unharmed. He looked at the others, and felt as worthless as he'd ever done: he was close to useless with his bow, he reminded himself, and he didn't have a freyal to try to fight with, either.

As it happened, two of the court elves did have other plans, and they were put into action before Mark knew what was happening. Flinnor and Planiss stepped forward, brought up their bows and aimed high, back into the caves. The others looked puzzled, for their bows were aimed well over the heads of the six spriggans, and it almost seemed that the bats were their targets. Their incredible arrows quickly came to life, but this time with wide, razor-sharp heads. Amazed and bewildered, Mark and Victoria watched the steady arms of the two elves, the green gems on their bracers catching the morning sunlight. They held their aim for many long, precious seconds, then suddenly the arrows were gone and the bows were lowered.

One shot was perfect. It sliced cleanly through the corner support rope of an enormous net high above the approaching spriggans. The second one was almost as good, but the rope was only partially cut and the net jolted to a halt with only one corner free. Without even a pause for a breath, both bows came up again and two more white arrows waited for their freedom. They soon got it, and the damaged rope was cut cleanly in two a second later. The net, now only attached by its two remaining corners, swung down in a huge arc, squarely onto the spriggans, completely smothering them in its thick, knotted cords and bringing a torrent of snarled oaths and curses.

Any remaining thoughts the stranded group may have had of returning into the caves quickly evaporated away as a hairy spriggan arm pushed a sword up through the net and started to slash at the cords and ropes around it. Before anyone could stop him, Mark was on his feet and sprinting the twenty paces to the boiling spriggan scrum, picking up a discarded spear as he went. He leapt up onto it, fighting to keep his balance as the netted bundle bucked and heaved, then swung the spear with all his strength around and against the hand gripping the freyal. There was a tremendous roar, and suddenly Mark was scooping up the precious sword then scrambling back towards the others … but he'd left it a moment too late.

Another hand sprouted from a gap close to his foot and grasped it, tripping him up and pitching him down onto the net. He rolled onto his back, ready to slash at the hand with his freyal, but before he could sit up, a hand also appeared near his head as another spriggan realised what was happening and joined in. That hand found the cord which was hanging from behind Mark's neck and grasped it firmly with a tight, white-knuckled fist. All the while, the roaring and bellowing filled the whole cave and echoed from every wall, as the trapped spriggans became steadily angrier.

Mark had changed from hero to victim in just three seconds. He was on his back, unable to do anything with his sword, and being garrotted by the tight cord around his neck as the ruthless spriggan pulled it downwards with a terrifying force. Mark wouldn't let go of the precious freyal, and his other hand went to his neck and tried to stop the cord from cutting into his throat. It was useless.

At the cave entrance, the others had already sprung up to help him, including Victoria, who was on her feet and leaping forwards with her thumb stick, ahead of the elves.

'WAIT!' ordered Agoriff loudly. It stopped them all instantly. 'Keep back! It is too dangerous.' Agoriff's order was clear, and he meant every word. Roall took Victoria's arm and stepped backwards with her.

The court elf of trees stepped in front of the others, knelt down on one knee, brought his bow up and drew it in one easy action. Mark was turning purple as the cord tightened, and his hand dropped away from his throat. But Agoriff already had a tiny target in his sights and he paused to ensure his aim was perfect. It had to be his most skilful shot ever, and nothing less.

The bow sang and the arrow flew eagerly across those twenty paces. Victoria gasped as it flew straight at Mark's head, but it was seeking the thin cord around his neck. It found it in the gap between his neck and the net, cutting the cord cleanly and freeing Mark in the same instant. The cord and its precious pouch disappeared down into the chaos below him as Mark sat up and swung his freyal at the hand which still grasped his foot. It was a fair swing, as a roar from under the net proved. He scrambled up, coughing, his free hand already groping at his neck, but not finding the cord he so desperately wanted to be there. His face fell in dismay, but he could only leap from the net and be thankful that another grasping hand had not stopped him ... they were suddenly appearing from everywhere, and two reluctant freyals were now slashing at the net and starting to make larger holes in it.

Mark ran back to the others, but he could hardly speak when he reached them, and his own words were choking him as Victoria threw her arms around him. Mark's arms dropped as if the life had been sucked out of them, and the tip of the freyal hit the stone floor and stayed there. He fought back his tears and whispered into her ear as she held him tightly.

'I'm sorry, Vicks, I'm so sorry! I'll get it back somehow. I will. You know I will.'

'I know *we* will,' she whispered back, correcting him. And she meant it.

There was no trace of resentment in her voice. The disappointment which was swamping her whole body and mind could not win over a lifetime of total understanding and trust.

'I know we will,' she repeated even more quietly, but with her eyes now filling with private tears.

Victoria looked up from his shoulder and through those tears saw the spriggans disentangling themselves from the net. She let go of Mark and pulled him back to the elves waiting behind her. They knew what a devastating blow Agoriff had dealt the youngsters, wielding the sharpest two-edged sword imaginable: Mark's life spared, Elspeth's cure lost. But he'd had no choice. Mark went up to Roall, but he couldn't look him straight in the eye.

'Far too valuable to leave behind,' said Mark as he offered the freyal to the bewildered elf. 'It's a shame we can't get under there and find the other two,' he muttered hoarsely, keen to keep the subject on swords. Amazingly, Roall pushed the freyal back to him.

'Thank you indeed, but you keep it for now,' replied the court elf. 'You will need it before long, I fear.'

Trifillo was lifted up onto his feet once more, and with a last glance at each other they burst out into the sunlight, turning sharply to the right and finding they had no choice but to claw their way up an extremely steep bank ... exposed to all. For just a few moments, the spriggans outside the cave were completely unaware that they'd had other unwelcome visitors who were now leaving, being fully occupied with the business of killing as many dark elves as possible.

In that short, valuable time, the group somehow managed to climb more than halfway up the bank, but Trifillo slowed them down horribly, even though he was dragged up unceremoniously by his skinny arms, lying on his back. Mercifully, they were able to find a little cover behind a few boulders there, close to a spring which seeped out of the hillside somewhere higher up and out of sight. It was barely a trickle, but just enough to scoop up and moisten Trifillo's parched lips.

Then the cry they were all dreading came from below them as they were finally discovered, and the rocks started to fly uphill instead of down, and spears, too. The little group kept their heads down as much as they could, but Roall pulled Victoria and Mark towards him so that they could hear above the yelling and the clattering of the rocks, which were suddenly flying about everywhere. The other elves were now defending the whole group with quickly aimed arrows loosed only a moment after they dared to stand up.

'You two must find your way out of this! We will cover you for as long as we are able.'

It sounded as if Roall was saying goodbye to them, and that these would be their last seconds together. Victoria began to turn pale as Mark held her close, and Roall looked straight into her eyes. He had more to say, but precious little time to say it.

'You *must* survive this and live to find the cure again! You have risked your lives to get it once, and you must not stay here and risk them further. I fear that we shall soon have a fight on our hands which our children's children will be hearing stories of when we are all long dead!'

Roall suddenly sounded tired and he stared down at his clenched hands. He opened one of them, and in it lay the iron key. He chuckled to himself.

'This is what these dark elves want!'

He closed his fingers around it, but then he paused and opened them again, his mind whirling.

'What is it?' asked Mark, who could see that the elf was struggling with a difficult decision.

'You should keep this, and look after it carefully.' He placed the key in Mark's hand and closed his fingers around it for him. Fifty yards below, a sharp-eyed dark elf lowered his bow and watched them, wondering if his eyes were deceiving him.

'If we die here,' continued Roall, 'then a dark elf or spriggan will soon find this pretty key. That would only bring even more death and destruction to our worlds, for with their hearts full of greed they would stop at nothing to get to the Witcher hoard. Keep this ... and come to Russell's Wood when you can.' He nodded towards the wood which nestled in the valley bottom a mile away from them. 'If we survive this we shall go there and find healing for Trifillo ... for all of us, even. Take it and go!'

Elf and mortal were now almost nose to nose, and Mark couldn't stop himself from looking deep into Roall's eyes. They were filled with trust, hope and urgency, and the colour of them was so intense that Mark doubted if he would ever see anything so astonishing again. As he stared at them, his fear that this was the last he would ever see of Roall, or indeed any of the court elves, grew to a sudden, intense dread – that they would be spirited away into their unseen world and never share his own again. Dear, wise Roall could see all of those fears in one blink of Mark's eyelids.

'If the spirits are with us, and what few powers we have left do not desert us, then we shall meet yet again, you will see. We still have unfinished business, do we not?' Mark nodded feebly and Roall gripped his shoulder firmly. 'Go!'

The court elf of meadows turned his back on Mark and

stood up from behind his meagre cover. He drew his bow and an instant later a dazzling arrow found the leg of a huge spriggan. The other court elves put their bows to good use too, in-between avoiding flying rocks and a blizzard of black arrows.

On their knees to start with, Mark and Victoria used tufts of grass and bracken to pull themselves up the top part of the slope, which was suitable for agile sheep and little else. Their cloaks helped, but black arrows soon began to thud into the hillside or ricochet off nearby boulders before they'd climbed very far. Two of them hit the loose part of Mark's cloak but didn't pierce it. Another even found Victoria's shoulder and the force of it spun her off her feet, down onto her knees, but the elfin cloth was too strong and the arrow was foiled. As they climbed steadily higher, a heavy spear, one which even an elf cloak would struggle to stop, sunk into the ground inches from their feet, but they struggled on upwards. The dark elves closest to the steep bank had now turned their full attention towards the light elves, who had become an easier target than the spriggans, and many black arrows streaked up towards them.

The youngsters fled, continuing their desperate climb to safety for several long and terrifying minutes, and taking a diagonal route up the side of the hill so as to lessen the gradient and give them more speed. They clung onto any plants not buried by the snow, but still slipped and stumbled as they scrambled upwards, expecting a lucky arrow to kill them at any second. Fewer and fewer came near them, though, and eventually they stopped all together. They could still hear the fighting from somewhere below, distant now and out of sight, but despite their instincts to go back and help, they knew that to do so would probably only make matters worse for Roall and the others. Mark's hand went to his bare neck, and Victoria noticed.

'We'll get it back, you'll see.' It was all that she said, between gasps for breath, and Mark was thankful for that.

Hope was fading quickly for the court elves. Of course, they could have tried to take the same way out of trouble that the youngsters had, but Trifillo would never have managed it, they knew very well. They'd lost him once before, and there was no question of leaving him behind again, even if it meant the end for all of them: an undying dedication to their mission in life, and to each other, ran through them just as surely as their blood did.

Agoriff's bow suddenly seemed alive. He'd found some good protection behind a rocky outcrop, and stepped out from behind it with virtually every breath, drawing, aiming and firing. Arrow after white arrow flew into the melee below him, sometimes finding a spriggan, sometimes a dark elf, sometimes wounding, sometimes more. He saw at least three dark elves slump forward clasping their throats or chests, or clawing at the white arrows which pierced them. But despite Agoriff's amazing skills and the bravest actions of the other light elves, they were all facing a disastrous defeat. It would be gradual and painful, but quite inevitable, for six light elves – including one unable to defend himself – couldn't withstand an attack from so many frenzied assailants for more than a few minutes. Indeed, they had only survived as long as they had because they fought bow to bow and not sword to sabre, and the rocks and spears were being thrown uphill, making them less deadly. These things apart, the courageous light elves were being slowly but surely overwhelmed. Much to the disgust of the rock elf, Stirran eventually took a blow to his shoulder from a boulder, which left him in great pain and unable to draw his bow fully. Roall was still stiff from his encounter with Malrin, and far from being on his usual best form, but his ears still worked well enough, for he could now hear deep, ferocious barking coming from the caves. His thoughts were

285

bleak, and he wondered what else could possibly go wrong for them before they all finally died.

One by one, the court elves accepted the fact that this was their last stand against terror and evil. Here, in the bright sun, with fresh snow under their feet, and the glory of Rosedale spread out before them like a lavish banquet, was where they would surely perish together. It could have been much, much worse.

*   *   *

It was Planiss who heard the call first, from the very deepest part of that valley. Perhaps it was to be expected, him being the court elf of springs, for the waters of the River Seven called to him now as they never had before. To begin with, it was no more than a distant whisper, or even a stray thought in his mind, but it was constant and unquestionably deliberate. The call came to him because Planiss was linked to that river just as surely as Agoriff suffered the pain of a tree being felled, or Flinnor felt the first change in the weather on his cheek an hour before the others did. It was a reminder to Planiss, an urgent reminder that the six of them were huddled together a few paces from a spring. It was only a trickle, admittedly, but it was still a spring.

As the whispering became steadily stronger, Planiss turned from his friends and the fighting, and gazed at the dribble of water as it followed a tiny channel it had cut for itself through the snow, along the route of an old sheep track which snaked its way downwards and sideways, away from the cave entrance. For a few seconds he was puzzled, but then he understood. It flooded into his mind just as the water would soon flood out from the earth. It was as simple as that. The water was under his control if he so wished it, and now he did most *certainly* wish it, with every fibre of his being. With a brief look at his fellow elves as they fought what might be their final battle, he touched the ground with his fingertips and willed the spring to grow and swell ... and so it did. The trickle grew and became a gush, and the gush soon became a torrent. It picked up rocks effortlessly and tumbled them down the hill, but still it grew and grew. The rest of the group heard it then. They lowered their bows and turned to see the water, as Planiss shouted for them to come over to him.

They didn't need a second invitation. Two of them pulled Trifillo up a little higher and dragged him as gently as they could towards the water, which was now coloured red-brown with soil, and erupting from the ground like boiling soup in a huge, over-filled cauldron. As several black arrows thumped uselessly into their cloaks, the elves shouldered their bows and rolled, one after the other, into the seething water. Such was its power that it took them in an instant, picking them up and carrying them, sliding, tumbling, almost drowning, down the snow-filled ditch in which a totally insignificant spring had so recently trickled. The snow was blasted from it instantly, as the elves, mud, water and rocks cascaded down and away from that dreadful place. They clung to Trifillo with all their strength, but he sucked in more than his fair share of muddy water as the others did their best to keep their heads above it.

Even from near the top of the hill, Mark and Victoria heard the rushing water and rolling rocks and turned to face it. From where they stood it was impossible to see everything that was happening, but they could both see a deluge racing down the last section of a ditch and bursting over the edge of the riverbank far away and below them. There was little chance of seeing what it carried along with it, but they both had a feeling that it was something to do with the light elves, and they hoped with all their hearts that they were right.

At the cave entrance, the dark elves stopped their brawling and watched the curious sight in the valley bottom, resting on their bows and shielding their eyes from the sun as they strained to see if there would be any survivors down in the Seven. Even the spriggans paused in the middle of their fighting, some with rocks or spears still in their hands, to stare silently down into the valley, or mutter curses on the good fortune of the light elves.

Just inside the cave entrance, one spriggan had finally managed to rip his way out from under the net which had snared him. Throwing the tattered remains of it angrily aside, he got to his feet and staggered out into the daylight with a throbbing wrist and an empty scabbard. A freshly cut cord and its precious pouch dangled from his fingers, whilst his face was a perfect study in fury. He'd lost his freyal, but worse still, he'd lost it to a mortal. He already knew that the keys had gone from the cells and strong rooms, too, along with a prisoner, and that some light elves and a couple of mortals he'd just seen escaping most likely had all of it. As the spriggans' very own whirlwind suddenly exploded onto the scene and obliterated the sun, he lifted his chin and added to the fearful noise, roaring out across the valley for all the unseen world to hear, shaking his head from left to right, flinging long, sticky strands of black spit everywhere.

Scribber had now suffered twice at the hands of the young male mortal, and to his way of thinking, twice was two too many. He couldn't remember the name that the girl had screamed out from the top of the crypt steps, and he didn't want to. Scribber just wanted to snuff out his miserable, interfering life at the very earliest opportunity.

The Seelie Court

(Three weeks later)

It was shortly before midday on a Sunday morning, just two weeks before Christmas, and Farndale had at last recovered from its thick blanket of snow and the interminable, messy slush which followed. The fields had been left waterlogged and there were puddles everywhere on the lanes, much to the delight of the younger children. Each morning, after the clear and frosty nights, they would smash up the smooth, fresh ice which had formed on each one, putting their shoes, and their parents' patience, to the ultimate test. On this particular Sunday, though, all that cold and ugliness was quite forgotten, as the valley put on its Sunday best for all to see.

The bright sun was coming around to the south, framed at the end of the valley by the sweeping curves of its clean, green flanks, which in turn soared up from the farmland to meet a sky of faultless icy blue. It was still low, though, perhaps worn out by the cold days and even colder nights, and unable to climb much higher than the heather up on the ridges. The shadows it cast were the unusually long, cut-with-scissors type, especially reserved for the middle of a sunny winter's day, but other rules of nature had been flagrantly broken, too. Although it was noon, the light was filtered in that startling 'end of the day' way, seemingly retouching every colour with a new brush and the very freshest paint. It could all so easily have been an oil painting by an overenthusiastic but accurate artist.

Victoria stood in the garden at Willow Garth, at that place which was so special to her, close to the wall. She was staring out across Farndale, admiring the pretty view as if it had been staged just for her, when a loud, tuneless whistle drifted up from somewhere down the lane. Victoria didn't move. The whistling got louder, and soon the visitor and his squeaking bicycle were shooting out of the lane and onto the gravel driveway next to the lawn. Mark used his feet as brakes and the bicycle skidded to an awkward halt. He jumped off and let it clatter to the ground – it was old, and a few more scratches wouldn't harm it.

Mark had used his morning off to cycle all the way to Russell's Wood again, on the far side of Rosedale. It was his fifth attempt to find the elves at the place they'd mentioned, and he was determined to continue until he did. Whether he liked it or not, he *had* to – for Elspeth's sake. He strolled across the lawn, which was still sodden from the melted snow, and towards Victoria.

'Hey-up, lass,' he shouted merrily as he approached her, wondering why she hadn't turned around straight away.

'Vicks? You okay?'

Victoria still had her back to him. She crossed her arms and tried to wrap them around her body. Mark came up behind her.

'Come on, Vicky. What's up?'

He put a hand on one of her shoulders and tried to peer over the other one to see her face, but she turned away. He could see that she'd been crying, and so he tried again.

'Vicks. Tell me what's the matter.'

She moved away from his hand, but stayed close to the wall. Mark waited patiently.

'It's Elspeth,' she finally mumbled with a sniff, but still

facing the valley. 'She's worse. I saw her yesterday and she was all right then – not changed much, really. Dad and Annie have just got back from seeing her.'

She was struggling now. Mark waited for her to carry on, but his pulse was already racing as he wondered what had happened.

'Christ, Mark, she's in intensive care! They moved her there overnight because she nearly stopped breathing.' Her voice was strained and broken.

She suddenly spun around to face him, and Mark recoiled slightly as he saw her swollen eyes and tear-streaked cheeks. Her whole face was filled with despair, and she was keeping her lips pressed tightly together to try to stop herself from crying again. Mark now wished that he hadn't arrived so cheerfully, and put a hand back on her shoulder. He wasn't sure how much holding she wanted: he was painfully aware that he'd lost the cure for Elspeth so soon after finding it, and a hug might not be *quite* the thing to offer, even after all these weeks.

'I don't know what to say,' he muttered. 'There must be something new they could try, surely. Can't they speak to some doctors abroad? America, say, or … or anywhere. Someone must know what to do, it's crazy.'

'It's not crazy,' she replied, trying hard to calm herself. 'It's just the way it is, that's all.'

Victoria turned back to the view which had lifted her spirits so many times in the past.

'Unless things change, she could easily die. They've told dad that, and I heard him telling Annie. He said … he said we have to prepare ourselves.' Her voice faltered again. 'How the bloody hell are we meant to do that?' She could hardly get the last few words out, and Mark suddenly felt sick with guilt.

'Oh shit, it's all my fault,' he groaned. 'I really messed up this time, didn't I?' He was giving her the chance to blame him openly, and knew it. He was fed up guessing, and needed to know how she really felt about what had happened back at the caves. A stray breeze moved her hair and she shivered briefly, despite the sun on her face.

'I won't give up though, Vicks. I'll find the cure again ... somehow.'

'I know you won't give up,' she replied. 'Let's face it, you've never given up on much before, have you?' She pushed her hair back behind her ear. 'I just hope we find it in time, that's all. But we need the elves first, surely. Is there any sign ...?' she asked, wiping her cheeks with her sleeve.

'Not yet,' answered Mark, trying to sound optimistic. 'Maybe they had to go somewhere else to rest – another wood or somewhere. P'raps there's been trouble in another valley, I don't know.' He knew that they would sound like excuses to her, not explanations, but it was all that he could offer.

As it happened, it didn't matter very much because Victoria's mind was already elsewhere. She was increasingly aware of a dread which was growing in Mark, because it was growing in her, too. She could hear it in his voice, just as surely as she could feel it starting to creep into her own thoughts. In the end Mark surprised her by bringing up the subject first.

'Actually, I've been wondering, Vicky ... well, for the last few days, I s'pose.' He fiddled with the strap of his watch and looked everywhere but at her, unsure of the best words. 'Do you think they ... they ...?'

Despite her fragile state, Victoria interrupted him and took control, to save his breath and stop whatever it was from flushing his cheeks even redder.

'I think you should stop worrying about them, Mark. There's no point yet, is there?' He looked down at his boots and studied the fraying laces as she continued. 'Sure, it would've been dangerous, but some of them may have made it down to the river in that flood.' She thought to herself for a moment, trying to be positive. 'And anyway, we have some things of theirs, don't we? The freyal, for a start. They're not going to forget *that* now, are they? Or the other stuff they gave us.' She nodded towards the front door where the remarkable thumb stick leant innocently against the wall. 'They'll show up, you watch.'

'Yeah. You're right, I guess,' answered Mark, quietly relieved. 'They'll come and find us if we can't find them, won't they?' he added, trying to convince himself.

'Bound to,' she replied absently, still staring at the view. She surprised him then.

'How about a bit of cake, or will it spoil your lunch?' She knew just how to distract Mark when needed, and the two of them crossed the lawn on their way to the kitchen.

Mark soon had his treat in front of him and he chatted to Victoria much as he would have in the old days, before elves and spriggans had erupted into their lives. He was clearly frustrated, determined to find the elves – and the cure too, if he could, but was shackled to his duties at Hill Garth Farm. More paid help would have been ideal, he politely reminded her, but there simply wasn't the money for it. In fact, he was lucky to get *any* time off on Sundays, given all the work there was to get through.

Victoria listened patiently and poured the tea. She knew that he often had a lot on his plate – in more ways than one.

*   *   *

He would have preferred it otherwise, but another long week passed before Mark had the chance to go to Russell's Wood again. As usual, he wore his bracer underneath his jacket, in the hope that it would help him find the elusive elves. It was the middle of the morning before he finally got the chance to jump onto his old pushbike and rattle off on his quest once again. His parents wondered why his precious spare time nowadays seemed mostly devoted to pushing the heavy bicycle up the hill to Blakey Ridge, and onwards to goodness only knows where after that, but Mark didn't care what they thought as he shoved the old machine up the same long, steep road he had climbed a month earlier in a snowstorm – with some very unusual company.

As he toiled away, he thought back to those unbelievable times with the light elves – the glade, the island, the caves, everything – and he even wondered what his family might have to say if he told them the whole story. But if he knew anything, he knew better than to make a fool of himself in front of them. Tales of elves with magical bows or huge hounds and murderous giants might not be taken too seriously, and who could blame them, he asked himself.

Half an hour later, and pleasantly cooled down by a long, effortless downhill ride, he arrived at Thorgill and pedalled his way through the sleepy little hamlet. He didn't see a soul, but he caught the mouth-watering smell of roasting meat at least twice, a reminder that he wouldn't be eating until a lot later in the day. He cycled as fast as he could, so as to leave the tempting aromas behind, and soon found himself in Rosedale village, riding past the remains of the old abbey there and the huddle of tiny cottages clustered around it. Several of them had smoke rising lazily from their chimney pots and once again the smells of home-cooking wafted out of a kitchen window or two, just to torture him a little more.

After a good deal of effort, he'd put all thoughts of hot food aside and was imagining entering the spriggan caves once again, secretly and by himself, searching for more of the cure, when he almost missed the track up to Russell's Wood, about half a mile past the village. As usual, he used his feet to stop the bike, and dragged it roughly around so as to face up the track. It annoyed him that he'd been daydreaming and missed the turn, but he was soon standing up on the peddles and making fast progress. A couple of tiring minutes later, the wood was looming up in front of him, and he wondered for the hundredth time why the elves should choose this particular place to rest, and not somewhere in Farndale, which was their true home, apparently. The wood consisted entirely of mature spruce trees, tall and deep-green, putting the bare branches of their nearby broadleaf neighbours to shame. Mark wondered if this was the reason for the elves' choice: he knew that they adored beautiful things and this wood couldn't really be described as anything else.

Sticking to his now familiar routine, he propped his bike against the first large tree he came to and wandered into that still, tranquil place, which now surrounded him like a great hall. Its roof was a translucent canopy of fragrant leaves, its pillars an army of straight, thick trunks standing smartly to attention, whilst its floor was a dry, springy rug of dead needles sprinkled with golden cones and even a few early snowdrops. He loved the total peacefulness and fresh smell, and even the wind had no power there to disturb either of them. As he zigzagged back and forth across the width of the wood, searching, he felt that he was intruding, even spoiling it somehow, but just as he had on previous visits, he followed the contours of the hillside, working his way gradually upwards and wishing he was fitter than he was.

There's no gain without pain, he told himself. It didn't help much, though, as he panted and began to sweat a little.

When he was halfway up, and in the very centre of the wood, he stopped close to a pair of particularly large trees, ready to call out the names of all six court elves yet again. The trees were only an arm's breadth apart, with all of their upper branches interlocked tightly together, and he was looking up into their dizzy heights, watching the slender tips fidgeting in the light breeze, when it happened.

Quite unexpectedly, two small hands covered his eyes from behind him, startling him so much that he jumped clear of the ground. By the time he'd landed again, he'd realised what was happening and relaxed, although he was surprised that a certain young lady from Farndale had finally bothered to follow him all the way ... and had been able to stay hidden until the last moment. Now *that* impressed him. The hands were soft and delicate, but with an underlying strength which he recognised. He decided to play his usual game, as it seemed that she was playing hers.

'Now, who's this sneaking around in the middle of a lonely wood? Jenny Broadbent? You should know better. How come you're following me about and not back home helping with Sunday lunch? There'll be talk, y' know.'

Mark hoped that this would get Victoria nicely stirred up, but the hands didn't move and there was no reply. He brought his own hands up then, and put them over hers to make up for teasing her ... but the smile slowly left his face. He could feel a ring on each hand, pressing into his palms. He opened his eyes against their warm skin as his heartbeat quickened.

It wasn't fear, although after the events of recent times it could so easily have been, and he knew that the hands were a girl's ... but Victoria never wore rings. He didn't move – he hardly dared to – but peeking out of the corners of his eyes, he could see that the arms were bare, which surprised him even more, and as he took the hands away from his eyes and looked at them, he saw that the rings on each middle finger held a large, bright stone. He stared at them both, for they were of no particular colour, and yet every colour at once, almost like the cloaks of the light elves. They caught the light and crackled with it – fascinating him at first, but then suddenly worrying him, although he didn't know why. He turned around slowly.

There was no Victoria. No Jenny Broadbent, even, whoever she might have been. A female elf was staring directly at him, straight into his eyes, but with so much purpose that it was as if she was looking *through* him. He didn't understand how it could be, but he instantly knew that she could see everything which made him who he was – his fears, his loves, his memories, even his hopes. All of them were hers in a few fleeting seconds, and he was completely powerless to stop it.

The irises of her eyes, which were a blue-green topaz, alight and shimmering, like the most stunning part of a butterfly's wing, encircled wide, fathomless pupils, whilst the outer parts were a radiant white. The image of those eyes burned into his mind and never left him again. As he tried to swallow, but failed, he looked at the rest of her face for the first time. It was perfectly beautiful. No other words would really do. Despite her young age, it was full of wisdom and tolerance, too, and her hair was the colour of autumn beech leaves and old gold, falling behind her shoulders then far down her back.

Still facing him, she then placed her hands on his shoulders and, as his gaze sank slowly to her bare feet, his mouth fell open, quite beyond his control. They were six inches above the ground, her toes pointing downwards as if she was standing on them, stretching up to him whilst hovering there without the slightest effort. She smiled and placed a finger under his chin, lifting it gently and closing his mouth, then she spoke, or at least the words came to him from her and he felt her warm breath on his face, but her lips barely seemed to move.

'I am sorry that you have had to search for so long, Mark, but now we have met at last. My name is Estraal.'

Mark was suddenly and completely convinced that he was dreaming. Despite his recent times with the elves and other creatures from their strange world, this elf, this ... living perfection, defied all his senses. They shouted out to him that she was an illusion, nothing more than the briefest glimpse of a reflection in a still lake. She was aware of his doubt as soon as it existed and so spoke again, trying to reassure him.

'There has been a great deal happening here, Mark, as you shall soon discover. Come!'

She lowered her hands before turning to the two trees beside them, and ushering him forwards. They moved towards them, and were about to pass between them when she stopped and dropped gently downwards, until her toes touched the ground. Then, as Mark watched, still entranced, she reached out and started to pull at what seemed to be a curtain of some sort ... he couldn't tell exactly, because it was totally invisible, and only defined by the scene behind it, which was revealed as she moved it aside and made the opening large enough for them to walk through. She invited him to do exactly that, and although he was inexplicably reluctant to follow her, he did. With her alongside him, supporting his arm, they stepped into a place of which there'd been no sign only a few seconds earlier.

In front of them was a small, open-fronted building of smoothly cut stone, twice as tall as he was and semi-circular, with walls curving up to form half of a dome-like roof. Deep-green ivy spread up one side of it, with new, young branches doing their best to take over the remainder, whilst close by, a wooden handrail protected the top of a curved stairway which twisted itself down into the ground and out of sight. Estraal let go of his arm and gestured to it, inviting him to descend.

'This way, Mark,' she said with a warm and knowing smile. 'The others are waiting.'

Mark grasped the handrail tightly. He was glad to feel that it, at least, was sturdy and apparently real, as he peered down into the spiral and saw the flicker of firelight far below. Estraal was still close behind him and so down he went towards it, following the tight curve of the steps and staying on the outer, widest part, which felt safer to him. There were a great many of them, more than he cared for, actually, and he was ready to run back up them pretty quickly if the whole thing turned out to be some kind of trick. As the daylight above him receded, the firelight below grew brighter, and soon even began to offer a hint of welcoming warmth.

Then, at last, they reached the bottom, and Mark stepped down onto a soft, thick rug of moss which his boots sank happily into. He and Estraal were standing together in a small recess at the side of a very large and quite incredible room. Mark felt his jaw starting to sag again, but he managed to control it himself this time, and snapped it shut noisily. The flickering light came from two vast and identical fireplaces which faced each other across the circular room, helped by a dozen flaming torches which burned just as brightly on the walls. Around the edge of the main room, he could see several other side-rooms. There were no doors or dividing walls, they just seemed to merge into each other like the petals of a large daisy, arranged neatly around its broad, colourful centre. Some of them were also well lit, but others were lost in shadows or complete darkness. The walls were all covered in fine panelling, and the ceiling arched upwards, carried on long, gracefully curving beams which soared upwards to one central point. Stunning though it all was, Mark couldn't drag his eyes from the middle of the room.

A vast host of elves was sitting there, on the moss-strewn floor. They all looked his way as Estraal's hand guided him forwards, and he had the most peculiar feeling of being exposed and vulnerable, as well as excited and awestruck, all at once. He was determined not to be shy and look down, though, as hundreds of eyes stared at him and the embarrassing silence dragged on. The sea of faces filled his view, and it was only when he made himself study one or two more closely that he realised that they were all friendly, welcoming ones.

At the far side of the room was a long, curved table, close to the wall. Sitting there, facing the throng in the centre, were a dozen more elves. He felt a rush of happiness and relief as he suddenly recognised Roall, Stirran and the others, but there were females amongst them, too, some almost as beautiful as Estraal, and like the rest of them, each wore a welcoming smile.

'Come in, Mark, come in! Estraal, please bring Mark over here.'

Mark was thrilled to hear Roall's voice again after weeks of doubts and fruitless searching, and he followed Estraal sheepishly around the edge of the room and up to the curved table. Over three hundred eyes followed him every step of the way, until an elf near the end of the table stood up and offered Mark a seat next to her. The room was still horribly quiet and all those eyes were still on him as he sat down, but despite this, he felt himself starting to relax at last. After all, he was once more in the company of light elves whom he knew and trusted. He noticed that Trifillo was sitting at the table, too, but looking a great deal stronger and cleaner than the last time they were together. His hand was touching the hilt of one of three freyals which lay on the table in front of them. Roall leant forward, and the countless eyes at last left Mark and turned to the court elf of meadows as he spoke.

'Welcome to our hall, Mark, welcome indeed – from every one of us.'

He waved his hand towards the others, bringing a subdued but sincere ripple of greetings from the centre of the room.

'Well, my young friend, you can see that we *did* all survive our escape from the spriggan caves, although we got a bit damp, and it nearly finished off poor Trifillo here.' Trifillo's cheeks immediately blushed to a colour close to that of his gingery hair. 'I might add that his recovery took many days and nights, even under his cloak, and with Estraal rarely being tempted away from his bedside whilst he was healed.' It was her turn to blush then. 'I am sorry that we could not meet you sooner. You see, we have been rather involved with other even more pressing business, I am sad to say.'

'Don't worry about that,' replied Mark, who surprised himself with the sound of his own voice and so lowered it at once. 'I'm just glad to see you're all alive,' he added shyly.

'Well, I am glad we are, too,' chuckled Roall. He sighed and looked down at the freyals in front of him on the table. 'We know that you lost something very precious in the caves, whilst you were winning something priceless for us.' He ran his finger down the blade of the freyal closest to him.

'You're dead right there,' agreed Mark. 'It was precious, for sure ... more than precious, if you ask Vicks – I mean Victoria. I still can't believe I lost it.'

He paused for a moment, rubbing the back of his neck as he recalled his struggle on the net. Agoriff smiled to himself, knowing that Mark could have lost a lot more than the cure for Elspeth if it hadn't been for an outstanding bowshot.

301

'Actually, that's why I've come,' continued Mark politely. 'I mean ... I mean it's great to know you're all okay, of course it is. It's brilliant. But Vicky's sister is really ill now and we need help to find the cure again.' He glanced around, hoping that he hadn't annoyed anyone. '*Your* help.'

The room went so quiet that the crackling of the flames in the two fireplaces seemed to fill the whole room.

'Your time will come again, I am quite sure,' answered Roall at last, 'and I realise that it must be soon if the little girl is to be saved. However, there is another matter which concerns us all – you included, Mark.' His voice dropped a little. 'A possible catastrophe, in fact. Listen ...'

The next hour – or was it three? Mark had no idea – passed very quickly. Every moment of that time, however long it really was, etched itself into Mark's memory. He could recall it all clearly, word for word, shrug for shrug, chuckle for chuckle: the warmth, the murmur of the voices, the firelight dancing on the walls and playing games with the shadows amongst the vast beams. None of it would ever leave him.

He heard how the small army of elves in front of him had been summoned from near and far, from Rosedale up above them to the neighbouring valleys of Farndale and Danbydale, Fryupdale and Newtondale, even Bransdale, so as to hear of 'grave tidings'. Roall's most cunning elves had been hard at work, too. Countless long, cold nights had been spent hiding close to the fires of dark-elf camps, or in the muddy entrances to goblin dens, squatting amongst the damp roots of hollow trees, listening carefully and remembering all that they heard. From every valley had come similar news, and as that news came, Roall's heart grew steadily heavier and his hopes for a joyful Christmas more futile.

Mark listened as the meadow elf told of a great threat, a

threat to himself, Victoria, both of their families, and other mortals, too. A threat also to the host sitting there with him, one which would require all of their resolve and courage to counter, as well as a great deal of careful planning and a sizeable slice of good fortune. A scheme was afoot, a nasty and altogether wicked scheme, conjured up in the depraved minds of Malrin and his followers. Mark could scarcely believe what he heard.

Everywhere the light elves had spied or listened out, there was talk of fire. There would be uncontrollable raging fires in the night, with houses and barns razed to the ground, leaving only charred, smoking timbers and crumbling walls pointing into the sky the following morning. The farmhouses at Willow Garth and Hill Garth were the first targets, and would be attacked without mercy, for they knew that the iron key had gone that way when it was taken from the spriggan caves. Everyone within those homes would die in their beds. It was simple, but unimaginable. Mark, Victoria and their families would all be burned alive so that the third Witcher key could be found, taken and used.

As Roall continued, Mark began to feel sick. He was sick with fear at first, knowing all too well what the dark elves were capable of, but then, increasingly, sick with anger. The senseless and greed-driven destruction of two entire families, just for an old key. It filled him with a rage which now clawed its way up in his throat and tried to squeeze it shut.

I've got that key hidden under a floorboard in my bedroom. I could just bring it to Roall and he'd make sure that the dark elves got it, then everyone would be safe again. It's so simple!

Mark didn't quite choke, but he did cough, and inadvertently got everyone's attention. The hall fell silent again and all eyes turned to him as he tried to speak with a mouth suddenly as dry as fire ash.

'If the iron key is the cause of all this trouble,' he licked his lips and tried uselessly to swallow again, 'why don't I just bring it to you, so you can give it to Malrin – or whoever else wants it. They'll leave us alone then, won't they?'

The silence would have deepened further if it could have, and the only movement came from those flames within the two fireplaces. Mark was now getting really anxious, and clenched his fists together tightly under the table.

'I can't see what else I can do to help. It's the cure for Elspeth that I need more than anything. Without that, Vicky's family would rather die in a fire anyway, I bet they would!' He suddenly felt far too warm, and a bead of sweat trickled down his temple as he ran his finger along the inside of his collar and looked at the concerned faces around him.

'Sadly, it is not quite as simple as that,' replied Roall at once. 'If the dark elves were to find the iron key – by whatever means – they could enter the mines at a time of their own choosing. It may be the same day, but it could be weeks later if it suited them more. That must not happen! We cannot make a gift of the key, either directly or indirectly. Not now, not ever!'

He paused then, momentarily struggling with his own mixed feelings, but the others waited for him patiently, and seconds turned to a minute as the wise court elf considered the risks of any possible plan. He had been hoping that another, less dangerous option would occur to him at the last moment, but he already knew in his heart that there was only one answer to their problems, and it would be exactly as he'd feared, ever since the first elves had returned from their missions a week or more earlier. He spoke clearly then, without a trace of doubt in his voice and a cool determination in his green eyes which no one there missed.

'No. The key must not find its way to them, but as long as we are careful, *they* can be brought to the key.' Mark was intrigued and suddenly impatient for more, but Roall paused again as he chose his words carefully. 'If it is *we* who decide what happens to the key, and when that should be, there is a chance – a *slim* chance – that we can take great advantage of their greed. To fail to use that advantage would be unfortunate to say the least, but if the hoard also ends up in their hands, they will have wealth beyond their wildest, warped dreams, along with the means to hire every evil creature in this county for their own despicable ends. The repercussions do not bear thinking of. Only the Seelie Court can stop this!' The few elves who were looking down quickly looked up again. 'We must all gather and do battle against them, just as we have done before. It is clear that they are planning to summon the entire Unseelie Court in order to carry out these attacks and that a Sluagh will soon be upon us all! That foul host will ride through or over everyone in its path, carried on its evil hounds or other beasts under their spells. No one in the mortal world will see it or stop it, but they will surely suffer its gifts – death and destruction. To the mortals hereabouts it would be two or three disastrous and unexplained fires, but we would know differently.'

Roall stopped again, looking at the many faces, young and old, which gazed up at him, and an aching sadness suddenly came over him as he realised the enormity of his words: many elves would surely die on the sabres of the dark elves, or in the jaws of the hellhounds. Some would be young, and have long, contented lives stolen from them. Others would be older, and leave their own families bereaved and shattered. They might *all* die if the good spirits deserted them completely, and then the moors would surely become a wild and unloved place, full of terrible deeds and hopeless souls. He turned to Mark.

'I know it must be very difficult for you. We *all* know.' Most of the others at the table nodded, and those who didn't were staring at their hands, each lost in their own dark thoughts. 'You may want nothing more than our help to find the cure again, and in different circumstances that might have been possible. At least we would know the way this time!' Mark's expression didn't change, but Roall's did, for something difficult had to be said.

'This is an opportunity for us, Mark, and a rare one, too. Remember Victoria's mother? You now know who killed her. He is only one of that foul host! It hurts me to say it, but I feel it is worth risking Elspeth's life – may every good spirit watch over her – to grasp this opportunity and use it. Her cure must surely wait!'

Mark's head dropped and he found himself staring at those clenched fists, but, as his disappointment seeped out of him, he relaxed and let his fingers uncurl. He knew in his heart that Roall was right. He was always right, it seemed. The court elf spoke again, but quietly now, and despite his best attempts not to show it, somewhat tiredly.

'Let us all rest a while ... and perhaps eat, too.'

He gestured towards one of the side-rooms close to a fireplace before standing up. Everyone at the table did likewise and Mark realised that he was indeed in the company of a great leader. As every other elf in the hall also rose to their feet, Roall walked over to Mark.

'I need to speak to you privately, Mark.' There was no smile and no promise of any relaxed conversation between friends. 'Perhaps when you have rested a little?' he added.

Roall left him and fell into deep discussion with Flinnor and Agoriff. Even in that crowded place, Mark suddenly felt very alone as he made his way around the edge of the hall, nodding rather awkwardly to various groups of elves as he passed them by. He was finally spared any further embarrassment when Estraal came out of a side-room and approached him.

'I expect that you are hungry after your journey here.' Her words flowed over him like warm water. 'Follow me and see if we can tempt you with something to keep your strength up.'

Mark was thankful for the friendly help and he soon found himself in a side-room where long tables were spread with a wonderful and curious assortment of food. In fact, he was too amazed by everything to be very hungry, but he managed to nibble at some exquisite biscuits which tasted of pure honeycomb, and drank from a leather tankard full of cool, sweet apple juice, better than any he'd ever tasted. Afterwards, he wandered back into the hall alone, and found a space on an oak bench at the edge of the room, close to one of the fires. He sat there quite happily and was starting to feel more relaxed as he sipped his juice and brushed the biscuit crumbs from his lap.

There was too much for him to take in all at once. He could see 150 bows propped against one wall, whilst another was covered with the now familiar cloaks of spider's silk, hanging in a long, neat row. The firelight played on them, transforming them into a shimmering ribbon of silvery cloth which he thought would definitely hypnotise him if he stared at them for long enough. Everywhere, groups of elves talked and gestured with their hands. Despite what they now faced, they even smiled and occasionally laughed, bringing a comforting jumble of murmuring voices to his ears.

Whether it was the warm fires or the tiring bike ride, he didn't know, but sleep sneaked up on him and dragged his eyelids slowly downwards once, then twice. He shook his head and tried to fight it off, but it soon won. The subdued conversations around him became a perfect lullaby, and he drifted off to sleep with his head back against the oak panelling behind him.

He was dreaming about a huge beehive overflowing with thick honey, and was stirring up a lot of trouble with its furious occupants when he heard a voice coming from inside the hive.

'Wake up, Mark, wake up.' The voice was familiar and not bee-like at all. Then someone was gently shaking his shoulder, but firmly enough to bring him back to the waking world. He awoke with a start and found Roall sitting next to him. Remembering his manners, Mark started to get up, but Roall stopped him with the hand that was still on his shoulder.

'Please sit, Mark. I am not half as important as you might think.' Roall laughed quietly to himself and was pleased to see Mark smile sleepily, too.

'I didn't know you were in charge of so many bees – I mean elves. Crikey! I hope I haven't been rude to you over the last few weeks without knowing it,' replied Mark anxiously. Roall swept his fears away with a wave of his hand.

'I lead them for now, that is true,' said Roall modestly, 'but that could change at any time, and there are many elves wiser than I to whom I answer ... when we occasionally meet.' He was smiling and frowning together, making it clear that such meetings were best avoided if possible.

'Anyway, it is not leaders and followers which I must talk of now, but other, far more important things.'

'I'll help you in any way I can,' answered Mark, sincerely. 'If I can, that is. I feel out of place here with all you elves and your magical skills. I don't really see how I can help.' Roall looked at Mark, admiring him for his plucky courage and determination, and not for the first time. He sighed as he came closer to Mark's ear.

'This business of the dark elves. You *do* realise how much danger your families are in, don't you? They are quite capable of carrying out their plans, you know.'

Mark had heard enough about dark elves to know that they were capable of virtually anything they put their minds to.

'Oh yeah, I realise all right,' he replied under his breath. 'Look, if you want me to fight them with you, I'll try,' he added. 'But I still think I'll just be in the way. I've used my bow half a dozen times and a freyal once, in the crypt. It's not much training, is it?'

Roall put his hand over the bracer which Mark still wore on his forearm.

'I don't intend for you to have much need of this,' he said, tapping one of its green jewels. 'But it is possible that you could help more than you might imagine ... if you really want to.'

'You bet I do!' replied Mark. 'Just say how.' He forgot where he was for a moment and said it far more loudly than he'd intended. He looked straight at Roall and lowered his voice before speaking. 'You'd do anything to protect your family, I expect. Well, I'm the same.'

'I cannot deny that,' said the elf. 'But it will be dangerous ... or worse than dangerous. Possibly fatal.' He whispered the last word and watched for Mark's reaction.

'Don't be so sure about that. There's no way I'm going anywhere without one hell of a struggle. Yeah – including heaven.' He grinned then. 'So what is this *fatal* mission anyway?'

Roall was delighted. Without Mark's help, Roall knew that any conflict against the Sluagh could indeed be deadly for far too many of those gathered in the hall.

'Very well then,' continued Roall, with obvious relief. 'Their greed for the hoard could be their downfall. *Could be*, mind you, for their sick minds can never be trusted an inch, or relied on, except in their unwavering dedication to evil.'

He looked at Mark for any sign of a change of heart, or mind, but there was none ... so far.

'You have Sir Henry's third key. They will come to it like a dog to a meaty bone on the kitchen floor. They must get to know that you will take the key to Three Howes Gate and enter the mines there.'

Mark had grown up with a healthy respect for the dangerous mines, but didn't know of anyone who'd actually been inside them. He frowned at the mere mention of the gate.

'Alone?' he asked.

'Perhaps,' replied Roall. 'If they believe that you want the hoard for yourself, they will come to stop you – and stop at nothing to achieve it. It may give us the advantage that we need.' Roall blew out his breath and prepared himself for a possible disagreement. 'There is something else, Mark. You have to tell Victoria about this, but you must tell her in the garden of her home, and nowhere else.' Mark looked puzzled as Roall continued. 'It appears that the dark elves saw me handing you the key outside the spriggan caves, and have had their spies watching you ever since. They will also have heard every word you have uttered since then, for they are desperate to know the exact whereabouts of that key. Yes, tell Victoria in her garden, and I am sure that some infinitely more pointed and dirty ears will hear you well enough. This is the best way for them to hear about Three Howes Gate and your intentions to use it, without them suspecting something. Then ... Well, we shall see what can be done.'

Roall waited patiently as Mark took it all in and searched his unwise mind for any alternatives once more. But there probably weren't any, he quickly realised. Wise Roall would have thought of them by now if there had been, and so the way ahead was clear at last. His eyes lit up as his silly, brave heart took control once again.

'Right, then. This ... um ... this Seelie Court will include me for once. I just hope I won't let it down.'

'I suspect that there is very little chance of *that*, whatever the outcome,' replied Roall, slapping Mark proudly on the shoulder. He stood up to go, but turned and looked back at him.

'By the way, when you go to the mines, take your freyal with you.' Mark's eyebrows shot up in surprise.

'Are you sure? I know what it means to you.'

'Quite sure, my friend,' confirmed Roall. 'I fear your need will be even greater than ours on that occasion.'

Three Howes Gate

The ancient granary at Bell Farm was gradually falling down, just like the rest of the buildings there. When the last tenant had died over fifty years earlier, no one else could afford the extortionately high rent demanded by the Witcher estate, and so, sadly, greed and stubbornness prevailed over common sense. It remained empty, year after year, until the gutters fell off and most of the roofs fell in, making a good home for pigeons and bats, but very little else. At least the granary had more roof remaining than most of the other buildings, and it was spacious. But best of all, there were no windows. In short, it was ideal ...

The ground floor had changed very little since the day it was last used, all those years ago. It wasn't as dry as it once was, with gaping holes in what did remain of the roof, and more of the same in the timber floor of the upper level. There were a few pieces of farm machinery, so old that a horse would be needed to pull them again, as well as a pile of discarded fence timbers and some broken tools, but no sign of any stairs, strangely.

The dark elves had seen to that, soon after they'd discovered the place. Out came the stairs, or what was left of them, and up went their own gear: stones for sharpening swords and sabres, boxes of stolen food and barrels of stolen cider. Straw bales had been added here and there as seats, with some ripped apart and spread out to form stinking beds – which probably crawled with many more visitors than the drunken good-for-nothings who collapsed into them each night. Without the stairs, they were as safe as they could be. If anyone wanted to prowl around, then it had to be downstairs, and that would be an extremely risky business given the pack of hellhounds which kept each other company in one of the darker corners.

The hounds were gnawing the last traces of meat from their supper bones. The noise of it was an effective reminder for everyone to keep their distance, and even their masters didn't get too close to them at feeding times. From higher up came the murmur of voices and occasional light footsteps. There was a red light somewhere up there, goblin light, which peeped through the gaps between the floorboards, or streamed down in bright shafts through the larger holes where rain had completely rotted the floor away. One such hole was a little neater than the rest, almost circular, but otherwise not particularly special at first glance. A small, hooded person suddenly appeared in it, silhouetted against the red light, then slid down to the ground floor as if he was on a rope. Actually, it *was* a rope, but an invisible one: the perfect way up and down for the granary's new residents, and of no use at all to anyone else.

He was a tree-goblin, so called because he happened to live deep under them and certainly not because he admired or respected them in any way. Another one quickly followed, and the two of them set to work pulling branches from a large pile of firewood which had been stacked well away from the hounds. Like all goblins and the rabble they mix with, they would be intending to keep their toes warm, and slow-roasting over a fire was a good way of making sure that their supper was really dead, as well as reasonably furless or featherless. They were soon passing the long branches to someone above them (who pulled them up though the hole with a lot of grumbling), before shinning up the invisible rope and leaving the hounds in peace once again.

Up there, in the dull, red smoke-haze from the smouldering fire, the Unseelie Court was gathering. The dark elves usually coped alone with the day-to-day business of stealing, tricking, maiming and occasionally killing their victims, but this time it was different, and the word had gone out far and wide for anyone who was qualified to ride with the Sluagh, to come along and join them. If they were evil, depraved, or uncontrollably violent, or preferably all three, they were invariably welcomed with open arms.

Many dark elves were there as usual, gathered in small, secretive groups, like murders of huge, scheming crows, but they had other company now. The wood-gathering tree-goblins were only two of thirty or more, their heads covered by hoods and their faces always in shadow. The end of a long nose appeared briefly now and again, or the tip of a darting tongue if one got overenthusiastic with his talking or eating. They formed their own private groups, and kept their distance from the dark elves. After all, the Unseelie Court was a malignant gathering of like minds ... not friends.

In a corner furthest from the fire, yet another small crowd had assembled. These were bogles, but bogles of the most loathsome kind. This motley bunch were far removed from the everyday variety so fond of dusty spaces under children's beds, or the impenetrable shadows cast by bright moonlight. These were like hollow trees, rotten to the core and devoid of all feeling: all wearing different, but equally grubby, knotted neck scarves. Long, curved daggers lay waiting under their sacking cloaks, and many carried a short length of cord, for tying wrists, or more often than not, tightening around bare throats. They liked nothing more than the thought of travelling fast at night, on bewitched horses or the broad backs of the hellhounds, wailing like tortured ghosts as they went, and hoping that something or someone would be foolish enough to get in their way. In short, their credentials were outstandingly good.

Closest to the fire sat two other figures. They were deep in conversation and paid little attention to anyone else around them. One of them was Malrin. He was poking the fire with his sabre, sending a shower of glowing sparks up towards the roof, whilst the other creature, evidently a goblin, was holding a long stick close to the glowing embers, cooking several mice which had been threaded onto it, nose to tail, like strange, furry beads on a necklace. A full black hood covered his face, with cut-outs for his eyes and mouth. His long, hooked nose was too large to be contained and protruded grotesquely from a final central slit, whilst an old red scarf was knotted around his neck. Despite the warm fire, he wore thick leather gauntlets, and appeared to be unarmed – although that meant very little in company such as this. Malrin seemed to be interested in his new acquaintance, for he was now leaning towards the stranger so as not to be overheard.

'I don't think I have heard of you or your boys ... Snilbog, was it? What makes you think we need you at all?'

Malrin glanced across to where seven or eight particularly underfed goblins were playing dice, and making a good deal of noise about it. Snilbog squeezed one of the hot mice gently to see if it was cooked, before answering.

'When it comes to the pinch ... at the gate, you'll soon see ... who you can rely on and ... who you can't. Just watch!'

The goblin sniffed loudly between every few words, despite the fact that his nose wasn't even dripping. It made the conversation rather odd, and Malrin didn't quite know what to make of it. The smell of burning fur filled the dark elf's nostrils as Snilbog spun the smoking mice over and spoke again, still sniffing.

'Surely you've 'eard about ... them drownin's at Fryup Bridge last month ... Who d'you think was behind them now? Some naughty kids from the ... ruddy farm next door? No it weren't ... T'was my boys and me!' Malrin looked at him with renewed interest. 'All we want is our ... fair share of any takings ... no more, 'n' no less. We fight like cornered wildcats and we ... don't take prisoners!' He almost spat the last word out through the slit in his hood. 'So are we in ... or are we out ...? 'Coz if we're out ... we've got other business to get to ...'

Snilbog started to get up, but the dark elf's sabre was suddenly resting across the goblin's knee, stopping him. Malrin was used to dealing with the likes of Snilbog. He was fairly sure that the strangers would be a useful addition to the Unseelie Court, as it seemed that they had recently 'arranged' for the road bridge in Fryupdale to collapse just as a tractor and trailer carrying several men home were crossing it. Two of them were horribly crushed and another drowned below the bridge in the unfortunate 'accident'.

Malrin concluded that Snilbog and his lads were quite capable of sinking to the required depths, and besides, he had a strong feeling that if he turned them away, they would probably be making their own plans to line their pockets, now that word of the hoard had spread amongst the local lowlife. It was better to have them close by, he decided, where he could watch them from a safe distance, but although they might prove useful, it didn't mean that he had to trust them. He moved his sabre and laid it across the stick and its half-cooked mice, in a subtle but threatening gesture.

'All right ... you're in. But *I* give the orders, is that clear?' He tried to see Snilbog's eyes, but couldn't.

'Clear as fresh running spring water, my friend,' sneered the goblin, suddenly sniffless.

Leaving a slightly puzzled Malrin to tend to his fire, Snilbog got up and went to join in with the dice game. He didn't share out the cooked mice, though.

* * *

Far away from the gathering in the granary, another individual was chewing over recent rumours that the Walker lad would be at Three Howes Gate the following evening – maybe alone, and maybe not, but definitely with the iron key in his pocket. Scribber sat all alone on a bench, leaning back against the damp wall of his cave with his injured wrist thickly bandaged in strips of old cloth – the leather sleeve of his jerkin had been slit open to make room for them. His only company was a solitary bat which seemed determined to pester him, but was skilfully managing to keep out of swatting distance with each pass. The spriggan picked up an empty jug and threw it at the bat as it flew past him yet again, but missed, which made him feel even worse. He was seething with hatred. It was almost coming out of his skin in his sweat. It was on his breath and in his spit. He hated his own bad luck, the other spriggans, and all the elves which lived, dark or light. He especially hated the bat, but most of all, he hated one particular mortal. Scribber knew that it should all have been settled a long time ago in the crypt.

''Ow did that scrawny kid survive the fight? He'd got a freyal from somewhere, okay, but 'e couldn't 'ardly lift it, let alone swing it.

Scribber plagued himself with the question for the hundredth time, and others, too.

And 'ow come 'e managed to get them light elves on 'is side, anyways? They got past our 'ound and stole the iron key from under our blinkin' noses. Gawd! I wished I'd known it was special – I could 'ave saved 'em the trouble.

He had plenty of questions all right, but not a single answer. He was far too distracted to work them out, even if he had the patience to try, which he didn't. His wrist burned as if it was being branded, that was all he knew or cared about, that and sending the mortal back to his maker the first chance he got. He stood up and kicked a bucket of slops into the remains of a smouldering fire in front of him. It hissed and steamed for a few seconds, then just smoked and stank. Tomorrow couldn't come soon enough.

* * *

Well before light the next morning, Scribber's first waking thought was of Three Howes Gate. Thirsty for violence, his determination to kill the boy there was so overwhelming that his appetite had disappeared the previous day and not returned – this had never happened to him before, and he put it down to an exceptionally large breakfast of boiled mutton two days earlier, and certainly not anything like bad nerves, of course. After a poor night's sleep, he crawled off his stinking bracken bed far too early, and had been ready to go for hours when he finally pushed back one of the two massive door stones and stepped out into the pale light of dawn.

So what. I'll just 'ave to 'ide a bit longer, that's all. Better than missin' 'im, for sure, he told himself, as he heaved the heavy stone back into place with a few grunts and groans.

He was glad to be on his way at last, and he shrank to his smallest size as he tramped along a well-worn path

318

between huge rocks, and up and down heather-covered hillocks, slowly gaining height as he did so. The daylight was little more than an uninviting glow in the eastern sky as he fingered the end of the dagger tucked in his belt, chuckling to himself as he recalled his convincing lies regarding the two identical ones he and Wipp had already lost, and how he'd just taken another one without permission. Generally, he would have asked, but on this occasion he had no time or patience for lengthy discussions about why he wanted it and for how long, or any other nosy questions. Taking it was easy. He'd saved a large mutton bone for the hellhound guarding the valuables, and had quickly helped himself to one of the remaining two freyals as the delighted hound had crushed the bone into sharp splinters between its powerful jaws.

An hour later, and only half a mile from Three Howes Gate, his feet suddenly crunched on the cinders of the old railway track and he peered along it in both directions, half expecting to see the doomed mortal in the far distance. Two partridges scuttled across the track in front of him and disappeared into the heather, but there was no other sign of life. It suited him perfectly. He didn't want any last-minute distractions or delays and, pulling his hood up, he headed south-east along the track towards the stump-like remains of the great chimney at Chimney Bank, along with the ruined kilns close to its base. Just beyond those kilns, and cut straight into the hillside a stone's throw from three ancient burial mounds which gave it its name, was Three Howes Gate itself.

Typically, Scribber congratulated himself for running to schedule so well – early though he was. He checked around him again before making his way to the crumbling brick archways which had once belched out black smoke or glowed with the searing heat of the kilns behind them. From these he had a perfect view of the gate's large doors, and an equally good hiding place. He settled down in one of them as well as he could, and quickly discovered that comfortable resting places and piles of old bricks don't necessarily go hand in hand, but he waited anyway, sitting on a large pile of them with one eye spying around the corner of the wall and along the track which the mortal must surely use. He tapped his long fingernails on the blade of his dagger and smiled to himself contentedly ...

Whether it was simply due to a missed breakfast, or the unusually sleepless night he'd just endured, it was difficult to say, but he was soon so well asleep that it took the shrill whinny of a horse to wake him. His head came up so quickly that it hit the wall beside him, but he somehow managed not to shout out as he fought to remember why he was there, and not in his cave. Then he did remember, and if he could have, he would have kicked his own sore backside for coming so close to ruining his clever plan. He scrambled to his feet and pressed himself against the kiln wall, trying to shake some life back into a leg which had fallen asleep almost as deeply as he just had.

A bay horse and its cloaked rider were a short distance along the track and coming his way. Scribber grinned and relaxed. The cloak was elfish – borrowed from his new friends, no doubt – and the hood was over the rider's head, hiding him and keeping his throat warm ... ready for slitting. The excited spriggan leant a little further out to see if anyone was following the lone rider, for just like everyone else in the unseen world, he'd heard that the Unseelie Court had gathered together and planned to take the iron key soon for themselves.

They can 'ave the ruddy key, he thought generously to himself, *as long as I gets the interfering little fool's blood first!*

Scribber had no wish to find himself stranded in the middle of the track with a Sluagh bearing down on him at breakneck speed, and so he knew that he must move quickly before the mortal used the key and disappeared into the mines, or a festering goblin robbed him of his chance for glory by getting to the boy first.

He watched impatiently as the horse reached the gate and the rider slipped expertly from the saddle. The horse was soon tethered to a large metal ring which still dangled from the wall a lifetime after a pit pony last used it – the narrow-gauge railway lines on which those ponies had pulled their trucks of ore still ran out from under the enormous doors and disappeared below the cinders. The rider now straddled those lines as he stood facing the doors, pausing for a last look up and down the track before reaching out for the huge, ring-like handle on one of them. He twisted it one way, then the other, and Scribber felt his hatred for the boy rising in his gullet.

'Does he really think it'll open for 'im after all these years, just like that?'

As the handle was tried again and again, Scribber decided it was time for action, particularly as the fearful racket the boy was making would make it even easier to attack him without any warning. It was a short dash to the gate, and Scribber was out of his brick hiding hole like a sprinter out of his blocks, with each pace greater than the last as he rapidly grew larger. By the time he was halfway there, he was over seven feet high but still growing, and the reluctant freyal in his hands was a long and deadly sword, lifted high above his shoulders in both hands. With six yards to go Scribber couldn't resist letting out a loud cheer of victory. The mortal was his at last.

Too late, the horse whinnied again, but in fright this time. It reared up, tugging against its tethered reins, and the cloaked figure at the doors only had time to turn around and face the noise behind them. It was impossible to say who was the more surprised of the two. Scribber's roar stopped short, but he was going too fast to stop himself. He didn't even have time to swerve when he realised that his prey wasn't the stupid boy, after all.

As for Victoria, her instincts to protect herself took over, and in that last second she brought up her thumb stick to face her attacker, thrusting the end of it against the sturdy door behind her. It was only an instantaneous and feeble attempt on her part to fend off the huge spriggan, but it was more than enough time for the stick to react. As Scribber took his last few paces, he sliced downwards with the freyal towards Victoria's neck ... but she was now grasping a long, slender lance. Scribber ran onto it and could only keep going, skewering himself like a pig ready for the roasting fire, whilst his freyal clattered uselessly against the doors.

Strangely, Scribber felt no pain at all, but he knew that something was very wrong. Even as he smashed brutally into Victoria and crushed her against the door, he still didn't realise that he'd already killed himself. He bounced backwards off the doors before staggering a few steps with the lance protruding a foot in front of him and six feet behind. Then he knew that he'd made his very last and fatal mistake, and as he stood there, sucking in his final breath, Scribber was true to form and blamed anyone or anything other than himself.

Yes, of course. The elf cloak tricked my eyes ... and the horse was just like the one the boy sometimes rode. That was it!

He dropped the freyal and looked down in disbelief at his stomach and its unfamiliar attachment, then, with his eyes staring wide but now seeing nothing at all, he sank slowly to his knees and fell sideways into the cinders. He was dead and gone before he even reached them.

In a way, Victoria was gone, too, but at least she was alive. Her cloak had helped her to survive the brutal onslaught, but the lance hadn't slowed Scribber down at all, and she'd been knocked unconscious by him for the second time in her life. Utterly lost to the world, she slid down the door and came to rest in a sitting position with her back against it, looking just as if she'd dozed off in the sun after a long summer picnic. Her horse, which had broken free in its distress, now stood close by and foraged amongst the heather for hidden grass. He couldn't know how close he'd come to losing his owner forever.

Half a mile back along the track, Mark knew that something was wrong at the great gate the moment he saw a horse grazing there, unattended. It was too much of a coincidence that a riderless horse should be at that exact place, and on that particular day. With his heartbeat quickening, he tightened his legs against the mare's ribs and eased her into an easy canter, his eyes fixed hawk-like on the distant horse. A quarter of a mile further on, his heart began to race in his chest, which felt like a hollow drum, as he realised that the horse was very much like Victoria's. He spurred his horse on as various explanations rushed through his head, but none of them were even remotely comforting.

Surely she's not here now, when it's so dangerous. She can't be … She mustn't be!

When he imagined that he could see a cloaked figure slumped against the doors, the horse willingly galloped for Mark, with cinders exploding from under its hooves and Mark half standing in the stirrups whilst it fled across those last 100 yards. Mark dismounted long before the mare had slid to a halt in a cloud of cinder dust.

Oh no, it's going to be her! The horse is hers for sure, and there's the cloak, too …

Her head had fallen forward and the hood covered it completely. Mark saw the dead spriggan just next to her. The body was small again now, and looked ridiculous on the eight-foot lance which still ran through it. There was blood everywhere, including the front of Victoria's cloak and legs. Mark's mind was twisting itself into a tight, painful knot as he fought to control the dread that was now filling it: if it was her, he was sure that she'd be dead. He knelt in front of her and lifted her head with his unsteady hands, desperately hoping he was wrong.

The quiet groan which came from her lips was simply the sweetest, most wonderful sound he'd ever heard. One side of her face was grazed and smeared with blood, but it was dark brown and Mark guessed that it wasn't hers. He kept holding her head with his hands whilst she drifted back to him and finally focused on his face, then, as she recognised him she started to smile, but stopped and put a hand up to her bruised cheek. They both started to speak together then, but Mark let her have the first word. He was absolutely sure that she deserved it.

'I thought I'd come and help you, but I was a bit early, I think.'

It was Mark's turn to smile then, thrilled to know that she'd cheated death, but amazed that she was in good spirits despite what appeared to have happened.

'Are ... are you really all right?' he stuttered.

As relief swept through him, he let go of her head and offered his hands to pull her up. She took them and Mark helped her to her feet, but she didn't let go of him.

'I thought you'd already gone in,' she half whispered. 'Then *he* came at me from behind.'

She looked down at the spriggan, who was curled up on his side like a sleeping child, still clutching the lance which ran through him.

'That's my stick, you know,' she added, proudly.

Mark could now picture what had happened, although he couldn't know that Scribber had actually been waiting for *him*. He pulled Victoria closer and her head dropped onto his shoulder as they stood there for several long moments, not speaking, each of them glad to feel the other one close and safe. Nothing else mattered for them now that they were together again, and Mark took her by the shoulders and looked straight into her eyes. They were filled with tears, and one of them was already swelling up and threatening to close, even as he spoke.

'He met his match when he took *you* on, though, didn't he?'

Mark shook his head in wonder, but he also meant what he had said. Victoria just nodded and tried unsuccessfully to smile again, whilst Mark went to her horse and calmed it with a few strokes of its neck before leading it back to Victoria. He handed the reins to her and went to the dead spriggan. Victoria looked away as he lifted the lance by its bloodied shaft, and with his boot in the small of Scribber's back, pulled it the rest of the way through the body. It glistened at first, wet with Scribber's dark blood, but as soon as it was out it quickly shortened to become her familiar polished thumb stick once again. Mark then noticed the freyal lying on the cinders where Scribber had dropped it, and let out a silent whistle as he picked it up and tossed it lightly in his hand.

'That's one more for the court elves and only one left in the caves, according to my reckoning.' He paused for a moment as he tucked it into his belt, then held it out to Victoria. 'You keep this for now, Vicky ... You mustn't stay here any longer, you know. I'm expecting some company and I don't think you should be around when they get here. From what I can see, they'd start dropping like flies if they upset you!'

He looked at Victoria's handiwork lying on the ground, then up and down the cinder track: he assumed that the light elves were hiding somewhere close by, but was puzzled and alarmed that they hadn't intervened when Victoria was attacked. He kept his thoughts to himself as he turned to her.

'Come on, Vicks. I'll give you a leg-up.'

Mark bent forwards, offering his cupped hands ready – and giving her very little chance of arguing about who should go and who should stay. In the end, there was no time for an argument, or even a decision. That was made for them before Victoria could place her foot in his hands or open her mouth to protest.

From deep in the valley came a hollow, resonating bark, then another, then many, like a distant pack of foxhounds onto a fresh scent. Mark stood up straight and listened. It could only be one pack of hounds up in this high country, and they would be hellhounds. The Sluagh was on the move.

*   *   *

He fumbled in his coat pocket for the large key and looked around anxiously, still clinging to the hope that the light elves would rush out from a clever hiding place and save them.

'Now you've done it, girl! You'll have to come in with me!'

He was deadly serious, and she knew better than to argue with him as she nodded quietly. He placed the key in the lock and tried to turn its large square handle, but the lock seemed to be jammed. He kept talking as he wrestled with it.

'Get ready to send the horses off!'

Victoria moved towards them and stood ready to send them cantering away to safety. The hounds already sounded a lot closer and Mark put all his strength into turning the key, but the old lock was still being stubborn.

He shouted to Victoria now, who was waiting with her stick held high.

'Hold it! Wait! If I can't open this, we'll have to risk riding out of here.'

He then drew his freyal, putting the short blade through the handle of the key and using it as a lever. It still wouldn't turn, but then the freyal started to grow, inch upon inch, with Mark now putting all his weight on it and turning red as the leverage increased with each of those inches. Luckily, the key turned before it broke, stiffly and noisily for sure, but the lock finally clanked open and Mark gave Victoria the nod she was waiting for. She put her stick to good use across the horses' hind quarters, and they galloped away as the young couple put their shoulders to the door and pushed. The baying of the hounds was growing steadily louder, but yelps and shrieks of delight were now mixed in amongst it all. There wasn't much time left.

Then, to Victoria's surprise, Mark started to chuckle to himself as he pushed. She stared at him as she pushed too, wondering what it could be.

'What's ... so ... funny?' she asked incredulously, between pushing and snatching breaths.

Mark controlled himself a little, but couldn't wipe away a smile as he turned and put his back to the door instead.

'It's reminded me ... when we were both eight, trying to get into my dad's big barn. Do you remember what happened?' Victoria thought back, then nodded.

'We both got a good hiding,' she grunted, as she pushed again.

'Nothing changes!' replied Mark, his face turning purple as he strained even harder.

The exceptionally heavy door hadn't moved for years, and so it only opened very slowly on its rusted hinges, but open it did, screeching like a rat pierced on the end of a pitchfork as it edged inwards, bit by bit. When the gap was just large enough, the exhausted pair slipped in, turned, and even more slowly it seemed, pushed it shut with a loud and horribly final clunk.

'Oh, Christ!' exclaimed Mark, in the pitch darkness. 'The key's still outside – I can't lock them out.' Luckily, he couldn't see Victoria's expression. 'We'll have to leave it. Let's go!'

They had no choice but to go blindly into the tunnel, walking for the first few yards, then jogging ... hoping that the way was clear, but holding their hands out in front of them in case it wasn't.

'In tunnels black,
You may see light'

The Sluagh was a heart-stopping spectacle. The hellhounds carried the first of them, just as the dark elves had trained them to. Whips of thorny briars lashed across their haunches, or sharp teeth bit into their hairy, muscular necks as their heartless riders clung on grimly. A score or more huge red eyes bobbed about as the hounds approached the gates at Three Howes, like a wild pack from Satan's kennels. Several dark elves rode on each one, clinging to thick leather straps which encircled wide, barrel-like chests and taught stomachs. Cinders and dust blasted from their huge paws and flew everywhere – including backwards into the rabble which ran, half blinded, in their wake.

In amongst them were many more dark elves of the lower ranks, along with Snilbog's hooded band of ruffians, all grotesquely bow-legged but still capable of running at an alarming speed. A swarm of bogles followed behind. They'd pulled their scarves up high because of the dust, and so their enthusiastic yelling and grunting was a little muffled. They were all swinging their strangling cords around their heads in blurred circles, though, barely able to control their bloodlust. At the rear came a dozen stallions, once tame, but now wild, stolen and bewitched in some secret way, each one reluctantly carrying an infestation of hooded tree-goblins. These demented creatures were digging their spurred heels viciously into the bloodied ribs of the terrified horses, or hanging on cruelly to their ears and manes if they were close enough to reach them. The Sluagh was nothing short of a seething, panting nightmare.

The sound of it was as terrifying as the sight. The baying of the hounds was all but drowned out by the wild screaming from on top of their backs, or from behind them in the dust clouds. Only fifteen seconds after the huge doors had closed with Mark and Victoria behind them, the Sluagh was sliding to a halt outside, paws, hooves and a small army of booted feet cutting deep furrows in the cinders. Two of the hounds were more excited than was good for them, and reared up in front of the doors as if they would happily tear them to pieces with their claws and teeth. Their riders held on like cockroaches and used their briar whips with renewed venom. It was an effective but brutal reminder of exactly who was in charge, and instantly brought streaks of blood from the rippling flanks of the crazed beasts.

Malrin was the first to slip down from his mount, and was at the doors before Snilbog could even rein in his own hellhound. Scribber's body lay close to the dark elf's feet. All it received was a splash of black spit – after Malrin had hit the door with his fist.

'Too late, he's in!' he snarled, before gazing down at the protruding key. 'But no matter. At least he's left it unlocked for us. *So* kind of him!' He looked up at the others, who had now gathered around. 'Shall we join him then, boys?'

He didn't wait for an answer. Images of the hoard now swamped each of their minds and no replies were wanted, or needed. The lower sections of the doors suddenly disappeared behind a dense, jostling rabble, all pressing shoulders or backs against them. The doors were soon wide open, and the truck lines at Malrin's feet were disappearing into the darkness a short distance ahead of him. A deathly, malignant silence settled upon the Sluagh as the last of the dust dispersed and even the cords stopped spinning, then dangled idly against legs: it was almost as if that silence had escaped from the mine, looking for a new home, but it was very short-lived. Of their own accord, the hounds suddenly became excited again, straining at their reins or turning in tight circles under the whips – they could now smell human flesh and were in the mood for sport. The deafening sound of their barking and howling raced into the mine to be immediately lost in a jumble of colliding echoes, but only after it had caught up with two small figures a mere hundred paces further into the hill as they stumbled forwards blindly.

Malrin remounted his hound, which reared up, snarling, before leaping between the open doors. The entire Sluagh surged forwards right behind it, and was instantly swallowed up by the red gloom inside, for many goblin lights started to grow in amongst the front runners. As the Sluagh poured into the mine, the tail-enders were almost lost in their own dust once more, but a one-eared bogle had a keener eye than most, and he sprang sideways towards Scribber's body at the last second. It was nothing more than a thin leather cord which had caught his eye as it hung from the spriggan's jacket pocket, but no right-minded bogle could ever have resisted it.

*   *   *

Further inside the hill, the two youngsters may as well have been blind. There were a few glow-worms high above their heads, but these could do little more than hint as to what might be solid, unforgiving wall and what was perhaps the less painful way ahead. The old truck lines were far more useful to them, however. As they ran onwards as quickly as they dared, hand in hand, Mark brushed his foot down the side of one of them, and so at least had some warning of any bends. Despite this, it was too dark to run quickly, but their blood was certainly running: running cold in their veins at the thought of what was close behind them, and catching up by the second. Mark couldn't understand it.

Where are the light elves? Surely they wouldn't let me down ...

But the awful truth was gripping him by the throat and beginning to make it ache. They were in this living hell all alone, and they would soon die, miles from their loved ones, their bodies thrown to whatever was howling behind them.

Mark could hear Victoria's sobs as they stumbled forwards: she was trying to hold them back, but she couldn't hide them completely. She was terrified of dying in the dark, far away from her family and with Elspeth left utterly doomed, but despite her terror, the same thought kept cutting through her mind, straight though everything else in it.

If Mark is going right in, then I go, too! That's how it is with us.

The faces of her sisters and father were swimming about in the blackness ahead of her, saying goodbye – or so it seemed to her. She could almost have touched them if she'd tried, as Mark held on to her tightly to remind her that she wasn't alone, but there was nothing he could say to make it any easier for her. Their freyals had grown longer, and they held them out in front of them, hoping for an early warning of anything in their path, but Victoria's arm soon ached with the weight of hers, adding to her misery. The sobbing continued and grew a little louder, with Mark sickened at having to hear her so frightened and yet unable to help her. He gripped his freyal tightly, so tightly that he thought his knuckles would burst, whilst the terrible noise behind them began to fill their ears and minds to overflowing.

Then, without any warning, they ran straight into something hard and cold. The freyals clattered noisily against it and twisted violently in their hands: Victoria's dropped to the ground as they hit a pair of solid steel doors which shut off the tunnel and blocked their way. They grunted as the wind was punched out of them and Mark hit his forehead badly, bringing a dozen bright lights – but only *inside* his head, sadly. The pair of them turned and leant back against the doors, feeling the penetrating coldness of the steel striking through their cloaks in seconds, and Mark's thoughts suddenly became as dark as their surroundings.

Huh, so this is where we die together ... Under a bloody mountain and as far from everyone and every place we know and love as we can be. Just brilliant!

Victoria's sobs had died already, and she dropped onto one knee and felt around in the dust for her sword. As she found it and stood up, Mark spoke to her. He wanted to whisper the words for some reason, but the din of the Sluagh was swelling, bouncing off every wall. He could hardly think, let alone speak, for he could now pick out individual sounds: whips cracking, the hum of the strangling cords spinning, a barbaric 'Kill! Kill! Kill!' from a large group of them, all of it mixed in with the relentless baying of the hounds and the screaming of their riders. A red glow suddenly started to push back the darkness from around the curve of the tunnel in front of them – like the first teasing glimmer of a new dawn. But this was a dawn from Hades. He shouted to her above all the noise, whilst she could still hear him at all.

'If this is really it, I ... I wouldn't want to die with anyone else, Vicky. You know that, don't you?' He stared at her, wide-eyed, blood trickling down his temple from a deep cut.

'I know it!' she shouted back hoarsely, but the emotion within those three short words almost choked her, and she gripped his free hand so tightly that it hurt him. 'Same here!' she added, meaning it more than any words she'd ever spoken.

The red light grew steadily, and soon they could see that in their blindness they'd run past the end of the tunnel without realising it, and were now standing at the far side of a high, wide, marshalling yard. The dusty floor was criss-crossed with many truck lines, whilst large pieces of derelict machinery stood along both side walls. Above the machinery to their left was a long, deep balcony with protective railings, cut into the solid rock. They could just make out the filthy walls and boarded-up windows of various abandoned offices and storerooms up there, festooned in sagging wires and cables which went nowhere. It was a depressing place to die in, that was certain.

There are probably ghosts of miners up there right now, leaning on the railings, laughing at us ... waiting for us, thought Mark morbidly as he lifted his sword and took a deep breath, for neither of them needed to speak another word.

The Sluagh spilled into the yard like overflowing sewage, and the goblin lights suddenly dazzled the two solitary figures standing with their backs hard against the steel doors – Mark wouldn't let go of Victoria's hand to shield his eyes, and he squinted at the incredible sight in front of them. Partially hidden in clouds of their own dust, the entire Sluagh had skidded to a halt ten paces away. It could be for no other reason than to gloat at their trapped prey, and gloat they most certainly did.

333

The Unseelie Court virtually filled that vast, godforsaken place from wall to wall. Six white hounds along each side twitched under the spurs of the dark elves straddling their backs, eager for fresh meat. The centre was filled, row upon row, with more dark elves, goblins and bogles, all jostling for a good view, whilst the larger ones shoved smaller ones aside with their shoulders or snarled at each other like the vicious, barbaric animals that they were. The stallions blocked the way out at the rear, some stamping their hooves and others rearing up in terror, forcing their tree-goblin riders to hold on tightly to their manes, or to each other. It was quieter now, though, as the dust tried to settle and the hounds were gradually whipped into submission, but there was still an empty space between the Sluagh and its prey, a no-man's-land for those last few moments before the kill.

Lost in the Hill

Malrin swung his leg up over the neck of his hellhound and slid to the ground. Snilbog was close by, standing with his bow-legged rabble, and he stepped forwards to join Malrin. Together, they walked into that open space and stopped five paces from Mark and Victoria. Then a heavy, brooding silence came, as both goblin and dark elf toyed with their quarry like cats with mice, their arms crossed and their contempt for the youngsters oozing from every pore of their skin. They noticed that the mortals each carried a sword, but the inevitable outcome would not be altered by such minor details, as far as they were concerned.

'It's *such* a shame that you got in our way,' said Malrin, always glad of the opportunity to intimidate his victims before he actually killed them. 'All we wanted was the key and a clear run to the hoard,' he purred.

His words were as smooth as silk, but Mark ignored them and decided to speak up whilst he still could. He would have, that is, but a certain person beside him beat him to it. She never ceased to amaze him. It could have been the inevitability of her death which gave her the courage to speak out, or just the famous Featherstone bloody-mindedness welling up in her, nobody could say which, but she lifted her long freyal and held it up defiantly, before letting go of Mark's hand and grasping the hilt with both hands as the heavy blade began to wobble at once.

335

'What gives you the right to … to …' she couldn't find the words she wanted and tried to compose herself, 'to kill or … or maim whoever you want … just because you *feel* like it?'

Her suppressed fury was plain enough to hear, though, and Mark felt a sudden rush of pride as he glanced sideways at her.

'You … you think that no one matters in this world apart from yourselves. *You're* the ones who should be destroyed, and you will be one day, you'll see! The light elves will see to that!'

Malrin gasped in mock horror at her prophecy, but then he smiled a crooked smile at her as she lifted her sword even higher and looked briefly at Mark. It was a look to say goodbye, and to remind him that her feelings for him were still as true and bright as they had been when they'd tried to get into that barn, so many years before. Mark looked back at her and nodded. They still understood each other perfectly, and he wasn't the least bit ashamed of the single tear which ran down his cheek. It was a tear of exasperation and sadness. Exasperation, for he knew that he couldn't protect her from what was about to happen, and sadness that he'd never know what might have been, had they lived. Malrin drew his sabre and the corner of his lip curled upwards in anticipation of extreme, sadistic pleasure.

*　　*　　*

Only sixty light elves could step out of the shadows and onto the long balcony without so much as a rustle of a cloak or the fall of a footstep – sixty elves who in the end had been unable to hide and wait for Mark outside Three Howes Gate, where the enemy could so easily have been scattered to the four winds and so live to fight another day.

Sixty elves who, with the help of the court elf of rocks and a long rope, entered the mines by a long forgotten and horribly narrow air shaft, directly into the marshalling yard. The risks to Mark's safety had been discussed and calculated with the utmost care, but they were taken in any case: unless he drew the entire Unseelie Court deep into the hillside, all would be lost. Unfortunately, the light elves had no way of knowing that he would do exactly that ... but with Victoria at his side.

That balcony instantly filled with light elves, as if by magic. Perhaps it *was* magic, for the movement was ordered and precise, but also awesome in its latent power. It was so silent and instantaneous that it didn't catch a single eye or ear amongst the mob assembled below. The bows of the light elves were fully drawn and empty, poised in a neat and unwavering row, waiting for a well-rehearsed, silent signal that the moment had come to unleash that same power. It came when Malrin took his next step towards the steel doors and the two helpless figures standing in front of them. Sixty silver arrowheads appeared, close to the fist of each archer. There was no other movement, though, as sixty deep-green arrow shafts grew back from those tips, and rested on the bowstrings, steady and slanting downwards towards their chosen targets. And then, as Malrin took his second step, a truly wondrous sight would have met Mark's eyes if he had glanced upwards: sixty perfect fletchings bursting into life from the shafts and soon nuzzling against the cheeks of those sixty archers. Each one was the soft green of newly opened beech leaves, full of life and promise, for the green arrows were their rarest and most destructive weapon. The Sluagh was about to pay heavily for terrorising a young couple who were prepared, however briefly, to fight their way towards what could only be a painful and bloody death, against ridiculously overwhelming odds.

The hail of arrows unleashed a deadly toll. One moment there was relative order below the balcony, albeit a cruel and evil one. The next, fifteen or more of those vile creatures were dead or dying, pierced many times by green arrows; through necks and cheeks or chests and bellies they went, it didn't matter which. They fell where they stood. Some didn't move again, whilst others writhed about noisily in the cinders and dust as their lowly comrades ignored them and sought cover behind each other. Many of the arrows were destined for the great hounds, and the most unearthly howling and snarling broke out as they all received numerous injuries of one kind or another. One of them crumpled forwards onto its chest, quite dead – five arrows had found their mark, close to its heart. Each of the others reared up or went berserk, all hit many times and crazed with pain as any riders on their backs who were still uninjured fought to bring them back under control. The horses alone were spared. They were innocent in many ways, and the light elves couldn't find it in their hearts to destroy them, but many tree-goblins dropped from their backs as well-aimed shots found their targets.

As the mayhem grew, axes were swung in readiness and countless sabres or curved daggers were drawn: the air almost sang with the ringing of steel. Bows were slipped from the shoulders of dark elf and goblin alike, and were made ready, but a second forest of green arrows already waited on the balcony and these suddenly streaked into the seething crowd. Their targets were mobile now and many shots failed to find their mark with such devastating accuracy, but despite this, more of the Sluagh fell and did not move again.

Mark and Victoria could hardly take in what was happening around them, but they stepped forwards bravely and did their best to help, swinging their swords as well as they could: they felt their freyals choosing their own targets, twisting or turning in their young hands and soon finding unprotected parts of hairy legs and arms. At times, the youngsters were completely exposed to attack from behind or to the side, but several of the light elves on the balcony were under specific orders to protect them at all costs: two large goblins were struck down together as they rushed at Mark with axes raised, shortly before a charging bogle collapsed inches from Victoria's feet with three green arrows sprouting from between his shoulder blades.

Then black arrows started to fly upwards, out of the chaos. Two found their way under a hood and claimed the life of a young and worthy light elf, but many more were foiled by the fabulous cloaks of silk, and soon it became clear that the Unseelie Court were facing defeat. Malrin could sense it already, and several arrows had struck him but failed to penetrate the light armour hidden underneath his cloak. He was one of only a few that were protected in this way, which pleased him greatly – the fewer survivors there were to claim a share of the hoard when he finally had it nestling in his arms, the better.

All his thoughts and actions were now dedicated to escaping from the onslaught of the light elves, before a lucky arrow found his neck. He leapt clear as another hellhound fell sideways just beside him, a long, bloody tongue hanging from its open but lifeless jaws – several arrows had pierced its head and neck, and some were already fading away, their task finished. Malrin took the time to look around him coolly. Despite the black arrows which were flying up at them, he could see the light elves still standing and firing shoulder to shoulder above him – if one of them fell, the gap was closed at once with another from behind. He also noted the bodies rapidly accumulating around his feet, their distorted faces frozen in pain or surprise.

Now Malrin had never been one to remain in a fight just to help out his comrades: his code of behaviour didn't include qualities such as honour or courage, and never had. As another green arrow glanced off his shoulder armour, he pushed his way through the rabble around him to the steel doors. Just like stone coffin lids, they were no obstacle for him. He held his hands close to the rusting sheets of metal with their countless rows of rivets, and in a few seconds the doors were moving sideways in their tracks, grating over the dirt and cinders trapped beneath them.

Up on the balcony, Trifillo was the first to see what Malrin had in mind, and he left the ranks of his brother elves at once, running to the stairway at the end of the railings. Another elf followed at his shoulder and the two of them were soon down the steps and in amongst the remnants of the Sluagh. Their swords were held high, and those close by soon saw that Trifillo's reputation for swordplay was well earned. Although several creatures ventured to attack him the moment his feet touched the floor of the yard, they were soon touching that floor themselves – either dead or injured. His sword was everywhere at once, deflecting blows or dispatching goblins and bogles.

The other elf, his protective hood of silk up, was equally impressive, back to back with Trifillo and protecting him more than once as the two of them started to fight their way to the steel doors which now stood a foot apart. Those doors were only seven or eight paces away, but it required all their courage and skill to cross that distance alive. Even as Trifillo dropped two bogles who tried to attack him from both sides at once, and his partner behind him felled a large one-eyed tree-goblin holding a dagger in each hand, a group of a dozen or so suddenly surged forwards and made a rush for the gap between the doors.

Snilbog was amongst them. Just like Malrin, he and the

others had the whiff of defeat in their nostrils, and any hint of an escape route was irresistible to them. They burst forwards, knocking Mark to the ground as they went, but Victoria was caught up and carried with them through the gap by their weight and speed. Malrin was also bundled through the gap by the same crowd, whether he liked it or not. It was certainly more company than he'd planned on, but whilst the other creatures with him were tripping over each other or deciding what to do with their sudden reprieve from certain death, he'd already formed a plan.

Victoria was quite convinced that she was about to be killed, so when Malrin grasped her arm and pulled her further into the tunnel, she was both surprised and terrified. Red light from the marshalling yard streamed through the gap between the doors, lighting their way for a short distance, but also revealing a wide oak door in a side wall not far from them. The steel doors started to close of their own accord, horrifyingly unstoppable as they moved towards each other: Malrin's trickery was still at work, shutting off a somewhat dubious means of escape for himself, but more importantly, not allowing anyone else to follow him, either.

Some of the escaping goblins were still picking themselves up out of the dust when Snilbog, Malrin, Victoria and a handful of ruffians reached the oak door – under Malrin's powers it soon swung open. Just as Trifillo and his battle partner reached the steel doors, Mark found himself at their sides. Victoria's stick lay trampled in the dirt at his feet and he swept it up as the two elves slipped through the rapidly shrinking gap. With only the briefest hesitation, Mark seized his last chance to follow them and squeezed through sideways just before the doors met with a loud clang of steel against steel.

By this time, Victoria and the others were through the oak door and it, too, was already closing behind them, blocking out several new red lights which now shone out brightly in the passageway beyond it. Mark sprang towards it with the two light elves following him, for with the fearsome noise from behind now shut off, he could plainly hear Victoria screaming. He could see the oak door shutting, but his tired legs felt weak and useless as he tried to sprint towards it. There was no chance of reaching it in time – he knew it before he'd even taken three strides. The door slammed shut and Victoria's screams became muffled notes of despair a world away from where he stood, helpless and devastated.

The court elf of fire didn't hesitate. The point of a white arrow burst into flames, poised on Trifillo's bow. Mark stepped aside just before it flew across the tunnel and buried itself into the oak door. Another followed, then another, until Trifillo had sent a dozen of them into its planks, and the door was lost behind a dancing curtain of fire. The flames grew and then roared, as if an immense blacksmith's bellows was blasting them into life, burning the oak away with a searing, white heat which nothing could withstand for long. Mark lifted his arm across his face as it prickled his skin, shielding his eyes from the glare. He realised that Trifillo wasn't a force to be taken lightly and was amazed at the change in the elf since he'd stumbled out of his spriggan prison cell a few weeks earlier. As he watched, the magical fire ate greedily into what remained of the door, until only the outer part of it was left: a rectangular frame of red, glowing embers.

Any one of them was willing to be the first one through, but it was Mark who reached it first, leaping bravely through the smoking hole as if he was practising a dangerous circus trick. The two light elves were close behind him and not a single hair on their heads was singed as they jumped cleanly through, running as they hit the ground on the far side. The thought of what might be happening to Victoria somewhere ahead of Mark in the darkness gave new energy to his tired legs. The three of them ran, and ran hard.

As he went, Trifillo held his sword up high, and strange, cool flames now leapt up from the end of it to the roof of the tunnel. The flames rolled along in front of them, burning nothing, but curling around timber beams, old pipes and cables as they went, lighting their way. They lost no more time as they sprinted forwards and tried to listen out for Victoria. Their lungs were heaving and their hearts hammered, but still they ran, deeper and deeper into the old mine. The tunnel eventually began to curve steadily around to the right, and they passed several smaller, closed doors to either side, before their way was blocked by a huge stockpile of wooden ore trucks which forced them to stop and squeeze their way slowly past. The delay was agonising, but it wasn't to be the last. They'd barely taken twenty more strides when they came to a stop yet again, for the single tunnel had become three, each with its own set of rail tracks, and each as dark, silent and forbidding as its neighbours.

They stood together, bent over with their hands on their knees, trying to get their breath back as Trifillo's astonishing flames paused and rippled above their heads in a slowly rotating ring of reds, oranges and yellows. The air was as cold as moonlit frost, and they could see their own breath in large clouds, tinted with all the colours of the elfish fire and drifting around them like smoke from hell's furnaces. The only sound came from their own heaving lungs, but it was enough to make it impossible to hear any noise which might be coming from the tunnels.

'Which one?' asked Mark between large gasps of icy air.

'You choose,' replied Trifillo, who really had no preference at all.

They all looked unpromising to the elf, and he was

beginning to think that they must have run past an opening or door which they shouldn't have, when Mark suddenly chose a tunnel at random. He had a sickening feeling that they would only be wasting even more time, but the elves followed him unquestioningly and the hovering flames came too. They still ran quickly, though, for they knew that things were now going badly for them, and that they were steadily getting lost in the hill just when they couldn't afford to be.

After two more minutes of hard running, Mark's fears came true – his chosen tunnel came to an abrupt end. There was nothing to see except a cold, wet rock face and a tall pile of truck lines heaped up to one side. The flames above their heads died down and rolled against the wall, defeated or perhaps just confused. Mark hit the wall with the palms of his hands and leant his forehead against it as fatigue overwhelmed his body and mind. He could feel his last tattered shreds of energy seeping out of him and disappearing into the ground under his feet, as the same words went through his head over and over again.

I must find her! I must find her!

Then, as they were just turning to run back, they heard an alarming sound growing in their ears, in the direction they'd come from. It was the sound of heavy, running feet, mixed with grunts of complaint and barbaric encouragement. For a moment, Mark thought that it could so easily have been a friendly tug-of-war team arriving on the village green back at home, but they all knew that this was no village fete ... or band of cheerful light elves coming to help them. No, this was *far* from that.

* * *

In another distant part of the hill, Malrin, Snilbog and four lesser creatures fortunate enough to have escaped from the marshalling yard unharmed, soon got fed up with Victoria's screams. The sweaty red rag which had been around Snilbog's neck was now across her mouth and tied far too tightly behind her head, digging mercilessly into the corners of her mouth. As well as this, her hands were tied behind her back with a bowstring which was cutting into her wrists. She soon gave up trying to call out. It was utterly pointless. They'd been running for fifteen minutes now, but it seemed like hours to her. If she tried to slow down, she at once felt the sharp jab of a dagger in her ribs or the small of her back: Malrin had snatched her freyal from her at the start of their run and had already found a use for it. Little did he know that even the hoard itself was of less value than that small weapon – to a court elf.

Incredibly, though, he knew more or less where he was, for he had distant memories of the network of tunnels and halls under those hills. When they'd been buzzing with activity a century before, he'd occasionally sneaked in with the miners and explored them, unseen and unheard for days or nights on end, always hopeful that he would overhear a careless word or two which would take him a step closer to his dream. He was a little older now, but wiser too, and he knew exactly where he wanted to be. There was only one way to get to the fourth and last Witcher key ... he would have to find some old acquaintances of his.

Victoria suddenly felt that she could go no further, poking daggers or no poking daggers. The rag in her mouth tasted like sick, and was half suffocating her, whilst her legs felt as heavy as milestones, and she realised that if she fell, Malrin would have to drag her along by her hair ... which he happily would, of course. He wanted this particular prisoner with him at all times, for he suspected that she might be extremely useful to him before the day was out, and the hoard was in a sack over his shoulder.

Luckily for Victoria, it didn't come to that. With

indescribable relief, she saw the red lights and blurred, jogging figures ahead of her come to a halt, and she fell onto her knees at their feet, too tired at first to even look up at their hideous faces.

The tunnel had widened out to make room for several more large pieces of abandoned machinery, and Malrin pulled Victoria up roughly by the arm, making sure that his nails dug into her. She tried not to scream out, biting hard onto the disgusting rag and squeezing her eyes shut, whilst Snilbog stood to one side, watching the dark elf carefully. He didn't trust him a hair's breadth, let alone an inch.

'What now ... my friend?' asked the goblin, fingering a knife which was concealed under his jacket and sniffing loudly. 'I take it you ... knows the way?'

Malrin answered at once, but his tone made it clear that he wasn't in the mood for too many questions.

'Oh, I know the way, all right,' he snapped (this wasn't perfectly true, but even Malrin didn't want any dis-agreements in a confined space, with several armed goblins of dubious temperament). 'But first of all we have to meet someone and get a little bit of information,' he added, trying not to let his growing excitement show.

Victoria was sure that she saw Snilbog's eyebrows shoot up in surprise under his black hood.

'Meet *who*, exactly?' quizzed the goblin, suspiciously. 'I take it we won't ... be 'avin' to share the takin's ... with any more than ... we 'ave already?' His annoying sniffs seemed louder than ever.

Malrin was almost amused, but he kept his thoughts to himself. It was possible that Snilbog would get a share – a *small* share, naturally – but the rabble with them would only be feeling the edge of his sabre across their scrawny throats when the time was right. He ignored what, to him, were irrelevant questions and got down to business.

'I want you lot to do just as I say. There'll be plenty of

time later for discussing shares!' He ran his finger along the back edge of his sabre, and there were no further comments. 'Right, let's whistle a tune. And make it loud!'

Snilbog had now had more than his fill of Malrin's ridiculous game.

'Now look 'ere! We ain't got time ... for any tunes, or songs ... or even poxy hymns. We want to get ...'

He didn't have time to finish the sentence. Without any change in his expression, Malrin calmly skewered one of Snilbog's two goblin associates with a single, noiseless and effortless thrust of his sabre in and straight back out of his protruding stomach. The unfortunate victim didn't make any noise, either, but he did look down in surprise before crumpling into the dirt like a puppet with cut strings.

'Whistle *now*, or say your goodbyes to each other,' hissed Malrin menacingly.

His black beard twitched and his lips tightened with anger as he wiped his sabre clean on his victim's shoulder, and although the others found it difficult to whistle at all, given the situation, those who could made a valiant attempt at it. Even Snilbog cooperated, and made a reasonable effort from inside his black hood. Victoria was saved from even trying by the rag across her tongue, but that was no bad thing, for she was without a doubt the worst whistler for miles around, and Malrin could well have taken her offering in the wrong way. As the others did their best, Malrin moved the tip of his sabre along in front of their noses, prompting more volume. It soon came, but it was an unpleasant racket, with each one attempting a different tune, and in various keys.

After far too much of this, and without any warning, a shower of gravel dropped down from the roof and onto one of the dark elves. He nearly jumped onto the goblin next to him, but Malrin didn't flinch, as if he'd been expecting it. For some reason, he wanted still more volume and he made this clear with his sabre, which he now started to use like a conductor's baton. The volume increased a little, and more gravel soon began to fall from holes the size of dinner plates above their heads.

'Now swear out loud!' shouted Malrin, who at once launched into an unbroken string of obscenities. The others naturally wandered if he'd suddenly lost his wits altogether, but the body lying face down at their feet in a pool of dark blood persuaded them that it was probably a good idea to go along with his demented game for now. Soon, each one of them was either whistling or swearing like a drunken sailor, and more deluges of gravel rained down on them, each one larger and more forceful than the last, as the bewildered group below leant first one way, then the other, trying to dodge them.

*　　*　　*

Almost one mile away from Malrin and his unhappy choir, Mark pushed himself off the wall and stood up straight and alert as he strained to hear what was coming along the tunnel towards them. Trifillo, though, already had a fair idea of who their visitors would be, and he moved Mark back towards the wall with his arm. The other elf slipped his bow from his back and stood alongside Trifillo.

'D'you think ...?' asked Mark, hardly daring to finish his question.

'I'm afraid so,' replied Trifillo calmly. 'But we'll know for sure soon enough.'

Mark pulled his freyal from his belt, wishing once more that he possessed the skill and strength to use it more effectively, but Trifillo seemed ready for anything, holding his sword in one hand and standing his bow against the wall beside him, ready. More flames suddenly leapt from the point of his freyal and up onto the roof, before racing away into the darkest reaches of the tunnel and at last revealing just what Mark had been fearing. Far away, but getting closer by the second, a band of large bogles was charging towards them. They filled the tunnel from one side to the other – and filled the group at the end of it with dismay. There were seven of them, each holding a curved dagger in one hand and a leather strangling cord in the other, and their sacking cloaks probably concealed something far more substantial, for Mark could already hear the continuous rustle of chain mail in amongst everything else. It would certainly help explain how they'd just survived an onslaught from sixty expert archers.

Trifillo moved towards his bow, but the other elf stopped him and stepped forward, bringing up his own. Mark looked at the elf's bracer. Its gemstones shimmered in the flames above their heads, but they weren't green. They sparkled like tiny rainbows, with every colour jostling for supremacy as the elf drew his bow and a perfect green arrow instantly grew backwards from the tip. A second later it was gone. The bow was lowered, and a brute of a bogle running at the front of the pack was stopped in his tracks as the arrow found his unprotected throat. He died running, but his so-called friends simply dodged around his body and kept coming, without any sign of hesitation or regret.

'Good shot!' cheered Trifillo, always one to give praise where it was due.

Once again, the other elf aimed and fired. An arrow streaked down the tunnel and another bogle collapsed, its shaft protruding from his gaping mouth.

'Even better!' said Trifillo, feeling genuinely impressed this time.

The bogle hadn't even finished sliding along the ground in his death throes when his neighbour suffered a similar fate.

'The best so far!' muttered Trifillo, who was now starting to feel just a little bit outdone.

The four remaining bogles shouted all the more and swung their cords with renewed energy: failure clearly wasn't an option for them. They were forty paces away when another one joined the trail of bodies behind him, with a horribly accurate shot to his groin. Trifillo shut his eyes and winced.

'Perfect ... but so cruel.'

He decided it really was time for him to contribute, and soon a flaming arrow was finding its mark in the forehead of the fifth charging bogle. There was no more time for archery as the last two survivors covered the final dozen strides at full speed and full volume, and Trifillo rushed forward to meet them wielding his freyal. Mark watched, open-mouthed, as the brave fire elf ducked below two wildly slashing knives, killing one bogle with a slicing cut across his belt as he ran past, and thrusting the other one against the side wall at the same time. The last of them rolled along the wall for a short distance, desperately trying to regain his footing, but he never did. The sword in Trifillo's hand moved as if it had a life of its own, and the bogle watched himself sliding down the wall and onto the floor a few paces in front of Mark – his ugly, blood-smeared head lay all alone on the other side of the tunnel.

'Not bad. Not bad at all!' said the other elf, who now spoke for the first time.

The hood came down and Estraal was shaking her hair free and smiling at her friends. Trifillo and Mark caught their breath. She was the last elf Mark expected to see in that terrible place. He remembered her rings at Russell's Wood and realised that the gems on her bracer were just like them. Trifillo was even more surprised. He stared down at the ground and shook his head in disbelief, fighting to resist a slowly widening smile. He was clearly thrilled to see her, without any doubt, but also shocked that she'd put herself in such danger, both there in the tunnel and even more so back at the marshalling yard. He didn't know whether to embrace or scold her, and in the end he managed neither. One sentence from Estraal settled the matter, as she looked straight at the fire elf with her startling eyes.

'If you think I spent two long weeks nursing you back to good health just to see you killed down here by yourself, you are sadly mistaken!'

And so Trifillo knew that she did indeed care for him, and didn't need any lectures about danger, either. Mark watched as they touched fingertips for a few seconds then shouldered their bows, and was just thinking how much she reminded him of Victoria when Trifillo spoke up.

'I think we took a wrong turn!' He sent another burst of cool flames up to the roof and beckoned to the other two.

Without another word, the three of them ran back up the tunnel, dodging the littered bodies as they went, with Trifillo leading Mark, and Estraal at the rear. As she ran past the last of the dead bogles, her keen eyesight caught a glimpse of something which stopped her instantly. With Mark disappearing into the darkness ahead of her, she dropped onto one knee beside the body, a pale green light already spluttering into life in her fist. The bogle, who only had one ear, was still clasping his curved dagger in one hand, and a strangling cord in the other. She pulled the cord from his frozen grip and held it up ... then away from her nose. A small leather pouch swung from it, and Estraal smiled to herself before closing her fingers around the light and snuffing it out.

Time was even more precious for them now. They knew that Victoria could be virtually anywhere under the hill after all their wasted time, and Trifillo wished that Stirran, Planiss, or any of the others were with them to help. They wouldn't be coming, of course, but as he ran, his mind and heart went out to his fellow court elves, wherever they might be.

As it happened, *he* was being missed, too. Back in the marshalling yard, relative calm had replaced the frenzied disarray of battle. Green light, not red, now shone down brightly from the high roof – that and the glare from a dozen flaming torches, courtesy of a very young fire elf and fourteen exceptional shots from his bow (he *was* still learning, after all). The floor was strewn with many bloodied corpses, including five of the hellhounds. The others had fled, with several of their less courageous masters clinging on to their necks and escaping – for the time being. Not a single green arrow was to be seen amongst the dead, for every one of them had vanished once their job was done, but several of the bodies were moving and one even required another arrow to keep it still.

As the air cleared of dust, there was the joy of victory for the light elves, but it was a muted joy, tainted with great sadness. Alas, up on the balcony, eight beautiful cloaks of silk lay over the bodies of eight fearless elves. They were beyond the help of their cloaks now – indeed, beyond any help – but they would surely be honoured by every light elf, either living or yet to live. For now, the victors wandered silently amongst the vanquished and prayed to the spirits of those gone before them that this would be the last of it. The eight were eight too many, but with good fortune, they might at least be some of the last.

Five court elves stood together close to the steel doors, unable to go to the aid of Trifillo and the young mortals. They didn't possess the skills to move such heavy doors, and as they stood staring up at them, feeling wholly inadequate, Agoriff picked up what looked like a discarded scarf which had been trampled into the ground. It was Victoria's cloak, but there was no pleasure in his finding it – not for any of them.

*   *   *

Malrin knew very well that knockers hate whistling and swearing more than anything else, and that given enough time, along with a sufficient quantity of either, they would make their presence known in no uncertain terms. He also knew that throwing gravel was their first, harmless but extremely annoying response to anyone who broke their rules, but that this would be followed by a face-to-face meeting, with some general unpleasantness thrown in for good measure, if the gravel failed to do the trick. Malrin's sabre kept the whistling and swearing coming loud and strong, despite the sharp gravel down the backs of their necks, and so it wasn't very long before some rather larger things started to fall from the holes above them.

First one, then another, then three knockers dropped the ten feet down to the ground, feet first, landing there without so much as a stagger. Malrin didn't move a muscle when they suddenly appeared in front of him, but the others all took a step back in surprise ... even Snilbog. They were strange little things, three feet high at the most and rather queer looking: their eyes were on the large side and far too close together, their noses were short and wide, so as to keep out of the way in tight spaces, whilst their hair was very long and untidy, purely from neglect. They looked indignant, as if they'd just been interrupted in the middle of something interesting, and the one nearest Malrin turned to face him with his arms crossed and his chin jutting out just a *little* further than was advisable, given whom he was dealing with.

'What's all the noise about?' he demanded curtly, looking up at the dark elf with his large, unblinking eyes. Malrin came straight to the point, much to the amusement of some of the others.

353

'Actually, we're here to take the Witcher hoard,' replied the elf casually. 'You see, I know the way – well, more or less – but I was hoping that you might be so kind as to ... how shall I put it ... to remind me of the last few twists and turns, so to speak.'

Victoria noticed that the other two dark elves, who were well used to Malrin's antics, shuffled half a step backwards towards safer ground.

'Oh, is *that* what you were hoping,' sneered the knocker rudely, as he glanced sideways at his friends and smiled knowingly.

'Is there a problem with you helping us, then?' asked Malrin, pretending to be concerned.

'Well, there could be,' replied the knocker, sounding just like a hopeful salesman.

'Yes, there could be,' confirmed the other two in perfect unison.

'You see,' continued the first one, trying to be patient, 'we never objected to giving the miners a few clues as to where to dig, back in the good old days. But we always got a little something back for it. We had a sort of *understanding*, if you get my meaning.'

The knocker had other memories going through his mind as he spoke. In the distant past, extremely valuable items had occasionally been found at the rock face with their help, and that 'little something' in return had sometimes been quite substantial, in fact. However, he carefully avoided mentioning precious gems or Sir Henry Witcher: he wasn't a genius by any means, but he wasn't stupid, either. Malrin scratched his head and looked convincingly confused.

'Ah, I *see*. So all you want is a small gift of some kind, and then you would be happy, even overjoyed.' Malrin was now at his most charming – and dangerous.

'That's about the long and short of it,' agreed the

knocker, who smiled at his friends again, and was obviously pleased with his bargaining skills.

'Yes, the long and short of it,' chorused the other two merrily.

Everyone jumped at the sound of Malrin's sabre leaving its scabbard, though it happened so quickly that no one really saw it move. It appeared to come perilously close to the knocker's neck, though, as it swept around in a wide arc on its way back to the dark elf's hip. The knocker was suddenly lost for words and seemed to be staring blankly at the wall behind Malrin. Snilbog watched with interest, wondering if the knocker was in shock, but Victoria had a feeling that something unpleasant was about to happen and she even tried to speak up through her soggy rag.

It was very strange in the end, for the knocker managed to stand upright for at least ten seconds despite his head and shoulders being separated. As Victoria shouted out loudly but uselessly in her rag, his neck slowly turned red and wet below a thin, dark line, just before his head toppled forwards, bounced once on the hard floor and rolled up to Malrin's boots. The rest of him collapsed into a pathetic, bleeding heap a few seconds later. As one of the surviving knockers darted into the safety of the dark tunnel, Malrin reached out and grabbed the last one by his hair, before bringing the sabre up to rest across his throat. The little thing hissed and spat like a cornered cat, but Malrin was having none of it.

'Well? Which way is it then?' he asked coolly.

The elf glanced down at the severed head next to his boot, before kicking it into the shadows.

'Perhaps you would like to join him?'

The knocker had enough good sense to know that his head was indeed dangerously close to joining the one already on the floor, and so he decided to tell Malrin most of what he needed to hear. He was only just in time, though, for the sabre was about to go to work.

'Go *that* way,' he muttered, pointing along the tunnel to his left, 'then go through the next door on your right.'

He paused, wondering whether or not to hold anything back, but another brief glance at the gory heap on the ground helped him to decide.

'Look out for a light from above,' he added, somewhat dejectedly.

Malrin was just imagining himself bathed in a shaft of heavenly light, with the hoard tucked under his arm, when a noisy shower of gravel suddenly shot out of a hole directly above him. It was enough to distract him for a split second, and more than long enough for the last knocker to wriggle out of his grasp and disappear into the darkness after his friend. Malrin was left standing with a long tuft of greasy hair in his hand and even more gravel inside his collar, but none of that mattered to him any more. After all those years of scheming and searching, he at last had the vital information he'd craved for every day and dreamed about every night. A few moments later they were all on the move again, and Victoria could do nothing else than run with them, trying to ignore the pain in her wrists.

The two knockers only stopped running once they felt that they were reasonably safe. They tucked themselves behind some old ore trucks pretty quickly, though, when they heard another group coming up behind them fast. As they hid there in the shadows, they were surprised to see two light elves and a young male mortal running past them, heading deeper into the mines. Although they were somewhat cut off from life in the daylight, knockers understood exactly what was what in the unseen world, and certainly knew that light and dark elves are sworn enemies. Within their cold, dark world of rock and stone, they would always retaliate against scoundrels or thieves, and happily so, but they felt a hint of regret as they pushed one of the small trucks as hard as they could, straight into a stout timber prop not far from them. The prop fell over and the roof of the tunnel above it collapsed with a tremendous rumble, completely blocking the tunnel in a few seconds and sending clouds of thick dust rolling away in both directions.

It was as simple as that. It couldn't be helped that both good *and* evil creatures would be trapped beyond this particular rock fall, but some things just had to be done. They looked at each other and nodded.

*   *   *

Malrin could smell the hoard now, or those with him would have been forgiven for thinking it, judging by the way he was running with his nose stuck well out in front of him. His globe of red light bobbed along above his head, keeping up with him, and the group following behind tried to do likewise. Victoria was longing for the knocker's 'door on the right' to appear, so that she could stop and rest – she could feel blood from her wrists running down her hands and dripping from her fingertips, but there was nothing that she could do about it. After another nightmarish quarter of a mile her wish was answered as the red light came to a stop, and soon they were all gathered together at a closed door. Malrin had everything worked out, as usual.

'The girl comes with me,' he puffed, out of breath, but with his eyes now alight with excitement.

Snilbog, who'd been polishing his dagger on his cloak, looked up in surprise, but Malrin was far too quick for him.

'You too, Snilbog. We can divide it up between us, as fair as fair can be!'

His sickly grin should have worried Snilbog more than it

appeared to, for the goblin merely nodded and returned to his dagger-cleaning. The other lowly goblin and Malrin's two lads shuffled their feet silently and stole glances at each other – they had their own plans about the sharing out of any rich pickings, but were wise enough to keep them safely in their heads for now. Those plans didn't matter in the least to Malrin as he moved towards them. A two-way split was bad enough, in his opinion, but a five-way version was quite unthinkable, so he felt that he needed to decrease the size of his little group, particularly in the goblin department. In fact, a two-way split was still one too many for him, and if the chance came to make it only one, he certainly didn't want a fair fight on his hands.

'You lot wait here, and watch out for trouble,' he said, looking at the three of them but easing his cloak away from his sabre.

The two dark elves knew their leader's methods and didn't move an inch. The wretched goblin opened his mouth to say something but had second thoughts and shut it again just in time.

'Very good indeed!' added Malrin, looking pleased with himself as he cupped his cold hands together and huffed into them like a safe-breaker preparing for work.

He lifted the latch and pushed the door open with his shoulder, revealing yet another long, but very narrow passageway, no more than two paces wide. He had no memories of this new place, and so his hopes were rising by the second as he and Snilbog careered down it together, with Victoria sandwiched miserably between them. Now it was Snilbog's turn to use the point of his dagger to encourage Victoria to keep up the pace, but she hardly felt it, as thoughts of Mark now filled her mind to the brim.

If you're alive, how will you ever find me down here? Oh, Mark,

358

I don't want to die alone and in agony. Please find me, Mark. Please find me!

The hopelessness of it all suddenly overwhelmed her as she stumbled along, her tears turning the dull red figure ahead of her into a fuzzy blur. She was fighting to breathe past the tight, sodden rag in her mouth, and her saliva was now running down her chin and neck to join the tears already there.

Crystal Clear

It had, of course, crossed Malrin's devious mind that the frightened knocker may have lied about this wondrous 'light from above', just to save his skin, so he was therefore delighted and a little surprised when he saw exactly that, some distance ahead. It spilled downwards from a circular hole in the roof of the passageway, but not brightly enough to stop him stubbing his toes on one of dozens of iron spikes sticking up out of the ground directly below it. It was amazing that showers of gravel didn't start dropping at once, as he hopped around between the long spikes, holding his throbbing foot and swearing horribly. Whilst Malrin was otherwise engaged, Snilbog stood at the edge of the deadly spikes, staring up at the hole. It was the bottom of a tall, straight shaft, almost the full width of the passageway, and the faint lamplight which lit his upturned face told him that there was someone up there, waiting.

Snilbog had watched with interest as the size of their merry band had steadily dwindled, and he was now absolutely certain that Malrin intended to take the entire hoard for himself when the time came. That could only mean one thing. As he stood to the side in the shadows and looked at the dark elf jumping around on one leg with his guard down, he knew that this was probably his best or even last chance of rearranging Malrin's plans. He drew the long, curved dagger from his belt.

He was past Victoria in a second, and lunging at the

dark elf the next. Malrin's sensitive ears warned him of treachery just soon enough for him to spin around and send his hand to his sabre, but the goblin was already upon him, and there was no time to draw it. Victoria stepped back to the wall and watched in terror as they fell to the ground beside the spikes, with Snilbog on top, but Malrin managing to hold his attacker's wrist away. They grunted and snarled with the effort of trying to kill and not be killed, whilst Victoria was torn between seeing who would remain to torment her further, or turning away from what was sure to be a grizzly end for at least one of them. Every muscle in Malrin's ugly face was strained tight as he fought to twist the dagger around towards the goblin wielding it – the dark elf looked as if he was grinning, and perhaps he was, for he had been over-confident all his long and wicked life. The goblin's breath was blowing and sucking his hood in and out around his mouth as he used his weight to bear down on Malrin.

'Thank you for bringing me all this way,' sneered Snilbog through his hidden teeth – and without a single sniff.

Malrin decided that it was time to see his attacker face to face, and he risked taking one hand briefly away from the goblin's wrist to pull his hood off as they fought. The shock of what he saw was his undoing.

'*You!*' was all he could gasp.

A moment later, the dagger found its mark and suddenly Malrin was writhing under the goblin, letting out a tortured, gurgling cry as first his throat, then his mouth, filled with blood and a pool of it quickly grew below his neck. The twitching body was soon still ... and silent. Malrin and all his evil schemes were no more, as Snilbog eased himself up and wiped the dagger across Malrin's chest. Victoria's freyal was still tucked into the elf's belt, unused, and he pulled it out at once.

361

'Another pretty prize,' he gloated, admiring its jewels and bright, faultless blade.

He laughed quietly to himself then, in self-admiration more than amusement, and turned to Victoria as she pressed herself even harder against the wall. Everything seemed inevitable to her now: she wasn't even frightened any more, and lifted her chin defiantly as she looked straight down at Snilbog. She could see that without his hood on he was just another small, ugly, blood-thirsty goblin, the next part of her nightmare, and the last part of her life. But in fact, he was far more than that. His real name was Redcap. Victoria couldn't possibly know it, but her mother's murderer now stood facing her.

He pulled her away from the wall roughly and spun her around to face it. She closed her eyes and waited for the dagger to do its work, past caring now that all hope of surviving had finally deserted her, but the goblin pulled her into the light and was soon slicing away the bowstring from around her cut and bleeding wrists. The pain trebled and she screamed into the rag as he tugged at them cruelly, but suddenly they were free at last, and she could bring them up to her face. He let her pull the rag from her mouth and it slipped down around her neck as she turned to face him, helpless but still unafraid.

Actually, Redcap wasn't being kind to her by untying her hands, for kindness wasn't an emotion with which he was even vaguely familiar. Just like Malrin, he'd done his homework thoroughly over many long years, gathering the information he needed: bit by bit, reward by reward ... murder by murder. Although he didn't know exactly what waited for him up there, he did know that he must climb up the shaft – and that the girl had to go up first. She would need her hands free for that. With his dagger close to her stomach, he grabbed her jacket and pulled her down onto her knees before bringing his face close to hers

362

– she reeled as his foul breath wafted into her face and the point of the dagger pressed painfully into her. Standing almost nose to nose with her now, his eyes darted from side to side as he looked at each of hers from under his red cap – left and right, right and left, as his greed finally took control of him and all his vile thoughts. His words to her were hissed out, as if by a viper.

'We both go up, but *you* go first, my dear.' She turned her head from the stench.

'Why me? I'll just get in your way,' she answered, surprisingly calmly, hoping that he would agree.

In fact, she was wondering how she could possibly climb up the shaft at all. She'd had enough trouble just climbing trees at home, she remembered, and even if she *could* somehow climb vertical stone walls as high as the church spire, her wrists were badly injured too. Redcap soon enlightened her, and all too happily.

'Oh, I'll tell you why, child! I know of this place. There are guards up there, and I think you will find that a rope will come down for you. But only for you!' His words were filled with hate, and she tried to shuffle a little further away from him on her knees. 'They would cut it quickly enough if they knew *I* was on it.'

Victoria's head swam as she looked up the shaft and a jumble of thoughts fought for answers in her aching mind.

Dear God, let Mark still be alive! How the heck can I climb up there, even with a rope? And why isn't he sniffing any more?

The goblin pushed her in amongst the sharp spikes – which she somehow managed to avoid. It suddenly occurred to her that she could refuse to cooperate and simply let her tormentor kill her: she guessed that she was going to die soon anyway, and at least it would stop him from getting to the hoard. But then she thought of Mark again, of fighting at his side in the marshalling yard, and knew that she would be letting him down if she died uselessly. That memory was enough to temporarily drive away any thoughts of giving up, and she gazed up towards the flickering light a hundred feet above her, wondering what she was meant to do next.

'Tell them you're here,' whispered Redcap, who was now standing well back from the spikes, in the shadows. 'And tell them who you are.'

Victoria obeyed him, but she knew that no good could come from it. Why would her name matter to them? She cupped her bloodied hands to her mouth and shouted upwards.

'I'm coming up! Hello ... Can you hear me? I'm coming up.' She was so tired that her words were croaked more than shouted, and she doubted if they would be heard by anyone so far away. For almost a whole minute there was only silence as she stood waiting amongst the spikes, then a voice came down to her. It was thin and high-pitched, almost child-like.

'Who are you?' it asked suspiciously. 'What's your name?'

'Victoria. I'm Victoria Featherstone,' she shouted back in amazement. 'I have to come up!' She was praying that they could hear her clearly enough, and that they would throw down a rope. There was another, much longer pause as her answer was carefully considered by whoever was up by the lamps. Suddenly, there was a more enthusiastic answer.

'Very well, you can come up – if you really are who you say you are.' There was another pause. 'So what's your mother's name, then?'

Victoria looked at the goblin, confused and suddenly alarmed at the mention of her mother.

'Her name is ... her name *was* Laura – Laura Featherstone.' There was another, shorter pause.

'That'll do for us!'

A thick, knotted rope snaked its way down to her and she stepped hurriedly aside as it jerked to a standstill a few feet above the spikes. Somewhere up there, the other end of it passed over a wheel fastened to the ceiling and down to a large iron ring set into the floor, where it was tied securely. Two small, plump creatures crouched close to the top of the shaft. They knew *exactly* who had any right to come calling on them, for the Witcher hoard was only for Sir Henry himself – or his true descendants. One of them was holding a sharp knife to the taut rope, ready for any trickery, whilst the other peered down into the shaft, waiting to see whether or not he liked the look of who was coming up. Redcap encouraged Victoria with his own dagger in the small of her back.

'Up you go, my girl,' he said, as if he was encouraging her to climb up onto a few bails of hay, not to scale a one-hundred-foot high shaft cut into smooth, solid rock. 'And remember, if there's any trouble, they'll cut the rope. So behave!'

Reluctantly, she stepped back into the circle of light and grasped the end of the rope as it drifted around lazily, then, with what she hoped was a last look back at her tormentor, she pulled herself up onto it, trying not to call out as shooting pains darted through her wrists and up her arms. She got her feet above the first knot and started to make her way up, biting her lip silently, but when she was eight feet above the ground Redcap skipped between the spikes and leapt onto the rope below her, almost shaking her off. Up they went together, knot after knot.

'Call up! Call up again,' came a whispered order from just below her feet. 'Tell them you're coming up.'

Redcap looked down anxiously at the spikes below him: he wanted to be sure that there were no fatal decisions made by anyone at the top of the shaft. Victoria stopped climbing and once again thought of putting an end to it all, but Redcap lifted himself a foot higher and bit hard into her ankle, until she dared to pull it away and risk falling off. She stifled a cry as it tried to leave her lips, to save what was left of her dignity. Looking down past the red cap just underneath her she realised that she was far too high up to see the bottom of the shaft, or the spikes which were surely waiting for her there. She shouted upwards as loudly as she could.

'Hello up there! I'm still coming. Please wait. It's me, Victoria Featherstone.'

She caught an odd word or two from a heated conversation, then felt the rope jolt in her hands. She held on as tightly as she could, and was swinging there gently, terrified and wanting to cry, when at last a reply came down to her.

'The longer you wait, the more likely you are to fall off. Get a move on!'

'A guarded place ...'

The keepers of the hoard were gnomes, the most expert of all treasure guardians, but these were somewhat overweight and definitely cantankerous gnomes, probably due to the incredibly boring and inactive nature of their work. Victoria guessed that their warning was well meant: her arms already felt like half-set jelly and she knew that unless she got to the top very soon, she would be arriving back at the spikes even sooner. She dug deep into her Featherstone resolve, finding a pocket of strength from somewhere inside her and hauling herself slowly upwards again, but the goblin was always close to her feet and ready to bite or stab if she paused for more than a quick breath.

It seemed endless. Exhaustion, terror and pain rolled together into one long, nasty dream, but she persevered, and at long last saw a round face with exceptionally large ears silhouetted against the light of an oil lamp. She prayed that whoever it was, they would somehow get her safely off the rope and be done with the brutal goblin that was so close on her heels – forever. There could be no other outcome in which she survived, for once the goblin was safely at the top, he was sure to kill her just as he'd killed the dark elf below her – mercilessly. As her numb arms heaved her body up past those last few knots, so tired that she hardly knew where she was any more, she suddenly felt guilty for tricking the little creatures up there, whoever they might be, and hoped that they'd forgive her ... if they were spared.

She wasn't sure how she managed it, but she did eventually arrive at the very top knot. A thin but strong arm pulled the rope to one side, bringing it close to a low, circular wall around the top of the shaft. Victoria made a grab for it with one aching hand and soon the gnome was helping to pull her to safety. When she was halfway out, he peered over her back to see if the shaft was clear ... but it was the last thing he ever did.

There was a piercing scream from the chubby little thing as a curved knife leapt out of the shadows in the shaft and ended his tedious life. The unfortunate gnome grasped the blade with his bare hands as it protruded from between two buttons on his jacket, almost as if he wanted to pull it out by himself, but he toppled forwards into the shaft, twisting the knife out of Redcap's hand and taking it with him to the bottom. He screamed all the way down, until the deadly spikes instantly silenced him.

The sickening sound of that fall brought three figures running from the passageway door, where they'd been told to wait – the goblin and two dark elves soon arrived at the base of the shaft to be greeted with a gruesome sight. Lit up within the pool of light, the dead gnome lay there for all to see, impaled by many of the spikes, and with his last scream frozen silently onto his twisted, terrified face. Malrin's body was close by, on its back. A large patch of blood-soaked earth was still growing slowly beneath his neck, and a black hood lay discarded beside him. His corpse was staring up at the roof of the passageway with a surprised expression in its lifeless eyes, and Malrin's lads didn't know whether to laugh or cry as they saw their greedy, ruthless leader lying there, dead. The wretched goblin was just as confused, but the horrific scene was enough to convince all three of them that they were a long way out of their depth. With a wide-eyed glance at each other and one more for the skewered gnome, they turned and ran.

At the top of the shaft, Redcap sprang into action. The second gnome was already sawing desperately at the rope with his knife, and Victoria was barely over the low wall when the goblin clawed his way up over her back and pounced at him, knocking him over. Redcap was up on his feet in a second and used his boot, not the freyal in his belt, as the gnome tried to get up. The vicious kick sent him hurtling back against a massive wooden post, which he then slid down with a long groan, dazed and winded. Redcap was on him a moment later, though, throwing off a leather gauntlet, grasping him by the collar and dragging him back up onto his feet. Victoria, who was now sitting in a corner and feeling as weak as a sick kitten, noticed that two fingers were missing from the goblin's hand, but also that he seemed to be managing well enough without them.

The unfortunate gnome had never encountered a goblin before, let alone a dreaded redcap, and so hadn't the slightest idea as to what kind of monster now pressed against him. His feet slowly left the ground as Redcap pushed him further up the post, squeezing the life out of him and enjoying it, too, judging by the grin across his whiskery face. He leant forward and came close to the gnome's pointed ear, the tip of which was now shaking just like the rest of him.

'The key, – where is it?' he snarled, barely moving his lips.

The last guardian of the hoard made the mistake of thinking about whether to answer or not, but Redcap wasn't in the mood for any last-minute heroism. He shook the gauntlet off his other hand and held it out open, close to the gnome's face, expecting the key to be dropped into it at once.

'I ... I ... I ...' stammered the gnome uselessly.

'I ... *what?*' whispered Redcap into the large ear, nearing the end of his patience.

'I don't have it!' bleated the gnome, before squeezing his eyes shut and starting to mutter to himself as his nerves finally went to pieces.

Redcap could only see jewels in his mind now, large piles of them, stacked up like sparkling fruit on a market stall, so if the stupid gnome didn't want to hand over the key, then he'd take it for himself – as soon as he'd killed him. He pulled the freyal from his belt and without so much as a blink stabbed it towards the gnome's throat. Redcap was extremely skilled with a dagger, having used one a great deal more than most, so he was surprised when the fatal jab turned into a harmless stab through the collar of the gnome's jacket, as the freyal moved unexpectedly in his hands. It pinned him to the post behind, leaving him hanging like a strange coat on an even stranger coat hook. Redcap would have tried again, but the freyal had decided that it would rather be stuck in the post, and there it stayed, however hard he pulled on it. This threw him into even more of a rage, and he would gladly have strangled the gnome there and then, had the little creature not managed to squeak out a few more words at the last second, in pure desperation.

'I ... never ... had ... it!' He was trying to pull Redcap's mutilated hand off his throat as he fought to get the words out. 'It's with ... the chest.'

He nodded towards a little door, set in a wall between two lamps which hung in high, arched openings. The lamps appeared to light two rooms – the gnomes' guardroom, and another one beyond the door.

'Excellent!' said Redcap, his excitement growing by the second. 'How civilised of you to arrange things so conveniently for me. Why, the tales I've heard about you gnomes are all quite wrong!'

The gnome forced out an unconvincing smile, quite unaware that Redcap would have gladly sent him down the shaft to join his friend if only he could remove him from the post without a great deal of effort. He let go of the gnome's throat at last and the pitiful creature took several gulps of air as the goblin turned and gazed at the small door on the other side of the room. All thoughts of gnomes, elves and mortals drifted out of Redcap's mind. Only one thing mattered to him now.

*   *   *

Far from that guardroom, Mark, Trifillo and Estraal had been searching tunnel after tunnel for any sign of Victoria and her captors. They'd not had the benefit of directions from knockers, but they guessed that Malrin most certainly had, having almost tripped over the headless body of one as they ran along under Trifillo's curling flames. After that, all they could do was search and search again, but with renewed energy. They opened any doors that weren't locked, and even some that were, breaking them down and rushing into whatever lay behind them. More than once, they found themselves in tunnels which seemed horribly familiar; with time being so precious to them there was nothing worse than discovering they'd been running around in huge circles.

Again and again, the cobwebs told them if they were on the wrong track. These were festooned everywhere, and were a sure sign as to whether anyone had passed by recently, or not. After countless wrong turns and far too much wasted time, their spirits finally soared when they went through an open door and found themselves in a very narrow passageway completely free of cobwebs – and one they definitely hadn't been down already. A few minutes later they found the bodies Redcap had left in his murderous trail: the impaled gnome was still eerily illuminated by the flickering light high above it, whilst another body lay in the shadows nearby. None of them recognised Malrin.

Mark grasped the rope which still hung there, and looked up the shaft hopefully: Trifillo and Estraal were at his side, standing gingerly amongst the spikes and also staring up into the dim light. Mark seemed to know that they were at the right place, for somehow Victoria felt close by, but he also had a sickening feeling that they were too late. Throwing caution to the wind, he bellowed up the shaft as loudly as he could. It snapped Redcap to his senses as he stood gazing at the little door, wondering how heavy the hoard would be.

'Victoria! Victoria! It's me ... Are you up there, Vicky?'

Mark couldn't wait for an answer, and in any case, there wasn't one. He shouted again, but Victoria was spent – she hardly had the strength to lift her head, let alone call back to him. She tried, but a dry whisper was all that she could manage. Redcap walked to the top of the shaft and peered down it, before cupping his hands and shouting, enjoying himself, 'Oh, she's here all right ... not that *you'll* ever see her again, though!'

371

Redcap looked at the young girl in the corner and put on his most compassionate, caring face, teasing her. He was thinking back to a year or so before, and could see the mother in the child, the mother whose life he'd ended with no more effort than putting out the candle by his bedside. He added a few more words, out of pure malice.

'She sends her love.' Redcap went back to the hanging gnome. 'I take it there *is* another way out?'

The gnome swallowed hard and looked down in shame.

'Well, yes ...' His eyes darted around and his face turned a pale grey as fear filled him again. 'Beyond the chest. But ...'

Redcap had heard enough. He went to the end of the rope and untied several large knots where it was fastened to the ring. Then, with a thin, cruel smile for Victoria, he opened his remaining fingers and let it go. It snapped up into the air and sped over the wheel in the ceiling, making it spin wildly, before disappearing down the shaft like a frightened snake. Victoria's head dropped onto her knees and there were no more voices from the bottom of the shaft.

Redcap dusted his hands casually and returned to the door which fascinated him so much. He knew that it would soon lead him to something that for many long decades he'd only dreamed of ... but it was such a *plain* little door, he thought. There wasn't even a keyhole or bolt, and it was so tiny as well – perhaps two feet high and about as wide as his shoulders: gnome-sized, he supposed. He got down on his knees in front of it, almost as if he was worshipping it, and lifted the simple metal latch. He did it slowly and deliberately ... not out of fear or caution, but more as if he was opening a long-awaited gift – a truly novel experience for him. The door opened easily and noiselessly. The helpless gnome, still pinned to the post, twisted his head sideways and watched in horror as

Redcap shuffled into the doorway and towards his heart's true desire.

Everything went very quiet. Victoria managed to lift her head up, still as curious as ever, and listened out, but there wasn't a single word from the goblin, or any other sound in that strange little room. As Redcap knelt in the doorway and took in the sight before him, he suddenly felt that he couldn't breathe. He gasped, then gasped again as he fought to suck air into lungs which didn't want to fill, with ribs that didn't want to lift. He was in deep, painful shock, but the pain of it was sweet and the depth luxuriously pleasurable. Beyond the door was another small, but even stranger room. Its high, arched ceiling was carved out of the living rock, but incredibly, it had no floor. He eventually drew in a long, laboured breath and leant forwards a little, to be sure that his eyes weren't playing tricks on him, but there were only smooth, stone walls reaching down and disappearing into pitch blackness. He fumbled in his pocket, found some of the knocker's gravel and threw it into the chasm, then waited ... and waited. But no sound came, or none that his ears could hear, and they missed very little.

In fact, it was the bridge which had robbed him of his breath, not the bottomless shaft underneath it. It sprung from the ground just in front of his hands and arched across the open space to land at another small door on the far side, much like the one he'd just opened. The slender structure, no wider than the span of his hand, was a thing of unimaginable beauty, for it was made entirely of clear, dazzling crystal.

'Oh wondrous sight ...!'

He moved his head to the left and gazed at it from the side. Ten thousand tiny, flickering oil lamps were reflected in ten thousand perfectly polished surfaces, and he marvelled at an intricate arrangement of crystal rods and tubes which cleverly supported it from below. It could so easily have been created on a wet, freezing night, where icicles and frost had replaced steel and wood, but with the very greatest skill or crafty magic built into every single part of it.

At the highest point of the arch sat a small but quite stunning chest, made of the same exquisite crystal. Redcap's eyes moved to it and fixed themselves onto the contents. He was utterly bewitched, and still barely able to breathe or move. The light from the lamps played on the fat emeralds which lay safely inside it, snuggling against each other, layer upon layer, all skilfully cut and positioned so that the lights seemed to ignite them. It was a green, sparkling fire. Silent, but perfectly radiant. Valuable beyond all comprehension. The fruits of a hundred years' toil by an army of secret miners. The knockers had helped to find every one of them for Sir Henry, and their rewards had once brought them untold wealth and comfort, but now the emeralds awaited a new and rightful owner to reclaim them.

With an unimaginable effort, Redcap dragged his eyes from the chest and ran his fingers over the smooth, cold crystal of the narrow walkway in front of him. His lips were suddenly dry and his tongue darted out to lick them, as if a banquet had been set out in readiness – and just for him. He didn't trust himself to stand up and walk across the bridge: even Redcap knew his limits. His hands were shaking with excitement, and so his legs would be too, most probably, and that certainly wouldn't do for *this* short journey. And so he remained on his knees and crept forwards, clutching the edges with his hands and wishing yet again that he had more fingers on one of them. Halfway to the chest he stopped and looked down. It was a mistake, of course, and he knew it at once, but he moved on after promising himself not to repeat it.

He was trying not to smile, but as he crawled up the gentle slope it just grew uncontrollably, until he finally came close to the chest and reached out cautiously to touch it, beaming from one pointed ear to the other. He noticed at once that the fragile crystal key was in its crystal lock, just as the snivelling gnome said it would be, and the elegant lid of the chest was smooth and curved, just like the bridge. He came closer still, and saw that many more tiny emeralds were scattered throughout it, cast into the crystal for eternity like a frozen cloud of green, twinkling dust. He was mesmerised, lost in his own dreamy world of greed and pride. Yes, pride. No one else could possibly have found it and claimed it as their very own, he reminded himself.

He could easily have plucked the chest from its resting place right there and then, and carried it back to the guardroom – with the utmost care, naturally, but Redcap only considered this option for a brief moment, as a far greater power began to take control of him. He must touch *them* first. He'd earned that pleasure, in his opinion, throughout all those years of planning and scheming, and after all, the key was already there and just waiting to be turned. Redcap stroked it lovingly with one finger, as if it was a pet mouse. It looked so delicate, so perfect, but he would be as careful as anyone could be, or even more so. He reached out with his good hand and slowly turned the key, as gently as if it had been a crispy, dried-out leaf, his tongue just showing between his broken teeth. He knew it! The wonderful little key worked perfectly. It was turning easily and noiselessly.

It was just then that he thought he really *was* dreaming, for someone called out his name – his real name.

'Redcap! You'd be wise to stop that, y' know.'

The vaguely familiar voice was clear in his ears, and it was no dream, either. His hand froze and he looked up over the chest, annoyed that someone should dare to disturb him at his work and postpone his imminent ecstasy. At the far end of the bridge, standing against the other door, was a short figure, cloaked and hooded. He had one hand on a hip – as if he was quite relaxed, and certainly not on a narrow perch at the top of an apparently bottomless hole. In his other hand he held a stout wooden staff. Redcap couldn't see his face and so had no idea who it was, but he did know that if this impertinent intruder expected a last-minute share of the hoard, *his* hoard, then he was about to be sorely disappointed.

'Stop?' snapped Redcap indignantly. '*Stop?* So that you can take it for yourself, do you mean?'

In the guardroom, the first mention of Redcap's name had brought Victoria's head up smartly, and suddenly she knew what it was to feel the blood run cold in her veins. As the enormity of the truth sunk home in her tortured mind, a shiver was born between her shoulder blades and quickly spread outwards to every fibre of her young body, like ice suddenly forming over a still pond. The colour was sucked from her face instantly, and her fingers and toes turned numb, no longer hers. She fought for her breath as that simple, appalling name repeated itself over and over again in her head. She knew before her second laboured breath that she *had* to try to do something: amongst everything else she owed to her mother, she owed her that, at least. She summoned what pitiful dregs remained of her strength and somehow managed to push herself up onto her lifeless, tingling feet.

The gnome, who was terrified but also curious, watched wide-eyed as she walked up to him stiffly and grasped the hilt of the freyal. He'd never met a real mortal, either, and for all he knew she was about to finish what Redcap had started. He wriggled for a few moments, but knew that there could be no escape and so closed his eyes as he hung there, waiting for the end.

Victoria pulled the freyal out of the wooden post with only the slightest effort, for the enchanted blade was still in control of its own destiny, even then. The surprised gnome dropped onto his feet before darting to safety in a corner, but he needn't have worried. Victoria had other unfinished business, and although there had never once in her life been a trace of premeditated violence within her, she meant to finish that business right then and right there. She walked unsteadily to the little door and fell to her knees, ready to follow Redcap. The freyal grew longer in her hand with each passing second.

*   *   *

Redcap had no intention of taking advice from strangers, particularly when it was startlingly obvious that the cloaked figure wanted nothing more than to delay him, or trick him, then rob him of his newfound wealth. Ignoring him, he looked down at the crystal key, then held it gently again and turned it just a *little* bit more.

> *'I warn you now,*
> *The last is weak!'*

There was a quiet click as the transparent works unlocked some hidden mechanism inside the chest and at last Redcap could lift the lid. He did exactly that, of course. He couldn't resist it in any way, irrespective of who or what was trying to distract him, and he'd lifted it less than an inch when, with a clear, ringing note like meeting wine glasses, the side of the chest closest to him suddenly dropped open onto the bridge, allowing a cascade of huge, perfect emeralds to rattle out of the chest and roll down around his knees. Virtually every one of them left the comfy home they'd known for so many years and fell into the dark void below, as Redcap grabbed and fumbled and grasped at them with what fingers he had. Only two particularly large jewels survived, for these found their way between his knees and rolled back down the bridge – before coming to rest in the dust just in front of Victoria.

Redcap stared into his empty hands incredulously, mouthing something incomprehensible whilst he turned steadily paler and sweatier. Then he peered down into the dark chasm and listened, but still there was no sound from below. Not a single clink, splash or tinkle.

> *'For others seek*
> *What should be yours.*
> *It waits there, still,*
> *Hidden deep*
> *Beneath my hill.'*

He glanced over his shoulder towards Victoria, wondering briefly where she had found the beautiful sword she was holding. Then he looked over the top of the empty chest and saw the short, hooded figure. Both his hands were gripping the staff now, and his hood was down on his shoulders, revealing a tangled mess of hair, and a strangely familiar, ugly little face. One of his ears was missing, too.

Redcap's eyes widened as he stared in horror, and once more his mouth moved silently. They may have been unspoken words of pure hate or anger, or they could equally have been a convincing plea for mercy – he was quite capable of either, but in the end the hobgoblin had the last word. He looked across the bridge at the goblin who'd taken his ear, the very same goblin who'd taken

Victoria's mother from her family and snuffed out the lives of countless other unfortunate souls from either world – both innocent and not so innocent. His voice was calm and his words clear and unhurried, for they'd been well rehearsed.

'You as good as killed me, Redcap. The hag took me into 'er cold water and squeezed the life out of me, but it was your greed what put me there in't first place!'

A small finger pointed straight at Redcap as he fought to think clearly – whether to attack or retreat, or even beg. The hob was relentless, though.

'I knew you'd get 'ere in the end, tho', killin' anyone what got in yer way, no doubt.'

Redcap had now pulled his cap off and was wringing it in his hands: his pale cheeks were the colour of moonlight and beads of cold sweat covered his forehead. The hobgoblin continued, but showed no mercy to someone who had never once given it.

'This 'ere treasure ain't for the likes of you ... *or* me. The girl behind you 'as more claim to it than most. It's in 'er blood at least.'

Redcap looked behind him again and Victoria saw that terror had replaced the fear in his eyes for the first time. Raw terror.

'I'm already dead and past savin',' went on the hob in a matter-of-fact way, 'but there's enough of me left over to put summat right what's been wrong for as long as I can remember.'

The hob lifted his stout staff and cocked his head questioningly at Redcap, allowing his hair to fall aside and show his missing ear, as a last reminder. They looked at each other, and although it was unlikely, it was just possible that Redcap understood the hob's silent question, and regretted his evil ways during those last few seconds.

The hob brought the staff down with all his ghostly

strength, onto the crystal between his feet, and with a deafening crack, the entire bridge began to shatter into ten thousand transparent fragments. Pieces all over it soon started to break away and fall, then most of the half nearest to Victoria totally disintegrated, right up to the door where she still crouched, its tiny shards falling away with no more sound than the rustle of melting snow falling from a hedge. The goblin was left stranded on the remaining part, alone with his empty chest, and on a structure with barely any strength – more pieces were already dropping from it and disappearing below him. He looked back at Victoria again, and wondered if he could leap back to the doorway.

If she'd just get out of the way ...

Victoria could tell what he was thinking. Suddenly, a memory drifted into her mind from nowhere, a bitter-sweet memory which both saddened and enchanted her. Redcap became an insignificant blur as it all came back to her and tears filled her eyes.

I'm small again ... coming home late ... It's too dark to be out for a six year old like me ... Mummy's running to me ... She'll be pleased I'm home.

But she's smacking me ... hard. Ow! Why did she? I don't understand. She's kneeling down now – and she's crying, too ... She's holding me tight, squeezing me ... Perhaps she still loves me, after all.

It was a newly unlocked memory of her mother, crystal clear, like the remains of the bridge in front of her, and here she was, holding her murderer's life in her own two hands. It wasn't a very difficult decision. As she crawled backwards through the doorway she saw the two emeralds lying beside her fingers and scooped them up with one hand ... before pulling the door firmly shut behind her with the other.

Redcap immediately took his last remaining chance and sprang from what was left of the bridge towards the closed door. He hit the wall hard, incredibly hard, but using all his strength and cunning, he ignored the pain and gripped onto the doorframe with his bare fingers as he struggled to find a toehold on the narrow slither of ground showing at its base. Considering his situation, he was ridiculously confident as he bent his mind towards the door, willing it to open for him, forcing it to obey his mental command. Suddenly, the latch was being ripped away from the timber behind it and the door was starting to open again.

Victoria immediately spun around and threw herself against it, trying to force it shut with her back as she sat in front of it – one of Redcap's feet slipped, but somehow he regained his balance and concentrated even harder. The door obeyed his will and opened a little further, pushing Victoria along in front of it, and again she forced it shut, pushing back with her knees, but her feet were slipping now.

Redcap made a final effort as he clung to the vertical wall like an inexpert lizard, but whilst Victoria was being pushed along for the second time, she looked down at her hands. One still clenched the emeralds tightly, but the freyal was in the other. It was now much longer, and she felt it come to life in her hand, as if it knew that it was needed. She didn't hesitate. As the door inched open wider still, she twisted around and thrust the sword blindly into the narrow gap. The freyal worked with her, turning her vague aim into the most accurate and deadly of strikes.

There was a scream from behind the door. It was an unearthly, ear-splitting scream, full of pain and surprise, perhaps anger, too, but it was followed by an even more unearthly silence as Redcap dropped away from the wall and down into the chasm waiting below him, with the empty chest and the rest of the bridge following a second later. He fell, tumbling and turning in amongst a blizzard of crystal fragments, his fingers clawing at the air and his legs pedalling uselessly in the black void which quickly enveloped him. Redcap would soon be reunited with his beloved emeralds, but he would never hold a single one of them between his greedy fingers.

Victoria was still drained and confused as she put the heavy freyal down, pulled open the little door and peered into the empty room. She saw that Redcap had really gone, along with his treasure and the ghostly hobgoblin, and that the door where the hob had been was now wide open. She somehow knew in her heart that it would take her to safety and freedom … if only she could reach it. She opened her hand and looked in it. The two emeralds were still there, almost the size of walnuts but infinitely more attractive, she thought, and she gazed at them for several long seconds, lost in their fathomless beauty.

Her exhaustion finally caught up with her whilst she explored their sharp edges and flat, perfect faces, each one a slightly different shade of green, for she suddenly felt that she was floating just above the ground and nothing around her was real any more. The flickering oil lamps, the freyal, the emeralds, the cowering gnome, even: they were all part of a most peculiar dream, as far as she was aware. The dream continued as she watched the gnome tie a spare rope to the iron ring in the floor, fastening the knots with hands which seemed far too small and shook far too much for the task. She saw him struggle to lift the heavy coils of rope over the low wall and tip them down into the shaft, but thought that she could hear voices again from somewhere a whole world away. The gnome smiled at her and she was pleased that he wasn't afraid any more.

He must be the forgiving type after all, she decided.

Somehow, she managed to stand up again and lean against the same post which the gnome had hung from, resting for a while and trying not to float away, for she was convinced that she was just about to. The gnome was peering over the wall and shouting out something to someone, then, a minute later, he was talking, not shouting, then encouraging someone, but she couldn't make out any of the words. She squeezed the emeralds together in her hand, seeking reassurance that at least *something* in that dream-like place was real, then somebody was holding her by the shoulders, just like Mark used to.

She looked up, and it *was* Mark. He pulled her off the hard post and held her tightly as she stood there with her arms hanging uselessly at her side – she wanted so much to put them around him, but they felt so weak and heavy. Then, suddenly, the two of them seemed to be back at the willows by the river. She could even hear his mouth organ playing one of her favourite tunes, but it didn't last for long. They were under the hill and far from home, but her Mark was with her at last and now she knew that he was safe. She knew that *she* was safe, too, and it was a lovely, warm feeling – just like lying on the rug in front of the fire at home, with Chopper asleep beside her.

She looked up from his shoulder, trying very hard to stop her eyelids from closing, and saw Trifillo standing next to a female elf she'd never met. Even in her half-dream, Victoria knew that she was the most beautiful person she'd ever seen – there was no trace of doubt in her mind. Estraal could feel the silent compliment and smiled back shyly just as Victoria opened her fingers and looked down at the emeralds again. They were still there, still alive in the lamplight, and so her dream was a very realistic one, if it *was* a dream ...

'You know it's your birthday tomorrow, don't you?' said Victoria sleepily, still wrapped in Mark's arms.

Mark laughed quietly to himself. As it happened, he *had* forgotten, but he was amused by Victoria's first words to him after what they'd both been through, and couldn't stop himself from chuckling.

'One of these is for you.' She stepped back, holding out her hand, and Mark's eyebrows shot up in astonishment. 'Tomorrow!' she added, snapping her fingers closed and yawning. 'And anyway, we still have to find a way across *that*!'

She looked at the little door and Mark went over to it, squatted down and peered through the opening.

'Oh, is that all?' he said casually, before walking over to Estraal.

She was already holding Victoria's thumb stick out for him. He grasped it, turned to Victoria, and tapped the end on the floor several times.

'I think I've got just the thing,' he said happily, grinning impishly from ear to ear.

*   *   *

Beyond the second small door where the hobgoblin had stood so bravely, steps had been cut into the rock. Five hundred or more of them were set into the entire length of a very long, cramped passageway, itself only just high and wide enough for one person at a time. Long though that climb was for the four of them, it also seemed effortless – even for Victoria, amazingly. The death of Malrin and Redcap had lifted their boots as much as it had their spirits, or so their tireless legs told them: soon the passageway was behind them and Mark was putting his back to the underside of a large flagstone which the last few steps finished up against. There was only enough space for one to work in, and so Trifillo, Estraal and Victoria could give nothing more than their encouragement as they queued up patiently, crouching on the steps close behind Mark and waiting for their freedom.

Up above them, in creation's very freshest air, and all alone, stood a cross carved from stone, twice as tall as any man could reach. It had been called Ralph's Cross for centuries, but Ralph, whoever he was, had long since passed into obscurity. Although it was alone, it wasn't in the least bit lonely, for it stood completely surrounded by its true home – the North York Moors. Its base was set deep into their very highest point, and so its view was usually uninterrupted.

It was the middle of the afternoon, and overcast above, but clear and bright enough below the white, scudding clouds. A lively wind had also sprung up from the north, carrying the promise and fresh smell of rain, and tugging playfully at the short heather which completely surrounded the cross. Only a stone's throw away, a small, square patch of heather suddenly twitched rather more than its neighbours. The twitch became a jerk and the jerk became a jump, as that square suddenly arched up into the air and fell back on itself under the weight of a heavy flagstone.

If Ralph's ghost had been close by, even *he* would have been astonished to see a young lad's head and shoulders pop up from the ground, soon followed by the rest of him … and a young lady with as fine a thumb stick as you could wish for. Ralph's astonishment might have turned to amusement, though, or even delight, as two light elves walked up those last few hidden steps and stood amongst the springy heather, alongside the young mortals. The brisk, northerly wind took their hoods, cloaks and hair and tossed them about, but had never been so welcome two days before Christmas. It blasted the dust and cobwebs off them in a few seconds and filled their lungs with the sweet, clean air for which they had craved all that day.

The four friends stood together in that very special place, facing each other, elf and mortal, mortal and elf, with no other desire than to gladly take each other's hands and form a square. As smiles turned to laughter, the corners of that living square leant back from one another, arms pulling on arms, heads falling back, hoods and hair hanging free, and then slowly turned ... and turned ... and kept turning. In that one, priceless moment, more precious than any emeralds, or perhaps even life itself, two startlingly different worlds truly became one.

Victoria's bloodied hands were the first to lose their grip, not surprisingly. She let go and sat down in the heather with a bump, still laughing, as the others staggered backwards, laughing out loudly too, then turning to face the wind and letting it pull at their cloaks. Estraal stopped laughing first. She stood gazing at a far horizon, acutely aware of the value of the small gift now in her hand, and what it would mean to the two young people she had come to know and admire. She turned and faced them both, but went up to Mark, knowing that it should come to him. *Back* to him, in fact. She held up the thin cord and its little leather pouch.

'I think that you will be needing this,' she said, and offered to him.

*   *   *

It was a long walk from Ralph's Cross to Farndale, but it didn't seem like that to Mark and Victoria. True, they were sad to say their farewells to Trifillo and Estraal, but after that, there was only a steady downhill trek back to their homes, with light and joyful hearts. They chatted together every step of the way. To begin with, memories seem to fill their minds – many of them happy, but a few of them appalling and only hinted at for now – then, as they passed the first of the cottages in the village, came hopes, with Elspeth's plight uppermost amongst them.

They went straight to Willow Garth, but Victoria became quiet on the lane up to the farmhouse, as fears and doubts suddenly sneaked up on her. Mark didn't interrupt her thoughts, knowing very well that she'd have them whatever he said to her, but when they reached the lawn, he stopped her. This was *her* time, not his. He held out the pouch and she stared at it for a few moments, almost frightened by its potential power, before she slipped its cord between her fingers.

'Good luck, Vicks,' said Mark. 'When you get to York, you'll have to get her all to yourself, you know. The doctors won't let you anywhere near her with it.'

'Probably not,' agreed Victoria distractedly.

'Especially if they get a whiff of it,' added Mark, trying to relax her a little.

'Yeah ... Still, I'd better try, hadn't I?'

'Definitely! Estraal would be gutted if you didn't.' Mark smiled and turned away. He couldn't do anything more.

Victoria walked across the lawn, thinking about the trip to York and how she would cope with everything there, but she was surprised to see Annie sitting in the garden by herself, looking down at the lawn. It wasn't something she ever did. Victoria changed course and went to join her on the bench seat.

'Been for a walk?' asked Annie, only half looking up.

'A run, mostly,' replied Victoria, before quickly sitting on her hands to hide them. 'What's up? You haven't been to hospital early, have you?' Victoria's stomach suddenly felt strangely hollow as Annie continued to look downwards.

'No. We haven't been.' Victoria waited for more. She *knew* there was more.

'She's come home,' whispered Annie. Victoria sat upright, about to celebrate, but Annie didn't give her the chance.

'She's not good, Vicky. She's ... she's not good at all. They thought she should come home to be with us for ... for a while, before ... before ...'

'What d'you mean?' demanded Victoria, who now forgot her blood-smeared hands and grasped Annie's arm tightly. 'She's *here*? Without the doctors? How *can* she be?'

Annie still couldn't look at her sister, despite wanting to so much.

'You should go in, Vicky.' She paused, struggling to find the right words, but failing. 'Dad's in there with her, I think.' Her voice trailed even further away.

Victoria sprang up, alarmed and suddenly wishing that Mark was with her. She wanted him to be there, more than anyone else.

He'd understand. He'd hold me and not say anything when I don't want to hear any words. Why didn't I ask him to come in with me? I must be crazy.

Her mind raced back to the glade and how he had held her after the hobgoblin told them about Redcap.

Redcap – huh, he's dead, and I killed him. But I had to, because he caused all of this. What's happened to Elspeth? Why's she at home? Oh my God, something's happened, I know it has!

She ran to the red door and threw it open, rushing into the house and leaving it swinging free. There was only one thing in her mind now. She *had* to be in time.

*   *   *

The following day was Christmas Eve, and just for a change, the weather behaved itself and did exactly what everyone really wanted it to. The snow started to fall at two in the afternoon, well before sunset. Most of the valley folk had finished their work – apart from those whose lives were ruled by milking parlours and full udders, that is – and for the younger children it was the perfect end to a day full of expectation and growing excitement.

In two neighbouring farms, two families had barely noticed that their fifteen year olds had been away a great deal recently, up to goodness only knows what. Whilst Mark and Victoria had battled for hours against unimaginable horrors and even the threat of death itself, only minutes had passed by for those left behind at home. Such is the way of the unseen world, and this time it was the best way, too. Their families did, however, notice that certain young people seemed to have no energy left in them at all, and that they had even wandered off to their bedrooms for a short rest straight after lunch. This was completely out of character for them, and particularly so for Mark, because this day was also his birthday.

Victoria wore a warm jumper all day long. It was definitely a warm jumper sort of day, and she particularly appreciated wearing it when the lanes began to turn white, but now there was another advantage: its long sleeves kept her injured wrists well covered, and any awkward questions about them at bay. They would soon heal, she knew, helped by a precious elf cloak which would be secretly wrapped around them through the nights.

In each of those two cosy farmhouses stood a fine Christmas tree, filling each room with the fresh smell of pine needles and draped with a dazzling array of colourful, glittering decorations and tiny, glowing lights. As befitted such trees, their bases were hidden, surrounded by a glorious but untidy pile of gifts, wrapped up with great care and no expense spared, judging by the wide ribbons and sumptuous bows which bound many of them.

With darkness cloaking the valley and the snowflakes growing larger, it was far too much for one particular little girl to resist. She seemed to know exactly when everyone's back was turned for a few seconds, and made straight for the irresistible tree in a series of awkward, uncertain steps. Her arms were outstretched and her chubby fingers spread wide, determined to grasp as much as she could, but Annie noticed her just in time. She turned and swept

Elspeth off her feet, swinging her up into the air sideways. A few baubles fell off the tree, nothing more, but Annie already had the best present she could have asked for, dangling from her hands. She was *everyone's* best present, in fact.

Each tree had another special present at its foot, though. They were undeniably small, even easy to miss amongst all the other gifts, but they were destined to change the fortunes of those two struggling families forever. The smart little boxes, one for Mark's parents, and one for Victoria's father, each with their tiny, deep-green ribbon, couldn't have held anything much larger than a walnut...

The End

Appendix

All of the more unusual characters in this tale are listed below, along with their most commonly held descriptions and habits. Whilst writing, I have added a few minor details of my own, hopefully for your enjoyment, and left some out, for your own protection and sanity. I trust that you will forgive me for doing so.

The author

Bogle

Known as bogills in Scotland, these fierce beings are reputed to enjoy torturing young, disobedient children, as well as lazy, uncontrollable or criminally inclined adults. When they are not in such a violent mood, their less wicked habits include entering houses and making a general mess, giving out strange, unnatural noises from around corners, pulling blankets off beds on cold nights, or hovering unseen, close to people's backs, causing a strong feeling of uneasiness.

Elf

These supernatural, human-like beings are either very beautiful (light elves) or equally ugly (dark or black elves), and indeed, the Celtic types are as tall as humans. Light elves have particularly strong links with trees, hills and waterfalls, and can have shining white skin: it has been said that they are 'fairer to look upon than the sun'. Elves have been an integral part of the culture of virtually every known primitive race or tribe, with British references to them being commonplace from the eighth century onwards.

Gnome
These small, dwarf-like creatures are often misshapen and ugly. They form part of a general group known as the elementals, being those most closely associated with the earth, with undines (water), sylphs (air) and salamanders (fire) making up the remainder. Gnomes nearly always live underground as sunlight is lethal to them, reputedly turning them into stone and, being subterranean, they tend to be experts at guarding buried treasure. They can pass through solid rock as easily as humans walk on the ground, and it is likely that they are in some way related to daylight-loving goblins and dwarfs.

Goblin
Goblins originated in France, but soon spread rapidly throughout Europe. They never establish permanent homes, preferring to live temporarily in amongst the roots of old trees. Varying between two and six feet in height, they are often described as a grotesquely disfigured type of gnome, occasionally playful, but very capable of evil tricks causing great harm to humans. A smile from some goblins will curdle the blood in the veins of a living victim, whilst their laugh alone can turn milk sour and cause all the fruit on a tree to fall instantly to the ground. They also have a great fondness for altering signposts, simply to be a nuisance.

Hobgoblin
These are impish, mischievous, but otherwise friendly little goblins, typically up to two feet tall, who for some reason

tend to prefer brown clothes. They like to get close to warm fires and avoid getting cold outside if at all possible, but are happy to live in dry farm buildings, often attaching themselves socially to one family. In these circumstances, the hobgoblin will even help out secretly with chores around the farm. They are fond of practical jokes if given the opportunity, but to this day there are farmers who put out fresh cream for their 'hob' each night, so as to avoid their wrath. Some hobs have been ignored or badly treated in the past, resulting in havoc. This was the case at Rudland Rigg, above the western slopes of Farndale, when the disruption was so great that a farmer was eventually forced to move from his farm. Unfortunately for this particular farmer, when he left, his hob was seen to leave with him, hiding in amongst his furniture.

Jack-in-irons

Jack is an extremely dangerous giant who, for years, has haunted the back lanes and trackways of Yorkshire. He is covered with chains and the heads of his victims, and often carries a large, spiked club.

Knocker

Usually between two and three feet tall, these creatures are invariably good-natured and always live in mines. With their loud knocking, they will guide miners towards rich veins in return for food or other gifts, and even give advance warning of impending cave-ins. They are prone to scaring miners with their peculiar faces, which they can change at will, but they have a keen dislike for swearing and whistling, and will throw harmless gravel when provoked too far, or even perform strange dances. In the Welsh mines they are called coblyns, or in Cornwall, buccas.

Peg Powler

Peg is a hag, or ugly old woman, with green skin, long hair and sharp teeth, usually living somewhere along the course of the River Tees. She grabs the ankles of her victims – from all accounts including the wickedest of children – pulling them into the water, where she sometimes drowns them. A Yorkshire version of her is known as Jenny Greenteeth.

Redcap

A redcap is a solitary and particularly evil type of goblin, who inhabits the ruins of castles, especially those on the border between Scotland and England. Their intention is to bring harm to all around them and they will murder any travellers who unintentionally stray into their homes, often by crushing them under piles of huge stones. They use their victims' blood to dye their hats (hence their name), and they must kill regularly in order to keep their hats damp with fresh blood, for they die if their hats dry out completely. They are very fast on their feet, which is surprising, given that they are often heavily armed.

Sarkless Kitty

Kitty was a young girl from Gillamoor, near Farndale, who drowned herself in a nearby mill pool in 1787. She believed that her young man, Willie Dixon of Hutton-le-hole, no longer loved her, and cast herself into the pool wearing only her smock (or sark). A few days afterwards, Willie's body was found in the same pool, with his horse wandering free nearby. Kitty's ghost had claimed her first victim, and worse still, her body had disappeared from its resting place in a barn close by. Kitty's ghost was seen at the pool many times until 1809, when a service of exorcism carried out at the pool by a priest finally laid her spirit to rest. By that time, though, sixteen more men had mysteriously drowned in that very same pool.

Seelie Court

This is a gathering of the kind and harmless host, including light elves, occasionally seen at dusk or dawn in a long procession. They are known for helping the poor with unexpected gifts of bread and other basic foods. Their name literally means the 'Blessed' or 'Holy' Court.

Spriggan

Spriggans are grotesque, ugly creatures who, although normally quite small, can instantly enlarge themselves to the size of a giant if they so wish. Both clever and dangerous, they are expert thieves, and will often rob human homes, even stealing their younger children. In such cases, a baby spriggan (sometimes called a changeling) or other 'gift' may be left in the child's place. They can control whirlwinds, using them skilfully to destroy crops or other property. When there is the need, they can travel extremely quickly over very long distances, and can be easily mistaken for a common cat if seen from afar in their natural (smaller) form, but just like cats, they are rarely interested in anything or anyone other than themselves. Their antics at Trencrom Hill, Cornwall, are particularly well known and recorded.

Unseelie Court

The evil counterpart of the Seelie Court, the 'Unholy Court' is set against mankind in every possible way and at all times. When the host flies at night it is sometimes called the Horde. At other times it can be known as the Sluagh, a version of the Wild Hunt. The Sluagh, which can be lead by huge and terrifying white hounds with red eyes, will assault any traveller they happen across, or even carry them along through the air, beating them mercilessly and forcing them to commit vicious acts such as attacking helpless cattle or sheep.